SMALL WARS

Also by Sadie Jones

The Outcast

SMALL WARS

Sadie Jones

Chatto & Windus
LONDON

Published by Chatto & Windus 2009

4 6 8 10 9 7 5

Map by Reginald Piggott.

First published in Great Britain in 2009 by
Chatto & Windus
Random House, 20 Vauxhall Bridge Road,
London SW1V 2SA

www.rbooks.co.uk

Addresses for companies within The Random House Group Limited can be found at: www.randomhouse.co.uk/offices.htm

The Random House Group Limited Reg. No. 954009

A CIP catalogue record for this book is available from the British Library

Hardback ISBN 9780701184551
Trade paperback ISBN 9780701184568

The Random House Group Limited supports The Forest Stewardship Council (FSC), the leading international forest certification organisation. All our titles that are printed on Greenpeace approved FSC certified paper carry the FSC logo. Our paper procurement policy can be found at www.rbooks.co.uk/environment

FSC
Mixed Sources
Product group from well-managed forests and other controlled sources
www.fsc.org Cert no. TT-COC-2139
© 1996 Forest Stewardship Council

Typeset in Perpetua by Palimpsest Book Production Limited, Grangemouth, Stirlingshire
Printed and bound in Great Britain by
Clays Ltd, St Ives plc

For Tim Boyd

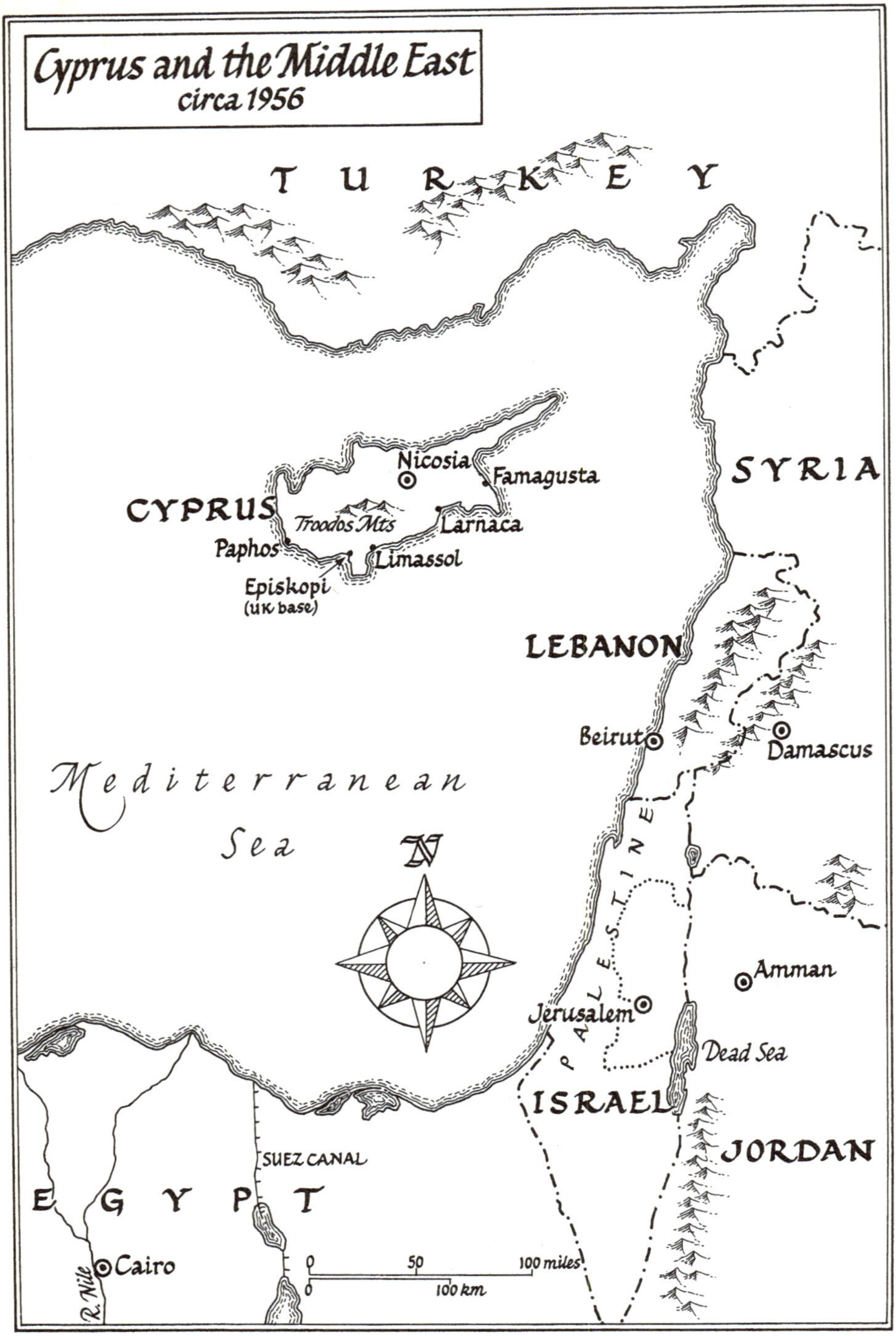
Cyprus and the Middle East
circa 1956
TURKEY
SYRIA
CYPRUS
Nicosia
Famagusta
Troodos Mts
Larnaca
Paphos
Limassol
Episkopi
(UK base)
LEBANON
Beirut
Damascus
Mediterranean
Sea
N
PALESTINE
Amman
Jerusalem
Dead Sea
ISRAEL
JORDAN
SUEZ CANAL
EGYPT
Cairo
R. Nile
0
50
100 miles
0
100 km

Almighty God, whose son Jesus Christ, the Lord of all life, came not to be served but to serve, help us to be masters of ourselves that we may be the servants of others and teach us to Serve to Lead, through the same Jesus Christ, Our Lord, Amen.

The Collect of RMA Sandhurst

– Yet when we came back, late, from the Hyacinth garden,
Your arms full, and your hair wet, I could not
Speak, and my eyes failed, I was neither
Living nor dead, and I knew nothing,
Looking into the heart of light, the silence.

T.S. Eliot, *The Waste Land*

Prologue

Sandhurst, July 1946

An English rain was falling onto the instruments of the band, onto their olive green uniforms and the uniforms of the cadets as they marched. The quiet rain lay in drops on the umbrellas of the families watching, on the men's felt hats and the women's gloved hands; it dampened the grey and green countryside around them and put beads of water onto everything.

The band played 'Auld Lang Syne'. The sound of the commands of the cadets and of the marching feet seemed to promise a bright future that was grounded in England and in discipline; the love of one made strong by the application of the other.

The families stood in a crowd ten deep, bordering the parade square. The small band and the marching cadets were between them and the long, white, columned building. The cadets held rifles and wore dark green battledress. The wool of their uniforms was dense and damp in the weather. The marching feet and rifles and tilted heads made patterns, so that their mothers could hardly tell one from another and felt embarrassed about it, but proud too, because their sons had become part of a greater body and did not stand out.

Some mothers and fathers had seen the passing-out parades

of other sons, and many of the fathers remembered their own. This parade, in 1946, like England herself, lacked opulence but had its own austere ceremony. It was not the sunny, decorative ceremony of established peacetime, but resolute and businesslike, as if these men, like those of only a few months before, would be dispatched immediately into battle.

There was almost no self-consciousness at the emotion of the occasion: it was designed to be emotional and there was nobody there who did not feel it. The only time Hal Treherne could remember his father choked with feeling was in describing the day of his own Sovereign's Parade.

Hal was not choked with feeling: he had only the desire to do well that he always had, immense pride, like a physical thing, and a powerful eagerness to meet his future and to conquer it. He wasn't thinking about these things though; he was thinking about the precise execution of this small part of his training, drilled, redrilled, and accomplished. It was afterwards, as they stood in silence for inspection by the Princess Elizabeth – rifles up to the shoulder, eyes front – then, suddenly, he felt it, a sort of overflowing, and he had to blink and focus carefully on the far trees.

There was almost total quiet as everybody watched the young princess walk down the line of cadets. Hal could hear the sound of the footsteps approaching. He knew that she was the embodiment of his country, that he was doing his best to please and that he always would. He thought of God – his hazy, humble idea of God – and dared to hope he could please Him, too.

Hal, flanked by his peers and not alone, thought briefly of his father, watching him from the crowd, with all his battles behind him, and of his mother, next to him, quietly satisfied.

Then his mind focused again on the exact present. The group of officers, aides and the princess came into the side of his vision, and across it, and his eyes didn't waver. He could see the top of her cream-coloured hat out of focus at the bottom of his field of vision. She paused briefly, she passed him and she moved on, and the small group with her moved on too, down the line.

Hal's girl was called Clara Ward. She was watching from the crowd with her parents and younger brother and later, at the Sovereign's Ball, she would dance with him. Clara was the sister of Hal's friend James. Hal had gone back with James to stay with his family a few times in Buckinghamshire, and that was how they had met.

Clara and James's family house was a village house, a wide red-brick villa, with white painted door and gate, white sills and sashes and a big garden. It had a lilac tree, apple trees, roses and a well-kept lawn that had a stream with a small bridge over it. Clara and her two brothers had grown up there and gone to and from their various schools and the house showed the small scars of their childhood in its crooked swing and worn carpets.

It was a house for Christmases and summers, for school holidays, rocking horses and chickenpox. It had seen wooden toys, rattles, satchels and raincoats and then, later, it had seen evening clothes and beaded bags on thin chains left on the hall chairs as Clara and James, tired from their parties, went upstairs to bed.

Hal had seen Clara for the first time one weekend, in the first weeks of his training.

They had arrived after tea on a Saturday. James had been talking to his father about money, and Hal had thought he'd better go out into the garden for a smoke and to be out of the way.

There was a blueish dusk just settling and Clara was coming into the drawing room; she had her arms full of wet flowers, and Hal – avoiding a small table – had almost bumped into her. He had apologised and they had shaken hands awkwardly. Her hand was wet from the flowers. Hal said, 'You must be James's sister,' and Clara answered, 'Yes, I'm Clara.'

She said 'Clara' as her brother did – to rhyme with 'dare' or 'fair' – and then, 'Are you Hal?'

'Yes. Hal,' and he had been silenced by her voice and the look of her, and had not known what to say.

They stepped around each other. He had gone out into the garden and had his cigarette; she had gone into the kitchen to put the flowers in water, but the picture of her stayed in his mind. She was pale and had dark brown hair, the colour of conkers or a bay horse, and her eyes were marine blue. She was seventeen then; he was nineteen.

Hal had set about seeing more of Clara with determination, and over the few months of his training he would come back with James whenever they were allowed a weekend.

His own parents' house was near Warminster, in Somerset, not far from Stonehenge. It was faced with dark grey and had a well-proportioned front and other older and more complicated sections attached and interlocking behind. It bore the wind that came off Salisbury Plain stoically, with barely a rattle of its Victorian windows. Hal was always happy to be back in the big chilly rooms, with their familiar echoes; the gilt-framed paintings, the grim colours of the house, and its coldness, were nourishing to him. Although before visiting the Wards, he had never noticed the look of his own house before, he still felt more comfortable with its discomfort than he ever did in that light village house. He was happy with the silent mealtimes and bare boards of home, but he needed to be near Clara, and tolerated her jolly, messy family well enough to see her.

Hal and Clara had written to one another, letters more intimate than they ever were face to face. He called her his 'red, white and blue girl' – for her colouring – and when he asked her to come with him to the Sovereign's Parade and ball it wasn't surprising, but it was significant.

Clara stood with her parents and younger brother, trying to pick out Hal and James from the lines of cadets, straining up onto her toes to see over the people in front, while twenty feet away, Arthur and Jean Treherne, in the front row, watched too.

Arthur Treherne and George Ward could not have been more different. George was a kind, fastidious man, and smallish. His trousers had one soft crease at the ankle and his overcoats spoke of dim offices and hatstands in domestic hallways. James was the first of their family to go into the army as a professional soldier, and they had watched his absorption into that world with something like dread.

George was a civil servant; he had gone to work every day from the red-brick villa in Buckinghamshire, returning each night to Moira, Clara and their two sons. He had fought briefly in the First War. It had been – still was – the unequalled crisis of his life. He didn't feel soldiering was anything one would choose to do, and was sharply aware that the greater part of his wish for continued peace in the world was so that his sons would not have to do the things he had done, and that his daughter would not have to be a soldier's wife. And yet here he was, his powerful distate – and fear – mixing with a pride that was almost beyond his control.

Hal's father, Arthur, was a soldier, had been a soldier, and would always, whatever he wore or wherever he went, be a soldier in every aspect. He had Hal's height and colouring – although his dark blond hair was faded now with grey, and his bones, like a steel frame revealed, were closer to the surface. Arthur watched the parade with none of the Wards' ambivalence, his leather-gloved hand clamped over his wife's as it rested on his arm. He had neither anxiety nor regret, but simple, deeply felt pride in his son, whose progression was expected, a long anticipated stepping-stone to a distinguished future.

The slow rain became no more than mist when the parade was over, carrying the smell of wet grass and rifle shot as the birds started to sing again. The new officers and their families stood in groups on the parade square. Around them was parkland, big vague trees undisturbed now by sharp volleys of fire. Women shivered in the chill summer air and held their husbands' arms. Clara Ward stood shyly by her brother James, and teased him, and hoped that Hal would come over.

Hal was with his father and mother, with very little to say after the congratulations were over. He twisted his head to look over his shoulder at Clara with her family and felt nervous suddenly of what they might talk about all evening. He wanted to be alone with her. He wanted not to have to get to know her – which seemed a frightening process – but to know her already.

The Wards went back to Buckinghamshire, after the Sovereign's Parade, to change into evening dress for the ball. The Trehernes went to a hotel they had found in the high street in Godalming because they lived too far away to be going back and forth. His parents drank warm gin and tonic in the downstairs bar, while Hal went up to his room, which overlooked the road.

He put his belt and jacket on the bed, paced up and down and thought about Clara. She was a foreign country to him, but one he felt he'd always known, like the countries coloured pink on the atlas, that he had been familiar with through his childhood. Like a far-off place of treasures and spices that still was English, in his mind she waited for his visit; she was India.

Clara's dress was midnight blue. The idea was that it would match her eyes. It was strapless, and had clear beads on the skirt, which was net and there was a lot of it. Her bosom felt very bare and white; she had tried several different ways of wrapping her stole around herself to cover up. Her mother's dress – a casualty of Clara's yards of net – was stiff, brownish taffeta, seven years old and making what she hoped was its last appearance.

James was wrestling with Bill on the landing, they were shaking the floor with their thumping. Bill was fourteen and already too old for wrestling on landings, and James really should have known better, twenty years old and still in his battledress from the parade.

Clara sat on the bed in her evening gown, listening to the noises of their fighting and laughing. She felt an intense nostalgia. They would all leave home. Everything would change. Clara felt she could reach out and touch her childhood: it was all around her in the house, still living. She rested her hands lightly on the edge of the bed, as her mother's footsteps came up the stairs and reached the boys on the landing. 'Do be quiet! Stop that!'

She came into Clara's room and sat next to her, lifting the material of her skirt away from her legs so as not to crush it.

'Silly boys,' said Clara.

Her mother took her hand. 'Shall we set your hair?'

Clara nodded but neither of them stood up; they sat together, quietly, with the sound of the boys fighting and a wood-pigeon in the garden outside.

At the ball, all the women were in long gowns, but only half of the men in black tie because the young officers were in the mess kit of their new regiments, standing out brightly against the sombre black dinner jackets of their fathers and guests.

Hal had waited by the door to the ballroom at the beginning of the evening and when he saw Clara walking towards him he felt again the odd stillness with which she affected him. It wasn't just being tongue-tied, or nervous – although that was part of it – it was more that he was overwhelmed by her.

She was with her family. His own parents had already gone away into the crowd. His father was with a large group of officers and retired officers at the other end of the ballroom and paying no attention to Hal, or who he might or might not be with, but the Wards hovered for a moment while Hal and Clara gazed at each other.

'Do you know where they're sending you?' said George, abruptly, to Hal.

'Clara has told us already, George,' said Moira, and she and

Clara exchanged a smile. George, though, continued to stare at Hal.

Hal had an uneasy feeling that this kindly man did not like him. He didn't seem the sort of father one would expect to be jealously protective of his daughter, but Hal knew his attention to Clara displeased George somehow. Hal wasn't somebody who'd ever had a conversation about the workings of his or anybody else's mind in his life. His own family limited their conversation to the dogs, occasional social engagements and his father's pronouncements on war or politics, none of which had equipped Hal to fathom the more intimate aspects of human interaction. He had no means with which to approach the problem of George Ward not liking him, and thought only that if he behaved properly, as he intended to do, it would somehow work itself out.

James was grinning somewhere near Hal's left shoulder, hoping to torment them.

'Go away, James,' said Clara, and – at last – her parents took him with them and left Hal and Clara together.

'Everything all right?' said Hal.

'Oh, yes,' said Clara.

He noticed she wore red lipstick, which she hadn't when they had met before. It suited her, but the glamour of it, with the dress, was unnerving. 'Would you like some punch?' he said.

'Yes. Where is it?'

'Over here. Come along.'

They went through the people together and arrived at a waiter with a large full tray.

'Or a cocktail?' Hal looked down at her, frowning.

'I don't mind,' said Clara.

'Right then.'

He took two glasses of punch and handed her one. 'Not sure what's in it. Something awful probably, if the food in this place is anything to go by.'

'I'm sure it's lovely.'

There was a brief silence of excruciating tension.

'We don't get to see an awful lot of girls. Sorry if I'm not up to much small-talk.'

She seemed relieved. 'You're fine. It was easier at home, wasn't it?'

'Yes. Much. Now we're all dressed up. Makes things trickier.'

'You've only seen me in slacks. With dog hairs on them probably.'

'Not that bad. Frocks anyway.' He paused. 'And you looked very nice.'

Clara looked down at her punch. Hal noticed she wasn't drinking it. The hand holding her glass was gloved. He wanted to take the glove off. He wanted to hold her hand. 'Would you like to dance with me?' he said.

'I'd love to.'

'I'm not awfully good.'

'Aren't you? I'm marvellous,' she said, and Hal laughed; he knew he'd been right about her.

They danced to 'Choo Choo Ch'Boogie', and then 'Fools Rush In', and then 'Mam'selle'. They danced until the supper interval, and wouldn't be interrupted by anybody.

The cadets, though commissioned into their regiments, kept the pips on their shoulder boards covered all through the evening. At twelve o'clock, it was the girls who pulled the short dark ribbons away, and completed their transformation into soldiers. Some chaps had their sisters do it or, God forbid, their mothers, but Hal – unaware of being watched now, or of anything else – would have Clara for his, and he wasn't frightened about the promise it seemed to make between them.

After this, and a few months in England on exercises, he was to be sent to Germany with his regiment. He would write to her from there, visit when he could, and when the time came – if she wanted it – he would marry her.

In the dissonant laughing countdown to midnight, Clara reached up to his shoulder to untie the ribbon – had to take off her gloves at last to do it – and smiled at him.

Hal saw nothing but the girl he was with and the service he was promised to, and in the deep silence at the centre of himself he made an absolute commitment to each.

PART ONE

Limassol

Ten Years Later. Cyprus, January 1956.
During the Emergency.

Chapter One

The army had rented them a house in Limassol, quite near to the harbour because married quarters on the base hadn't been sorted out for them yet.

Hal knew the weather had been bad on the crossing from England – even after Gibraltar – and he pictured Clara and the girls laid up in their cabins all the way from Portsmouth. He hoped they hadn't been too sick; Clara wasn't a good sailor. He had enjoyed his own journey from Krefeld, flying in bumpy weather with the countries of Europe and wrinkled blue sea passing below, like a clay model you could stick flags in, and move imaginary armies from place to place.

Hal had been promoted to major, and transferred from his battalion in Germany to this one, alone, not knowing anybody. Everything had been new to him. He had set about the business of leadership and his new rank with steadfast energy, and was rewarded by a smooth transition. Sleeping alone in that house for a month, as he had, he missed the company of barracks, and the isolation was grating.

The Limassol house was narrow, in a cobbled street, with no outlook to speak of and barely a lock on the door. It made Hal uncomfortable to think of it, the unsettling lack of security, and that you couldn't see anything from the windows other than the crooked windows of other houses. If someone were to approach, or set a booby-trap, there'd be no stopping them. A few months before, in Famagusta, an EOKA terrorist had lobbed a bomb through the open window of a soldier's house as his wife was putting the children to bed. Hal knew his instinct – his agony of responsibility – must be tempered and that the Housing Officer was doing everything he could to get him married quarters at the garrison. But the other soldier's wife, in Famagusta, had lost half her arm in the explosion. Hal had spoken to the Housing Officer again that morning, reminding him, but beyond doing that he had no power: he must trust everything was being done that could be done. If he didn't have faith, he wouldn't manage, but with it, he could live with the knowledge of the other soldier's wife and still have his own come to be with him.

He lay in the bed that was too big for him, but would be too small for them both when Clara came, and imagined her leaving England for Cyprus. It had been a vicious winter all over Europe. Hal pictured a cold day at Portsmouth harbour, HMS *Endeavour* vast and cold too, and Clara waving to her mother.

Hal was right. Clara had been sick on the voyage. Meg and Lottie hadn't seemed affected by the heaving boat at all, perhaps being small and low to the ground their bodies weren't so disrupted, and she'd had to run after them, bent over, up and down the slippery metal corridors of the *Endeavour*, what felt like all day, every day, for the whole journey. The twins were sixteen months and had discovered exercise, exploration and teasing their mother.

Clara, whom Hal had taken to calling 'Pudding' during her pregnancy in Krefeld, had lost all of her baby weight, and with being seasick all the time and no German – or even English – stodge to sustain her, now barely filled out her clothes at all. She hoped she wouldn't be too skinny for Hal. He loved her curves.

When she wasn't chasing the girls up and down the *Endeavour*, or leaning over the metal bowl of the lavatory, she read to them. She read the new books she had bought for them in London, and she read the old books her mother had allowed her to take from the shelves of the nursery. She held the loose-spined books gently, reading to Meg and Lottie about fairies and trains and England, until all three fell asleep.

The *Endeavour* made its slow floating entry into the deep east of the Mediterranean. They passed Greece, and the long reaches of Crete. The ancient seas slid away beneath them, the boat throbbed and heaved, the islands and the skies surrounded them. Now she stood in the drizzle, watching Cyprus coming towards her out of the mist.

She had travelled out with an odd assortment of people: an Italian nightclub singer, a young teacher for the English school, who was a shy man barely out of school himself, and a Welsh businessman, with 'interests' in Nicosia, who was very boastful; he liked to frighten them with stories of EOKA's terrorist atrocities, and make them feel as if they were entering a proper war zone, not just a long-held part of the Empire having a little trouble with a few insurgents. 'It's hardly the Blitz, is it?' Clara said to the young teacher one night. It made her feel braver.

Despite the recent war, she had never felt herself a foreigner in Germany: it had the northern European restraint and ragged bombed greyness of home, and she had felt unthreatened there, even as she missed her family. She thought her sense of belonging might actually spring from the war between them, that England and Germany were like two siblings, badly bruised, but forced to carry on in the same house and learn to get on. Cyprus, though, was another thing altogether. Part of the Empire it may have been, but the island was a virtual chip off the Middle East too, Byzantium, Turkey, Greece, all of these parts in crisis, under the British flag, and her husband charged with part of its protection; Clara couldn't help but feel nostalgia for the dull concrete barracks and modern flats of Krefeld, and Brunswick, that she had called home for the six years of her marriage.

The group of civilians clustered together on the metal deck while all around them troops prepared to disembark and the *Endeavour*'s crew brought her into dock. Clara knew they were in the way; she was trying to get mittens onto the girls, but kept dropping them, dangling on their elastic. The soldiers were National Service ones, noisy, desperate to be on land. Clara and the other civilians had kept apart from them on the voyage and it was disconcerting to be surrounded now. The Italian singer, who had put on a sort of safari suit with a cinched waist for their arrival, held one of Meg's hands, and Clara, with Lottie on her hip, held the other. Rain stung her eyes.

The arms of the small harbour were around them now as they drew closer. Clara could see the houses of the town all along the straight front and the waves hitting the sea wall and splashing up. She could see the fishing boats and navy craft bobbing and bumping together on their moorings. She saw black cars and Land Rovers and soldiers, and behind them the jumble of plaster and stone buildings, warehouses, storehouses and the big metal mooring posts, which were mushroom-shaped with giant thick ropes tightly wound around them. She saw soldiers and Cypriots milling about, knotted in groups, waiting. She held onto her children's small hands tightly.

She saw Hal.

He had seen her first and was smiling, with his eyes squinting against the wind. He raised his hand. Now there was just the waiting for the big slow ship to close the distance between them.

The front door stuck.

'We've had a lot of thunderstorms,' said Hal.

The girls peered past their mother's legs into the darkness of the house.

'Well gosh, it's not awfully Mediterranean, is it?' said Clara.

'Not today.'

Corporal Kirby, Hal's batman, began to bring the cases in from the Land Rover. Clara was forced into the kitchen; she and the girls pressed themselves against the wall as Hal and Kirby lifted the biggest trunk and took it upstairs.

Clara took off her hat. There was a stove, a small table, a sink and a food safe with a front that opened downwards to make a shelf. The brown louvred shutters were closed on the window at the front, and at the back of the house there was a door with a curtain over it. The little girls silently watched Clara go to it and push the curtain aside. It slid awkwardly on the plastic-covered wire.

The neighbouring houses backed onto a small courtyard where there was a washing bowl for clothes on the tiles, and a tree in a pot that was dead. She turned back to the room. The girls were pale and top-heavy in their buttoned-up coats.

'Your things are wet, aren't they?' said Clara, and took off their woollen hats. 'Shall we go and see what Daddy's up to?'

In the front bedroom, Hal and Corporal Kirby were trying to find space for the trunks and smaller cases. Hal turned to Clara as she came in. He looked serious and embarrassed.

'What a lovely house!' she said, and he smiled at her.

'That's fine, Kirby. Leave it, will you.'

'Right, sir.'

They heard his boots down the stairs, and the door, and then the Land Rover starting up. Meg and Lottie stared at their parents.

'How's it been?' said Clara.

'Not bad at all.'

'Better than Krefeld?'

'Well, not half so luxurious, as you can see.'

'We don't mind.'

'Don't you?'

'Of course not. We'll make the best of it.'

Clara went to him slowly. She put her face against his shoulder and the girls came over too, and rested their hands on their parents' legs. Hal put his head down and felt Clara's smooth hair against his cheek. 'A month was too long,' he said. He put his arms round them all as the sound of motorbikes and Cypriot voices and the banging shutters of other houses came up from the street.

Chapter Two

The Episkopi Garrison was west of Limassol. The narrow road left the town and crossed the big headland, with the Akrotiri RAF base fence on the left, then went back towards the sea through orange groves, flat fertile land and a long avenue of cypresses.

After the orange groves, the road went up steeply and climbed the cliffs, first with a cutting through them, then with big views of the sea and the long coast behind. After that part, the land was empty and more remote for a stretch and then there was Episkopi.

After you drove through the gate and along the small road into the garrison, there was a mixture of freshly made concrete buildings and Nissen huts, signs to different areas and rows of Land Rovers, three-tonners and large tented sections too, with rutted tracks between them, where permanent buildings hadn't been sorted out yet. There were too many troops coming into Cyprus to accommodate them all properly, a feeling of movement all the time, and a shifting of plans.

Happy Valley was at the far side of the garrison, with the mountains behind it, and had been tented, but now white houses for officers were being put up, with front lawns, and the track to the stables and polo field was half laid with tarmac.

Below the garrison was the beach, an arc, which for most of the year was good for swimming and exercising horses on the sand. You could walk through a long straight tunnel in the high cliff to get to it, or you could negotiate a very steep track down the front of the lower cliffs where they were sandy and had grass in patches.

The officers' mess was a new, concrete building, painted white, with shallow steps up to the narrow porch, and on the evenings that women were invited it was sometimes strung with dim bulbs. Hal thought the bulbs rather pathetic looking, and that they highlighted the general shabbiness, but women always said, 'How lovely,' so he supposed he was wrong. There was a big garden at the back of the mess which you could get straight out to from the bar.

Clara was trying not to get mud on her evening shoes and didn't notice the bulbs. She had hated leaving the twins with the Greek girl on their first night. On the drive over Hal had felt foolish pointing out donkeys and goats and the oranges on the trees, trying to cheer her up.

The mess bar was low-ceilinged and modern, filled with soldiers and their wives, and the floor was carpeted like a golf club.

'Colonel and Mrs Burroughs,' said Hal.

'How do you do.'

'Mark Innes.'

'How do you do.'

Mark Innes, an even-featured, open-faced man of about Hal's age, smiled and shook her hand. 'It's a pleasure to meet you,' he said.

'Another of mine, Tony Grieves. Grieves, my wife, Clara.'

Grieves – a crumpled-looking man of twenty-three, quite drunk – made a sort of lurching bow. 'Mrs Treherne, how do you do.'

'How do you do.'

A Turkish Cypriot waiter in a white jacket brought over a tray of cocktails.

'White Ladies,' said Mrs Burroughs. 'Would you care for one? We've all sorts of other things if you'd rather not. But White Ladies are *it* at the moment.'

'That's lovely. Thank you.'

The waiter held the tray in both hands, Clara noticed, as she took the drink.

There was a bar, hard sofas and armchairs, and a fire at one end of the room. A glass case held silver cups, and yet the whole place had a hasty, brand-new feeling, like a stage set, she thought. She sipped the cocktail, and the sharp lemon juice stung her lips.

'Have they managed to sort out a house for you yet, Hal?' said Colonel Burroughs, and put a hand on his shoulder, turning him away from Clara as Mrs Burroughs closed in.

'Don't be overwhelmed,' she said. She was long-faced and kind, speaking quickly in a powerful voice. 'You'll get used to us all. There's always a crowd at the end of the week, but you won't find wives here all that often. There's more fun to be had in town, at the club. My husband is terribly impressed with yours. He's young to have been made up to major, isn't he? His father must be awfully pleased – are Arthur and Jean well?'

'Yes, I –'

'I should think you'll both find it quite different from Germany. But you didn't come directly from there, did you?'

'No. I took the girls to my family in Buckinghamshire for a few weeks.'

'Lovely. What price Buckinghamshire now, eh? It is *freezing* this evening, isn't it? Very often we have beautiful warm weather in January, but this winter has been very harsh. You'll find the spring pleasant, I should think, although the summer's absolutely draining. We have most things here, and once you're on the base you'll be more or less comfortable, I'm sure. It is a shame you're stuck in the town, typical army muddle, but really there's very little trouble. I don't know what you've heard.'

'Hal says it's been a bit quieter recently.'

'Well, there was an incident in Limassol last week, but mostly we're managing to stop these ghastly things before they happen, that's the plan at any rate, but these Cyps are so damned sneaky and the law of averages says they get away with one or two things, however careful one is.'

'I met a man on the boat who said they make bombs out of car exhausts and food tins.'

'My dear, they'll make them out of absolutely anything. They have them on timers and tripwires and goodness knows what. They've no scruples whatsoever. We've had to put poles on the fronts of the vehicles to catch the piano wire they stretch across the road before it can take off our poor lads' heads – now what sort of a terrible mind thinks up a thing like that?'

'I noticed something of the sort as we drove in,' said Clara, remembering she had been worrying about the girls and hadn't asked Hal what they were for. She'd rather not know, she decided.

'Another drink?' said Mrs Burroughs, and led Clara away

from the bar towards a group of women at a card table, playing whist.

'You must join our reading group at the club. It's terribly good fun, and we often read plays aloud – do you enjoy the theatre at all? We were thinking of starting a dramatic society . . .'

Later they were driven home by Kirby through a very black night, stopping for the gates to be opened by soldiers, who peered in at them, saluted and waved them through. The headlights picked out the barbed wire that was looped on the tops of fences or stretched tight between posts.

Away from the base the road felt lonely; Clara was glad to see buildings ahead of them as they came into Limassol. There was almost no street lighting, and nobody about, just the dark houses and alleyways between them.

'I'm sorry I was so grumpy earlier,' she said.

'Don't be silly,' said Hal. He put his arm around her. 'You'll see the girls in a moment.'

'I'm sure they're fine.'

'I'm going to be kept pretty busy,' he said. 'Do you remember the blokes in Krefeld, shooting up wrecked old cars just for something to do?'

'This will be better.'

'Yes,' he said firmly.

He was happy.

In Germany Hal had distinguished himself, been promoted to captain and served six years after that without having seen a shot fired in anger and it had been hard to take the inactivity. Even with his joy in having Clara at last, after their long engagement, he had been frustrated. His main challenge was keeping his men up to the mark and occupied, and Clara had come to understand that it was not blood-lust that was being thwarted in Hal, but something cleaner than that, and natural. He'd been trained to do a job; he should have liked to do it.

The car stopped. Kirby got out, opened the door for them and looked up and down the street, short-fingered hands resting loosely on his Sten gun, as they let themselves into the house.

The Greek girl was sitting on a chair in the kitchen. She stood up and smiled. Hal took out his wallet and Clara went straight upstairs to the back bedroom and pushed open the door.

A candle was burning on the tilting chest of drawers.

Lottie was asleep on the bed and the cot was empty. After a very short moment of terror Clara saw that Meg was in the single bed, too, in the shadow behind the heaped-up blankets. She went to the bed and sat down. The twins were jumbled together in sleep. She felt their faces, as she had when they were smaller. She always told herself there was no need to do it, but still, whenever they slept, she checked to make sure they were breathing.

She picked up the candle and went to the top of the stairs. 'Where's the girl?' she said.

'She's gone.'

'She left a candle in the room.' Clara heard her voice shaking. 'It's very dangerous. They're not babies now, they might have pushed it over. Will you tell her next time?'

'We won't use her next time.'

After a moment, she said, 'Don't worry, I'll get used to everything.'

Hal came up the stairs. He blew out the candle and, in the sudden blackness, kissed her. 'I'm not worried,' he said.

Chapter Three

Even up in the hills, the walls of the village houses were covered with graffiti. Some of it was in poorly spelled English, although any schoolboy could have read the Greek: '*BRITISH OUT. EOKA. ELEFTHERIA I THANATOS – freedom or death. ENOSIS – union with Greece*.'

The trucks crawled as the road got steeper. The engines whined, and sometimes the tyres skidded where the roads were still running water from the heavy rain. The villages were built onto the sides of the steep foothills, and the fields beneath them were stepped to make them workable. Hal could see the three-tonner ahead full sideways now, because the road had taken a sharp bend to get around an outcrop before disappearing into trees. The trucks ground and toiled up the steep incline and around the long corner.

This was how many of Hal's days were spent, patrolling the villages, conducting searches. At least there was more to do than in Germany where he had been in his office most of the time, signing papers concerning the minutiae of the movement of supplies, or overseeing exercises and patrols that were almost uniformly without incident. The glory of the regiment had been demonstrated mainly in the boxing ring, and the silver cups that were awarded decorated the officers' mess wherever they were sent. He had envied James, whose first posting had been to Eritrea, and whose letters, almost gritty with desert sand, were full of action.

Hal's father had gone into the Great War a lieutenant and come out of it a major. His uncles – those who survived – had had their promotions the same way, in the big conflicts of big battles. His grandfather had fought in both Boer wars, Lieutenant Colonel Henry Treherne – Hal had kept his medals in his room when he was a little boy. In Germany, Hal's regiment had spent a year living in a palace formerly occupied by Nazi generals. There had been a gold banqueting hall. His first office was a music room and his desk Louis Quinze. It wasn't Ypres. Now, in Cyprus, England was fighting to hold her territory, and Hal could serve her in some small measure.

As the last of the convoy made the turn, the road forked, with one narrower part going into the trees and the other climbing up to the left.

The sky was white, the tops of the mountains were hidden. If they went higher they'd be in mist. They took the wider, left-hand turn and the first village they came to was compact, with a café in its centre.

The men in the café all stood up and watched as two trucks stopped and the others and the Land Rover drove on through, nearly touching the houses on each side, the soldiers holding their Sten guns and staring back at the old men.

The second village was more spread out along the road with no clear centre to it. The two three-tonners pulled over and Kirby stopped the Land Rover close behind them. Hal got out and met Lieutenant Grieves, who had climbed out of the truck in front of him.

'Mandri, sir.'

'I'll try and find the chief. You can get going when I come back.'

Hal took Kirby and went to look for the village headman.

He found a bar that was set back from the road with a ragged tree in front of it and metal chairs stacked against the outside wall. Kirby pushed open the door for him, and Hal stepped inside, taking off his cap and looking around. There was a good smell of Greek coffee. At a table in a corner, five men stopped playing dominoes to look at him.

'Good morning,' Hal said in Greek, and the old men nodded and said good morning back.

Hal asked for the *mukhtar* and was told he lived next to the church. He thanked the men and left. As he walked back past the trucks he was aware of Grieves watching him and scowling; he was impatient and bored with waiting and the men were bored too. Well, they could wait some more: relations with the Greeks must be respected.

There was nobody on the street and just a girl staring from the darkness of her house as he and Kirby walked to the church. In the crooked square, a small boy stood by the corner with muddy feet and Hal felt the presence of the people inside the houses without seeing them.

He chose the larger of the houses next to the church – although it was still a pretty rough-looking dwelling – and knocked. The door opened, and a woman in a black dress, holding a broom, greeted him. Hal asked for the *mukhtar* and was shown into a parlour to wait.

The walls were plastered but the floor was stone and there was a damp chill in the house, with no sun to warm it up. Hal put his cap on the polished table, which was the only piece of furniture in the room. Kirby, standing in the street outside, coughed and lit a cigarette, and the *mukhtar*, who was in his fifties perhaps, with dark skin and a moustache, and the voluminous Greek trousers that many of the men in the villages wore, came into the room. 'Yes?' he said in English.

'Good morning, sir. My name is Major Treherne.'

The man nodded. Hal didn't think he hated him, but he couldn't tell; it was often hard to tell but it was an important thing to know, to understand how much danger there was. 'I ask permission to search the village houses for suspected terrorists,' he said. It was a sentence he used often.

'You'll do it with or without my permission,' said the *mukhtar*, in thickly accented English.

This was true. If they had intelligence beforehand they skipped the asking of permission.

'If I must,' said Hal. 'There are many terrorists who use their families to shield them. I come here as a courtesy to you.'

There was a silence while the *mukhtar* looked at him – Hal thought there was every chance he was a terrorist himself. Then, 'You may,' he said.

The soldiers' searching was methodical and polite, embarrassment rather than belligerence characterising their entry into people's homes. Hal moved back and forth between the groups. It was so routine as to be tedious, but there was always an undercurrent of tension – at least, it was important to stay sharp. He was only needed if something had been found, or if there was a problem, so when Private Francke came to fetch him, he followed immediately.

Hal stood in the tiny house and looked at the wreckage.

The table was on its side. A pool of olive oil moved silently over the floor from a cracked jug. The food cupboard had been emptied and jars shattered. The bedding, which he could see in the back room through the door opening, was tipped onto the ground and the mattresses bayoneted in places. There was china on the floor, too, mostly broken. Hal moved his boot away from a small plate painted with birds and olive branches. 'I don't see what you called me in here for, Francke.'

'It's the empty tins, sir. Who needs that many tins?'

Hal looked at them. There were ten on the floor near the door into the back room. 'I can't arrest somebody for some empty tins. What sort of people are they?'

'Cyps, sir.'

'Yes, Francke – how do they *seem* to you?'

'Dunno, sir, pretty browned off.'

'And?'

'An old couple, sir.'

Most of the lads showed an instinctive tact in the dealings they were required to have with the locals, even while calling them wogs and Cyps, but Francke was a bully, and had probably been one all his life. Hal didn't know the names of all the men in the company; it was the ones who turned up in his office on a charge who stuck in his mind. Francke was one of those.

'Francke.'

'Sir?'

'It seems to me you've gone about this with undue relish.'

'Sir?'

'You may have heard the phrase "hearts and minds" bandied about in regard to this campaign.'

Francke gazed at Hal densely.

'It's been hard to miss, Francke. It's been the backbone of what we're trying to achieve here. This island is under British sovereignty – that means protection as well as rule. We are here to root out terrorism and to protect the population from it, not to give people a grievance and send them scurrying for the hills to grab a bomb with which to murder the next squaddie they see. In other words, this,' he gestured to the room around him, '*is too fucking heavy-handed. Do you understand me?*'

'Yes, sir.'

'This is *no good*.'

'No, sir.'

Hal sent Francke ahead of him out of the house. He picked up the olive-branch plate and put it on the table and then he went out into the street.

About fifty villagers had been herded into the square and were being guarded by Ellis and Trask, who looked embarrassed. A woman was shouting angrily in Greek that Hal had no hope of understanding. Another woman joined in the shouting, some of the men too and the soldiers answered in English, as you might talk to animals, conciliatory and threatening at the same time.

Ellis and Trask squared up to them, gripping their Stens in both hands. Sergeant McKinney stood nearby, with his legs wide apart and his chin jutting out, overseeing the whole thing with an air of comfortable immovability.

Lieutenant Grieves came towards Hal out of a side street with two other soldiers. He hadn't exactly been distinguishing himself with his leadership qualities in the last two hours;

Hal hadn't seen him since the damn thing started. 'There you are, Grieves. Put those people in the church.'

'Sir.'

Grieves went off – shuffled off, thought Hal. The WOSB must have been having a slow week when they'd made him a lieutenant, a sneery grammar-school boy with chips on both shoulders and Bolshevik tendencies. No one liked drinking with him and he was hell sober. Hal had nothing against National Service boys as a rule, but Grieves, with his too-civilised-for-soldiering attitude, counting the days to demob, irritated him.

It wasn't a big village, no maze of streets and blind alleys to contend with, just the houses along the road and the square, and more houses in a modest sprawl up the hill with rutted goat tracks leading to them. Most of the villagers were in the church and every house searched.

Hal looked into the back of the truck where a Greek boy, the one arrest, was sitting with his head in his hands. He was flanked by Tompkins and Walsh, who were sharing a fag. On the sandbags at their feet was a muddy stack of EOKA pamphlets, two good-sized clasp knives and a piece of piping, crudely welded closed at one end.

The boy looked sideways through his fingers at Hal.

Hal picked up the piece of piping, pushing the leaflets with it. They were familiar to him, distributed by EOKA in their thousands, and although he couldn't read the Greek, he knew the meaning: '*We have nothing else to do but shed blood.*' He examined the pipe, then put it down on the floor of the truck again. 'Are these yours?' said Hal to the boy, who didn't answer. 'Tompkins – was the pipe in the same house?'

'Yes, sir, he had it hidden up in the fireplace.'

'You're sure it was this boy's house?'

'Yes, sir.'

'Was he alone?'

'His mum was there.'

The boy looked about nineteen. Old enough to know better.

Hal looked around him at the valley, where the mist was shifting, and then up the hill towards the church. He could see the people drifting back to their houses, and the rest of the soldiers coming down the hill towards him, lighting cigarettes and talking.

He looked back at the Greek boy, who hadn't moved. 'On you go, then,' he said to Tompkins. 'Good.'

Tompkins nodded and shoved the boy along into the dark of the truck, to make room.

Kirby was smoking in the Land Rover, with his collar well up, and hunched down in the driver's seat.

'Kirby. Come,' said Hal, and Kirby got out. He was a knock-kneed, heavy young man, whose every movement was reluctantly forced from clumsy limbs.

He and Hal started up the hill together towards the *mukhtar*'s house, as the trucks rattled away from them.

Hal stood in the parlour, the *mukhtar*'s housekeeper – or wife, or mother – poked the fire and the *mukhtar* maintained his silence.

'What's the name of the man we arrested?'

'He's a good boy.'

'Name?'

No answer.

'You're not doing him any favours.'

'Your soldiers have damaged property here today. They have destroyed houses. They distressed the women.'

'Any complaint you have can be made in writing to the British High Commission,' Hal said.

The *mukhtar* spat. The woman looked at the spit shining in the firelight on the stone floor.

Hal said, 'Are you going to give me the man's name?'

'No.'

'Then thank you for your time and co-operation,' said Hal, and turned to leave.

Kirby let him go out and then followed him. The door of the house closed behind them.

'Fucking cheek,' said Kirby, as they walked away. 'You could do him for that, sir.'

Hal laughed.

The two platoons were back in Episkopi at dusk. Tompkins and Walsh marched the Greek boy off to the guardroom, with Walsh carefully carrying the evidence. Hal didn't think about him again, but went to the mess and had a drink, then Kirby drove him back into Limassol, to Clara and the girls, with Hal sitting up front and both mostly quiet, comfortable with one another.

Chapter Four

Clara lay against Hal in the close darkness. The blankets on the bed never seemed quite dry, but they were warm and heavily tucked around them.

Obedient to convention, the first bed they had ever shared was on their wedding night, in a hotel in the New Forest, to be near Southampton for the boat back across the Channel the next day. Hal, newly promoted to captain, only had a few days' leave and they couldn't have afforded a longer wedding trip anyway. The hotel was accurately, but still somehow misleadingly, described as 'an old coaching inn', and had been recommended by a friend of Hal's. It was a disappointment, and the bed most disappointing of all. The room had uneven, poorly covered floors. Clara's going-away suit hung neatly in the wardrobe as their every tiny movement was announced through the pipes, boards and hollow bulging plaster of the cold building, a wedding night broadcast to the world at large.

It had not been everything the four years of their engagement had promised. Before that viciously creaking bed, four years of writing letters and visits – far too short, far too infrequent – when they had kissed incessantly. Clara's family saw a tall, cool-faced young soldier, plainly uncomfortable in their presence but somehow needing their daughter badly enough to stay in various cheap boarding houses and bed-and-breakfasts to be near her, never going anywhere else, always faithfully there, while Hal and Clara, alone in knowing what they were together, frustrated themselves kissing. His fingertips on the pulse of her neck, her lips on his knuckles, his thumb on her temple, her hairline, his arms circling her – they had been in a long daze of need for one another and that hotel, that room, that bed did not deliver them from it.

But the night had its own success because Hal and Clara had, almost despite themselves, a deep affinity. In their love and flirting, they liked to point out their differences, but their observations were similar, as if they had been brought up together some forgotten time and only now found themselves with contrasting lives. They easily made a world to inhabit when they were together. They played within it. They had not slept all night, the night they were married, had boarded the boat bright-eyed with dazzled exhaustion and strange joy, and every bed they had been in since then – all more satisfying than that poor beginning – still had a little of that first bed in it, those first long hours of their free companionship.

This bed, like that one, rested on an uneven floor. There was some light coming from the bulb at the top of the stairs so the outline of the door glowed.

Her head was under his chin and he couldn't see her face, but he could see the shape of the blankets over her body and feel her pressed against him inside the warm bed, her head fitting well into the hollow there. He was holding her hand. He could feel her wedding ring and the small diamond next to it under his thumb. He didn't think they needed a bigger bed. He liked to be so close to her all the time and not miss anything. When she spoke, he felt her voice in his chest, through her back. 'This bed is definitely tipping towards the window.'

'It's the floor I think,' he said.

'Did you try to prop it up?'

'I tried!'

'I wake up all squashed against you –'

'And me almost on the floor –'

Then the bulb on the stairs went out with a small popping noise and there was total darkness.

'Hal!' She had whispered his name so he couldn't feel her voice any more.

'Just the bulb,' he said.

'It's too dark.' There was absolute blackness around them. 'The girls –'

'I'll see to it.'

Then there was a very dull boom, almost too deep to hear. It shook the windows of the house. Clara sat up suddenly, and Hal was out of bed, finding his lighter in the dark. He flipped it open and Clara blinked at the bright flame.

'Here.' Hal handed her the lighter and pulled on his trousers. He took his pistol.

She closed the lighter and burned her fingers doing it.

Neither of them could see anything at all now. He listened. There were engines in the street and running footsteps. He couldn't tell if the footsteps were coming to their house.

He left the bedroom, went fast down the stairs, with his hand against the wall for balance, and stopped at the door. We've got to get out of this house, he thought. It's completely impractical.

The feet were running past the house, not to it, and he

heard sirens and realised that the light going out had nothing to do with the bomb – if it was a bomb – and he opened the door a little way, with his pistol ready.

'Hal?' said Clara, from the bedroom.

'It's all right,' he said. 'I don't know what happened. I'll bring a bulb.'

He heard her getting off the bed – the springs were noisy – then he saw the glow of the lighter as she left the room to check the twins.

He went to the kitchen. Moonlight was coming into the back of the house. There was no bulb in the kitchen drawer, but he found candles and took three plates from the cupboard above. He went to the front of the house again and up the stairs to where Clara was sitting on the end of the girls' bed. She had Hal's lighter on the floor in front of her, still burning. The girls were fast asleep.

Hal lit a candle and blew out the lighter, which was too hot to pick up. He dripped wax onto the saucer, stuck the candle down and lit the other candles, and while he was doing it Clara started to cry.

Hal had finished lighting the candles. He didn't move now, just stayed kneeling on the floor with Clara crying, thinking how much he hated it when she cried, and not knowing what to do.

'Sorry,' she said.

He got up from his knees and sat next to her on the bed. The three plates of candles lit them both quite brightly from underneath and flickered on the cot bars. Hal put his arm around Clara and felt her softness. 'It was just a fright,' he said.

Then there was banging on the door, very loud – Clara jumped. Hal stood up and left the lighted room.

'Yes,' he said, going down the stairs.

'It's Kirby, sir.' Hal opened the door. 'They've bombed the bloody police station in Hellas Street.'

'I heard it. I'll come now. You were fast.'

'I can be.'

'Just a moment.'

Hal shut the door again, thinking how much he liked Kirby, and ran up the stairs. 'I need to go. The police station has been bombed.'

Clara was just where he'd left her with the girls still sleeping. She looked at him bleakly.

'It's all right,' he said deliberately, having to explain, 'it was nothing to do with us,' and he closed himself off from her.

He went into the bedroom, put on his jacket, his cap and his boots. He didn't go back into the girls' room but holstered his pistol as he went down again.

'How long will you be?'

She was at the top of the stairs.

'I've no idea.' His hand was already on the door. He didn't want her to say anything else, and she didn't. 'Go back to bed,' he said. 'There's nothing for you to worry about.'

Hal left and shut the door behind him.

Clara sat down on the top stair because her legs were shaking. 'Buck up and don't be so ridiculous,' she said, in a whisper.

She got up, and took a candle from the floor of the girls' room, placing the others out of reach on the table. She went downstairs, with the small flame throwing shadows against the walls of the house, and drew the chain that Hal had screwed onto the thin door for them a few days before.

The dark kitchen was behind her, with the glass out onto the courtyard uncovered. She turned to it. The curtain wasn't closed over the door. She went into the kitchen and the tiles were rough under her bare feet. She put the candle on the counter, and picked up the table, having to stretch her arms as wide as they would go to grasp both edges, leaning forward unnaturally. She carried the table with tiny steps, holding her breath because it was heavy, trying to be silent. She put it against the back door; she pressed it up snugly, feeling the horror of being observed from outside. She pulled the curtain across the glass, it was stuck behind the table, it wouldn't close properly.

She left the kitchen and went up to sit on the bed, with the girls sleeping, tucking her legs under her and wrapping her arms around her knees. The house was empty and evil around her, hiding itself, no protection from anything that might come. It was a nothing house; she couldn't hope to be all right in it.

The sleeping children near her had peace all around them, like a shield, and she edged closer to them. She felt very guilty for being comforted by the presence of defenceless babies.

She didn't want Hal to see the table against the back door because then he'd know how silly and frightened she was. Perhaps she could put it back before she unbolted the door for him when he came home. She didn't want him to think she wasn't coping. She thought of him setting off not just fearlessly, but with relish, to see what could be done, and smiled. Her girls slept on. His daughters had inherited his colouring; perhaps they would grow up with his fair outlook, too, perhaps his courage. A shutter banged – first loudly, making her jump, then again in sluggish repetition – and a dog began to bark. She thought of Hal's belief in her and how she loved his admiration. She hugged her knees again, listening to the dog barking, the rumble of engines and a distant alarm bell ringing. She closed her eyes, clenching her jaw tightly. Words of hymns often helped. It wasn't God, she didn't think; she wasn't sure what it was. Determinedly, in the prison of her mind, she sang: *'Praise, my soul, the King of Heaven, to his feet thy tribute bring, ransomed, healed, restored, forgiven –'*

The police station was burning. Two Turkish Cypriot policemen and a Royal Military Policeman had been killed. Another Turkish Cypriot officer had his legs blown off, and would die before morning. A double victory for EOKA then: both Turks and British successfully targeted.

The soldiers were trying to keep people back, forcing the staring crowds into a semi-circle, and the fire engines, RMPs and other troops trying to fight the fire had to force their way through.

Hal had his men evacuate the nearby buildings and make the area safe; there was no point getting into it with the locals now, and revenge was an empty concept to him. Whoever had pitched the bombs into the police station was long gone, congratulating themselves on victory in some distant safe house or mountain camp.

The breeze grew stronger and Hal could smell the salt on it. He thought of it blowing the smoke inland over those dark sheltering mountains.

The fire was loud and the roaring flames were fanned by the sea breeze that came between the houses, like a draught sending flames up a chimney. Inside what was left of the police station, the plaster ceiling and wooden frames cracked and crumbled. The three dead men and the wounded one had been taken away before the fire took hold and were peaceful, or lying quietly at least, in the hospital. The fight was to keep the fire from spreading, and it took until dawn to do it.

The early morning was mild and grey, long streaks of smoke mixing with the cloud in the sky over the town. There would be days of activity as the bombers were sought. They would not be found. Somebody might be found, somebody else, another terrorist, another sympathiser.

The rubble of the police station was still smoking. The soldiers left the streets to the morning traffic, and people going to work made the day normal again.

Kirby left Hal at his door. He only remembered Clara when he opened it and the thin chain snapped tight. 'Clara!'

Clara had fallen asleep leaning against the wall, with her neck stretched uncomfortably. She woke up with small hands on her face and Meg saying, 'Mummy,' then a few moments later Hal's voice downstairs.

She wrapped a blanket around herself and ran down. She went as fast as she could to the table and dragged it back from the door.

'What are you doing?' said Hal, laughing, shut out.

Clara slid back the chain and he stepped inside, smelling smoky with a dirty face. 'Everything all right?'

'Yes of course.'

'Good. Two Turks bought it, and an RMP – bloody bastards. I need to get cleaned up. I'll have breakfast at Epi. CO wants to see me.' He went loudly up the stairs.

'Hello darling!' he said to Meg, cheerfully, and Clara went up after him, gently rubbing the soot from her hands where she'd held his arm.

Chapter Five

Clara was upstairs with the children and Adile was sweeping the stairs. Adile was Turkish Cypriot, about sixteen years old. She had been recommended by Mrs Burroughs and had five brothers and sisters so was presumably well used to children. She spoke not one word of English, which Mrs Burroughs said was probably a good thing, as anything one wanted her to do was easily communicated by sign language, but Clara found their relationship impossibly strained.

She missed the girl who had helped her sometimes on the base at Krefeld, who, although German and a citizen of an occupied country, seemed to bear no grudge – at least, not towards Clara and the babies. She had spoken English well, and been extremely cheerful. Cheerful to the point of backwardness, Hal said, but Clara had found her easy company. This girl, Adile, was silent. She arrived on time every morning and never looked Clara in the eye.

Clara had been making a game of dressing the girls – putting their socks on their hands and heads first to make them laugh – and it had taken a long time to get ready. She was trying to teach them how to put on their own dresses; they weren't awfully interested.

The quiet slap of Adile's slippers on the stairs, the light

sweep of the broom, and the door was pushed open. It creaked. Adile bowed her head slightly. She had a gentle face. Clara knew the Turkish Cypriots were more consistently friendly to the British, but Adile was a Muslim, and more foreign than a Greek would have been. Hal said the Turks were reliable policemen and did a good job, and Clara worked to overcome her prejudices. Adile always wore her scarf wound tightly around her head and under her chin, and had very big brown eyes. Clara wondered how long her hair was.

She got up from the floor and dusted off her dress.

''Lo there!' said Lottie, who was very chatty, or tried to be.

Meg was quieter. Clara hoped that they weren't going to be divided like that so obviously all of their lives: the quiet twin, the jolly one, the pretty one, the plain one. They weren't identical and she was relieved about that. Their being two halves of the same personality would have been an uncomfortable thought.

Adile smiled, but didn't speak.

'Good morning,' said Clara, briskly, and stepping around Adile, took the girls downstairs. The stairs were very narrow, it was a lengthy business with the girls' tiny feet on the tiles, slipping on the wooden edges that were worn thin.

There was a knock on the door.

'Who could that be?' said Clara. She sensed Adile behind her. 'It's all right, Adile,' she said, not expecting an answer. 'I'll go.'

The knock came again.

'We're coming!' said Clara.

They reached the door.

'Who is it?'

'Evelyn Burroughs!' came the operatic answer.

Clara opened the door. Mrs Burroughs, big and beaming, briefly transformed all of Cyprus to England.

'Hello,' said Clara.

'Not having a telephone puts one right back in the nineteenth century,' said Mrs Burroughs. 'Not that I would remember, I hasten to add!'

She laughed and Clara smiled at her. 'Come in. Look, girls, it's Mrs Burroughs.'

'Silly girl, call me Evelyn.'

'Evelyn. Come in.'

Evelyn came into the house, which seemed to shrink around her. The children stared up. 'How's the Turkish girl doing?'

'She's fine. Very helpful.'

'So you're all right?'

'Yes, of course,' said Clara, firmly. 'Absolutely fine.'

'I must say you've been an awfully good sport about it. I would've kicked up a hell of a fuss. Your husband must be proud. It makes all the difference in the world to have a wife who doesn't make things harder, don't you think?'

'I'm sure.'

'Still, it's a rotten show and I've been doing my damnedest to get you a house up at Epi and I may have succeeded.'

'A house would be nice.'

'Yes, it's no good here. I've brought a car. I've one or two things to get and then shall we go up to the base?'

Clara felt gratitude verging on the adoring. 'I'd like that,' she said.

'We just need to pop by Costa's or whatever it's called on Anexartisias Street – and then we can head off. All right?'

'Lovely. I'll get our coats.'

'There's no need. Have you seen the sun's out?' said Evelyn, and opened the door wide to the street where bright light was striking the first floors of the houses opposite.

Evelyn had organised everything. She had invited three more officers' wives and lunch was very busy and noisy. There were other children, too, though none so small as the twins, and they were all given lunch in the kitchen. The women competed to impress Clara with their welcome and were eager to show her that Cyprus wasn't such a bad posting.

'What about a walk on the beach? It'll remind you of Cornwall in summer . . .'

So, after lunch they left the children and went down to the beach, by way of the stables, where shiny horses looked over their stable doors at them as they went by and Clara touched their soft noses carefully.

The beach was wide and sandy and a shallow sea broke white-topped waves along it in a homely rhythm. Clara felt her cheeks getting pink as they walked. She imagined kissing Hal and telling him about her day.

When they got back up to the Burroughses' bungalow, Captain Hayes was there on behalf of the housing officer. 'We've a couple of houses for Mrs Treherne to take a look at. Shall we go along now?'

The house Clara chose out of the two offered her was brand new, the still-damp plaster had just been painted. It was a short walk from Evelyn's and next door to Deirdre and Mark Innes. They could drive or walk to the officers' mess. The plot was called Lionheart, a half-built miniature suburb, with front gardens but no fences and a brand-new road through it.

* * *

The night before they moved Clara and Hal lay in the tilting bed of the Limassol house for the last time and Clara allowed herself to feel how very much she hated it.

'I'm glad we'll have you safe and sound at Episkopi,' said Hal, holding her close to him, both arms around her. 'I might be away next week, and I would have hated to leave you here.'

Clara allowed only the smallest of pauses. 'How long will you be away for?' she said.

'I don't know yet.'

'Proper fighting?'

Hal laughed.

Clara pressed herself close up to him. Let him think her a girl-woman if he wanted. 'Proper fighting, Hal?' she repeated and he laughed again.

'Well, a bit of action, anyway. If I'm lucky,' he said.

Chapter Six

The boy Hal had handed over to the Special Investigations Branch was called Andreas. He was interrogated by them, but the talking was done by an interpreter, who was a gentle young Englishman, a classics scholar before his National Service, and not inclined to – or often able to – translate the more colourful language of the two SIB plain-clothes officers he had been attached to. The transformation from Homeric to modern Greek had been achieved by a hasty language course in England at the end of his basic training when the WOSB had discovered he had a classics degree.

The interpreter was one of life's diplomats, and his answer to 'What did he say?' was often a tactful approximation: 'He said he doesn't know, sir,' rather than 'He said you can rot in hell.'

After three months in Limassol, the interpreter had begun to see himself more as protector than questioner. In Nicosia he had worked for the Special Investigations Branch attached to a different regiment, and wished he was still there, where he could honestly say he had never felt ashamed. These two were harsher. They were both quiet men, who kept to themselves, not making friends around the camp, standing out in their suits as the outsiders they were. The sight of them going about their secretive business was chilling sometimes even to the soldiers who worked alongside them.

The interrogations he was asked to leave were the ones he felt he'd failed at, and often he thought he was under more pressure to get results than the SIB themselves, because he so badly didn't want anybody to be hurt. He didn't want this boy to go onto the next stage of questioning, the more unpleasant stage. He tried to explain to him, without meaning to threaten, that if the boy would be helpful, then he would be unhurt and even protected, but if he was stubborn he – the interpreter – couldn't say that he would not be hurt, and perhaps seriously. Often prisoners took this the wrong way, and were defiant, but sometimes they accepted that the young officer was trying to help them. His uniform was less frightening than the incongruous dark suits of his two superiors; it was honest, and his face was honest too, and kind. Sometimes they gave up their secrets, if they had any to give. Sometimes they didn't.

The moment where a variation of 'All right, Davis, we'll take over from here,' was said to him, and he was dismissed – leaving them with a soldier and the prisoner in a closed room – was a relatively rare, but deeply uncomfortable one for the interpreter. He saw the prisoner again an hour later, or the next morning, when the phrase he used in his mind for that was 'a little the worse for wear'. A face that was a little the worse for wear was not a pleasant sight. It might not be bloody – although he'd seen that too – but it was always changed.

The interpreter knew he was a necessary part of a larger process; he tried not to feel responsible when the process went on without him. He had been told harsh methods were justifiable, and he believed that to be true, but he had never seen an English death brought about by terrorism, he felt no animosity towards the Cypriots, and he could not help feeling that violence was like cheating, and unfair.

This boy, Andreas, was not a hard nut to crack. His defiance on arriving at Episkopi Garrison faded to sulkiness within an hour of being locked up. He was given food and water and spoken to by Davis, and when the evidence of his feeble crimes was laid before him on the wooden table he became actually chatty. He had an uncle, he said, who had been talking to him and his friends for months about EOKA. His uncle hated the British – Andreas gave his name, pausing politely for it to be spelled correctly – and would do anything to drive them out of Cyprus. He was in a camp up in the Troodos, and rumour was that he was with Axfentiou, but he couldn't say for sure. He had another uncle, though, the black sheep of the family, a sort of cousin of an uncle, in fact, and the British were after him, too. Photographs were brought. Andreas identified him in the booklet handed out to every British officer of EOKA's 'most wanted'. General Grivas and Axfentiou, EOKA's leaders, were at numbers one and two, and Andreas's uncle was there too, down the list, at number thirty-four. Andreas described a farmhouse in the foothills near Kaminaria where he knew they were storing weapons and where this man was hiding. Encouraged by the enthusiasm of his questioners, he gave places and names; they were all good friends. Andreas himself had nothing against the British, and was keen to point that out, but he had been persuaded that fighting for Greece was a fine thing to do, and he regretted it now.

'Davis, tell him if he behaves himself, we won't tell the whole village he's a toad and he won't get his throat cut.'

'Andreas, we will take you home. We won't betray you to your village, if you don't betray us. We are all trying to stop more violence. Yes?'

Andreas was to do one more thing for them before his release: he was to show them exactly where the farmhouse was. He agreed immediately to this, and it crossed Davis's mind that the boy could lead a hundred soldiers into an ambush very easily and be a hero. It was impossible to tell from his dark face what he was really thinking.

SIB briefed Colonel Burroughs about Andreas's black sheep of an uncle, whose name was Loulla Kollias, and Burroughs briefed Hal. Hal devised a plan, his first, with particular care, and then – like a schoolboy having his prep inspected – went over it with Burroughs, who was thorough and helpful and questioned everything.

Loulla Kollias's photograph also hung in Colonel Burroughs's office, in his rogues gallery and opposite his picture of the Queen. It showed a middle-aged man who could have been a shepherd or a farmer, with a large black moustache, thick eyebrows and a frayed and faded sweater with a neck that stood up. The photograph had been taken for EOKA propaganda. In it, he was squinting manfully into a wind, with his hair blowing up from his head and the camera at a low angle. The only thing distinguishing him from any other Greek man between the ages of twenty-five and forty was the bullet belt slung diagonally over his body and the nose of his rifle, which could be seen poking up from behind his shoulder. He was responsible for the death of an American government official in a car bombing. He organised roadside ambushes and riots. He was close to General Grivas, and a chief recruiter for EOKA. He was a man who believed in a Cyprus independent of British rule and took his army straight from school, transforming romantic Greek schoolboys into soldiers – or terrorists, depending on your point of view.

Three hours before dawn, three days after Andreas's capture, Hal left Clara pretending to be asleep in their brand-new bedroom on Lionheart Estate and joined Kirby and a convoy of trucks and Land Rovers, which left the garrison, heading north into the Troodos. Andreas was in the Land Rover behind Hal's, flanked by soldiers, with the interpreter, Davis, sitting in front, very nervous.

It was still dark. The trucks crawled slower and slower, the drivers keeping to the hard-packed centre of the road, looking for disturbed ground where mines might be hidden, and the soldiers stopped talking and stayed quiet and watchful. There was no protection in being in a vehicle; they would rather have been out of them and on foot, where they could listen better and move more carefully and the ground away from the road had no mines hidden in it.

There had been burns casualties from a roadside ambush in the hills the week before. The terrain was good for it – scrubby and plenty of low cover – and there were caves, too, and not all of the island was mapped thoroughly.

The threat of ambush takes everyone differently. Some spend all their time imagining what may happen: in the front of a truck at night they sit to one side to avoid a bullet from a sniper who might use the headlights to gauge the position of their head. They get superstitious and try to second guess the mind of the man who may have hidden a mine or tripwire in this place or that place. Then there's the other kind, who don't think about it imaginatively. They limit their thoughts; they aren't interested in chance and they don't give any choice power over another choice because they know they'd spend their whole lives doing it and dying a different way each time. Hal was one of those.

He knew it was a decision to be like that, and understood how you could lose your nerve and start imagining things and he didn't know if he would be as cool in combat. He hadn't had the chance to find out yet. Perhaps he would now.

He could smell the damp pines, the mineral rocky ground, goats and, faintly, diesel. He felt his body quicken in readiness for what lay ahead and he was thinking about that, not worrying about imaginary mines, as the trucks made the climb towards the tree-line.

The farmhouse was deep at the bottom of a very steep valley. A river ran along it with a bridge, and the main house and outhouses were along the river and hidden beneath trees. There was one road in, and one road out, and each of the narrow roads made several hairpin bends, doubling back and forth deeper and deeper into the invisible valley or higher and higher to the top of the black hills that met a black sky almost no different.

They left the trucks and blocked the roads at their dividing. Then there was a long wait while half of Two Platoon went the long way around the valley to block the second road before they went forward on foot.

The soldiers spread out across the hillside, making the best of poor cover, creeping down into the dark crack in the earth that was the valley.

When dawn came, it would reach this place last; a more

acute and crevice-like hiding place would be hard to find. It was a sharp sudden valley and it wasn't fanciful to consider it sinister, with the slithering hard stones and earth that went steeply downwards. For most of the day it would be in shadow. Hal had seen the gradients on the map, but was still surprised by the extremity of the land and that anyone would choose to build a farm there, so deep.

The soldiers moved slowly downwards.

Hal's platoon had the interpreter and Andreas at their rear. Andreas was jittery, flanked by soldiers, and the interpreter, Davis, was hanging back and wishing himself home. Mark Innes and Two Platoon, coming down the other hillside, had the better time of it because they were in trees.

Hal could hear each sound very clearly. He was concentrating intensely, except for the small part of him that felt the eagerness to be getting on with it. He couldn't see the ground in front of him, or the house, and could only sense the men to his left and right and the mountainside opposite him, but as they went down, and dawn approached, the high line of the mountain showed him where the sky was.

A dog began to bark, then more dogs, and the sound was very loud, breaking the stillness. They all stopped, but no lights showed where the house must be. They continued their approach, holding their Stens close to their bodies. The hill was almost vertical, and they had to cross the flat road every fifty yards. The approach took a long time and their legs shook with the effort of the slope and with crouching so low to the earth.

At the banks of the narrow river the soldiers stopped. The bridge was wooden, and Hal was very near it. The water, where it broke slowly over big boulders, and around the supports of the bridge, gleamed white.

The dogs were still barking, but rhythmically, not in hysteria, because they were being ignored. Hal went along the edge of the water until he reached Trask, who was gripping Andreas by the arm.

He could just see a dark shape behind him, which he took to be Davis, and he hissed to him quietly. Davis came over to them. Andreas spoke to him urgently, and Trask yanked his arm to keep him quiet.

'He wants to go back,' said Davis, weakly.

'Just keep quiet, and wait,' said Hal, and then, to Trask, 'Keep them well back.'

Hal went away from them along the river again. He could see the shadows of men and moved towards them, identifying McKinney. They crossed the river through the water, which was shallow and icy cold, seeping into their boots.

The dogs, who were chained, began to choke themselves in their excited barking and, at that, McKinney gave the word and the arrest group moved quickly towards the house.

Hal, McKinney and Kirby were in the cover of some bushes, Hal itching to get in after the others, but for the rest of the platoon there was no more stealth. Over the sound of the dogs, scaring them, came the light spat of gunfire from the house as a shutter was broken open and bullets touched the ground and the trees.

Very quickly the soldiers surrounded the building, the door was kicked in and there was the harsher sound of a Sten fired inside and shouting, the high scream of a woman, and the banging of furniture going over.

There was no more gunfire.

The soft dimness was moving with the blacker shapes of running soldiers. The house, every small building and the big barn too, were surrounded. There didn't seem to be anybody in the outbuildings but it was difficult to tell anything above the barking dogs and the voices of the soldiers. It was fierce agony for Hal to wait, watching, counting seconds, his blood aching with the need to move.

Then, in the new light, a man could be seen running away from the back of the house towards the dark hill.

The familiar shout of 'Halt! *Stamata! Dur!*' and the man flung himself flat to the ground and was held there.

It had been a stupid dash anyway because the whole yard and house were full of soldiers and he had no chance. He only lived because there was no clear shot at him without one of their own being in the line of fire.

From inside the house Hal could hear boots on the wooden floors upstairs, and voices, but the first rush of the attack had eased, whatever confusion there was – and there hadn't been much – subsiding to nothing. Corporals' shouts of 'Clear' followed one another, and guarding positions were taken up.

Now that it was lighter, Hal could see the positions of his men and the exits blocked. His plan, as drawn, was adhered to. Even the dogs had quieted.

Now –

'Right, then,' he said coolly, and started with McKinney towards the house.

There was no one in the outhouses, just animals. The soldiers stood with their guns held ready, looking towards the shadows, at the house and Hal walking towards it. The man who was pinned to the ground wriggled a bit under the soldier's boot. Hal went inside.

A corporal, in a strangely domestic pose, was lighting the

oil lamp on the table. He turned up the wick and the warm light grew. The Sten fire hadn't hit anyone so there was no casualty to deal with.

'One got out the back when we were coming in,' said Amery.

'Yes, let's bring him in,' said Hal, and Amery went out past him.

There was a woman in a corner, in her nightdress, with two children clinging to her legs, one hiding his face, the other staring, with huge eyes, at Hal. Two men lay on the floor, their arms wide and palms flat, Walsh and Leonard's Stens at their heads. They were in their nightclothes, too, one man's naked legs splayed and hairy, the other in baggy trousers but shirtless.

Hal's mind was moving so fast that everything seemed to slow down, and in calmness he could absorb the detail. The room was like a photograph with all of it in focus for him to study. He saw the wooden beams disappear into the shadows of the roof. He saw the bones inside the children's hands where they gripped their mother's nightdress. He saw the men's boots lined up against the wall near the stove and little pieces of bread on the table by the lamp, the crumbling walls around him and heard the breathing of each of the people in the house.

He knew the woman was screaming before the sound left her, saw the movement of the man on the floor reaching up for his child and felt Francke panicking beside him. The woman rushed at Hal, throwing her children behind her, before she saw Francke's Sten raised to her chest, and Hal caught Francke up short with a word and put his own pistol to the head of the man who was trying to get to his child and told him to be still.

He held his hand up to the woman and looked at her. 'Calm,' he said, in Greek, and for a moment they were all motionless.

Amery and another soldier came back in with the prisoner in front of them. They turned him to face Hal. He knew immediately that they had found their man.

'Are you Loulla Kollias?' he asked, and when the man didn't answer, he sent for the interpreter.

When Davis came in, Hal had the woman taken into the other room. There was some screaming and panic as the men tried to fight, as if they thought there was something to protect the family from. Hal kept it brief and attempted to establish names and who owned the house, the broadest of connections between them all, but the prisoners weren't in the mood to assist him, so he had them dress themselves under guard and stood them outside to wait.

Outside, the sky was pearly and only black in the west, where there were still stars. The captured men were secured and the outhouses searched while the dogs resumed their helpless barking. The woman and her children sat in the kitchen with a rather embarrassed Leonard to watch them. Once most of the soldiers had left the house, the children cried very loudly and their wailing was a background sound to the searching.

It did not prove fruitless. There were guns in the main house – not a farmer's hunting rifles but two Brens and a rich stock of ammunition. Hal's men found pipe bombs in the well nearby and some dynamite stashed in a wooden crate under some grain sacks in a half-wrecked barn away from the house. With each discovery the mood took a step towards triumphant.

Searching the farm buildings took a long time; the sun was up over the high hill, hitting the mountainside and the loops of road opposite. The three prisoners were bound and marched under escort with Two Platoon, to keep them away from Andreas, who was exhausted and guilty and had been crying.

It took an hour to reach the vehicles, then they loaded up the prisoners and the weapons and headed down towards Episkopi. The engines whined and rattled over the dirt roads, grinding metal on metal in low gear, and Hal went over the things that had happened, thought about what had gone well and what he might have done differently. His plan had been sound, although it was unfortunate that in cordoning the house the soldiers were effectively disarmed, for fear of casualties amongst their own.

He was concerned for the woman and her children and, recognising humanity in himself, felt untroubled.

Hal had a boyish habit he'd never lost. He would score the outcome of things in his mind as if they were sporting results. It made him smile to do it. At school, getting news of the war in assembly or chapel, he would say in his head, England three, Germany one, or RAF, four hundred for four, Luftwaffe, all out for thirty-five. As he grew up, he knew it was absurd, wrong, even, but he still had to do it. Now, at thirty years old in a Land Rover in Cyprus he did it automatically: EOKA, out for a duck.

Looking around him, and above, he noticed that the sky was blue all over, with nothing in it but light. It was the sort of blue you might see on a ceiling with angels painted on it, now high, high above Cyprus, instead.

Chapter Seven

'All right, Davis, thanks very much.'

Davis, the interpreter, left the room.

The interrogation cell was in the guardroom, a building that wasn't far from the recreation ground for the troops and held corporals being punished for falling asleep on guard duty as well as Cypriots suspected of terrorism. The walls were fairly thin. The roof was metal and the cells were simply small narrow rooms with good locks on heavy doors. Loulla Kollias was in one of these.

Davis stepped out into the corridor, which had windows along it onto a yard at the back. He wanted to get away from the door because he didn't want to hear or know what was going on. It wasn't as if it was happening to him, but he found that his hands were sweating and his mouth was dry.

Very recently, three soldiers had been court-martialled for causing bodily harm to a prisoner. Their fate was supposed to be an example, but it was known amongst the SIB that the interrogation in question had elicited information about EOKA that, followed up, had stopped a hijack. The SIB had been encouraged, not deterred, in their methods.

Davis walked away from the closed door and along the corridor to the end, where there was another door that opened onto a small yard at the back. He went into the yard and lit a cigarette. There was a ten-foot wire fence right in front of him, and past that, a hill sloped gently upwards. It was a warm day. The sun heated his skin.

Inside the room Loulla Kollias, who was fifty-two years old, was tipped back in the chair he was bound to. The soldier fetched big metal jugs of water and wet cloths were placed over Kollias's face, his head gripped still while the jugs were poured onto his mouth. The cloths made it very hard to breathe. The heavy wet layers filled his mouth and his throat with the water as he gagged and suffocated. It isn't an extreme method of interrogation to nearly drown a man when you're saving lives.

Davis waited in the yard for fifteen minutes, then he walked away from the guardroom and across the recreation ground onto the long road back towards the main garrison. Below him, along the edge of the polo field, two horses were being exercised. A woman, one of the officers' wives, was being given a lesson, she was giggling as the horse trotted and bounced her in the saddle. Davis walked along the path and watched them and missed his home. He thought of his study in Cambridge, and afternoons spent reading, and wondered how he would ever forget these things happening here in Cyprus, or get over them.

A Land Rover was coming towards him; he recognised Major Treherne in the passenger seat and stepped aside, saluting. He liked Major Treherne, who seemed to be a good man, as far as he could tell, although it was hard to fathom soldiers – professional ones. He wondered what would happen if he were to stop him that night in the mess and say, 'They've been torturing the prisoner you brought in. They nearly drown him . . .' But his imagining stopped there; it was unthinkable, and anyway, he wasn't sure what went on, he couldn't have sworn to it in court, he was just guessing. Torture was probably a silly word, an exaggeration. His mind went around like that, excusing himself, condemning himself, lost in notions of responsibility, while the major's Land Rover passed him, throwing up the dust.

Hal was hoping Clara would be at the beach. He nodded to the interpreter – whom he always thought a worried-looking fellow – and the Land Rover bumped over the narrow road past the guardroom to the tunnel through the rock, accelerating towards its entrance.

The darkness swallowed them very quickly. The tunnel smelled of stone and earth; Kirby had to put the headlights on, and the lighted disc ahead grew bigger as they drove towards it and then, suddenly, they burst out into the light.

The beach was very sunny. Hal saw Clara and the twins – their outlines sharpening as the glare settled – with bare legs and covered tops, playing by the water. He jumped out of the Land Rover while Kirby was still turning it on the sand to go back through the tunnel and ran towards her. 'Having fun?'

Clara grabbed him and held onto him, full of joy.

'I went home but you weren't there,' he said.

'We were here.'

'So I see.'

He kissed her, he wanted to make love to her and held onto her tightly, trying to let go but not able to yet.

The twins were jumping about. He looked at them at last, went down onto his knees and let them push him over.

The skin on their bare legs was dusted with fine sand. He tickled them, carefully, one after another, their sand-gritty feet pressing into the palms of his hands. They giggled and choked with laughter as he put his face into their tummies and pretended to bite them, as Clara lay on her back and closed her eyes, smiling.

With the sun blinding them and the cliff above them, they played in the sand.

That evening they left the girls at home and went to the Limassol Club. The Limassol Club was where the British went for a change of scene from the mess, and to entertain their wives. It was a big white building, well guarded, in the part of town near the governor's mansion.

Mrs Burroughs had organised a reading of *The Tempest* in the garden and had chairs set up in a semi-circle. The women had to share roles, but there weren't very many men interested so they had whole reams of text to themselves.

The men Evelyn Burroughs had roped in were two young subalterns, and they read their parts blushingly, grateful to be asked and for the gentle attention of married women. There were lanterns in the garden with moths around them, and the dark night behind was springlike. The women wore cardigans or wraps over their dresses and held their books near the lanterns to see.

Inside, the bar was crowded, noisy laughter and cigarette and cigar smoke drifted slowly from the open doors.

Hal knew that he was tired, but didn't feel tired. Every few moments, almost without realising, he felt a small tug on the invisible thread that tied him to Clara and glanced out into the garden.

It was good for her to have a night away from the children. He tried not to, but just occasionally he resented the strain the girls put on her. He was very proud of the way she had managed the move to Cyprus, dimly aware, and ignoring the feeling, that this was a danger time for her. He was relieved they had moved onto the base – he could sense a relaxing in her and he thought she really was happy, not just pretending for his sake.

Clara, in the garden, was enjoying herself. Hal may have had his first small triumph as a soldier, but she'd had her first triumph as a real army wife. She hadn't cried and clung to him and told him not to get blown up. She had spent the day having lunch with Deirdre Innes, taking the children to the beach, and when he'd come back she hadn't cried either, but laughed.

She hadn't been listening to the reading, but was lulled by the language and her own thoughts.

That morning she'd had letters from home, and from James, now stationed in Malaya. Her mother understood it was the everyday things Clara wanted to hear about. Just as Clara wrote to her mother about where she did her shopping and the beaches, so her mother wrote back to her about a sudden hailstorm that had battered the spring flowers – she had spent a morning kneeling in the wet soil, to tie them to stakes – or a trip to London to see about finding a flat for Clara's younger brother, Bill, nearer to his chambers in the City. She didn't write of missing the children, or her own and George's constant anxiety for Clara and her brother. Clara kept the letters together, and read parts of them to Hal, whose own mother's letters were brief and tedious.

A third man came across the garden to them.

'Ah – there you are! Does everybody know Lieutenant Davis? He hasn't been with us all that long. He's the interpreter attached to the regiment.'

The young man nodded to them all, not making eye contact, and Clara moved her chair a little to accommodate him.

'How long will you be with us, Lieutenant?' asked Evelyn, summoning a waiter.

'Oh, I'm not sure. I go where I'm told to,' he said.

'We've run out of copies, I'm afraid, but I'm sure Mrs Treherne will let you look over her shoulder.'

'Of course,' said Clara. 'Here.' She held her book near him. He sat hunched forward, and his uniform made stiff folds across his chest. Clara smiled at him. '*The Tempest*,' she said.

'Yes, I remember. I saw the noticeboard.'

They were near the end of Act One, and took Davis's arrival as a signal to pause. Deirdre Innes giggled. 'I must say,' she said to Lieutenant Castle, who was next to her, 'you're attempting a rather masterful Prospero!'

Deirdre Innes was flirting, thought Clara, and Castle's attempt at masterfulness – if he had made one – had been entirely unsuccessful.

'Ought we to move inside?' asked Evelyn. 'It's a little dim out here, but rather suits the play, don't you think?'

They all agreed to stay outside. Deirdre Innes made a show of shivering inside her wrap and holding her book nearer Castle – or the light behind him.

'Do you know the play, Lieutenant Davis?' asked Evelyn.

'We did it at school.'

'Well, jolly good, then. You can read Gonzalo.'

Clara didn't think Davis wanted to read Gonzalo, but Evelyn was irresistible.

‘Carry on,’ she said leaning towards him, and staring over her spectacles.

Davis had a biggish, aquiline nose, and hair that fell forward. He peered at Evelyn, and his eyes, which were surprisingly large, were fearful. She nodded. He glanced down to the text and – without even the benefit of a cocktail – began.

‘“Beseech you, sir, be merry,”’ he cleared his throat several times, ‘“you have cause, So have we all, of joy; for our escape Is much beyond our loss . . .”’ He stopped. ‘I'm sorry,’ he said, ‘I –’ and then he stopped again, blinking down at the page.

This wasn't shyness. They had all been shy. This was some form of discomfort that stopped them all, and Clara recognised it. Lieutenant Davis was staring downwards, as if bewildered by his own silence. Clara said, ‘Poor man, he's only just arrived. Shall I?’

Evelyn was grateful to her, and in her gratitude didn't argue that it was a man's role, but said, ‘Clara. Please,’ and Clara began,

> ‘. . . for our escape
> Is much beyond our loss. Our hint of woe
> Is common; every day some sailor's wife,
> The masters of some merchant and the merchant
> Have just our theme of woe . . .’

The waiter brought Davis a drink. He took it and drank it down.

The little party of readers continued, quite a few cocktails were drunk, and it became what Evelyn had wanted, a Very Jolly Time, but Davis, and Clara beside him, had another experience, of shared, unspoken sympathy that was mysterious and comforting.

When the play had ended, they smiled at each other.

Clara said, 'I'd better go and find my husband,' and got up.

He stood up too, while around them their fellow readers gathered bags and glasses and prepared to go inside. He didn't seem to know what to do with his hands, which, coming out of sleeves that were a little too short, were long-fingered.

'Are you all right?' said Clara, thinking it was odd to be talking to a man who was younger than her.

'Much better, thanks,' he said, and grinned at her.

'Oh, good,' she said, and she walked away to find Hal.

The SIB had got their information from Loulla Kollias, not because of the near drowning or because of the beating the Turkish Auxiliary Policeman had given him, which was not severe, but because of the very kind words from the interpreter, Davis, that followed it. He had told him, as politely as he could, that if he would only tell them where Demetriou was hiding, his family would be safe and he would keep the families of others safe, too. Loulla Kollias had conceded.

He was left on his own then to sleep, but confined by physical pain and the shame of his weakness, he didn't sleep. In the dark part of the night, after the moon had gone and before the sun came up, he died. He died of a heart-attack, which couldn't have been prevented, and perhaps was nobody's fault, but it was a very lonely death, and fearful.

Chapter Eight

In March and April the hillside behind the garrison and even the cliffs below were bright with wild flowers. It hadn't been a bad winter, compared to English winters, but it was good that the thunderstorms were over and the roads were better.

The houses on Lionheart Estate were small and semi-detached; Clara thought living there must be what being working class might be like, except for the outside lavatories. She didn't know how anybody lived with those. Deirdre and Mark Innes were on one side and another officer and his family on the other; she felt a stronger sense of community than she had ever felt, even during the war. In Germany they had moved around a lot, and married quarters for a captain and his wife were very different from those for a major with a family.

Sometimes Clara could hear Deirdre and Mark arguing next door and she hoped they couldn't hear her and Hal making love. The twins were unwakeable, but she pictured Deirdre and Mark, sleepless in their beds, overhearing them. She tried to be as quiet as she could but it was difficult. Hal was virtually silent when he made love to her, perhaps a legacy of the etiquette of the boys in their lonely beds in the dormitories at school. He would please her, sweetly, and hold off and wait;

the more intensely he felt, the quieter he would become, and Clara felt closer to him than if he had demonstrated noisy masculinity. He would hide his face in her neck, forced closer to her, made vulnerable by his silence.

And laughing afterwards, too, was noisy. She would cover his mouth and her own with her hands and feel his breath on her palm.

In Cyprus there were strawberries in the early spring.

A grocery van owned by a Greek Cypriot named Tomas visited the houses on Lionheart, Marlborough and Oxford Estates almost every day. Tomas was something of a favourite with the officers' wives. He was flirtatious and unattractive – but pleasantly so – the father of four children. Sometimes one or two of his children came with him, and sat on big bags of Cyprus potatoes in the back, getting streaks of red earth on their legs. The van was small and dark green, with corrugated sides that rolled up and a diesel engine you could hear stopping and starting along the curved roads of the estates. The wives would go out with baskets or string bags to buy lettuces, vegetables and fruit.

Clara's first strawberries of the year were bought from Tomas. It was nine o'clock, and Hal had just left. They had made love that morning – even more quietly because it was daytime – and she had stayed in bed with her legs stretched out, listening to him downstairs, getting ready to go. He had brought the girls in for tickling and Clara felt very happy with the early sun coming in onto the creases of the white sheet and the girls' hair, tangled from sleep. It was a slow ecstatic morning. After breakfast she heard Tomas and they went out to catch him.

Clara stood in the road, which was quiet and empty. Tomas handed her the strawberry box last and she walked back with it in her hand, not putting it into the shopping bag. The corners of the cardboard were stained pink. The string of the heavy bag was digging into the fingers of one hand and the strawberry box was light in the other. The girls walked behind, slowly, not in straight lines.

In front of their house Clara put down the string bag and sat on the grass. She took the first strawberry. It was warm from being in the passenger seat with the sun coming through the windscreen. 'You can't get these until the summer in England,' she said.

''Tis-it?' asked Lottie, and then Meg:

''Tis-it?'

Deirdre Innes's front door banged behind them as she came out with her little boy, and they all turned. She had on her sunglasses and a bright green dress with a white belt. Deirdre was irritable even in pleasure, and her light mouse hair always fought to fall out of the curl she tried to keep in it. 'Picnic?' she said, dropping her keys into her big straw basket and trying to take her little boy's hand. He was called Roger, and would soon be three.

'Here.' Clara held a strawberry out to her.

'How marvellous.'

Roger, who wore pale blue cotton rompers and had fat legs, stared at Lottie and Meg, who stared back. Deirdre threw the strawberry stalk away from her. 'We're going down to Dodge. Coming?'

Dodge City was the nickname for the row of shops on the base. It had a wooden walkway along it and the buildings had been hastily thrown up, giving it the appearance of a frontier town in the Wild West – hence its nickname. There was a hairdresser and a small general store. Greek-run and friendly.

Deirdre and Clara walked to Dodge and the children went so slowly it took a long time. They chatted and finished the strawberries, looking up occasionally at the dark blue horizon of the sea.

'Cyprus – the Sunshine Posting,' said Deirdre, with bitterness, and Clara didn't draw her out, preferring to relish her own happiness as precious.

At Dodge, she waited outside the shop for Deirdre, leaning against the wooden post of the walkway with the sun on her face and Lieutenant Davis came out of the barber's, rubbing the back of his newly shaved neck. He noticed her and looked oddly surprised. 'Hello,' he said.

'Good morning. Nice haircut?'

'Well, I won't need another for a while at least,' he said, smiling.

'I'm just waiting for Deirdre Innes.'

'No shopping to do?'

'Not today.'

Davis looked at the girls, who were hunched low and close to one another nearby, examining some ants and squashing them occasionally with their short fingers.

'Savages,' he said.

'Shocking, isn't it? First instinct – destruction.'

He looked at her. 'Are you on Marlborough?' he asked.

She had thought he was going to say something quite different, she didn't know what.

'Lionheart,' she said. 'We were in town before, which was horrid, so I'm glad we're up here now.'

'Yes, much better off. Did you feel in any danger?'

'Everyone was very friendly, actually. The Greeks seem so hospitable. Hal says it's a shame a perfectly amicable situation can be spoilt by a few troublemakers.'

'Does he? I suppose that's one way of looking at it,' he said.

'What do you mean?'

'Well, how would we like it if a lot of Greeks moved into the Houses of Parliament and told us what to do?'

'It's not the same thing at all. And they didn't complain about it when we were defending them from the Germans, did they?'

Lottie got up and went over to Clara, leaning on her, pressing her dusty hands against her skirt and twisting her neck to smile up at Davis with self-adoring charm.

'Hello – you're a sweet little thing,' said Davis.

'This is Lottie. That's Meg.'

Meg was absorbed in the ants still and didn't hear.

'Twins?'

'Yes.'

'I was a twin, but my sister died when we were two.'

'Oh.'

Clara was at a loss for a moment. Her girls were nearly two; it didn't bear thinking about. 'I'm sorry,' she said.

'Well. You know.'

This remark seemed to finish the topic and Clara searched for another. She wished Deirdre would come out. Lottie wriggled and kept smiling up at Davis, then went over and smiled at him even more, hoping to be picked up, and Clara felt embarrassed, as if Lottie's behaviour were her own.

'Lottie, what's Meg doing?' she said.

Davis, unused to children, just smiled down at her. 'I say,' he said suddenly, 'I've got my batman down here. Shall I give you a lift up to Lionheart? I'm meeting your husband to – Well, we have to go up to one of the villages, but I've time, if you don't mind coming along now.'

'You're with Hal today?'

Davis looked at her for a second, then said, as if he hadn't heard, 'Should you like a lift up?'

'Yes. Thank you. Right now?'

'Right now would be best. I don't want to keep the major waiting.'

Clara picked up Lottie, put her on her hip and went to the door of the shop, leaning into the grocery-smelling dark. 'Deirdre? Lieutenant Davis says he'll give us a lift up – will you be long?'

'Oh, jolly good, Roger's fading. Right now?'

'Yes.'

'I'll just finish up.'

Clara was relieved Deirdre would be with them.

Deirdre sat in the front of Davis's Land Rover, leaning her arm restlessly on the open window and holding Roger around the middle, and Davis sat practically on the gearstick between her and his driver. Clara and the girls were in the back. Deirdre was quiet, the engine noise made it hard for Clara to speak and she had to keep the girls pinned down over the bumps.

The Land Rover stopped at the first street of Lionheart, by the Devonshire Road sign. 'Will this do?'

'Lovely,' said Clara.

'Will you be seeing Tony Grieves later?' said Deirdre, suddenly, and Davis said,

'Yes, I should think so.'

'Well be sure and tell him hello, won't you? From Mrs Innes.' She said it challengingly, meeting his eye.

'Certainly. Goodbye.'

She opened the door and put Roger down first, then climbed down after him and hauled her basket out. Davis jumped out and opened Clara's door for her. He nodded to her obligingly and smiled. He was a little smaller than Hal, possibly, and narrow. His narrowness was boyish.

'Abyssinia,' he said.

'Yes,' she laughed, 'I expect so.'

He turned to Deirdre. 'Goodbye, Mrs Innes.'

'Yes – don't forget what I told you.' Deirdre was impatient, and cross with Roger about something, walking away from them, so Clara and the twins waved off the Land Rover as it turned and drove away.

At Episkopi Garrison, after lunch, the officers often headed home or to Evdimou beach, which was in the next bay along to the west. The café at Evdimou was run by a Greek named Gregoris; they could drink and relax without the formality of the mess. Hal often went there with Mark Innes, and whiled away the afternoon hours when Mark didn't want to go home to Deirdre. He never said so, of course, but it was understood. Hal would keep him company, staring at the horizon, drinking bottles of Keo beer and resting his mind in peace, between the business of soldiering and the business of Clara and the girls.

That afternoon, though, as Davis had said, there was a job to be done. Kirby was driving Hal and Davis to find Loulla Kollias's wife, Madalyn. After the raid on the farmhouse and the arrest of her husband, she and her children had gone to stay at her sister's farm on the plains in the middle of the island.

Davis had a book with him on the journey, which he tried to read, whenever the road was smooth enough. Hal found himself irritated by what he took to be an affectation. There was something about Davis that got his back up, a slouching, sixth-form sensibility; he seemed unable to put himself aside for the job in hand, and at one point had said, 'Rich, isn't it, sir? Public relations exercise for the widows and orphans.'

Hal responded coolly: 'It's procedure, Davis. A man died in our custody. D'you expect us to put him out with the rubbish?'

It took three hours to get there from Episkopi; a long drive, not improved by Davis's company. They made a detour to the local police station where there was a muddle about who was going where, and arrangements for collecting the body from Episkopi. Then Kirby had got lost and driven around the dirt roads, swearing, for a while. Now he was waiting out by the Land Rover as Hal, Davis and the two local Greek policemen approached the house. Hal knocked on the door.

Around them were olive groves, the silver leaves touched by a low sun.

They stood, Hal, Davis and the policemen, surrounded by silence that felt deeper after their loud knock than before. Nobody came to the door. Hal glanced around the yard and into the beginnings of the quiet lines of trees, trying to see if there was anybody there. Some chickens pecked about in the dust and perched on the low wall that crookedly circled the house, but apart from that, no life that they could see. Hal thought it was a very peaceful scene that he had come to with the news of death.

* * *

Madalyn Kollias stood in stony earth between the lines of vegetables she had been working on, and heard about the death of her husband.

Hal looked up from her hands which were twined together; with soil under the nails and in the cracks in her skin. He looked into her face – carefully not into her eyes – as he explained to her levelly that her husband's body was in the hospital at Limassol. He relied on Davis to translate for him, pausing between his sentences. The police stood at a respectful distance, with their caps in their hands, looking down at their feet.

Hal told Madalyn Kollias that she was not under suspicion, he didn't want to cause her any unnecessary suffering. He was distracted by Davis, who was emotionally agitated. Hal could sense his untrained feelings, near him. He kept looking back and forth between Hal, Madalyn Kollias and the Greeks, stumbling over his words. When Madalyn Kollias pressed them for details of Loulla's death – which Hal was unable to give – Davis's voice faltered, and when her children came close, he lost concentration.

Madalyn Kollias didn't get hysterical or violent, which Hal had been warned might happen. She was as brave about it as an Englishwoman might have been. She seemed dazed by the news more than anything.

The Greek police stepped forward and began to talk to her about her husband's body, the transporting of it back to the village, and offering to take her with them. She refused, stepping back, the shock seeming to slow her as her eyes looked confusedly at them. There wasn't anything more to be said.

Hal didn't want to start playing nursemaid to the woman

but it seemed equally uncivilised to leave her standing by a patch of melons in her sudden grief. He debated whether he ought to suggest she go into the house, or find her sister, so that she would have somebody to be with.

'Tell her she should come back to the house – if she wants to,' he said to Davis.

She nodded. She even took Hal's arm. They walked slowly across the ridges of soil onto the golden grass and back towards the farmhouse.

He wished she might behave with wog hysteria and make herself foreign to him, but she didn't seem to hate him. Her sister would be back soon, she said. Hal nodded to the policemen, whose funereal faces showed relief, and turned to leave, but Davis said something else to her, quietly. He went close to her, bent down to speak into her ear and touched her arm. Jolted and upset, she pulled back from him.

They left Madalyn Kollias by the door to the house. Hal had recognised the faces of her children, as they followed her, and felt sure they recognised him too, from the raid on their house when he had taken their father. They were too frightened to come any closer. He realised, with sudden disgust, that he was the frightener of children. Still, it couldn't be helped.

'What did you say to her just then?' he asked Davis, as they approached the Land Rover.

'I said I was sorry for her loss. Something like that, sir. I don't know,' Davis answered casually, looking away.

There was no need to go back to the village; they left the police at the crossroads. Neither Hal, Kirby nor Davis had spoken since taking their leave of them. The Land Rover roared along the dirt track towards the road, the mountains casting immense long shadows, like night come early.

The dirt road ran out and the Land Rover bumped up onto smooth British-laid asphalt. In the relative quiet that followed, Hal turned to look at Davis in the back seat. He was slumped down with his hand up to his mouth to bite a nail. 'Davis,' said Hal, 'that was an unpleasant job. It didn't help the woman that you allowed your feelings to show. It was self-indulgent. And it certainly didn't help me.'

'What do you mean?' Davis was surprised and belligerent.

'Davis, Kollias was responsible for the deaths of soldiers and an American diplomat. You know the details of his crimes far better than I. Do you think his wife didn't know what he was up to? We could have left it to the Cypriot police. The CO dispatched a car, a driver and two officers to find her and tell her – respectfully – about his death. It's not my business to pass judgment on the British Army but, if pressed, I'd say we behaved rather well.'

Davis expelled air in a mixture between a laugh and a groan. Kirby kept his eyes front, but he was listening.

'If you have concerns, express them appropriately. Do you understand?'

There was a moment's silence.

'Yes, sir.'

'Do you have concerns?'

'No, sir.'

'Anything to add?'

'. . . No, sir.'

Hal nodded. He resumed scanning the mountains and considering the roads that traversed them.

Chapter Nine

The three years of the conflict so far had seen restaurant bombings and soldiers' vehicles ambushed on remote roads, street fights, graffiti and countless arrests. It had seen a fledgling desire for independence harden into a terrorist campaign, and the British government, having missed the opportunity to negotiate early on, was backed into a corner.

In February that year, with the indoctrination of schoolboys one of EOKA's key tools, the British had ordered the schools not to fly the blue and white Greek flag. There had been riots, and British troops fired on the crowd. Only one Cypriot schoolboy was killed. Nothing would happen for weeks, then a truck full of soldiers would be attacked, there would be deaths and maimings, more troops brought in, more villages searched and more villagers herded into wire pens. It was a war of intelligence. It was a war of subterfuge and rumour. General Grivas wanted a guerrilla war, and the British swept the mountains in their thousands for training camps, but the actual fire-fights, over three years, could be counted on your fingers.

Archbishop Makarios, known not just to sympathise with EOKA but to be at its very core, hand in glove with Grivas, was deported in March. There had been a general strike, more riots, curfews, the searching of monasteries and churches by British soldiers. The interrogation of priests was done with distaste, but it was done.

British helicopters dropped leaflets telling the Cypriots not to be seduced by EOKA propaganda. EOKA leaflets told of the torture and rape of Cypriot women and children in prison camps.

There was no truth. It was a nothing, laughable Mickey Mouse conflict; it was a sinister time of terror and repression. The British were misguided and ignorant; the Cypriots were lethargic and foolish. The Cypriots loved the British; the Cypriots hated the British. The British were torturers; the British were decent and honourable. EOKA were terrorists; EOKA were heroes. There was no heart to it. It had become a thing driving itself with no absolutes to unravel.

'How is the Emergency this week?' and 'What should be done?' were the endless circular discussions at dinners from Government House to the mess at Episkopi, and never a solution and never, like the conflict itself, a final truth you could point to and say, 'There! A solution,' because what is a solution? History doesn't end. Places that are fought over are always fought over, and will always be fought over, and there will never be an end to it, and each conflict is just adding to the heap of conflicts that no one can remember starting and no one will ever, ever finish.

So, conflict is normal and battles are normal, just as White Ladies are drunk within wired compounds and pipe bombs are made in the front rooms of village houses while supper is cooked. Domestic life continues. As the Special Investigations Branch shared information with Colonel Burroughs in his dim office, and Hal's next target was identified, and as three young men met a fishing-boat that held a stock of rifles and carried them in crates into the darkened mountains, Clara, in her semi-detached house on Lionheart Estate, took Meg's temperature, found she had a fever and wondered whether or not to bother the doctor with it.

Burroughs was a good soldier and a fair man and Hal liked him. He had become used to these meetings in the colonel's office. Whatever time of day it was, the office had the same slightly removed feeling, an atmosphere of order. It wasn't exactly luxurious either – a concrete room with louvred blinds, a cheap desk, maps on the wall, and the photograph of the Queen and the EOKA pictures facing it – but it had the richness of rank, and that was enough.

Hal and Burroughs stood in front of the big wall map, a minutely detailed, not always entirely accurate, Ordnance Survey.

'Kollias was a very busy fellow. We have reports of his contacts and associates all over the island . . .'

Burroughs had a light-timbred voice reminiscent of film actors of the recent past – Errol Flynn, perhaps, or Robert Donat as an upright sort of chap in a tight situation – and pale grey eyes that would have been fishy, being slightly bulging, but for the thick, well-shaped eyebrows and strongly boned face. He had old-fashioned ease that inspired confidence. Hal had heard many times from his father what a good man Burroughs was, and felt privileged now to have his leadership.

Burroughs stood three feet from the map, pointing at areas of the Troodos that now he knew as intimately as the lanes and coastal paths surrounding his house on the south coast of

England. Hal watched, visualising the terrain. They had put in the groundwork, were on the brink of reaping the rewards, and they felt that a real victory was in sight.

Kollias, at the time of his arrest, had been engaged in the movement of weapons up to a secret camp where it was believed a man called Kyriakos Demetriou – codename 'Pappas' – was hiding out.

Kollias had been close to Axfentiou, Grivas's second-in-command, and Demetriou was another of this select group. Some said that Axfentiou's time as favourite had passed and Demetriou was the closer of the two now to Grivas, having fought alongside him against the Turks as a young man. To fight alongside somebody, to lose and to survive is a very great bond.

Now, with Kollias's information on what – luckily for him, probably – had turned out to be the last night of his life, and other information exhaustively gleaned by the SIB, they had an exact fix on Demetriou's mountain hideout. The question was, how to get to him?

It was to be a big operation, with troops from two battalions, and from Famagusta and Paphos as well as Episkopi. Secrecy was very important. Nobody but the essential people knew where, or exactly when, they were going. Rumours, guesswork and tension raised the energy at the garrison as supplies and weapons were ordered and checked, with the utmost quietness: there were Cypriot staff all over the base. Even the wives weren't told exactly when they'd be on the move.

Clara ate supper alone. She put the wireless on to drown the muffled noises of argument coming from the Inneses next door. When Hal was there she didn't notice so much. The soothing sounds of Forces Radio accompanied her joyless meal and then she went up to check on Meg.

Meg had looked pale earlier but now, in sleep, her face was flushed. She had been coughing all day. She moved restlessly, spread out on her back, and Clara looked across at Lottie.

Since she had been a very young baby Lottie had slept on her front with her bottom in the air and her knees tucked up, arms down by her sides and her face sideways into the sheet. It was comical and bizarre. Clara and Hal loved to watch her, and to push her over sometimes, gently, to see how she bunched up her legs again to get back into position. She was in deep sleep, clean from her bath, her lips full and open to her sleepy breath.

Clara looked back at Meg, sat down next to her and felt her forehead, which was clammy, her fine hair stuck to it. She was always quieter, always the lesser person almost, the shadow, and Clara, feeling guilty and protective for thinking it, stroked her cheek again.

The fever and vicious cough had started after lunch. Clara wanted to talk to Hal about it; she wished he was home. Listening for his car to turn in and stop, and Kirby's 'Goodnight, sir' over the idling motor, she thought what Hal would say. ('Don't worry about it now. Wait until tomorrow.') She got up, still worrying, knowing she would check again in a few minutes, and went downstairs.

She had put Hal's plate in the food safe, laid out the coffee things, ready, and wasn't sure what to do with herself. She went to the back of the house and opened the door. Fresh air came in onto her face, along with Mark Innes saying, 'Well, what, then? Limassol?' very unhappily, and with frustration.

She closed the door again. There was the sound of the Land Rover from the front of the house and she ran to the door – no: she made herself stop and walk so that she wouldn't seem panicky.

'Right, sir.'

'Good.'

She opened the door.

'Hello, darling.' He knew immediately. 'What's wrong?'

'Nothing. Meg. She's got a temperature.'

'Let me get into the house first.' He came in.

She took off his cap and kissed him. 'Sit,' she said. 'I'll get your supper.'

'All right. Hang on.'

He ran up the stairs and she could hear him in the bathroom, washing his hands, noisily, and then Meg started to cry.

'Damn,' said Clara, and went up too.

'Sorry,' said Hal, waiting to be told off.

'Don't be silly, she's not well.'

He finished drying his hands on the small towel and put it back, neatly folded, in the bathroom. Clara had gone into the girls' bedroom. She sat in the shadows, holding Meg across her body.

Hal stood in the doorway, looking at them: Meg's damp hair and flushed cheek, held against the dark blue of Clara's dress. Clara's bare arms were around her baby, arms that were lightly golden now, he knew, in the sunlight. 'What?' she said to him, seeing his look.

'Where's my dinner?'

'Sh! Go down.'

He went, and sat at the table, and Clara came downstairs, fetched him his plate and the bottle of beer she'd had standing in cold water, some lemonade for herself. She sat opposite, watching him eat.

'Does she have a temperature?' he said.

'Yes.'

'What else?'

He tore the bread and made a sandwich of the slices of lamb and cold potatoes.

'She's been coughing. And she was very pale and now she's very red. And I think she has a headache because she doesn't like the light.'

Hal put down his sandwich. 'I'm leaving tonight,' he said.

'Oh – it's tonight?'

'Yes.'

He started to eat again, not looking at Clara, letting her get used to the idea.

'This is the big thing you were talking about?' she asked.

'Yes.'

'How long will you be gone?'

'Can't really say. Not long.'

Clara felt tears hurt her eyes and tried to tighten her mouth. *Stupid. Self-pity*, she said to herself, but it didn't help.

'Will you ask for the doctor?' said Hal, either pretending he didn't see her face or really not noticing.

'Well . . . I think I'll – not worry about it, and see how she is in the morning,' said Clara, strangled by tears, and put her hand to her face to hide.

The sight of that was too much for Hal, who had been pretending not to notice her upset, letting her fight it. He sat there, opposite her, and his chest hurt to see her break up like that. 'Stop it,' he said.

'Sorry.'

'No – just – It's all right. Meg will be fine. This is what I must do.'

'Don't *say* that! I *know* you must do it. I'm just being silly.'

Hal felt helpless and clumsy, knowing he had hurt her but not what to do about it. He was still holding his sandwich. He looked around the room. 'Clara,' he said.

'I'm fine,' said Clara, and looked up and smiled at him.

Her eyelashes were stuck together. He wanted to kiss her. How ridiculous that he could feel shy of her still, after being married for so long. The table was between them: he wasn't sure how he could get up and go over to comfort her without creating a drama in some way. 'All right?' he said, quite cheerfully.

'Yes. Better. Sorry.'

'Don't be.'

'Well, eat up, then,' she said.

Hal ate up, and quite soon they were back to normal, repeating comforting plans about Meg, and he was telling her his day – the bits he was allowed to tell her.

He went outside to smoke, because it was a nice night. Clara poured him a Keo brandy, and they shared it, and the cigarette, standing on the small terrace behind the house. Deirdre and Mark weren't shouting any more, but there was no breeze at all.

Chapter Ten

After the high hills there were the plains. You reached the top of a hill and expected mountains or a valley ahead of you, but instead there was the barren landscape that went away to nothing. It was enormous, foreign to all of them, and daunting that to their enemy it was home and as friendly as pasture.

'Who'd be prepared to die for this?' Kirby had said to Hal. 'It's just rocks.'

Hal didn't remind him that, by definition, they were prepared to die for it, too.

They knew the location of the camp they were looking for. Hal had his three platoons spreading out in lines, with other battalions from the north-east and the west forming a circle. There was radio communication between them and everybody alerted to the possibility that Demetriou – Pappas – with a force of unknown size, might try to rush them, or slip out in darkness. The job was to keep the lines tight and avoid friendly-fire incidents. Some of them – not Hal's unit – were coming through wooded areas, across the mountains where the danger of sudden ambush was greater.

The soldiers made temporary camps on rough ground at night and kept watch. There was no chance of secrecy. It was to be a much trickier operation than the cordon-and-search before: no house had been identified, just a description of a camp that was sometimes tented but more often in caves, and the caves were hard to see. Kollias had pinpointed the camp to within a one-mile radius. The terrain was very dry and appeared flat, but the plains were punctuated by sudden deeps or honeycombed chambers in the rock that the hiders knew well and the seekers didn't.

The days were very long and boring, with the officers and NCOs patrolling the lines to keep them tight and, for Hal's unit at least, no incident, but the nights were tense and they knew they were being watched. Once there was firing from the dark and the whole camp descended into Keystone Cops chaos for an hour. The firing hadn't hit anything, and it was a miracle there weren't casualties amongst the frightened soldiers shooting into the dark, half out of their sleeping bags. They sent armed patrols into the darkness, but the enemy had melted away.

They were a big fat English target, and they knew it. Once Hal, having a piss outside the almost non-light of the camp, looked into the dark, with a picture in his head of a pheasant he'd seen once, tethered as bait for foxes and flapping. It wasn't a frightening image but a comical one, and he'd buttoned up his flies and gone back to bed, but they were bait, just waiting for the fox to strike so that they could take the fight to him.

They had known one of two things would happen: Pappas would either try to make a break through the lines or hope to elude them by waiting it out in one of the dozens of hides. They came upon several small, recently deserted camps, and caves that had been hastily abandoned, some littered with dusty kit and even weapons, so they knew they were close.

It was only the officers who had this overview; most of the men had hardly any idea what they were doing, or why, or how great the prize was. Hal tried to impress upon those he spoke to – usually to tear a strip off them for gaps in the lines – that they weren't walking for hours in the glare and sharp wind for his entertainment. There was a rumour that their friends in the R— N— had let a group of four EOKA slip past them. They were leading a donkey, and had touched their caps. The donkey, presumably, had been carrying the weapons. They were young soldiers, falling for cheap tricks because they weren't looking sharp. Hal wasn't going to let that be his men. He worked the line tirelessly, and kept the ineffectual Grieves up to it too, when he could.

All three battalions spent a second night under canvas in their various positions, and then moved on.

On the third day, Hal's company were crossing the moonscape of the rocky high plain. They were squinting in the glare and the wind was blowing dust up into their faces. Then, out of the wind, a spatter of shots was fired, spitting up dirt and fragments of rock from the ground around them.

All of them went flat onto their bellies, trying to cover their heads. No one was hit.

Hal, Kirby, and the two nearest them, rolled or crawled into the shelter of a wedge-shaped rock that was about three feet high and Hal, flat on his front, thought, We must be getting very close if they're trying to engage us.

'Where was that fucking from? I couldn't see nothing ahead!' Kirby was at his shoulder, breathing heavily.

Time had slowed for Hal again. To his right there were six soldiers – one a lance corporal – spread out across about four hundred yards, lying flat too, but with nothing to protect them, then the ground rose up and he couldn't see any more. To the left he couldn't see anybody, because of the rock that was lined and ridged, the thin edges sharp against the sky.

Hal signalled the lance corporal to get over to him with the other men and, from their position behind the rock, started firing rounds for cover. As they got up on their feet they came under fire again – high-velocity rifles. The lance corporal and the five men with him bolted towards them, trying to keep firing in something like the right direction, skidding feet first into the small safe place where Hal and Kirby were. No one hit, just a jumble of heaped-up men and weapons, boots gouging stones from the ground.

'Hello, ladies,' said Kirby and the lance corporal answered, 'Very cosy.'

There was breathing, and quiet apart from that, then more shots, not in their direction but from their own lines off to the left, and a return of fire from the unseen enemy.

According to the map, there was a cliff ahead, dropping straight down into a narrow crevasse, but they couldn't see it yet. They had thought there might be caves at the bottom and there was every chance, with the enemy stirred to action, that this was the main hide they had been searching for. They had poked a snakes' nest and the snakes had betrayed themselves. Now they just had to keep the enemy engaged, send back to the radio operator, keep the lines tight and not fail.

Still, there was no doubt they were in something of a tight spot. Hal checked his watch. It was midday exactly.

Meg's fever hadn't gone down after Hal left. It didn't go down all day, and the following day it was worse, and Lottie was not her normal jolly self but coughing as well. Clara stayed quietly at home until lunchtime, trying to read to them, with the wireless on sometimes.

She decided it was just a normal cough and cold, sacrificing instinct to her need for calm. She didn't notice how extreme the situation had become until at three o'clock in the afternoon she realised they were all lying in darkness because whenever she opened the flowered curtains both girls cried with pain.

Dr Godwin was in barrack dress, and quite unofficial-looking. He had black hair, a ruddy face, and was about thirty-five. Clara showed him upstairs to the girls. He sat on the bed and said, 'What have we here, then?' and Clara was emotional with relief.

He looked at the twins – into their mouths and ears, pulled up their nighties to examine their stomachs and the skin on their arms and pronounced that, in all likelihood, they had measles. Clara didn't know of any contact with anybody with measles, but they had been in Limassol amongst crowds and on the beach.

'You just need to sit it out,' said Dr Godwin.

He asked Clara if she had had measles and she said she had.

'The rash should show itself within a day or two. There's every chance they'll just feel a bit poorly for a few days, and by next week you'll have forgotten all about it.'

Clara knew of a boy who'd gone deaf from measles, and another who had been epileptic ever since having it. She thought you could develop polio straight afterwards, but she wasn't sure of the connection and was too frightened to ask about it.

'Do you have any questions?' he asked, with the soldierly directness that comforted and intimidated her.

'No,' said Clara. Then, 'Except . . . you said "every chance" we'll have forgotten it – but . . . ?'

'Measles is a common enough childhood illness, surely you know that?'

Clara was embarrassed and said that she did. She was incredulous at her own meekness, and despised it. Apparently she was more concerned with showing the doctor she wasn't panicking than asking perfectly normal questions.

'You can call me out again if the fever reaches a hundred and four. Tepid baths. Water if they'll take it. Boil it first, of course.' He couldn't wait to be out of the house.

Once he was gone Clara felt outrage and irritation, and had dozens of questions for him, but it was too late. She hated him. He probably felt looking after children was beneath him and wanted to be splinting people's legs on battlefields.

She went upstairs, picked up the thermometer from the side table and shook it down. She put the thin glass stick under their arms, one after the other, holding each arm close to the body to keep it there, tucked into the tiny hot gap. Their temperature was 103. The room was very stuffy. She tried to make them drink water, wishing they weren't so compliant and sleepy.

Clara felt the overwhelming need for company, and went downstairs and out of the back door. She hadn't seen Deirdre go out that morning. Often they dropped by each other's houses, calling, 'You there?' before leaning over the low fence that divided them. Clara stepped into Deirdre's garden, and looked into the house through the window, which was a sash, and divided into four panes. The kitchen was dim, and darker as it went towards the front of the empty house and the kitchen door. Clara knocked anyway, then, hearing one of the girls coughing convulsively, like a baby seal, and crying out, she went back to her own house.

Adile had just arrived. Clara jumped when she saw her. Adile checked the scarf wrapped so closely around her head and said something Clara didn't understand, pointing upstairs at the girls.

'No,' said Clara. 'No, I don't understand you!'

Adile made rocking motions for 'baby', and then said something else.

Clara felt suddenly that perhaps Adile had been up to see them, or had frightened them, staring at them or touching them while she was gone. She knew she was being irrational. 'The babies aren't well,' she said, smiling resolutely, 'thank you, Adile,' and she went past her up the stairs.

She sat with the girls while Adile cleaned. She gave herself a very strict talking-to, but her babies' eyes glittered with fever, watching her.

Clara, going back and forth to the bathroom to rinse out the flannel with cool water, and wiping it over the twins' shivering hot bodies, thought almost constantly of Hal. Hal, after two hours in the shallow scraping underneath the sharp rock, getting men out one by one, and word back to the signaller, didn't think of Clara at all; if he'd heard her name he wouldn't have recognised it.

As he'd thought, the EOKA forces, such as they were, hadn't had enough firepower to engage in a fight for long. Further north and west of them there had been other incidents, as

EOKA, defending Pappas's hiding place, ambushed troops, but only one casualty.

By late afternoon Hal's company had advanced to the edge of the crevasse. It took another hour to get troops in position all around the edge.

It was a long slit of a place, about two hundred yards wide and ending in sharp angles at both ends. The R— N— were providing a much wider ring, a mile back, with Brens and snipers for Hal, too. Now they just had to wait. Pappas could have no thought of escape, and British morale was very high. Hal felt the determined cold sureness of his enemy's defeat.

The sun caught the far end of the crevasse; the caves could be seen very clearly in their blackness – small, gaping holes. As night fell, the ridged bones of rock made their own deep shadows, and the patterns were confusing, but Hal's men knew where they were now, and even Pappas's position, from the occasional helpful glint of the low sun on the metal barrels of guns.

The descent needed to be examined minutely. There must be another way in, apart from virtually abseiling: they'd be picked off like ducks if they attempted that. Night fell, with no change.

Clara had both girls in bed with her all night. She lay awake, and they coughed, whimpering their pain, coughing till they were sick even, phlegm and froth into Clara's shaking hands. All her instincts were wrong: she wanted to wrap them up but they were too hot already; she wanted to feed them but they couldn't eat.

* * *

Through the same night, the soldiers changed guard every four hours. They had patrols out, trying to find easier ways down the cliff, and Hal found he could sleep for two hours then be awake for two, and that way rested quite easily.

There was a bright moon, large and silver white. Its revealing beams lit up the crevasse through the night as if the heavens, too, were on the British side.

Chapter Eleven

The sun rose pinkly, touching the tops of the mountains above Hal and the white walls of Clara's bedroom, moving down slowly to light them both. Clara checked the rash that now clearly marked the girls' skin and found their fevers had cooled.

They had breakfast and now Hal and everybody with him focused on the dark bottom of the crevasse.

A loud-hailer was brought for Hal. Grieves – with Davis's help – stated the situation to Pappas, in English and Greek, and told him to surrender. The response was a volley of shots, which did nothing but reveal his whereabouts more specifically and Davis was sent back to the R— N— line to be out of the way.

During the night, patrols had found a track, almost a line, or a ledge, that goats might use with impunity but soldiers with less confidence. Still, it was a way down, and angled behind the sight-lines of the caves, so it was conceivable they might get a small unit down there. Once they'd done that, they could draw Pappas out, or else send more troops down and storm the place. The problem was, unless Pappas and whoever was with him came out, they would have to go in, and they didn't know how deep the cave went, how many men were in it, or how long their supplies might last.

At seven o'clock a section of ten soldiers made the first descent down the cliff. They were covered by fire from the edges on both sides. The moment they gained the crevasse floor they poured fire into the cave too: a heavy rain of bullets, followed by burning oil-soaked rags to smoke the enemy out. There was no response from inside. Another section began the descent.

There was, however, another entrance to the cave that the patrols had failed to find. It was a hole, barely the width of a man's shoulders at the surface, but opening out as it went down. The shaft was at forty-five degrees to the inside of the caves, making it a good hundred paces east of the scattered rocks at the cliff-top, a clump of bushes concealing it with hazy shadows.

Pappas had eight men with him in the cave. If they had all tried to get out that way they would certainly have been killed, but one man, easing head and shoulders out of the opening, under the cloud of thorny brush, could pull his .303 out after him, be very close to the British and still be hidden.

The man they chose was the best marksman they had, but the gun was an old one: it had been loaded and unloaded from crates, stacked against rocks, in bundles and on the floors of boats for fifteen years, and bore the scars of that. The soldier he pointed it at was fifty yards away, crouched over his mess tin, with a roll-up behind his ear for later, eating his breakfast and talking to another soldier.

The first bullet, aimed perfectly at his chest, went into his thigh instead and the bullet broke up on hitting the bone and made an explosion of flesh. Metal fragments flew, bloodied, into his face as well. He went over instantly, backwards to the ground, the other soldier jumping up and away while the men nearby took cover or hit the ground.

'Down!' and the second shot hit the same man in the soft part of his stomach, and the shooter slipped back into the shaft, pulling the thick stiff sacking that was the same colour as the ground over the shadow made by the hole.

The bush, only slightly disturbed by his movement, ceased to tremble.

The soldier who'd been hit was making deep, breathy sounds and convulsing. He was losing blood fast as it surged out of the wound, thick and pulsing. The man who'd been with him, who was very young and shaking too much to move well, ran back to him and tried to drag him to cover and keep his hand over the wound at the same time. Another ran to help.

The shooter pushed back the stiff sacking once more and the light dazzled him. His eyes adjusted, and he could see soldiers, all looking around and frightened, aiming into the middle distance. He could see the body of his first hit, sideways to the ground, hunched up. He felt a curious delight that even in the face of terrible defeat he could have this triumph. He took careful aim, aware of his risk, and shot one more British soldier clean through his head – although not so clean as the soft bullet acted like a small explosion in the skull – and the man fell immediately.

Then he really did retreat and slithered backwards down the shaft as fast as he could, keeping his gun up behind him and pointed at the opening as he descended. No light poured in after him, though; the ground made small tremors where booted feet tramped over it unknowingly.

At the other end of the crevasse the two shots weren't heard at all because of the blanket of fire as soldiers came down the cliff. Everybody was waiting for a reaction at the front of the cave.

Once news of the soldiers being shot reached Hal – about fifteen minutes after their deaths – there was an hour and a half of reassessment, an avoidance of confusion, more searches and the eventual finding of the tiny shaft opening. Nobody could be proud when the thing was found; there was no excuse for it not having been discovered at any time in the last sixteen hours and two lives would have been saved.

As well as the forty men they had now at the bottom of the crevasse there was a second force, an ambush group, led by Mark Innes, at the eastern end, surrounding the shaft opening. Lee-Enfields, a Bren gun on its tripod, Stens and even a couple of .38s were all trained on the little clump of gorse-like bushes that were putting forth a few spring flowers.

The sun made the sky a deeper and deeper blue above the hard ground, heating the rocks and the soldiers waiting on the surface and down in the deep crevasse too. They had radio communication between the two groups now, with a signaller near Hal at the top and another with the ambush group, but there was nothing further to communicate.

The morning went by. It was hard for Hal, with nothing to do, not to dwell on the killing of the two soldiers and remember things about them. Their faces, which before their deaths he would have been hard pressed to put names to, were now clear in his mind. It wasn't anger or outrage he tasted, it was the dark knowledge of his responsibility.

He began to dread the afternoon going by, the loss of light and another night, where in darkness the smallest defiant act could extinguish another British life. He felt them around him, each man moving and breathing amongst the dead rocks, subject to risk weighed and assessed by him, lives depending on choices taken or not taken by him. He needed to move forward.

Earlier in the day the sun had thrown the rockface into deep shadow but now the sun was directly above them. Another afternoon was beginning. He didn't want another night.

After he had eaten something, and stared at the ground while doing it, Hal walked away from the small group he was with. He stood with his back to them, facing the grey-brown paleness of the wide land. Ahead of him, small whorls of dust blew up from the plain; he watched them. Two of his men were dead. His soldiers had been taken by surprise twice now. They were a massive force, held up and halted by this tiny group, whose resistance was maniacal and hopeless.

Hal, alone in his command, could feel the shifting mood around him. It was like being in a ship, with full sails, set fair towards a point, then seeing the moving sky, feeling the canvas lose tautness, the sheets slacken as the weather changes. He felt the flat unease before a bad wind springs up. There had been the clarity of purpose; now there was division and grief. He didn't want to go into another night with those terrorists still under the ground, hidden, and no resolution brought. He needed to act.

* * *

'Kirby.'

'Sir?'

'Get hold of the CQMS.'

'Sir.'

'Tell him to move forward a hundred and fifty gallons of benz. As soon as he likes. We'll need cotton waste, too, for burning.'

'Yes, sir.'

It took four hours to bring twenty jerry-cans of petrol brought from the forward operating base. The terrain, the moonscape of it, dry and cut through with gullies, that the men had crossed chasing Pappas, was covered by mules this time, and the petrol arrived at four, in the deepest heat of the afternoon.

Twenty-five hours after the siege had begun, Hal gave the order for the ambush group to pour the petrol down the exit shaft of the cave. They followed it with grenades. The explosion caused a cloud of fire to blow downwards, filling the back of the cave with flame at the same time as the tunnel collapsed halfway down its length.

Outside in the bright sun, small showers of rocks fell from the cliffs around the soldiers with a smattering sound, and there was the deep rumble of imploding rock. A blast of hot air came from the cave, but not fire, and they couldn't see fire either, because it must have been very deep inside. Then there was the screaming of men.

At the sound of the explosions, and at the high screams, a sort of hotness went through each of the men watching and Hal felt it, too.

The screaming inside the cave was drowned by more

explosions, much louder and echoing, which must have been the weapons stores inside.

All eyes and weapons were on the cave mouth. A first man could be seen coming out, blackened and either burned or bleeding. He didn't have any fight to put up at all, but was like an animal rushing for the light and air. He was shot down, and another behind was shot down too – the soldiers, in the first effective cleanness of the assault getting down and clear, positioning themselves carefully, even in the heat of it. Another man came out, wandering drunkenly, but was dead before any bullet reached him.

Then there was a very short wait.

Hal was at the top of the crevasse on one knee, looking downwards, with the runner back and forth from the radio telling him what was happening with the second group. He was holding binoculars but not using them. His eyes could find every detail they needed to. He was unaware of himself physically, just the ecstasy of watching.

A huge black curving billow of smoke issued from the cave mouth. Another, smaller puff, like a dragon's breath, came from the smaller cave above. The soldiers were forced back, turning away from the smoke and wiping their eyes with their forearms, coughing, and checking and reloading their weapons when they could.

The black cloud appeared to throb, then dissipated, mistily, filling the crevasse, until the rich bitter smell of burned flesh and hair and the sharper, celebration smell of dynamite were everywhere. The smell reached Hal, and he breathed it, curiously, deep into him.

There were still screams from the cave, and shouting, but no one else came out. It was time to go in. A section prepared to go forward. They could see about twenty feet into the cave, then nothing.

Led by their corporal, the ten men went into the cave, slowly, weapons pointing into the blackness.

The light went quickly once they were inside, and the smell of burned bodies was stronger. One soldier's foot nudged something soft in the darkness and, kicking it away, he realised it was a leg, mostly torn off the trunk of the man it had been attached to, whose head was not to be seen. He felt himself go liquid inside, then went on, forgetting.

Very soon they reached the darkness, and there were gunshots, from a deeper cavern, ricocheting viciously off the cave walls and sending up sparks. The soldiers went flat to the sides of the cave, firing back into increasing resistance, until above the sound of the bullets, their own corporal gave them, 'On me now!' and they backed off and got out of the mouth of the cave, back to bright daylight and cover.

Hal watched the ten soldiers hastily scrabble backwards out of the cave and swore. 'Don't know when they're beaten,' he said to Kirby. 'Can we safely drag those bodies clear and try to identify them?' It was done. Then, 'Send word to B Company to get some more benz down there from the back. It can't be a tight seal – we could pump it in. If we can get a couple of hundred gallons down there we could get a real fire. We could light it from some other point. Get on to it.'

It was discovered that there was indeed a way to get more petrol in, fresh cracks being found in the rock above the caves, and when it was done, the burning was intensified, as Hal had wanted.

There weren't any screams now, and another section was sent forward to try to get into the cave.

Grenades had caused rock falls and the sweet roasting smell wasn't any better for the heat. The hundred men on the crevasse floor, and on the ledges surrounding, kept their positions and watched as the first section was sent into the cave mouth again. Grieves preceded their advance with more, largely unintelligible, announcements over the loud-hailer as the ten men disappeared into the shadow.

Now there was virtual silence, except for the wind that had picked up and made low organ-like sounds through the ridges and caverns. There were just the dissonant chords of air through rock, the men watching and the small streams of smoke blowing across the ground; everything under the wide sky was part of the pursuit of a conclusion.

Then, from deep inside the cave, there were shots – they could have been British or Greek – then more silence, then two separate pistol shots, a few seconds apart.

The soldiers emerged from the dim cave, dragging a prisoner. Everybody made a small move forward, as if to greet him, then stopped. The crevasse had become like an amphitheatre, and the soldiers entered the brightest lit part of it, letting the prisoner fall to his knees, but not letting the nose of the rifle detach from his soft temple.

Crouching under sacks drenched in water, in the smallest of hollows in the honeycombed rock, the last survivors had escaped burning with the others, but when the soldiers had entered the cave at last, there had been no more ammunition left to fight with.

The pistol shots had been from Pappas who, with his last bullets, had killed his remaining comrade and then shot himself.

The prisoner, as it turned out, was his son, whom he had apparently been unable to shoot, when it came to the end, so the pistol still had one cold bullet left in the chamber.

Lance Corporal Scott was an amateur photographer. It would have been distasteful, especially in the presence of officers, to photograph the heap of five burned and shot-up Greek corpses – there were only five as two did not invite reassembly. He did, however, in the fading light of the evening, photograph the prisoner, and circulated the picture all over the barracks before sending it home. It showed the section of ten men who'd made the final entry into the cave, standing over Pappas's son, who was seated on the ground. Scott had held the Coronet straight, and still enough, too, to get a good clear picture. The soldiers looked proud, holding their weapons, or leaning on them, with one foot stuck out and some of them grinning.

It struck Hal as surprising, when he saw the photograph, that the prisoner was looking into the camera. He would have thought he would turn away but, like a lone member of a losing team, he conformed and looked into the lens with a depressed expression, recording his role for posterity.

Chapter Twelve

They'd had to open up the mess to drink, because it was closed at one o'clock in the morning when the trucks rolled in, but there had to be some sort of celebration, none of them was ready to turn in. They'd sorted out rum rations for the boys – the whole of the camp was lurching into life out in the barrack room and none of the officers was ready to go either. So the watchman was hauled from his bed and a barman found. The light switches threw the place into semi-brightness and now they were drinking – drinking and breaking out the cigars.

This was exactly where he wanted to be. There was just this, drinking, remembering the triumph, and the knowledge in the back of his mind that he would be home later, with his wife. Hal wasn't much of a drinker; he'd drink along with whoever he was with, but he didn't have in himself that need to push things further that he saw in other men. There had been times when he was younger when he'd got stupid drunk and enjoyed himself, except for the illness the next day, but now all that was less interesting to him, except as a good way of loosening up sometimes.

Everybody else was pretty fairly all-out drunk, though. Grieves was slack with drink and it was only the wall that was holding him up. Mark Innes was with Hal; they were having pleasingly aimless conversations that were emphatic and trivial, laughing at each other's jokes and happy with themselves. There was enough smoke to make the bar seem like being inside a cloud up a mountain somewhere, and even with the doors open it didn't shift. The heat came off the bodies of men near him too, most of whom had cleaned up somewhat since getting back to the camp, but were not all dressed as they should be. That in itself lent sharpened energy to the place, like having mud on your boots after hunting but standing in the drawing room. Hal had washed his hands and face but he could feel the dirt from the rocks and the wind up on the high plains in every crease of his skin. It had blown in behind his ears and the place where his neck touched his collar. He could smell the last three days on himself: the sweat, not just under his arms but coming up from his clothes, the dirt off his boots, and the smell of burning too, the clinging smell that at first had been so foreign but now felt part of him. They all smelled of it. The spring night coming in didn't clear it any more than it cleared the cigarette smoke.

Mark Innes was going on about some private or other, and the boils he had on his neck, something to do with pus and it was funny and disgusting and they were both laughing stupidly but all the time, flashing in Hal's eyes in the dim, smoky room, were fragmented pictures of his victory; he thought Mark had that too, and perhaps everybody did, but no one could say it, or knew how to. He was in the mess bar, and it was night, and full of men, but then his mind would flash blue sky at him, or the sound of rockfalls, echoing up from the crevasse, or sudden black smoke that smelled of meat – not meat: bodies and burned hair. All at once he needed to get back to Clara. He hadn't felt the lack of her while he'd been away, but he felt it now, in the muscles of his stomach whenever he thought of her. He didn't have her face in his mind, just this need for her. Mark and he were joined by some others and somebody started to play the piano, a silly drawing-room song, with filthy words put to it, and the cigar smoke hung in wraiths, like ectoplasm, over their heads.

He went soon after, passing Grieves, who was face down on a table in the corner – he patted his shoulder, and Grieves suddenly heaved himself up. His face was dead white. 'Jesus. God,' he said.

Hal, who had felt unusually well disposed towards him, shuddered and went on by.

He left them – all the rest of them – happy and drinking, and wandered around looking for Kirby outside but couldn't find him.

It was very dark on the drive and hard to tell whose vehicle was whose, and he was a little drunker than he'd thought, now that he was out in the air. He felt irritated, not being able to find Kirby. He cursed him and went through the cars and Land Rovers, looking and getting more and more frustrated, and finally back inside to get keys from Sergeant Burns, who took care of transport for the officers. All of this took about twenty minutes. Hal's impatience was fighting with his euphoria and making him short-tempered. Burns was drunk and annoying. He had to get to his office at the other end of the building for the keys, and Hal followed him along the corridor, cursing his back. In the small dark office, Burns fumbled with rows of keys on nails with numb fingers.

'Bloody hell, man, can you get on with it?'

'Sorry, sir, coming up,' said Burns, managing to speak and move his hands at the same time.

Why did everybody move so slowly? It was a miracle the bloody army ever got anything done, with cripples like Burns in charge of essentials.

'Here – it's a Ford.'

'Well, which bloody –'

'Reg – regi . . . 's on the ticket label.'

Hal thought Burns might fall over. 'Try and sober up, Burns.'

'Sir.'

Hal took the key, with its brown label on a string and the registration written in pencil, and left him, walking fast down the corridor, out of the main entrance to where the vehicles were. The sounds of shouting and singing from the bar reminded him of his happiness, the music and his thoughts crowding round and round in his head, as he found the car and pushed the key into the lock – Empire 500 runs, not for no wicket, this time, and he shouldn't think of it like that, but Empire 500 for *two*, it was 500 for fucking two, and EOKA all out. EOKA all out anyway . . .

The engine fired and turned over. He pulled away from the mess and up the hill. The Ford's suspension was shot and the gearstick needed a whack to jolt it out of second, but the cool air felt good on his face through the open window. It wasn't far.

The unfamiliar car entered the empty road.

He stopped by his house, left it and went straight up the path, anticipating the feel of her, and of being home, so that he could taste it.

The door opened when he was halfway up the path and Clara was there. He had wanted her, and there she was. 'Hal!'

He took her, buried his face deep into her neck so he could smell her; she was almost insubstantial in her cleanness.

He got both arms round her, aware of his uniform, thick and rough between them, and thinking how narrow she was and that he was pleased she didn't have a bra on because she was in her nightdress.

'Hal –' she sounded cracked and upset; he kissed her.

'Hello,' he said.

Her mouth was beautifully soft. He wanted her very badly. He'd forgotten to close the door. He backed up, and pushed it shut with his back, not letting go of her, and Clara drew her head away from him, bending uncomfortably to look up at him and said, 'Hal – listen. The girls haven't been well –'

'Are they better?'

'A bit – but –'

'Thank God.' He kissed her again and she kissed him back but not properly.

'What?' he said, stopping, feeling embarrassed, the embarrassment hardening. 'What?'

'Darling,' she said, 'you're home –' but she made it sound sad.

He kissed her again to block out the details interfering with his wanting her, and the wanting came back. He put his hand up onto her face and rubbed the flat of it over her cheek, across her eye and hairline and kissed her harder. He wanted to get her onto the floor, or back her against something, he had to feel the inside of her mouth and get into her, and he felt her breath fast in his mouth as he kissed her.

Then she pushed him away with both hands, quite angrily. He stopped and looked at her, or tried to: there wasn't really enough light to see her face by.

'Hal! Will you please! God –'

'What?'

'It's been ghastly,' she said. 'It's been awful.'

'The girls,' he said. His voice sounded far away.

Both their voices sounded as if they were on the wireless with the volume turned down. It was unnerving.

'Yes! The girls, Hal. We haven't left the house – I haven't known, I've been so frightened –'

'Do you want me to see them?'

'No!'

'Well, what?'

'The doctor came. They've got measles.'

'Just that?'

'Hal, I haven't slept!'

'Silly.'

'They've been coughing, they've been terrible –'

She stopped, staring at him, and he could see her looking at him, but couldn't seem to recognise her frustration. It didn't mean anything to him. His own self was overwhelming him and everything else was far distant.

She turned furiously away from him and went up the stairs. He took a breath, and followed.

The white door to the girls' room was ajar, and he followed Clara into his own bedroom. No light was on, just the slightly paler windows behind her. He stood in the doorway as she took off her thin dressing gown. She wore the white cotton nightdress she always wore. The room felt extraordinarily small to him, and very clean. He was too big for it, and not welcome.

'Well, shall I look at them?' he said.

'No!'

She was half turned away from him and doing something to her hair – why would she do that now? Lifting her arms to do her hair was an invitation. Her face was turned away from him, he could only see her body, stretching up. She looked vague, her hair a dark cloud, the nightdress misty white, with no smell and no noise, as if she weren't really there. He felt something like panic. He was suffocating in it.

He took the two steps towards her and took her arm, it felt solid, his hand held her bare arm, his other brushed cotton, cool, not hard enough, he took hold of her –

'Hal,' she said.

His hand was on her waist, needing more, needing to feel something more than this small vagueness. If he kissed her, if he could touch her better –

She wasn't strong, and it was very easy to move her back to the bed and then he pushed her down, leaning down to kiss her and pressing her shoulders backwards. There.

'Hal!'

Again, the volume turned too low for clarity. He heard his voice, from nowhere, 'They're all right, then?'

'Who?'

'The girls –' and he put his hand under the cool cotton of her nightdress, up onto her thigh that felt secret, well known and beautiful to him. This was real at last, this made her real. She opened her legs for him, or he opened them.

He got his belt off, and the holstered heavy pistol slipped to the tiled floor with a clunking sound. It was quick and easy now to undo his trousers and he kept his hand on her neck – soft, pulsing – while his other hand got him close to her, he pushed inside her suddenly; it was so hard not to grip her very tightly and push deeper, not to be rough, just to have her quickly and be as far into her as he could. She made a noise. She sounded so far away to him. They were too low off the bed. He had to pick her up with two hands around her waist, staying inside her, and pushing her back from the edge so he could do it easier to her, and have both of their bodies on the bed –

'No. No – Hal – stop,' she said, and for strange halting seconds his mind absorbed that she was crying and he took that and mixed it with his need for her, her breath on his fingers, her clean skin, all the other parts of her that were his, and he lost it there.

He needed her badly. She loved him. He wouldn't make her cry, but he pushed very hard into her, pressing his cheek against hers, and felt her breathe faster just by his ear. It felt so sweet, but her body seemed to go away underneath him, not firm and pressing up to him, as it normally did.

He needed to be far deeper into her, all of him inside her, taken in, he closed his eyes and pulled her up onto him and kept his fingers on her face feeling her lips on his fingertips, and then sharp need went through him that was like rage, and he forgot about being careful with her.

Chapter Thirteen

In slow half-sleep, Hal heard Clara washing herself and the girls, and going downstairs.

When he got up it was later than usual and the room was hot. He had breakfast with a strange out-of-time feeling, because the rest of them had been up before him and he'd been away. The girls, their faces mottled with faded red, were playing at his feet, refusing their breakfasts, and Clara was trying to make them eat, worrying. Hal drank his coffee, watching them.

Clara came over to him and kissed him on the forehead, with her hands on either side of his face. Her dark blue eyes were infinite; he couldn't fathom them.

'Is everything all right?' he said.

She spoke carefully. 'Yes, Hal. It's all right.'

After that she was very busy with the girls.

Adile was cleaning downstairs and Clara went upstairs.

The bedroom smelled different from the rest of the house. It smelled of the night before. She looked around the room. It must have been coming up from the sheets where he had lain on them. The air was thick and burned-smelling. She went to the bed, pulled the sheets from it and bundled them up in the corner, and then she opened the window wide.

She thought that it wasn't as if he'd hurt her very much – she'd had two children hadn't she? There was no need to make a fuss about it.

She breathed in, putting her hand up to push her hair from her forehead, but the same smell was on her hands – she pulled back from it, sickened.

She went back from the window, into the bathroom, and washed her hands very carefully with the hard soap. She dried them on the towel and put the towel into the basket to be washed, but on the landing, she caught the smell again, through the open bedroom door. The clean air from the window was blowing it through the bedroom onto her.

She closed the bedroom door. The room could still be aired with the door shut, she thought.

PART TWO

Episkopi, July

Chapter One

There were no more slow mornings stretched out on sheets that were lit up like landscapes. There was no more sudden brightening of the day on seeing one another. It was at odds with everything around them. Hal was successful; he was beginning to live up to the expectations put upon him.

He had written to the families of the two dead soldiers, trying to find, in their deaths, something of which their mothers could be proud. He could not say he was proud. In the quiet times, when he thought of the siege on Pappas's mountain camp and its conclusion, he felt doubt, like a betrayal, shadowing him. Hal had known these things happened in wars; he had thought the wars would be different.

Lottie and Meg had got over their measles, and were out of quarantine. They had been pale and difficult for a few weeks, but now their legs were brown between their short cotton frocks and white ankle socks. They would be two years old in August, and Clara took them to other children's birthdays at the officers' club, where there was cake and ice-cream – much better ice-cream than there was in England, but Clara missed her home. Her mother sent packages to her, wrapped and over-wrapped with brown paper, bound tightly around with tough string in double knots against the foreign post. 'The assistant assured me they would fit two-year-olds but they seem terribly big to me,' she wrote, and 'Your father says eucalyptus puts off mosquitoes, if you don't want to put Deet on the girls. But how on earth would you apply it?' Clara opened the packages meticulously, absorbing the faint traces of England.

This party had been for Deirdre and Mark Innes's boy, Roger. They'd had donkeys brought up to the club and decorated their halters with coloured crêpe paper, and given rides round and round the circular drive outside. Afterwards they had all gone back to the garden, where tea was laid out on long tables and Clara had tried to persuade her girls of the merits of egg and cress sandwiches, but ended up eating most of them herself. Mark and one or two other men had been there for a while, looking a little lost in their uniforms, but mostly it was women, with parents' frowns and party smiles.

Clara was sitting on a rug in the shade of a tree on the lawn. It was the time of day between tea and drinks: waiters and yard-boys were clearing up fairy-cake cases and paper cups and getting ready for the evening, when the strings of bulbs would be lit and trays of White Ladies would come out. Clara knew she ought to go before then: young children at cocktail hour would not be welcome. People who had no children, or sent them away to school, lived a very different life from Clara's.

Lottie and Meg were together, walking without looking at one another, around a circular flowerbed, planted with roses. They had bows at the backs of their short dresses. Roger had been taken away by Deirdre some time before and Clara knew the girls would be bored soon.

'Lottie! Meg! Time to go, darlings. Come along.'

At the front of the building they walked between parked cars towards the road. Clara's eye was caught by movement in one of them and she looked again.

Through the back window she could see the top of the blond head of a child. There didn't appear to be anybody else in the car. Clara, still holding the twins' hands, looked around. There was nobody. The windows were closed tight in the car, but the child's hand appeared then, flat against the glass, streaking it.

Clara walked towards the car. She let go of Meg and Lottie.

'Stay there. One minute,' she said.

Nearer now, she could see that it was Roger. His face was very pink and sweaty from the heat, and he was crying. He looked at her with recognition but no communication. He was shut in a car; he had no plan what to do about it.

Clara, feeling embarrassed to interfere, tried the handle of the car, but it was locked. She went around to the other side. Then she saw – on the asphalt, almost crushed against the front tyre – Deirdre and a man tangled together, kissing. They would have been just out of sight of Roger in the back seat of the car, and partially hidden, at least, by the car next to it. Deirdre's hands were clinging to the man's jacket. Her legs were splayed like a traffic accident, and his whole arm was hidden beneath her skirt. His knees were on the ground and they were both breathing hard against the black driveway and the dirty tyre.

Clara, absurdly – trained up by Hal to notice these things – saw from the pip on his shoulder that he was a second lieutenant. She thought she ought to go, but then Deirdre saw her and almost yelped, her eyes flying wide open. The man scrambled to his feet. He was very dusty. His face was covered with Deirdre's rather violent lipstick. It was Lieutenant Grieves. Clara thought immediately that Hal didn't think much of him.

'I'm awfully sorry,' she said.

'God!' said Deirdre, sounding cross more than anything.

'I'm so sorry – I saw Roger.'

'He's fine,' said Deirdre, and Clara glanced back into the car at Roger who was crying with his eyes shut, saliva stringing his gaping mouth.

She remembered the girls, trying to think how long she'd taken her eyes from them, and saw that they hadn't moved from the spot but stood there in their party frocks, like little dolls – except that the frocks had chocolate cake on them.

'Just coming!' she said, although they hadn't asked. She tried to look back at Deirdre and Grieves without seeing them, and backed away. Then, suddenly, and with anger, 'I think he's a bit hot. You oughtn't to leave him in a car like that!' She took the girls' hands and left, more embarrassed for having said that than for having seen Grieves's hand up Deirdre's skirt.

With her back to Deirdre now, she said, 'It's his birthday!' in a rage, to nobody.

She realised she was dragging the girls and slowed down for them, trying to feel calmer, loving them, and loosening her grip on their hands. She felt the plumpness of their small fingers and stroked them with her thumbs, gently, as she walked, nearly crying.

At her house, she took off Lottie and Meg's dresses and ran them a tepid bath. She was washing them when she heard Deirdre calling from downstairs. 'You there?'

'Yes, wait, just coming.'

Clara took the girls out of the bath, dried them and put them to bed, taking her time about it, concentrating on brushing their hair and reading them *The Story of a Fierce Bad Rabbit* quite slowly.

'. . . "He doesn't say 'please', he *takes* it!"'

She forgot about Deirdre downstairs.

Deirdre had helped herself to a gin and tonic – at least one. 'I hope you don't mind.' She was standing in the middle of the floor, near the cane chair. She looked at Clara defiantly and put her drink down. She lit a cigarette. 'I didn't know how long you'd be or I would have made you one.'

They went outside. There were two white garden chairs, metal, on each terrace of the Lionheart houses, and Clara and Deirdre sat on them, with the white metal table between them.

'Promise me you won't tell Hal.'

'Hal?'

'He hates Tony anyway.'

Clara couldn't think who Tony was. Of course: Tony Grieves. 'No, he doesn't.'

'Yes, he does. I'm not even bothering about Mark, because I know you wouldn't let on to *him*.'

Clara looked at her and thought, This is what an adulteress looks like – I must be very naïve. 'No, of course –' she said.

Deirdre looked angry with her, which seemed unfair, and had her usual irritable restlessness, which always made Clara frightened of crossing her. She wouldn't tell anybody. She wanted Deirdre to go.

'You're my first proper friend,' said Deirdre, looking at her quickly and almost guiltily. 'I've never got on with other girls all that well. They were all bitches at school.'

Clara didn't want her confidence.

Deirdre leaned towards her, 'You and Hal . . . everything is so *nice* for you two,' she said.

Clara felt too warm in the close evening. She thought of Hal on top of her, smothering her; felt the inside of herself contract, a hard lump in her chest as Deirdre went on, 'Now you think I'm the original scarlet woman. I wish you hadn't seen.'

'It's all right.'

'You must think we were mad to be doing it *there*,' she said. Then, quietly, 'God, Clara, that's part of it, can't you see?'

Clara thought of Mark Innes, who was kind, and a good soldier. She felt pressed in by pleasure and pain. 'Let's just forget about it,' she said briskly. She stood up.

Deirdre was surprised. 'Shan't I tell you then?'

'Tell me?'

'About Tony. About Mark. Everything.'

'I'd rather you didn't.'

Clara, standing over Deirdre, realised she looked as if she was throwing her out. Deirdre stared up at her, scorned.

'No,' said Clara. 'I just think it's better if we don't go into it.'

Deirdre's mouth twisted a smile. 'I see.' She got up and stamped out her cigarette on Clara's terrace.

'I'd better get back to my little boy,' she said. 'I can't leave him alone, can I?' And for a second Clara had a feeling Deirdre would spit, or hit her, but she just smiled, then said, 'Look, why don't you two come for supper tonight?'

'Tonight?'

'No hard feelings and all that?'

Clara pushed open the door to the girls' room. The beds were at right angles to each other. The room was dim and soft and full of sleep. It was so clean. Clara bent over each of them and kissed them. Then, not able to leave, she sat down on the floor, in the narrow wedge-shaped gap behind the door, and rested.

Her mind ran over the scene with Deirdre and what she had seen. There's gossip, she thought, trying to smile, but couldn't make light of it. She thought of Deirdre's legs, the heels of her shoes scraping the asphalt, of her own bare feet trying to find purchase on the cool floor as Hal pushed her up higher onto the bed to accommodate him, not hearing or seeing her. The girls' breathing lapped and overlapped in the room.

She heard the door open downstairs and Hal's heavy boots on the tiles. 'Hello!' he called.

Clara got up slowly. She had better go down to him.

Deirdre had her maid cook something, and brought the covered dishes to the table herself, putting out her cigarette to serve the waxy potatoes.

The mutton, unidentifiable, swam in grease, the thick sheep smell rising up from the coarse meat. They drank thick white wine, tasting of resin, and there was a tomato salad, scattered with oregano.

Clara wasn't hungry. She watched Hal sitting back in his chair with his legs crossed. He seemed a bigger presence now even than before. Mark, next to him, was slight and tentative.

The day before, there had been a bomb in a café near Larnaka, and a British civilian had been amongst the wounded as well as soldiers. The morning papers – English and Greek – had been full of it. Clara had found herself reluctantly seeking out every detail. The day had been spent with the tiny print read and reread and the thin pages damp under her fingers, trying to look after the girls, sickening in the heat and stuffy closeness of her house.

'Deirdre's been getting all the gory details about this Arapiddou business,' said Mark.

'Oh, I have too!' said Clara, grateful to talk and smiling at Deirdre, who didn't smile back. 'I don't want to know, then I find myself looking. It's silly.'

'You shouldn't. It just frightens you,' said Hal.

'I'm just so curious,' said Deirdre. 'I live for the papers. Whether it's who's bombed who, or who'll be wearing what in London this autumn –'

'Yes. She's a heartless person, my wife,' said Mark, and Deirdre gave him a quick, contemptuous look.

'Are you shocked by me, Hal?' she said.

'We all like to read the papers,' he answered.

'Especially those of us all cooped up and not out seeking the action like you, probably,' said Deirdre, with a look at Mark. Mark, as Hal's 2 i/c, spent most of his time in the office, only out on ops when they were short-handed. It was an often thankless job, and Deirdre resented it, calling him Hal's secretary to tease.

Mark handed round the plates of mutton, and Deirdre's spoon dug into the bowl of big thick potatoes, piling Hal's plate and Mark's, with just one or two for herself and Clara. Clara looked down at the dark meat, and oil, then up from her plate to Hal's cool look and felt shamed by the judgement she read there.

Hal tried to smile at her, but she had looked down at her plate again. She wasn't going to eat; he could see she didn't want to.

After supper, they stepped onto their own terrace and said goodnight. Hal closed the sliding doors and locked them as Clara turned away.

'Wait,' he said.

She stopped, passively. He took her hand to go upstairs.

In the bedroom, she turned away from him to undress. Every part of him wanted to be close to her but her back was eloquent, and he was obedient to it.

'That wasn't much fun,' he said, to make conversation.

'No.' She undid her pearls. 'Deirdre and your lieutenant – Tony Grieves – are having an affair. I saw them today.'

'Really?'

'At the club. Kissing by the cars.'

'Christ. Poor old Mark,' said Hal.

She didn't turn towards him. He wasn't sure what more there was to be said. He felt silly, surplus to requirements. 'Were you feeling all right?' he said, thinking of her not eating.

'Just not very hungry.'

He nodded, although she couldn't see him do it, and sat down on the bed, beginning to undress, slowly, so that she could use the bathroom first.

Hal dreamed of the high plains and black smoke. In his dream the clear air, made bitter by smoke, was the main thing; the images – blue sky, bright sharp rock – were jumbled and not like any real scene, but the smell, the black cooked smell, was burning his nose; it was filling him up –

He woke with Clara's hand on his face. It was hot night, not glaring day and –

'Hal,' she said, 'you were making a noise. Bad dream?' and he, remembering, defended himself.

'No . . . Not bad,' he said.

She could not comfort him, then.

Chapter Two

Hal walked through the dark narrow tunnel towards the lighted beach. He had left the house after breakfast, asking Clara if she wanted to bring the girls down, or leave them with Adile and come alone with him, but she hadn't wanted to. They might all have walked by the sea before the heat of the day, but he hadn't imagined doing it alone. He didn't really understand going for walks: he didn't know what you were supposed to do on them, but once he'd said he was going, he had to go, and leaving the house, said, 'Well, perhaps I shall see you down there, then?'

Now he couldn't help listening for her voice behind him.

His boots echoed on the floor of the tunnel.

Hal's company might have been the heroes of the hour, but EOKA were unaffected by Pappas's defeat – if anything, they were stronger. It seemed that however many of the mountain gangs were destroyed the British could not bring peace to the island. In May, the tensions between the Greek and the Turkish Cypriots worsened, too. This was partly because of the British policy of turning the two populations against one another – using the minority Turks to police the majority Greeks – and partly that they hated one another anyway. Hal spent long hours with Burroughs in his dusty sun-filled office, drinking cups of tea and discussing the various machinations of governments and empire. British troops were pouring onto the island not just for Cyprus itself, but from their bases in Egypt, too. President Nasser had banished them and was being armed by the Communists, while America, Israel and Europe looked on and made deals of their own – and then there was Cyprus, immovably British. If Cyprus was lost, they were saying in London, then the whole Middle East was lost. Any British offensive in the area would be launched from sovereign Cyprus, tucked as it was in the far east of the Mediterranean. With the Suez Canal threatened, and oil supplies with it, Cyprus might have been a small island but its sea was the wide world.

The tunnel ended and the bright sun blinded him. His eyes adjusted to the light and the enormous view.

The long crescent of sand stretched whitely away to his right, and to the left ended in giant rocks that were different yellows and rainbow-striped. Far away, some horses trotted towards him through the shallow waves.

He could just make them out. There were four, he thought, straining to see. One was being ridden and one led, and then, behind them, two more, one with a rider. Hal walked towards the edge of the water.

He hadn't wanted to come alone.

He remembered Clara turned away from him that morning and other mornings – nights too.

The horses were clearer now: he could make out the thin leading ropes between them and their tails, carried high, blew softly to one side.

Perhaps he could persuade Clara to spend a proper evening with him in Limassol. That might cheer her up. Strange, though: when he imagined suggesting it he felt certain she would say no. He felt her presence, ghostly, pushing him away in mysterious rage, although she had never so much as reproached him.

He had reached the water; the tiny waves touched his boots. He took a small step back, wet tidemarks on the shining leather, the thought of Clara filling his mind with obscure shame.

He looked up and to the right again; the horses were much closer but he couldn't hear them yet over the sea. He could see the sun-glittering water thrown up by their hoofs, and that all four were bays, dark as conkers next to the bright blue sea. They shone; the sun was hitting them brightly.

He tried to work out who was riding them; one horse swung wide and he saw slender legs and hoofs trot out nicely to catch up through the dusty dry sand. Then – from one small moment to the next – the picture broke. The sand blew up in giant spouts around the horses. Hal didn't understand, but then his mind caught up, the noise of the explosion, coming surreally after the sight of it, was a muffled ripping.

All four horses were hidden by the huge feathery spouts of sand. The sand seemed to float, hover in the air in columns, and then fall, soft as water. Then sound came back to him, with the shrill shrieking of a wounded horse, and he began to run towards them. His boots were deep in the dry sand; he veered towards the edge of the sea where it was harder.

Two of the horses, unhurt, had scrambled up and they bolted towards him at a flat gallop with the reins and lead-ropes flying outwards. They were in a pair, like horses tied to a chariot, in a blind panic. Hal kept running, straight, and thought they would hit him. They reached him, one on each side with the gap between them very narrow. A knotted rope-end hit him full in the face, he thought one of the horses had hit him but they went past – he felt the heat of them – and he was in clear air.

He was yards away now, running towards the fallen men and horses, trying to assimilate what he was seeing. His legs stopped under him. The sand had settled and, with it, pieces of man and horse, huge splashes of blood that were like spilled pots of bright paint and hard to connect with reality.

There was a horse very near him with both front legs blown off. It was trying to get up, not realising, and throwing up its head with the effort. Its chest was flat to the ground, where it shouldn't have been, and it was screaming; its snorting head was very close to Hal, sweating and big. The man who had come off the horse was on the ground too. His face and head were covered with blood, but he was yelling, so Hal looked past him to the other man, one he recognised, a corporal – Taylor – who worked with the horses.

Taylor was lying on the sand and his leg was missing and it looked like part of his arm too, but it was hard to tell because of his being buried in sand and blood. The horse with no front legs was still trying to get up and still screaming.

Hal ran to Taylor and got down into the sand by him, grabbing him, with his back pressed against the back of another horse, a dead one – its huge insides spilled out behind him – and his knees grinding into the sand.

He pinned Taylor's chest down but his head was straining up, the mouth wide and soundless. Hal was shaking with the effort of keeping him down. He tried to look at the rest of him. His arm was there – Hal pushed the sand off it – but there was something wrong with it so he didn't touch it again. The two of them were writhing in a grotesque struggle, Taylor fighting him with impossible strength, his good leg thrashing around in the sand, which spat up into Hal's face and eyes, and the stump moving wildly too.

Hal was aware that two people were running towards them – it was Grieves and Scott – and he began to give orders without hearing himself. He sent Scott to the other wounded man and Grieves came over to him but didn't help him immediately. Hal was holding Taylor, struggling and convulsing, shouting for help with him; he would die very soon from bleeding, and his speechless scream was so close to Hal's face he could smell the fresh blood, like a butcher's shop, and more of it congealing on the warm sand. There wasn't time. Hal kept shouting orders, and Grieves finally got down with them in the filthy sand and was yelling for the doctor. There wasn't a doctor – he was such a fool and good for nothing – Hal grabbed Grieves's arm, and forced it onto Taylor's chest to hold him, gripping his hands to put on him, but he still kept pulling back and panicking while Hal yanked the stirrup leather from the saddle of the dead horse. It was clamped tight and hard to get free. Grieves was gibbering about something just by his ear while he pulled at it. He thought he was saying, 'Help help help' – but he didn't listen. The horse was still screaming so loudly that there almost wasn't any other sound, even with Grieves so close to him.

He got the leather free, and it didn't take long to tie it around Taylor's upper leg, but he had gone quiet and Hal wasn't sure that he was alive.

When Taylor went still, Grieves was still, too, and seemed to be in shock.

The horse was screaming with a constant shrill broken sound. At the side of Hal's vision he could see that the other man, Scott, was with the other casualty – the one he had passed by – and that he'd pulled off his shirt to press it against his head.

'Stay here. Hold here,' said Hal to Grieves, showing him, and stood up.

He took his pistol and went over to the screaming horse. It took too long because it was throwing its head around and he couldn't keep the gun against it. He gripped the bridle tightly with slippery bloody fingers and fought hard to keep it still enough. When he shot it, the horse's head fell straight down in a dead weight, its neck sideways on the sand, and it felt like silence afterwards because the screaming had been so loud.

In the deaf frozen quiet, Hal saw Grieves kneeling by Taylor, who seemed lifeless. The shining pale pink insides of the dead horse were curled and cleanly wet – they looked alive; the other horse, with no front legs, lay at his feet. Scott was kneeling in the sand holding the other wounded man, holding him tightly, cheek pressed against bleeding cheek. Just nearby lay a horse's hoof, blown clean off. It looked like a miniature version of an elephant-foot ashtray that a friend of Hal's father had, on a stand. Then the distant sound of an engine broke the silent shock.

He heard the quiet murmuring of Scott as he soothed the man he held, their faces close, and Grieves's rasping breath. A Land Rover came out of the black tunnel, the engine noise suddenly much wider, and roared towards them very fast.

He looked at the Land Rover, as it swerved to a sandy halt, all the doors opening at once. Dr Godwin and other men with stretchers got out. Help hadn't been long in coming – it was perhaps only seven or eight minutes since the explosion.

Taylor was lifted onto a stretcher. Hal saw him move, but

his face was white and sunk deep onto the bones, as if he were very old. They carried the other man, and Scott with him, to the Land Rover, and inside it, then it reversed, gears changing as it headed back into the tunnel.

Immediately the Land Rover had gone, running feet could be heard in the tunnel, then men came onto the beach and towards them. Grieves had sat back now. He had his head on his knees, with his arms covering it, as if he were under fire.

Hal moved his head to look. All around him the beach was pale and untouched, with just the limited carnage where he stood, just this small grouped wreckage.

There was blood and sand all round the dug-out space where Taylor had been lying in front of them. The horse Hal had shot had sand on its breathless muzzle. He could see Taylor's leg, with the brown leather riding boot still on it, nearby. There was no reason why the riding boot would have come off; it just looked odd. His eye went past this to the craters in the sand, about four feet deep, with the little waves coming in and running over the edges of them, foamy, and then running away again to the sea.

He thought that normally when you saw holes in a beach, there was a heap of sand next to them with a wooden spade stuck into it.

The soldiers had nearly reached him.

'Fall back,' he said. 'Mines.'

Chapter Three

The garrison was almost empty. The buildings of the barracks and NAAFI were quiet through the long afternoon, the flags lying still and just the sound of birds singing.

The troops descended on Limassol. At the beginning, some officers tried to control them but many did not. Perhaps they were relieved to have their own distress avenged.

The orders from Colonel Burroughs, such as they were, were for the questioning of men between fifteen and fifty and the rounding up of suspects.

The soldiers put up barbed-wire pens in the streets and squares, and herded people into them. There was a pen outside the cinema, opposite the church, others in other squares, near bars and grocers, outside shops that sold cotton dresses and trousers on hangers around the door. Where there was not enough space to erect the cages in the narrow streets, the soldiers lined the men up, faces to the wall, and kept them standing with their hands above them, leaning.

Suspects were loaded into trucks, and in heat and increasing chaos, rules were forgotten. The people were made to lie down on the floor of the trucks, because there were so many of them, and if the soldiers made them lie down, they could be layered, to make room. There were reports of suffocation, from this stacking of live bodies, but later, the British, investigating, found no bodies.

Each company took a section of the town to search. They cordoned off their area – from the port to Anexartisias Street and back as far as Gladstonos – and then the soldiers not involved in manning the barricades divided into sections for the business of searching.

The knot at the end of the horse's lead-rope had pulped the flesh over Hal's cheekbone. A nurse saw to it while he waited in the medical centre to hear about the wounded men. The rest of the garrison was mobilising to go into Limassol, with Mark Innes commanding. Hal, responsible to these men first, waited.

The man he hadn't recognised on the beach was a private called Jenson. Hal hadn't known who he was because he couldn't see his face properly for blood. The MO, Dr Godwin, tried to help him, to find some way of patching up his head, but it was beyond anybody's skill; he was dying. Hal went to him in the operating theatre. He wouldn't be moved out onto the ward.

It was just the two of them in the room, and Hal took Jenson's hand, because he couldn't see and was frightened. Jenson did not die easily, there was nothing gentle in it; his senses were taken from him one by one. Still, when Hal held his hand, the fingers closed tightly, and his breathing changed; it slowed.

Hal sat with him, he didn't know how long, and was there when he died, and briefly afterwards, not risking the abandonment of him while any shred of life might be left. Then he went in to Taylor, who had woken up.

Taylor had been under anaesthetic for them to work on the remains of his leg and since then had been given morphine. He didn't understand what had happened to him most of the time, then did understand for long moments. He kept arguing, and saying, 'No, I feel it, I feel it,' trying to reach down to touch his leg.

Hal, calm in his care for him, would look him in the eye and say very steadily, 'Don't think about it now, Taylor. Rest now. Just don't think about it,' and Taylor would recede again into sleep or unconsciousness.

Hal lost his sense of time. His only experience was the thickened bloody sand on his own skin and clothes, the anaesthetic smell of the sun-warm room in the medical centre and the two men, close to him. Distress presented itself to him – it tried him out – but he denied it. The damage hadn't been done to him but to the two men whose need he served. It would be an indulgence to dwell upon anything else now, and probable weakness to dwell on it later.

Tony Grieves should not have been in Limassol. In the urgency after the beach explosion, no one thought to stop him going. He wasn't injured, after all.

Immediately the casualties had been taken care of, Grieves was expected to take orders and to give them. He was to get back to his quarter and cleaned up, take command of his platoon, secure vehicles, become part of the military reaction to a personal crisis he had barely begun to absorb.

Changing his bloodied clothes with shaking hands, steeped in the horror of what had just happened, he felt as if he were stumbling in the wake of other men. He had been crippled by fear and revulsion on the beach, the nonsensical pieces of bodies on the blazing sand around him, God only knew how many other mines hidden from sight, and Hal yelling at him for help, as he nearly pissed himself in his terror. Now he was expected to take command and be an officer. It was a concept that meant little to him, and now he was appalled by it.

As a lieutenant, Grieves gave orders to his men in an ironic tone that at best approached chumminess and at worst was insulting, revealing his belief that they were stupid to have enlisted, unlucky to have been called up and he would rather be anywhere but there. He always tried not to speak to the men directly but through an NCO, fearing insubordination.

He hadn't known either of the injured men on the beach, or wondered who they were, but with Taylor's blood barely wiped from his skin, and the sting of his own cowardice fresh in his mind, he went with the others to Limassol.

At first he acted blindly, barely conscious of himself, but the violence and chaos of the troops, the hot current of vengeance that flowed through them began to flow through him, too. He was infected, gratefully replacing weakness with rage and the illusion of control. He allowed, encouraged, guided what became little more than a riot in places, and as the town began to look like a backdrop for chaos and calamity, so more chaos and calamity were heaped upon it. As Grieves, and others like him, lost their identity, so Limassol lost its identity, too. It wasn't a town any more, but an assortment of places for beatings and concealment, just hundreds of windows, chairs, news-stands and shelves to be overturned and broken. It was a fast degradation. The outrage of the collective frees the individual to commit terrible acts.

Grieves had brought Davis with him from the port, and

tried not to lose sight of him as his platoon patrolled. He was comforted to have him there, another officer, and one who could communicate for him. Davis didn't seem to appreciate the attention, and was very quiet.

The job was to get the men and boys into the pens for questioning. One of Grieves's sections had come off the main street after some stragglers and he'd gone after them. The section broke up as he lost control of it, soldiers scattering out of his reach; some returned to the main road and Grieves was reduced to a follower.

The street they were in was long and very narrow. It had been blocked off at one end to stop it being a rat-run from the main road, but the stragglers had gone up it anyway, and the soldiers after them, running away from the crowd. They were only four men, now, including Francke and Miller, with Davis tagging along next to Grieves at a run-hop walk.

Some people stayed locked in their houses as the running feet passed, but others came out into the grey evening to watch or interfere, thinking they could argue with the soldiers or help the escaping men. The youngest got away fastest. Francke and Miller went after them, sprinting, then skidding to a stop to shout, 'Halt! *Stamata! Dur!*' but shooting as they said it, and chasing again, as the bullets went into air.

The slowest man was caught. Giving chase had got their blood up, which was heated anyway from the skirmishes of the day, and they cornered him against the doorway of a locked house. The soldiers laid into him, kicking him, keeping him down, hunched up into the corner of the door and the stone step.

Grieves skidded into the group, just as the door was opened wide.

A girl of about seventeen and her mother were in front of the soldiers, screaming for them to get out and trying to drag the man into the house with them. The soldiers, interrupted in their orgy of kicking and blinded by it, panicked at the suddenness of the door opening, and pushed the women backwards, inside, with the butts of their guns and flat hands. They got the man into the kitchen as well, checking it quickly, kicking open doors, making sure nobody else was there. The women's clothes and bodies were much more yielding than men's to push against.

Davis was hanging back in the street, and Grieves yelled at him to follow.

It had happened fast, the whole group crushed into the tiny room suddenly, and the rest of the section outside somewhere.

They began to question the women, search the house, breaking things up, accusing them all of knowing one another, having some plan and being involved with EOKA. Davis, by turns protesting and translating, eventually backed into another room and stayed there, silent.

Grieves lost his temper with Davis when he wouldn't obey him, and his anger was blind screaming, but once he couldn't see him he forgot him. He turned his attention to the Greek man and the women sheltering him, and felt the power of his rank.

'Get them to stay still,' he ordered Francke. 'Shut them up.'

Grieves, who had never felt like a real soldier before, felt like one now. He had found a strength, greater than the distress of the morning; it wiped everything clean from his head – the maimed man, Hal pulling him down into the sand and blood. His rage comforted him. He could back it up: he was finding the guilty and punishing them.

Francke questioned the women, made them sit and slapped them – their faces – and Miller stood over the man, bending down to shout questions close into his face. Realising that responses were elicited when they hit the women, Grieves – according to his rank – encouraged the two soldiers to hurt the women and to touch them under their blouses and the long skirts covering their legs. It became a game, the mocking of the women and the teasing of the man, who was restrained and could do nothing. Each of the soldiers was exquisitely liberated by the others, the officer encouraging them was absolution, and they were anonymous in the group, and entitled.

The moment demanded completion: the rape of the women was inevitable. It was both celebration and rite – more about each other than the women themselves. They couldn't have recognised them afterwards, it was just the raping them, one after the other, the specific act, and hurting them. The women's foreignness made it easy: they didn't smell like English girls, but like the prostitutes they were entitled to anyway.

Grieves did not rape the women. He watched. He restrained the Greek man, who was barely conscious, with his foot on his chest. Francke, after he had buttoned his fly again, looked across at Grieves, then at the man on the ground.

Grieves looked down at him, too. They had both been watching Francke and Miller with the women, but they were not together.

With purpose and clarity, he nodded to Francke. Francke took one clean step towards him. He put his Sten on to single shot; the bolt was stiff, and his fingers slipped, doing it. The man, seeing what he was doing, began to struggle, and Grieves kept him still with his foot. Francke fought with the stiffly sprung bolt, and it clicked into place. He bent down slightly, put the nose of the gun against the centre of the man's moving forehead, and shot him, with Grieves's boot still on his chest. The only sound afterwards was the uneven breath of the women.

Miller was the first to get to the door, the other two following, with one last casual glance at the women, who did not look up. No one would believe them anyway. No Englishman, at least.

As they left, Grieves looked around for Davis, but could not see him.

Davis stood in the dark of the room he had hidden in. There was no door on the opening: he had seen everything. The moment Miller, Francke and Grieves had gone, the women, unaware of him or their own injury, went to the body of the man on the floor. The younger one fell at his side, pulling at his hand, while the older grabbed the body, lifting the lolling head to her, revealing, on the wall behind, the grey and red contents of his skull. She did not recoil: she clutched him. Davis took his opportunity, and blindly passed them. They were oblivious to him, and he left the house and ran away, as far from them as he could, taking gulps of air into himself, as if he were drowning in what he had seen.

The daylight faded from that small house, from the narrow street, the bigger streets and from the wire pens of caged men; the light dimmed over the roaming groups of soldiers, left the windows of the bars that had been smashed open, stopped shining on the broken windows and all the other varied scenes of destruction.

* * *

At Episkopi, an orderly came to tell Hal that Colonel Burroughs was there for him. He went to the entrance, where Burroughs was waiting. He was silhouetted against the evening light, which poured smoothly into the hallway and onto the wooden desk where a nurse sat, writing up notes nearby.

'Are you all right, Hal?'

'Yes, thanks.'

Burroughs placed a firm hand, briefly, on Hal's arm, then withdrew it. 'Managing all right, then?'

'Yes, sir.'

'Good man.'

Burroughs told him the troops in Limassol had been what he called 'understandably overzealous' in places. Now some restraint was needed. 'You'd better get down there. Let's hope they've got some of those EOKA bastards,' he said. 'Clean up first, though, Hal.'

He hadn't thought of it until now. 'Yes, of course, sir.'

Burroughs left him, and Hal waited in front of the medical centre for Kirby. It was after five. He was surprised that so much time had gone by, thinking that the mine on the beach had exploded some time after nine. That meant he'd been with Jenson and Taylor for something close to six hours. He saw a car driving towards him. Clara was sitting in front, next to Evelyn Burroughs.

They pulled up and Clara got out. She had on a tiered Greek-style skirt in bright colours – the skirt was the main thing he noticed because the colours were so intense: his eye kept being drawn to it. It was as if everything else was bleached out, just Clara's skirt drawing attention to itself. She ran towards him. 'They told me you weren't hurt!'

'I'm not.'

'I've been with Evelyn. I've been at her house all day. Everybody is – nobody can believe it,' she said. She fluttered her hand up to her face, shrinking away from him, it seemed.

Hal remembered he needed to get cleaned up. He was aware of his blood-stiff clothes, and the feel of his skin. His eye was dragged to her skirt again. 'What?' he said.

'Those men, the horses – how could anybody do that? How did they put it there?'

'During the night, I should imagine.'

There was a pause.

Hal heard an engine gunning up the hill in the sleepy quiet and then, over Clara's shoulder, he saw Kirby turning in. 'I'd better get going.'

'Where?'

'Limassol. Will you be all right?'

'Yes, of course.'

'Good.'

Hal walked past her and got into the Land Rover.

Clara, watching it drive away, wiped her sweating palms on the bright skirt. The sound of the engine faded.

Evelyn leaned out of the car. 'I told you!' she said to Clara, but not harshly. 'Come along now.'

Kirby drove him home without speaking to him or looking at him, leaving him his privacy. Hal changed his clothes quickly – fast enough not to notice the scrubbing of his skin and the smell – made sure everything was in order and went back down.

'Good,' he said.

* * *

Even at Kolossi, the tiny village nearest the garrison, there were signs of crisis. Land Rovers parked crookedly at the roadside, men with their hands up, held with guns by soldiers, the women looking on. Hal caught glimpses but didn't stop, and Cypriots, out of their houses, followed his vehicle with their eyes.

In the orange groves the sharp smell of citrus leaves filled his head.

The first checkpoint looked to be completely abandoned. There was nobody around at all, just low concrete houses with looped electricity cables between them and rubbish smelling in the heat. A three-tonner and two Land Rovers were parked, and left there, one with the keys in it still.

'Well, that's fucking marvellous,' said Hal.

They heard distant orders being given, in a house, or behind one, then a woman shouting and the banging of furniture going over, and more orders, in English.

'Jesus Christ,' said Hal, beginning to wonder what they'd find in Limassol. 'Let's get on.' Kirby pulled the Land Rover wide around the other vehicles and they drove on into town towards the port.

There was a curious exhausted tension now, as late afternoon set in. There was never any sunset in Limassol – it faced the wrong way – just more shadows. At the port, the big ships were moored out on the flat silver sea. The area between the Customs House and the water had become a yard for a holding pen and men were being loaded from that into a truck.

As the Land Rover stopped, Hal could see that the soldiers, as well as loading the men, were facing a small knot of boys and young men who were goading them and throwing sticks and bottles. Other soldiers were milling about, in pairs, with startling vagueness, and there was a lazy, sporadic violence that was too unfocused to be a stand-off, too dangerous to be nothing.

Hal stood up in the front of the Land Rover as Kirby cut the engine and scanned the crowd for Mark Innes. He couldn't see him. He looked for McKinney, Grieves, Trask or Fry – anyone who could have been said to be controlling the situation. There was nobody.

'There,' he said, pointing, and Kirby started up the Land Rover again, and crawled towards the road out of the port, to the east, where the waterfront of the town began, and the sea lapped up against the wall.

They stopped again, between the crowd of boys – now staring and quiet – and a soldier, brought to quick attention by their arrival. Hal addressed the soldier: 'Clark, is it?'

'Maplin, sir.'

'Who's your section commander?'

'Corporal Trask, sir.'

Hal asked quietly, 'The whereabouts of Corporal Trask. Any idea?'

'He was over there a minute ago, sir.'

Maplin was filthy and fidgeting.

'Where's Sergeant McKinney?'

'I ain't seen 'im, sir.'

'Lieutenant Thompson?' Blankness. 'Lieutenant Grieves?' Nothing. 'Quite a day then.'

'Sir?'

Then he saw Mark Innes coming from behind the wire pen, walking fast, smiling like somebody who'd forgotten how. 'Never mind.'

The soldier went on, and Mark reached him.

'This doesn't look like much fun,' said Hal.

'It's been a fucking shambles. Just getting some order back now. I sent McKinney with – Your face all right?'

'Yes, thanks.'

'Private Jenson died?'

'Yes. He didn't know anything. Half his brains had gone.'

'Taylor?'

'He'll be all right.'

'Fucking Cyp bastards.'

'We need to get this curfew enforced.'

'You think this is bad? Should've seen it earlier. The – it –' He had a look about his eyes, slightly staring. 'It hasn't been a good day, Hal.'

Hal nodded. 'It's all right,' he said firmly. 'Let's get it sorted out, shall we?'

It took hours to mobilise troops and vehicles into order. Truckloads of prisoners were deposited up at Episkopi Garrison guardroom; dozens of others were taken forty miles to the prison camp, Camp K, for questioning. Then, like soldier Pied Pipers, Hal and the other officers drove through the streets, with loud-hailers and whistles, flanked by men with Stens ready, and all around Cypriots melted away into their houses, and soldiers, remembering themselves, came out of bars and brothels and people's homes. Hal found Corporal Trask, in a bar with three others, no barman to be seen, and drunk, helping themselves. He got him and the others out of the smashed-up bar by the scruffs of their necks and tore a strip off Trask, but kept his temper. Being angry with Corporal Trask would be like being angry with one animal in a stampede.

The rest of the city, under different command, had fared no better, but it was cold comfort. There had been a failure. Hal hadn't been responsible for the orders, they had come from Colonel Burroughs, but he hadn't been there to oversee their execution, and they had all forgotten themselves. They had forgotten themselves because of the loss of one man, and the wounding of one more. They had forsaken all, forsaken discipline, for some blood on the sand, horse-hoof ashtrays.

And then, at the end of that day, Hal lay in bed with Clara.

She had waited, tactfully, to see what he would do when he came in. There had been nothing to do but eat, and climb the stairs to bed. They hadn't spoken. He had washed again, with soap, flannel, nailbrush, and shaved. The hot water, limited at the best of times, ran cold while he washed. Cold water, strong soap, the repeated scrub of the flannel, scraping. Clara sat downstairs, listening to him, waiting.

The sheets were cool. He laid his head on the smooth pillow and the cotton touched his cheek. His limbs and skin were unconstrained inside the loose material of sheets and pyjamas. It was as if these soft things were happening to him for the first time and he, like a snail torn out of its shell, smarted at the contact.

He turned onto his back. Clara turned too, towards him, her nightdress and hip slightly touching him as she went onto her side.

She rested her cheek on her hand. He couldn't see her, but he knew that was what she always did when she turned towards him like that. He knew the line her body made then, too, all curved, like an English landscape.

He made an effort to steady himself. He would find comfort.

Without looking at her, he took his eye down her horizon – small hill for head, little steep valley into neck, hill of shoulder, deep valley to waist, lovely hill of bottom, long slope of legs, running away down to . . . sea? A coastline at the end of the bed? A cliff. Deep water. Not a home landscape then, an island. He felt a lurching disintegration and struggled for control.

'Hal?'

'Yes?'

He felt her move in the dark, and then she took his hand and held it. It was as if she held the thread that would unravel him.

He took his hand away from her.

Chapter Four

They had been told that the beach was safe. At eleven o'clock in the morning, two days after the explosion, Clara stood at the entrance to the tunnel with Lottie and Meg. They had their buckets and spades with them. She had felt a sort of reckless defiance before leaving the house – some version of the British indomitable spirit, she decided, and had felt proud of it. Now she didn't feel proud. She felt stupid, and very frightened. The black tunnel, not much wider than a Land Rover, with the two hundred feet of sheer cliff above it, went away to its far point of light ahead.

The girls were pulling at her hands. She couldn't go through the tunnel.

'Come on, darlings, let's go and play at the club.'

'No. Let's go beach!' said Meg.

'Let's go beach' had been one of their first phrases and remained a favourite; they went to the club every day.

Clara knew they were going to make a scene. She had, after all, packed the beach bag and brought them down here; it was only fair they should want to carry on. She contemplated manhandling them both all the way back up the path.

'What about the horses?' she said.

'*No*,' said Lottie, her face like a child's picture of crossness: Mary Jane contemplating her rice pudding.

'The horses miss us,' said Clara, cajolingly.

She tried to turn them away from the tunnel, hot little hands and tipping-over beach basket making her clumsy. The tunnel had always frightened her – too small, straight and black, and too much rock above it. Whenever she walked through it, even before the bombing, she was frightened, had played echoing games with the girls just to make fun of it and prove her courage. She had dreamed once of it falling on her when she was halfway through and Hal on the outside with the children. The falling had been soft and suffocating, not the noisy rockfall of reality, but the thick foam darkness that nightmares have.

She stood there, half turned away from the tunnel, trying to avoid a fight with the twins that could only be won by force, with the path, polo field and all the dusty pointless bushes and hills around her, not pastures for playing in or grass for sitting on, just this hot-place landscape that you couldn't properly walk in, or lie on, that seemed to stare at her. Being with the children made her feel helpless and vulnerable, heaving them about, never able to explain herself to them, but always covering up with nursery platitudes and motherly confidence that she did not feel.

She was hot and panicking and felt imaginary Cypriot eyes upon her. She had started to feel that all the time now. When she was in her bedroom she imagined them watching her house, when she was opening her front door she imagined tripwires across it and had begun to check, without letting anyone see she was doing it. Whenever she got into the car, part of her was expecting it to blow up. Every sound she heard had both a benign and a sinister interpretation, and she would have to remind herself to keep to the real world and not be drawn into her fear completely, not let it overtake her.

Sensible people always said it, didn't they? The chances of being a victim of one of these things were infinitesimal – even when it had happened to those horses, even though that poor boy had lost his leg and would go home to his mother ruined, and the ruin would spread ripples.

She was still standing there with the children. They were quiet. Did she frighten them with her distress? Without even crying, without even saying, *I'm frightened, I want to go home, I miss my husband. I miss him even when he's there . . .* Did they know, anyway?

'Now, come along, and let's not be silly. Those poor horses haven't seen us for days. Let's go and give them some apple. Do you think horses like bread?' she said, in her mother voice.

'Horses,' said Meg, kindly. She was more pliant than Lottie, allowing herself to be captured.

The covered line of stables was dim and sawdust smelling. She found Private Morrison, who cared for the horses. He was eager for her company. She chatted to him, both thinking about Taylor, Jenson and the two horses that had died, and not saying a word, but he stroked the face of the horse he stood by consolingly, she thought.

He brought out one of the small ponies for the girls, and led them bareback up and down the line of stables, past the empty stalls of the dead horses, and the live ones, leaning curiously over their doors and blowing gently through soft nostrils, their eyes shining.

Clara leaned back against the wooden wall and closed her

eyes. No one could see her. She sang a hymn in her mind, a quiet one, this time. *Lord of all hopefulness, Lord of all calm, Whose –*

'Hello.'

Clara opened her eyes.

It was Lieutenant Davis. He was in barrack dress, the summer version, which was longish baggy shorts and shirt, with a webbing belt, boots and socks. His legs were very white and thin and his face red from the heat, with damp hair stuck to his forehead.

'Hello,' she said, wondering what she must have looked like. 'How are you?'

'I came out for a smoke.'

'You can't smoke here – you'll burn the place down.'

'Are you . . . quite all right?'

Clara had been going to say, 'Of course,' but instead she said – quietly, so that Private Morrison wouldn't hear her, 'It's too dreadful. I can't take it in, still,' and he answered,

'Yes. It really was. Awful.'

The moment of sympathy between them was a relief, like a glass of cold water – soothing. Clara felt gratitude to him, and realised with shock that she and Hal had not made any allusion to it, not even this most basic recognition of what had happened.

Davis was staring at the ground, his eyebrows drawn together in a deep frown.

'You look terribly hot,' said Clara.

He looked up. 'I came from the guardroom.'

'Quite quickly?'

'Yes.'

Clara glanced over at the girls, and Private Morrison, leading them patiently, one hand on the rope, the other on Lottie's back. The dusty quiet air felt slow with sadness, and Morrison's hand on Lottie's back was gentle, his head bowed as he led her. 'Have they found them?' she asked.

'Who?'

'The EOKA who did it.'

He laughed mirthlessly. 'No,' he said.

Clara looked at him.

'You sound as if they won't.'

'Of course they won't. This is all . . .' he gestured, '. . . this is all just . . .' He didn't have words for what it was, then. 'It's just punishment. It's just a game. Back and forth.'

'Not a nice one.'

'No.'

There was a pause. Then, 'Look, Mrs Treherne –' He had said 'Look' to her, but he was the one looking, searchingly, right at her. 'Look,' again, 'I wonder if I might speak to you?'

'Of course.'

'How about that cigarette?'

'Away from the horses, then,' she said.

'Yes. Over here.' He gestured some way away. 'Do you mind?' He was mysterious.

They walked a little way towards the trees at the edge of the polo field, where there was shade and a dog, sleeping, with Clara looking back over her shoulder at the twins, who didn't notice her. She thought they were probably safe for now, and no one would put a mine under a tree, would they, where people seldom walked? The ground didn't seem disturbed. They stopped. She reflected that EOKA had done what they had intended to: they had terrified her.

He lit his cigarette and offered her one, and she took it, to be companionable. She normally only smoked with Hal, after supper, and associated the fresh-lit taste with him. Davis blew smoke up into the weeping dappled leaves above them.

'What's your husband like?' he said, very abruptly, then looked down at his boots.

Clara was shocked. 'What do you mean?'

'No, no, I'm sorry. It's just that – I've been thinking of talking to him about something that's happened. The day before yesterday. I don't know if I should. I don't know if there's any point at all.'

Clara paused, considering how best to answer. 'Try him,' she said firmly.

He walked away from her, leaned one hand on the silver tree and rubbed his eyes with his thumb and forefinger, pressing quite hard into the sockets.

'You ought to know what he's like,' said Clara. 'He's your commanding officer.'

'He's your husband.'

'We don't want him for the same things, I shouldn't think.'

'Is he *fair*, though?'

'Fair?'

'Is he fair and does he listen? Will he listen to me?'

He was still rubbing his eyes. Clara hadn't been smoking her cigarette and she put it out carefully under her shoe. 'Hal says you should always be able to go to your commanding officer. It should always be the first place you go.'

'Yes, they *say* that.'

'Well – there you are.'

'But will he do something? Or is it all just a sham?'

'I ought to get back to the children.'

'Will he listen?'

'I don't know! Stop it!'

He let his hand fall from his eyes, and was still. 'I want to go home,' he said.

Me, too, thought Clara, *me too*, but – 'Where's home?' she asked.

'West Sussex. At least, that's where my family are from. I've just – I'd just come down from Cambridge. It was because of the Greek, you see – that's why they want me for this. Otherwise I would have just been a normal soldier for my two years. None of this Special Investigations mess, none of this interpreting. Interrogations.'

'Well, I should think you're very helpful. No one else can speak a word, can they?'

'No. I'm very helpful.'

He left a silence. Then, 'When I was on leave last time, they shipped us off to Athens – I had a week. I saw the most beautiful things. I did some sketching, which I'm awful at. I travelled outside the city and I saw the most lovely things. I saw Delphi – I'd always wanted to. You don't know my name.'

'What?'

'You don't even know my name. If we were at home, after we'd been introduced we'd call each other by our names. Don't you think it's extraordinary that you don't even know my name? Don't you think it's actually inhuman?'

'Well – what's your name, then?' She glanced back towards the stables.

'Lawrence. Lawrence Davis. Won't you say it?'

'Say it?'

'Yes. Please.'

'Lawrence.' Clara was embarrassed, but then, seeing his face, she softened. She wasn't used to seeing need in a man, certainly not in Hal. She smiled. 'How nice to meet you Lawrence Davis. People do use first names here, you know, when they know one another a little.'

Davis heard her voice soften, and saw her look kindly on him. 'I haven't really got to know anybody. Clara Treherne, is it?'

'Yes. Clara.'

'Like "air"?'

'Yes.'

'Good,' he said.

'There. Happy now?'

'Yes. Thank you.'

'And you'll talk to Hal?'

'Yes. I'll talk to him.'

Later, when Clara stepped across the lawn to Deirdre's house, and knocked to ask if she would like to bring Roger over for cucumber sandwiches and cake on their terrace, Deirdre, looking up from her magazine, raised her eyebrows and said, 'Oh, thanks, we might.' Roger was playing near her feet with a small red metal truck. But then, as Clara turned to go, she added, 'By the way, what were you chatting about so earnestly with the handsome Lieutenant Davis? This afternoon by the stables. I saw you.'

There hadn't been Cypriot eyes watching, after all, but English ones.

Chapter Five

Lawrence Davis was glad he had pursued Clara Treherne to the stables; talking to her had helped him, and that afternoon he went to her husband's office, just as she had suggested. He sat down, and Hal observed him across the desk, noting that he looked untidy and hoping he wouldn't take up too much of his time: he had spent the whole of that day, and most of the one before, sitting opposite errant privates and corporals and had run out of disapproval.

Hal hadn't slept since the explosion on the beach. Every time he closed his eyes, it was projected onto his eyelids with magnified brightness, and the sight of those things, revisited, made him too disturbed for sleep. It was easy to feel reassured, with Clara lying beside him, and to relax, but then the dense live curtain of his memory would tear and things would escape from it. It might be the feel of his own knees bedded into the sand as he tied off the pulsing stump of Taylor's leg, or something else – anything – and he would have to jerk to consciousness to put it away again, and himself back in the room. He wasn't surprised at being haunted like that; he blocked out the distress as well as he could, but he thought it would be better if he could learn to control his night-time hours as well as he did the daytime ones.

Hal shifted more upright in his chair, to sharpen himself up, and looked at Davis expectantly.

'There was something I wanted to talk to you about, sir,' said Davis.

'Yes. Obviously. Go on, Davis.'

'I'm not sure of the procedure.'

'Well, first you speak, and then I respond,' Hal said drily. 'We go on like that, until we reach a conclusion.'

'Yes, sir. Of course. It's just it's rather a difficult matter.'

'Lieutenant Davis.'

'Sir?'

'Get on with it.'

'Sir.'

Davis had the dry mouth of confession. He felt the power of Hal's authority, and his impatience, and was sharply aware that he was placing his trust in him. He began: 'In Limassol – on Monday – I saw, I was witness to a crime,' he felt child-like, 'committed by British soldiers. A murder. And rape. Some women –' He stopped.

Nothing about the way Hal was sitting or looking at him had changed perceptibly, but Davis felt a seismic shift in the atmosphere in the room.

He could hear orders echoing from the drill square, and the snipping sound of shears near the window.

'"Some" women?'

'Two women.'

'Where was this?'

'In a house.'

'Can you identify the soldiers?'

'Yes.'

'Could you identify the women? If you met them again.'

'. . . I don't know.'

'You know where the house was? Exactly.'

'Yes, sir.'

Hal leaned back in his chair, picked up his pencil and studied it. 'Who were the soldiers?' he asked, quite casually.

Davis thought briefly of Clara Treherne saying, *Try him*. He found that his voice was shaking. He felt inexplicably ashamed of himself as he named them. 'Lieutenant Grieves. Private Miller, Private Francke, sir. It wasn't Lieutenant Grieves. I mean, he watched. He ordered it.'

'He ordered it?' Hal was looking at him intently.

'He watched.'

'He watched or he ordered it?'

'He . . . encouraged it.'

'Who shot the man?'

'Private Francke, sir. In the head. Do you know about this already?'

'What was your role in this?'

'My role? I was the interpreter.'

Hal held the tip of the pencil with one finger, balancing, its sharp point digging into the blotter and his finger pressing it down from the top. The very end of the pencil crumbled slightly. 'What exactly do you mean?' he asked.

'I need to tell you everything,' said Davis.

Hal had kept Davis in his office for two and a half hours. He had made notes. At some point in the afternoon Mark Innes had put his head around the door and said he was going off for the day, and then they were alone. Hal asked Davis question after question after question, not aggressively but with no let-up, no glimmer of a decision over what would be done, least of all what he thought or felt, about Davis or anything that had happened. Then he'd dismissed him with 'Thank you very much.'

Davis had gone straight to the toilets at the mess and cried, with his hand jammed over his mouth, because it had been so disgusting to play the scene over and over in his head, the way Hal had made him. All the other things he had seen in the past weeks flooded his mind too, and his own weak presence, watching. Then, when he could stop crying, he went to the bar and had a drink, a big one. He thought about home, his mother in the kitchen, his father working in the garden. Then he thought of his study at Cambridge. Then he thought of Clara.

When Davis had gone and left Hal alone, the room itself seemed grateful for the silence, after the things that had been described. Hal's coolness had been a sham; his impartiality an effort of will, for Davis's benefit, so that he might have the comfort of professionalism in which to unburden himself.

After a few moments, Hal began to go over the notes he had written. He made sure he cleared up details because he might not be able to trust his memory. Davis's words painted a vicious picture: the torture of women, the easy killing of the man, who was not a threat, the degraded collusion of the soldiers, excited by their violence. The details. He wanted to hide from it, un-hear it, and he wished he did not know, but he had crossed a boundary and could not go back. He had not known he was such an innocent.

He stood up. Taking his handkerchief from his pocket he wiped his palms dry, and refolded it carefully. Clara had put his initials in red chain stitch on all his handkerchiefs, years before: H.T. ('We don't want anybody sneaking off with them,' she'd said.) He sat down once more, straightened his chair, then the stack of notes before him. He picked up his pencil again.

If British soldiers did these things, their essential damning sin was not only against God – although it was against Him – but England, too. The sin infected Hal, the company, battalion, regiment, army and country, and the only victory could be their trial and punishment. Still, the prospect of turning on men under his command seemed to tear his loyalty inside him, and the disgust he felt was not just with them but with himself, at what he was preparing to do, and he resented it.

Hal's eyes closely read and reread the densely written lines. Every quarter page, he sharpened the pencil again, just to have the moment of its correction to a point, and to see the neat curls drop lightly into the wastepaper basket by his chair. He added the pages to the stack of reports he'd made since the mess on Monday night in Limassol: crimes ranging from the destruction of property, to drunkenness – and now this. When he had finished, it was six o'clock.

The soldiers had long since left the drill square, and now there were only the evening songs of birds.

He had to be very careful. He had to be sure.

Hal walked over to the hook by the door and, taking his cap from it, lifted it to eye level, facing him.

He looked at the cap badge, looked carefully at the castle, oak leaf and banner against their blue heaven. The image was as familiar as the British flag, and even closer to him than that. He didn't remember the first time he had seen it – on his father, perhaps, as a child, or with his grandfather's old uniforms, revered and visited in their preservation against moths. The castle – embroidered suggestion of a castle that it was – had been King Arthur's to him, Prince Hal's; the oak leaf was gold against a pale blue sky, stitching with thin shining thread, England and the air above, making God and country one. The badge was the very picture of his country made small, and worn proudly.

Those were not the words that came to Hal, looking at it and making his decision; he could not have said it out loud. His word was 'everything'.

He looked at the badge for a long moment: castle, oak leaf, banner. The deep quiet land that had bred him was as close as he might ever feel to God, and he served it. He felt the comfort and reassurance of responsibility. He crossed to the desk, and picked up the telephone. 'Colonel Burroughs,' he said and, after a moment, 'Colonel, sir, Hal Treherne . . . May I come up to the house? There's something I need to discuss with you . . . Thanks.'

Hal replaced the receiver, bowed his head an inch, put on his cap and left the room.

Chapter Six

The colonel's house was distinguished by its size, being set slightly apart and having lawn all around it. In other ways it was similar to the other officers' houses: it was recently and cheaply built, painted white, with blue window frames. It wasn't the colonel who had to bring in the heavy metal gas bottles when they ran out, but they still had to be brought in, and if he had an extra member of staff or two, he still lived as near to the officers under his command as made little difference. At home he would have had a long driveway and not been amongst them.

Hal sat silently in the Land Rover, going over what he would say to Burroughs and trying to banish the pictures Davis had put in his mind: the vision of a faceless girl with her legs jammed wide, her mother restrained. He told Kirby to wait at the corner, and walked up to the house alone. He found he was breathless, as if he had walked all the way up the hill from the office.

He had been to the colonel's house once or twice before, but always at Evelyn's invitation, and with Clara. The door was opened by an African servant. He was barefoot and nodded politely as he allowed Hal inside. Hal removed his cap and held it. He could smell women's scent and shampoo from upstairs; Evelyn must have been dressing for the evening.

He followed the servant through the house and down two steps into the living room. Hal's footsteps were loud on the marble chip tiles but the servant's were silent.

'Here is Major Treherne, sir.'

Burroughs was sitting on a planter's chair by the door to the terrace, he got up as Hal came in.

'I'm sorry to disturb you, sir.'

They shook hands.

'Quite all right, Hal. Drink?'

'Not for me.'

'Get me a brandy and soda,' said Burroughs, to the servant, who withdrew, and they went out onto the terrace.

It was half past six, and dark, but there weren't any stars yet and the sound of crickets was just starting up; it hadn't reached the rhythmic throb of night-time.

'I should think you've had quite a day of it.'

'Yes, sir.'

'Especially after Monday.'

'Yes.'

'Are you all right?'

'Yes, thanks.'

'You've leave coming up.'

'Should do, sir. Couple of months.'

'Spent the day sorting out the rotten apples, have you?'

'Yes. Monday night was –'

'I'm always surprised how many of them cry when they get hauled in. If they don't, they bloody ought to. Makes you feel like a schoolmaster – or, heaven forbid, their father.'

Hal, who normally found Burroughs easy company, had nothing to say. He recognised an extraordinary tension in himself, which separated him.

The servant brought a tray with the colonel's brandy on it, and looked enquiringly at Hal.

'Have a beer at least, Hal. It can't be that serious.'

'Thanks. All right.'

The servant went away and Hal said, 'Davis came to see me this afternoon.'

'Lieutenant Davis? The interpreter?'

'Yes. There was an incident on Starsis Street.' Hal prepared to continue. The second's silence was a thick barrier to be forced through. He spoke. 'Sir, Davis witnessed Private Francke shoot a man, at point-blank range, no provocation, with Lieutenant Grieves looking on.'

Hal saw the servant coming out of the kitchen with his beer, and said quickly, 'And he – Francke, that is – and another man, Miller, raped two women. According to Davis.'

The servant reached them and put the tray down. Hal watched him slowly pour the beer into the glass.

Colonel Burroughs turned away. He put his drink on the low terrace wall and stood with both hands deep into his pockets.

The servant handed Hal his beer, took up the tray, flat to his chest, and quietly left them.

'Have you had these men arrested?' said Burroughs.

'Not yet, sir. I just came from my office – from talking to Davis.'

'Davis.' The colonel tried the name carefully. 'I haven't had too much to do with him. He can be relied upon, can he?'

'In this, yes, sir.'

'No personal axe to grind?'

'Not that I know of.'

'Does anyone else know anything about it?'

'Not that I'm aware of.'

The colonel turned to him. The terrace light caught the side of his face, illuminating his pale eyes and the sharp bones. 'Not much space left in the guardroom,' he said.

'Just my thought, sir,' said Hal, laughing briefly, but with bitterness.

'What about Mark Innes in all of this?' said Burroughs, looking for blame, and Hal thought – with sudden anger – *They were your bloody orders, and they were sloppy, too,* but he said, 'Mark did his best. There were several hundred men down there. Being in the town made it difficult to keep tabs on everyone – the men were pretty worked up. Not to put too fine a point on it, there wasn't much he could do.'

'And you weren't there,' said Burroughs, eyeing him thoughtfully.

'No.'

Hal revisited lost hours spent at Jenson's side, his ugly companionship with death.

There was a silence.

'*George!*'

The strident sound of Evelyn Burroughs's voice came from upstairs, and the colonel looked at Hal and rolled his eyes. 'Duty calls,' he said, and went inside at a fast trot.

Hal smiled. The CO's CO, he thought. He drank his beer, while it was still cold, and stood looking at the ugly rockery until the colonel reappeared. 'Why can't women do up their own necklaces?' he asked, stepping onto the terrace. 'Mind you, I couldn't manage my own tie to save my life.'

He came over to Hal, and stood next to him, putting one foot up on the low wall, resting his arms on his knee for a moment. His closeness was familial. 'Well,' he said.

A lizard flashed onto the wall by his very shiny shoe; it was delicate. 'We'd better lock all three of the bastards up, and investigate the whole bloody business. It's a damn shame. Why do people have to be so stupid? If Davis hadn't seen, they could've kept their depravity to themselves. As it is, the whole damn island will know about it, and the press too, I shouldn't wonder. So much for bloody hearts and minds. Makes the lot of us look like murderous thugs.'

The lizard ran away down the wall and disappeared. Colonel Burroughs straightened. 'You'll see to it?' he said.

'Yes, sir,' said Hal.

'And, Hal, come to the mess tonight. It's best not to be on your own. We're all devastated by what happened to Jenson and Taylor. Not to mention the bloody horses. You acted very fast. You did everything you could.'

'I don't know about that.'

'You know what my first thought was when I heard what had happened?' He looked at Hal directly, unveiling some small pain within himself. 'First thing I thought – was it King's Man? Didn't give a damn for the humans. I'd hate to lose that horse. Then, of course, you remember the truth of the matter, and think about the man who died, and poor old Taylor losing his leg. Was he a good soldier?'

'Taylor?'

'Yes.'

'He's only been out here since January,' said Hal. 'Came out on the same boat as my wife, in fact. National Service lad. Quite capable. Jenson was just a very good groom, loved his horses. Came into the army to work with them. Couldn't shoot straight to save his life.'

'Didn't have to.'

'No.'

Hal thought of Jenson, whose face had been a mess of blood and lumped flesh. He was still unrecognisable when he died because they couldn't clean up his wound without pulling away too much of him. Hal had never held a man's hand before. He hadn't known if it had been spasm, or an attempt to fight loneliness, or death, that had made Jenson grip his fingers so hard.

Evelyn's heels were heard on the marble stairs, then she appeared, striding towards them, in an evening gown, mottled chest straining against the satin.

Hal watched her walk to him; her smile was momentarily grotesque, and he was jolted back from Jenson's bedside to the warm terrace.

'Hal! Shall I blame you for keeping my husband from his ablutions?'

Hal gathered his thoughts, he pulled his scattered thoughts, which had escaped like startled roaches into corners, back to himself. 'Guilty, I'm afraid,' he said, 'but I was just leaving.' He made polite conversation with them both, not referring to the arrests he was about to make or the reason for them.

'You will send our regards to your parents when you write, won't you?' she said, and Hal promised that he would.

Chapter Seven

Hal left Burroughs's house and walked back to the Land Rover. He glanced at his watch, thinking he should let Clara know where he was, but then he forgot about her, focusing on what was ahead, not on his wife, who was safe at home with supper and children, and not concerned with any of this.

Clara put the twins to bed. Hal hadn't come home. Nobody had come to tell her where he was. Adile was finishing downstairs; her presence wasn't companionship.

Deirdre wasn't home next door, she couldn't hear anything from the other houses, just the night-time sounds in the grass and the unseen bushes, little creaks and rustles coming through the open doors.

She came downstairs. She hated the feel of the darkness outside. She knew Adile was watching her as she closed the back of her house and pulled the curtains across.

The room became impossibly stuffy and hot. Clara checked her watch every few moments. Half past seven. Twenty-five to eight. Adile finished the kitchen and opened the low cupboard where she kept her bag and things. Clara looked up quickly. She got to her feet. 'No! Adile. Stay, please?'

'Madam?'

'Please stay.'

Adile nodded, and sat down at the kitchen table with her hands folded in front of her.

Clara stood still where she was. The two women were at either end of the room. 'I need to go out,' Clara said suddenly. 'Out. Stay, please. Watch the girls. Please?'

Adile nodded again, politely not meeting Clara's eye.

'Good,' said Clara. 'I'm going to the mess. I shan't be long.'

Clara walked all the way down the hill. She kept her eyes on the three feet of road in front of her that she could see. She wouldn't stare into the dark, like a frightened animal. She wouldn't look over her shoulder. Her heels slipped on loose gravel. How pathetic, she thought, how pathetic you are to cry with fear over nothing, nothing at all. They've bombed us already. If we're on our guard, they aren't going to get at us again, not here – but the picture of terrorists, creeping in darkness, laying hidden bombs in the soft sand, multiplied in her mind, her brain eagerly feeding on it.

She arrived hot and breathless in the brightly lit normality of the bar and her fear drained like sea-water into a dry beach, leaving her dizzy. She wasn't dressed properly. She must look a fright. She dabbed at her forehead with the backs of her hands. She ought to get to the lavatory and try to tidy herself up –

'Clara!'

It was Susan MacKay, sitting with Deirdre.

'Everything all right?'

'Yes. Hello.'

They were playing cards. They had White Ladies.

'Join us,' said Susan. 'No Hal?'

The bright lights and noise washed over her. She sat down next to Susan. 'He isn't home yet.'

'Will you play?'

'No, you go on. I thought he might be here, actually.'

'We haven't seen him, have we, Deirdre?' said Susan.

'Not lately.'

'I didn't dress. I'm afraid I rushed out.'

Deirdre glanced up coldly. 'Rushed out to look for your husband, Clara? Didn't leave your girls alone, I hope?' she said.

'No, of course not.'

Deirdre twisted her mouth into a smile, and slapped a card down onto the table. 'I should hope not,' she said.

Susan smiled too, but a friendly smile. 'Don't be silly. Nobody minds,' she said, 'but I've a comb and compact, if you're desperate.'

Clara watched Susan and Deirdre play gin rummy. They passed the odd remark about the cards, or people who walked by the table, and Clara let her eye move over the crowd. She couldn't see Mark anywhere – perhaps he was with Hal, or on the other side of the bar. Blue cigarette smoke hung like a banner over the people's heads. The gramophone in the corner was playing and the talk was loud above it, so that she couldn't hear the words.

She didn't know what had possessed her to try to go to the beach that morning; the horror of what had happened was only now finding its natural scale. The atmosphere in the bar was a little like people sheltering in a pub on moorland or a cliff-top, waiting for the bad weather to pass, a certain heightened welcome. Down the stairs, and across the bar, Clara saw

Davis, as he made his slow way through the people. He didn't speak to anybody, and nobody spoke to him.

He stopped by the door to the terrace, glancing around, searching faces, biting the side of his mouth. What was it? she wondered. What was it he had needed so badly to tell Hal? She followed his eyes as they fixed on somebody. Tony Grieves. Why would Davis be staring at him? Her eyes went back to Davis and he, at the same time, looked over the crowded bar at her. Their eyes met briefly, and instead of acknowledging him, Clara found she looked down to her lap, in shyness.

'What-ho, the major,' said Susan, and Clara twisted round to see Hal coming in.

He didn't notice her; he looked exhausted. He had lain rigidly in bed next to her the night before, silent, the air ringing with tension around him. Clara got up and went over to him. 'Darling, where have you been?' she said.

'What are you doing here?'

'You look tired.'

He was scanning the room. 'Long day.'

'Oh – telling off soldiers?'

'Yes, look, would you mind awfully going home? I need to do something – I'd rather you weren't here.'

He still hadn't looked at her, but then he glanced down, as if to say, *Still here?*

'Oh . . . I'll –'

'Kirby can take you up. He's outside. Tell him to come back here afterwards.'

Clara's voice was quiet; she was hoping only he would hear, wanting him to listen very badly. 'I was rather nervous at home,' she said. 'Frightened.'

'There's nothing to be nervous about.'

'That's what everybody said about the beach!'

One or two people turned their heads. Clara was aware of Deirdre and Susan watching them. Hal faced her squarely, and dropped his chin an inch to look into her eyes. 'Clara, come along. It isn't the right time to talk about this. I'm still working. Shall I see you later?'

Clara felt her cheeks get hot. 'I can *be* here, can't I?'

He, low, 'I'd rather not,' but then, 'All right, if you want.' And he turned sharply away from her.

Clara didn't wait. She passed him, heading towards the ladies' room, the one place she could walk to legitimately. She paused at Susan and Deirdre's table. 'I think I will borrow that compact, if you don't mind.'

Susan handed Clara her evening bag, without comment, and, taking it, she saw Deirdre's eyes narrow in amusement.

Clara washed her hands. She felt slightly sick. She splashed her face with water, and powdered, and when she came out, she saw Hal, with Grieves, walking out of the bar again. Nobody had stopped to observe their leaving, but she felt it had some significance of which she was ignorant. Then, walking back to the table, she saw Davis, again across the crowded bar. He was watching Hal and Grieves leave, too.

She put Susan's bag down, and went towards him. 'Excuse me,' she said, pushing past men who were drinking and hadn't seen her, 'Excuse me, I'm so sorry,' and she had entered the more crowded part of the bar, the part the ladies didn't normally go to, but waited on soft chairs to have their drinks brought to them. Davis's eyebrows went up, seeing her coming.

'Can you tell me what's going on?' she asked him, and felt some satisfaction in his embarrassment.

'I don't follow.' He glanced at her.

'What was this urgent meeting with Hal?'

'Oh.' He was uncomfortable. 'Hasn't he said?'

'I haven't seen him all day. You see more of him than I do, I should think. Now he's disappeared off with Tony Grieves.'

'Not disappeared with. Arrested.'

'He's arresting an officer?' She was shocked. 'What could be so bad?'

'Would you like a drink?'

'No. I should like to know what's going on. Hal has sent me home.'

'Sent you?'

'Yes.'

He touched her bare upper arm with his fingers to guide her towards the wall a little. She shivered and he bent down towards her ear. 'I don't know if he's a friend of yours, but he's a –' He stumbled. 'He's disgusting.' The way he said it was so final, so English, the tone of it – *disgusting*. 'And now they'll deal with him.'

For a moment Clara thought of Deirdre and Grieves, on the dirty asphalt, and that, yes, he was disgusting. She had the mad idea they were arresting him for having sex with Deirdre and wanted to giggle.

'What is it?'

'Nothing. What did he do?'

'I'd rather not say to a woman.'

Clara, despite his pomposity, felt a chill of horror. What could have been so bad?

'Are you leaving?' he said.

'Yes, I suppose so.'

'I'll walk you out.'

They left together, and Clara stopped to say goodbye to Deirdre and Susan. Deirdre stood up. 'I saw Hal,' she said. 'He's with Tony.'

'Yes. I know,' said Clara, and left.

On the driveway there was no sign of Hal, or Grieves, either. She looked around for Kirby who, seeing her, turned on the lights and eased the car towards her.

'Is that your man?'

'Corporal Kirby, yes.' She would be alone with her little children in the house.

Davis stood quietly next to her and she said quickly, 'I know that soldiers – you, Hal – face things all the time that are actually dangerous, and you don't seem to be scared.'

'Well,' he looked at her, 'one just has to get on with it.'

'I'm scared here,' she said.

'Well, after Monday –'

'No. All the time.'

Kirby got out and opened the door for her, 'Evening, Mrs T.'

'Hello, Kirby.'

He went back around the car, slowly easing his body through the warm night. Clara turned away from the open door and the black inside of the car. 'It's silly,' she said. 'Hal's the one out in the villages, or driving along those cut-off roads miles from anywhere. Here I am, safe as houses –'

Davis pushed his hands into his pockets and rocked on his feet, hunching up his shoulders. He smiled. 'Funny old expression, safe as houses. Particularly after the war. You'd think it would have died out.'

'Yes.' She laughed. 'Safe as Morrison shelters, perhaps.'

He spoke in an undertone, but Kirby couldn't have heard over the idling motor: 'When my enlistment notice arrived, I went into a blue funk too. Visions of an inglorious death in battle. Turns out I'm not in battle, and if I were – well, as you say, I'm not frightened. Not in the way I thought I would be.'

'There you are. Perhaps men are just braver.'

'I brought a sort of charm with me, used to carry it everywhere.'

'What was it?'

'A rather lesser Ancient Greek deity – the goddess Iris. She's supposed to be good luck.'

'Not so obvious as a St Christopher.'

'No. It was just a bit of Victorian tat I saw in a junk shop in Cambridge, but it did make me feel better at the beginning.'

'Yes. I can imagine it might.'

'I'd never left England until last year.'

'It's not being *away*. It's being here.' There was silence for a moment. She knew she ought to go. 'I don't even have a cross,' she said.

There was a pause, in which Kirby cleared his smoker's throat carefully.

'Well, I should go,' she said.

She got into the car.

'Good night, Lawrence,' she said, not meeting his eye.

'Good night – oh! Thank you for making me talk to your –' he seemed to stumble over the name '– Major Treherne,' he said. 'It was the right thing to do.' He grinned.

Kirby let out the clutch, and the car pulled away from him.

* * *

Hal still wasn't home, and Clara was in her nightdress, drying her face, when there was a knock at the door. She jumped, and went to the top of the stairs. Looking down to the ground floor, she could see that something had been pushed under the door. It looked like a piece of paper, folded. She padded down, hearing a car driving away.

She bent to retrieve the paper, which had a damp, often-folded softness. Unwrapping it, she found a small cameo, such as would have hung on a thin chain. Its edges, of cheap gold, were bent. She took it to the light. The background was blue, and the cameo itself a clumsy relief of a winged goddess, carrying an urn.

Clara touched the little piece of jewellery with her finger. She seemed to sense comfort, as if it were pleasantly haunted. She thought of Lawrence Davis driving out to her house and pushing it under her door. I hope he won't think there's anything between us if I keep it, she thought, and then, How kind of him. She refolded the paper, with the cameo inside, and went upstairs. She would find somewhere discreet to keep it.

Davis drove away from Clara's house. He was glad he hadn't mentioned that the goddess Iris was the messenger of Aphrodite, as well as a good-luck charm. He thought if he had brought the word 'love' into it, she might feel inhibited, and he wanted her to have his present, and to keep it. He turned off the road towards the barracks. He wouldn't go back to the mess. He felt some relief that Major Treherne and the Military Police were the ones directly involved in the wretched business of arresting Grieves, not himself. Soon people would know about it, and connect him with the whole sordid mess; he didn't like to face them. He would rather be alone.

Hal had taken Grieves to the side of the building, out of sight, to make the arrest, delivering him into the custody of the RMPs and, once they had gone, he stood on his own, just resting in the peaceful dark.

Grieves wasn't to be put in the guardroom with the other ranks; he would be at home, with Lieutenant Cross guarding. His disgrace was to be kept separate, with neither the condemnation nor the camaraderie of other men's company.

Grieves had been propping up the bar, as usual, when Hal got to him. 'Hello, Hal,' he'd said, and taken a gulp of his drink.

'Listen, Grieves –'

Then Deirdre Innes had appeared, insinuating herself between them, and looking up at him over the rim of her glass. 'I see your game,' she said, teasingly, 'waiting for Clara to go home so you can have some fun.'

'Would you excuse us for a moment, Deirdre?'

'Well –'

'Can you come with me?' Hal said to Grieves.

'Certainly, sir.'

Deirdre, affronted, watched them go.

'What's all this about, old man?' Grieves asked him, as they went through the people, but Hal ignored him.

Outside it was fresher. The bright hibiscus flowers on the big bushes were crimson glowing under the electric light. They had gone round the side, and Hal, seeing the RMPs and Lieutenant Cross waiting, felt again the repellent wrongness of the whole situation.

Grieves, oblivious, had stopped on the driveway, and pulled out his cigarette case, moving his whole head in a small circle to focus on its contents. 'My bar bill is a bloody disaster,' he said. 'I don't know about you, but –'

'Grieves. The captain is here to arrest you.'

'What?'

He appeared to notice the RMP captain for the first time. The captain, Lieutenant Cross and the other RMP man, a sergeant, all stepped forward. There was embarrassment.

Hal nodded to the captain, who came up close to them and said, 'I'm arresting you on a charge of accessory to murder and to rape.'

Grieves went pale and let his slack fingers rest on the row of cigarettes in the case. 'You must be fucking joking,' he said.

He turned his face to Hal in appeal. Hal thought he looked drunker now than he had a moment before. He would have thought being arrested would sober a fellow up.

'Sir?' said Grieves. He had begun to sweat.

Hal didn't want a scene. 'Just a moment,' he said, to the RMP captain, and the corporal behind him looked disappointed at not being asked to collar Grieves in traditional copper fashion.

He walked away a few paces. Grieves followed him, eagerly. 'Tell them something!' he said.

'Don't be silly.'

'This is absurd. I haven't done anything. Are they talking about that wog the other night?'

'Look, you need to go with them, and try to do it quietly, all right?'

'What the hell are you talking about?' His voice had the shrill, whining note of an aeroplane in a nose dive. 'Look – do you think I don't know things went too far? This whole fucking place is a crime – Hal? Come on, man!'

'Keep quiet! You won't get any favours from me. You're a disgrace.'

Grieves gave a yelp of laughter. In response to Hal's look, the captain moved towards Grieves and grasped his arm.

They had taken him, as simple as that, and left Hal alone in the dark, with the lights from the windows shining out, making wide black bars around him; he could hear the sounds of his friends and fellow officers inside.

Hal took off his cap, dropped his head and rubbed his eyes and forehead. He felt tired. Straightening, he smoothed his hair and put the cap under his arm. He glanced in, through the window, at the noisy crowd, walked round to the front, and across the asphalt to the door.

Inside, the talking, smiling, companionable faces of his friends were brightly lit by the cheap-shaded bulbs overhead and shining with sweat and laughter. Smoke, the smell of hair oil, brandy, the friendly welcome of men, like one man, that he had always known and been part of.

'Hal!'

It was Mark, with one or two others, grinning with the schoolboy grin he got when he'd been drinking, and forgetting his wife hated him, and just remembering his own easy self. 'Hal, come and have a drink –'

Hal went over to him. The waiter, an old pro, in his wrinkled white jacket, who always managed to keep his tray steady and the drinks on it, however thick the crowd, arrived at his elbow. 'Sir?'

'Thanks.' Hal took a drink and the cigarette Mark offered him.

'I had Trask in my office on a charge today,' said Mark, striking a match for him.

'Along with the rest of them,' said Hal.

'Yes, along with the rest of them. But he's a good man, Trask, and I told him, I said to him, "Trask,"' Mark was somewhere between half and three-quarters cut, and bursting with delight at himself, '"Trask, for God's sake man, you're a corporal now, you've an example to set," and some other guff, normal old rubbish, and he said to me,' Mark laughed, 'he gave me a terrible sort of sad look, Hal, and he said to me, "I believe I forgot myself, sir." "Forgot myself". He forgot himself, Hal, like the bloody rest of them.'

Mark was laughing. Hal nodded, wasn't listening. The drink in his hand was untouched, and there was no point in smoking the cigarette, with the smoke as thick as blotting paper in the room. In the morning they'd all know about a lieutenant being under guard and that he'd been the one to do it. He felt a shadow, even with Mark laughing and leaning forward to him as he spoke, as if he were looking back on a place he had left. Davis was the only other man who knew about it now, and Hal, in his loneliness, glanced around for him, but didn't see him there. He felt impatient with himself, and not proud, and shook himself inside, like a dog in from the rain. 'Right, then,' he said, under his breath, squaring up.

He reached for the ashtray, on a stand a couple of feet away, and put out his cigarette, crushing it hard into the heap of stubs and ash, wincing with distaste at the filth getting on his fingers as he did it. He caught the eye of the waiter and deposited his untouched drink on the tray. 'I'm off home, Mark,' he said. Then, feeling fond of him and oddly emotional, he patted him briskly on the shoulder. 'Good man. I'll see you in the morning.'

Hal left the mess and found Kirby waiting for him. He would go home to his wife, and pray to God she was asleep already when he got home, or at least pretending to be.

Chapter Eight

The summary hearings were held immediately, within forty-eight hours of the crimes being reported.

Both Colonel Burroughs's and Hal's offices were too small to hold all the people required, so they were assigned a room at the club that was sometimes used for private dinners. There was a big polished table, various dim photographs on the walls and louvred blinds to keep out the sun. Grieves would be first.

The procedure was as official and court-like as possible, given the circumstances. The room was full of people; Grieves was under guard, and pale. Officers from the army and the RMP, as well as a plainclothes SIB man, were there, and Lieutenant Davis, who came in last.

Much time was spent deciding where everyone ought to stand, with murmured politeness and shuffling of papers.

Hal was on Burroughs's right; he stood rigid and correct. Physically uncomfortable as he was, he felt peace bordering on the blissful.

The heat of all the men, in their stiff uniforms but sweating underneath them, thickened the atmosphere quite quickly and the smell of Greek cigarettes mixed with the air. Tumblers of water, glinting, were arranged next to a jug in the middle of the table and were untouched. There was a thin white cloth over the jug, with beaded edges to stop it slipping, so that no flies could get into the water but flies circled and landed and circled all through the hearing.

The colonel asked the questions, and occasionally spoke in an undertone to his adjutant, who was the only man seated, and held a fountain pen, although he did not write.

Francke was sent for; he came in under guard. He stood opposite Hal and the colonel, flanked by privates.

Hal tried to see something in Francke that perhaps he might have seen before. He pictured him hitting the women's faces, holding their hair to keep their heads still, as Davis had described. He imagined him kicking the Greek man as he lay down, and saw him on top of the women. He remembered, suddenly, that it had been Francke who had ransacked the old couple's village house that day. He remembered the bayoneted bedding, smooth oil on the tiles and the olive-wreath plate in pieces. He had known Francke was dangerous. He ought to have checked him. He ought to have done something.

Colonel Burroughs began to question Francke, with Hal's notes held firmly in front of him, referring to them.

Francke had decided confidence and bluster would get him through. His answers were bold, almost swaggering:

'Reasonable force, I'd say, sir – only reasonable. But we had to stop them, didn't we?'

'No, sir, there was women there, but we never touched 'em.'

'I saw him coming for me and I shot him – he was coming at me, sir.'

And on.

After Francke, it was Private Miller's turn. He, too, apparently, had only the vaguest recollection of any women present and didn't remember Davis being there either. He had seen Francke shoot the man, though, 'And thank God he did, sir, 'cos if he'd got to him he would've killed him, sir.'

Hal was facing the room, with Davis at about a forty-five-degree angle to him. He allowed his eyes to move left until he could see his expression. Davis was agitated; his mouth was working, biting his lip or the inside of himself. Hal wanted to reassure him, to communicate his amusement and dismay, but he kept a neutral expression.

Then it was the turn of one of the RMP sergeants. Yes, he said, there was a body, recovered from the house on Starsis Street, and yes, the bullet had gone through the head, but the range from which it was fired was impossible to tell without a more detailed post-mortem. The body had been sent to Nicosia: the morgue there had chilling facilities, the one in Limassol was just a marble-lined basement.

Burroughs asked about the alleged victims, where they were, and if statements had been taken. The sergeant was regretful: there were rumours in Starsis Street, but all their best efforts had not discovered any women prepared to come forward.

'Neither of the women?'

'No, sir.'

'Nobody who knows them?'

'No, sir.'

Davis gave his evidence. He kept his answers short and simple; Hal was pleased with him. The silence in the room grew heavier as they moved from the account of the street, and who was with him, 'Lieutenant Grieves, sir, Private Francke, Private Miller . . .' to the getting down of the men in the doorway, 'I would say excessive force. Kicking. A torrent of blows –' to the appearance of the women. Once inside the house, though, his story changed.

At the first false note, Hal felt his head jerk up a half-inch, alerted to the difference. He had read the notes over and over. He had heard, exactly, what Davis had seen; two or three times in life and innumerable times in his head ever since. This was different.

'The room I had entered was to the left. There was a curtain over the door. I heard struggling.'

Heard. He heard struggling. Hal shifted his head slightly to look Davis full in the face. His eyes were locked with the colonel's. The question and answer between them drew out, a protracted rally, a slow screwing-down of detail.

'So you were in the other room?'

'Yes, sir.'

'What exactly did you see?'

'I saw an attack.'

'Did you see Private Miller's face?'

'Not exactly. I knew it was him.'

'At what angle were you standing?'

'It's hard to say.'

'Behind the curtain?'

'Yes.'

There was a curtain.

'Were you in this "other room" all the time?'

'Yes, sir.'

'Just . . . watching?'

'No. I was conducting a search for weapons, sir.'

He was conducting a search.

'You say here – you "heard" the rape?'

'Sir?'

'Can you explain to me what a rape sounds like?

The room was getting hotter and a thin trickle of sweat moved slowly down Hal's temple, then his cheek, from the inside of his cap where the leather band pressed on his head. Davis's eyes did not leave the colonel's face. Hal stared at him, willing him to return his look, but even when he was dismissed, turning – with uncharacteristic accuracy, in fact – to leave, he didn't glance at Hal once.

Another RMP sergeant who had attended the scene was summoned.

Colonel Burroughs asked him if he had visited the house, whom he had seen there, and if he had spoken to the women.

'Couldn't persuade them to talk to us, sir.'

It seemed the re was no witness to the alleged rape and murder but Lieutenant Davis, and no physical evidence at all – except the body of the young man, on its way to Nicosia.

And then it was time for lunch.

Burroughs and Hal lunched together at Burroughs's house, by an open window. with a white cloth on the table and their caps on the ledge beside them. Evelyn wasn't at home. The view from the back of the house, from the window, was wide and bright.

Hal was silent, trying to organise his thoughts, trying harder to keep his temper.

'Well. Quite a morning,' said Burroughs, putting his napkin on his lap.

They were brought chilled cucumber soup with bread rolls and there would be roast lamb and boiled potatoes afterwards.

'Yes, it was,' Hal began, 'quite a morning. Look, sir, Davis has –'

'It's a very tricky business. Particularly a rape. Very hard to get anywhere.'

'Yes, sir, but that's not –'

'It's always very hard to get concrete evidence in a case like this.' The colonel was hungry, and making quick sawing movements with his knife on his bread. 'And, you know, Hal, there's a brothel on every other corner in Limassol. For a lot of the men, raping one or two of them is rather like shoplifting. They just don't see it like you or I might.'

'It's not bloody shoplifting.'

'Voice down. Calm down.'

Burroughs's tone was the tone you'd stop a charging dog with, and make it cower.

'Now, look, Hal, I don't know what business you had bringing this to me at all.'

'You saw my notes, sir.'

'Yes – what were you thinking? I can't take this business any further. A lot of hearsay. Davis is obviously completely unreliable. I'm only glad he spends most of his time with the SIB. Not the sort of fellow –'

'No! He was perfectly clear before. Perfectly. He's changed his story.'

'In twenty-four hours? Pretty poor memory. Seems to me you should have made sure what sort of a witness, what sort of a *chap* he is, before stirring up all of this. Well, quite frankly, Hal, it's a mess, and I'm very disappointed indeed. You've dragged everybody through the mud. I don't need to remind you it was your company who behaved like a gang of thugs on Monday night –'

'Following your orders!'

'What did you just say to me?'

Hal was cornered by honesty and sought to free himself. 'Sir,' he frowned, 'the arrest and questioning of what amounts to half the population of the town was a – tall order. It was bound to result in some loss of discipline, I think.'

Silence. Colonel Burroughs smiled coldly. 'A loss of discipline is never "bound" to happen, Hal,' he said quietly, 'and you, as an officer, ought not to accept it so easily.'

Then, very calmly and with precise movements, Burroughs began to eat his soup. Hal was quite still, absorbing the sting. When Burroughs put his spoon down, his voice was friendly again. 'Also, don't forget, there's the shame of the women to be taken into account. It's very shaming for them. Particularly these Orthodox women.'

Hal brought his eyes back to meet the colonel's pale look.

'I need to have at least a reasonable hope of convictions,' said Burroughs. 'The purpose of these hearings is to establish whether or not that's likely. A court-martial, for any of these men, as I'm sure you've gathered, Hal, would be an absurdity. Their overzealous questioning, and the use of violence, can be dealt with at company level. Obviously the death of the man is a quite different matter, and will be approached with all proper seriousness. I'll review Francke's position myself, in light of what will, no doubt, thanks to your rashness, be a very nasty scandal indeed.'

Colonel Burroughs took a sip of water, then looked back at Hal. 'Now, shall we have some wine, or do you think we'll nod off this afternoon? It's terribly hot in there.'

Chapter Nine

Lawrence Davis wasn't surprised when his batman came to tell him Major Treherne wanted him.

The hearings finished for the day at half past four and Davis, after going back to his quarters to change, had walked up on to the cliff-top and then made an uncomfortable slithering descent to the tiny cove next along to the east from the one below Episkopi. Sweat and tears of rage mixed with the dirt on his face. He had undressed on the small beach, and swum in the sea. He swam quite far out, to look back at the coast.

He had floated in dark salty water that was a deep blue. He reminded himself of the vastness of the globe and the breadth of human experience in an attempt to calm his misery. Being one of a billion ants didn't comfort him today, though, not with the memory of the bare-faced lies he had told.

The sun had begun to go quietly down behind the hills as Davis dried himself and dressed. Then, back at his quarter, his batman found him. Major Treherne wanted him immediately, and he was 'in a rare temper, sir'.

Hal was in a rare temper. He met Davis at the outside door to his office – had been waiting there, in the deepening night, for him, barely able to control himself. 'What the fucking hell are you playing at, Davis?'

He turned and strode ahead of him, putting on the lights, with Davis following, reluctantly, until they reached his office. Once inside, he shut the door firmly, and the adjoining one to Mark Innes, too, even though there was no one but themselves in the building.

They faced one another. Davis couldn't hold Hal's look, and dropped his gaze, blinking with anxiety.

'Explanation,' said Hal.

'I don't know what you –'

'No. Explanation.'

Silence.

Davis began, and his voice was weak. 'I was persuaded that the good of the regiment would not be served by the public – what I was told would be the very public trial of Grieves and of all of them. That vilification –'

'You were "persuaded".'

'Yes.'

'And it had nothing to do with your own good? The good of the regiment is uppermost in your mind, is it?'

'I –'

'And your reputation as a liar, as well as a toad, are you persuaded *that* will do you any good with your fellows and subordinates?'

'Well, I – well, no, but I'd pretty much burned my bridges in that department anyway. I'm pretty unpopular –'

'And you thought you'd burn mine too?'

'Sir?'

'Never mind. *Persuaded*. By whom?'

'My superiors.'

'Special Branch? Major Eggars?'

'Yes, sir. All of them. They seemed all to be in on it. They said just on my say-so the case would never get anywhere.'

Silence.

'The witnesses, Davis, the victims,' said Hal, very slowly, 'did anybody go and talk to them?'

Davis seemed to shrink away. 'We . . .'

'Speak up!'

'Yes. Last night.'

'You went to the house on Starsis Street last night? You sought out those women, and "persuaded" them, too? And then just went ahead with the whole thing today –'

Suddenly Davis broke, appealing to him. 'I had to! I was following orders! They made it clear I had to! We didn't threaten them. Nothing like that! What good would it do? Making those poor women talk about it –' He stopped abruptly.

Hal walked over to his desk. He stood with his back to Davis for a long moment, then turned to face him. 'Lieutenant Davis, it could not be said of you that you are a man of *conviction*, could it? It could not be said of you that you are *morally courageous*. You are, in fact, a cynical, self-serving coward. Would you say that was true?'

Davis's face began to break up. A sixth former, disgraced. 'Sir –'

'You have sacrificed what you know to be right to save your own skin, haven't you, Davis, with no thought but for yourself?'

'I was following orders, sir.'

'You were following orders?'

'Yes, sir.'

'Not good enough. All right. Dismissed. Go.'

When Davis had gone, Hal, alone, paced his office back and forth, sifting, shifting and reshifting things in his mind, finding order, making patterns, moving and re-moving. Then he stopped, picked up his cap and left.

'Kirby, the colonel's house.'

'Sir.'

He let Kirby go at the end of the road, walked fast up to the house on his own, and rapped hard on the door.

The African servant answered, just as before, but this time the colonel was visible, coming down from upstairs. He dismissed the man and stood in the doorway himself. He hadn't been expecting visitors; he was in a pale blue short-sleeved shirt and shorts. He looked older. His hand rested on the door. 'What is it, Hal?'

'I need to speak to you, sir.'

'Can't it wait?'

'No,' angrily. Then, 'Just for a moment.'

'All right.'

They were out on the terrace again, but there were no drinks offered this time. Hal walked away from Burroughs, in the open doorway, stopped and turned back to him. 'I want you to tell me how much you know about this,' he said.

'I beg your pardon?'

Hal modified his tone. 'Are you aware, sir, of the situation?'

'Situation?' Burroughs asked drily.

'This Starsis Street business, the victims have been – intimidated.'

'Intimidated?'

'Told not to come forward. The Special Branch have been over there, sir, and the RMPs too. Did you know that?'

'Hal, I think you should go home. You ought to calm down.'

Hal spoke quickly, the words falling out of him: 'I can't believe you don't know about it. This must have come from you.' There was a reckless release in being able to say what he wanted. 'This whole mess, this cover-up came from you. There's no other way of putting it.'

'This is highly inappropriate.' Burroughs walked towards him. 'I don't like your tone. Am I to take from these questions that you are accusing me of something?'

'I just want to know!' He knew he was shouting. He walked away, in a small circle. Then, close to the colonel, he said in a low voice, 'This wasn't some *infraction of the rules* to be overlooked and indulged –'

'*Do you think I don't know that?*' The colonel kept his voice almost to a whisper and his face had turned a deep red, his pale eyes shining out of it and fixed on Hal's face. 'Do you think I'm unaware? I'm disgusted with it, Hal, but what am I to do? Am I to drag us all through the mud?'

'Just them! Grieves. Miller. Francke. Just them!'

'There is no "just them"!'

'Rape and murder – hear me? Rape and murder!'

'Yes, and murder is a hanging offence. Even murdering a wog.'

'Then Francke should hang.'

'He should hang, should he? And have the world know about it? You'd throw us all to the dogs for your principles?'

'Not *my* principles . . .' Hal searched for the truths he'd never challenged '. . . not just me, the *civilised world*. You aren't above that.' Hal went at him in his anger. 'You have no fucking right!' and the older man, retreating, put his foot out to steady himself, lost his balance and stumbled, one foot slipping off the edge of the terrace onto the uneven grass.

Hal, appalled, grabbed his arm to steady him, but Burroughs pulled from his grip in outrage. His normally dry, narrow lips were wet with spit. '*I won't have this!*'

Hal was standing crooked – half turned to help Burroughs, half backing off – his hands trembling with shock at himself, the sight of his superior, pulling away from him, the strange jumble of words and actions that had left them like this, in disarray. He put both hands up to wipe his face, then down to his sides and stood like that, in the cataclysm of his insubordination, eyes down, for a long moment. When he raised them, he said, as he must, 'I have to apologise, sir.'

'Yes.'

'I spoke out of turn, sir. I'm sorry.'

Burroughs allowed the silence to settle over them. Hal's eyes were wet, oddly hot. He thought of Davis, breaking up the way he had, his cowardly, trembling fear, and understood it.

At last, Burroughs spoke. 'We'll say no more about it,' he said. 'I hope you know you can speak freely to me, Hal. Within the proper boundaries.'

'Yes, sir. Thank you, sir.'

'Regarding this matter, and in answer to your question,' continued Burroughs, 'I did indeed ask others to speak to Lieutenant Davis. If I need to, I will speak to him myself. I should accept some blame, too, that I allowed matters to get this far. Military law is as rigorous as civilian law, Hal. It requires more evidence than the accusations of one man to put others on trial.'

'I see, sir. Yes.'

'Lieutenant Grieves ought to leave Episkopi. There are a

number of places he could go and be useful. It's a pity we can't dispense with Davis, but I'm afraid he's not easily replaced. I think we ought to separate the others, don't you?'

'Yes, sir.'

'You can see to it.'

'Yes, sir. I will.'

The colonel walked him through the house to the door, and opened it wide. 'As long as lessons are learned, there's no need for the public beating of breasts.'

Hal, facing the night, said nothing.

'Hal? We can comfort ourselves,' said the colonel. 'God sees.'

Hal looked at him. 'God?'

'Yes, He sees, He punishes.'

Hal walked away, along the unfinished roads towards home, determinedly.

The colonel's house was at the end of a new street, facing, and the semi-detached terrace on one side was incomplete. Hal walked past a hundred feet of white-painted wall and plaster, with doorways but no doors, empty squares of windows, and then a long black gap and sea breeze, before the buildings at the corner turned into another crescent.

Episkopi was scattered across the uneven land: barracks, polo fields, tents, stables, empty and half-built houses, and ones with people in them, going about their little tasks, all circled with barbed wire. Above him, like the glass dome of a child's snowstorm, was the glittering sky.

Hal walked blind, aware of that high view: himself, making the short journey from his commanding officer's quarter to his own.

What was right, and what was proper had always been inseparable, but in this perhaps one, like a Siamese twin, must be severed and destroyed for the other's survival. If it had to be done, then he must do it.

Calming himself, controlling his thoughts, he did not understand why, instead of the cool comfort of discipline, he was suffused with heat, a weakness like drowning, the blank surprise of a poor surrender.

Clara was putting the girls to bed.

'I'm back,' he said, to nobody.

'Come up,' she called down. 'We're having a story – a bit late!'

Hal went up and kissed the girls, who were clean, their fine hair smelled of soap. His heavy pistol, inside its holster, rested on the edge of their beds as he leaned down to them. He stood in the doorway and waited for her.

He realised he hadn't taken off his cap, or his belt, and did so, as Clara held the girls' small hands together, smiling, and said for them, 'The day is done; O God the Son, look down upon thy little one. Amen.'

Adile was tidying, finishing up before going home. Hal and Clara stood by the kitchen counter and Adile collected her bag, a string bag, that had some things wrapped in newspaper.

'*Hoşça kalın efendim*,' she said, quietly.

Clara, for some reason, didn't speak to her.

'Thank you, Adile, goodbye,' said Hal, and Adile left. He looked at Clara. 'Why don't you talk to her?'

'I don't know.'

He put his gun, Sam Browne and cap in their usual place, out of the children's reach, by the door. 'Do you never talk to her?'

She didn't answer him. He went to the fridge and opened the heavy door. He took out the glass jug of boiled water and poured himself some, and some for Clara, but she didn't move to pick it up. He went into the sitting room and sat on the sofa, putting the wet glass on the table in front of him.

He leaned back and shut his eyes. He had his hands on his knees, with his legs open and his head back against the wall.

When his eyes were shut there was a pleasant darkness. Perhaps it was almost as good as sleeping, to rest like this. Perhaps he should forget about nights altogether and, instead, take short naps during the days. The dark was nice. His hands were too still, though. They felt much too still. He couldn't be sure they were there. He opened his eyes.

Without moving his head he watched Clara. She was walking around the room very slowly. She had taken her shoes off. She started at the front door. She bent down slightly, to check the rubbish bin – for what, he couldn't tell – then moved on to the large potted plant at the foot of the stairs. She looked all around the rim, and in the clay tray that the pot stood in. She wasn't aware he was watching her from his half-closed eyes.

She went to the cupboard under the stairs, which was white-painted, like the stairs themselves, and had a small catch on it. She opened it, with a little metal clicking sound, and the door showed darkness inside. She opened it further and peered in carefully. Then she shut the cupboard and fastened it, and moved on. She checked under the small wooden table that stood against the wall. She examined the mirror. Hal wanted to say something but he didn't dare move. He kept his head still, and tipped back, watching her step lightly on her bare feet.

Soon she was opposite him. When she glanced over her shoulder at him, he closed his eyes. When he opened them again she was looking underneath the desk, and then behind the vase –

'What are you doing?' he said – and she jumped.

'Nothing.'

'Well, you're obviously doing something.'

His voice was hard; he didn't recognise it but felt removed. She stood in front of him with her hands behind her back, nervously.

'What were you looking for?'

'Nothing.'

'Have you lost something?'

'No. I –'

'You?'

'It's silly,' she said. 'I was looking for bombs.'

Hal said slowly, 'You were looking for bombs?'

'Yes. After they found that one in the NAAFI at Larnaka – and the beach.'

'You weren't on the beach.'

'No. You were.'

'Yes. I was.'

'I saw a picture in the paper of –'

'We've all seen those pictures, Clara.'

'They can make them out of anything. Olive-oil tins.'

'Yes. I know.'

'I feel better when I check.'

'Why don't you stop?' he said. 'There's nothing here. Adile has been here. Think of all the security. We're safe.'

'Just let me finish.' She went back to the desk and carefully opened the drawers.

Hal stayed still. If there actually were a bomb in the drawer, he thought, she'd trip the switch and blow her hands off to the elbow, at least.

He shut his eyes once more, but the sound of her checking and touching and fiddling with things was intolerable. She was nearby. He could sense her movement. He half opened one eye. She was kneeling, checking under the small table by the sofa.

With no warning that he was going to do it, no moment's check on himself to stop, he jumped towards her, big hands grabbing her viciously by the arms. 'Just stop it! Just fucking stop it!' He shook her, gripping her soft flesh, both of them on their knees. 'There's nothing there!'

He let go of her suddenly – realising. He tried to take her hands, but she pulled away. She was cringing in fear of him.

'God, Clara,' he said, as if all the world had stopped at what he'd said to her, at what he had done.

He found he was kneeling by the sofa with his head down on his arms. 'Clara,' he said again. 'I'm so sorry. I'm sorry. I'm so sorry. I'm sorry . . .' He shut his eyes, as tightly as he could. He stayed hunched away from her, hiding, until at last he felt her hands on his shoulders. Her fingers on the back of his neck.

'No, don't,' she said.

Her fingers stroked him, small strokes, where his hair met his bare skin, in absolution.

There was silence.

'It's all right,' she said.

'No. It isn't.'

'There. Silly, you haven't even taken off your jacket. There . . .'

A little later, it was supper time. They ate together in loving complicity, but Clara's arms hurt still where Hal's fingers had gripped the muscle. She felt the gentle ache, knowing she must absorb this, too, and forgive it. 'Hal,' she said softly, 'what's happened?'

'What do you mean?' He looked at her in surprise.

She was patient. She took a small mouthful, chewed it. 'Will you have to go to Nicosia for the court-martial?'

Hal's voice was quiet and even. 'There wasn't enough evidence.'

Clara was startled. She put down her knife and fork. 'What do you mean?'

'We're not going to take it any further,' he said.

'But that's not fair!'

'We have to think of the greater good.'

'The greater good?'

Hal, implacable, continued to eat his supper.

'But, Hal, Lawrence Davis –'

'Don't get worked up about it, Clara, there's no need.'

All control, he put an end to it effortlessly.

'All right,' she said.

'Eat up.'

She looked down at the table.

'Clara?' He spoke gently. 'I'm sorry about earlier. I don't know what came over me. I don't know what could have happened.'

'It's quite all right.'

* * *

When Hal went outside with his brandy, for his after-dinner smoke, Clara stayed sitting at the table.

She thought of Davis placing his trust in Hal, as she had done. He'd had so much feeling. *Disgusting*, he'd said, and that they would be punished. She was sure he would have fought for the principle of the thing. She remembered his silly youthful face thrust towards her, questioning. 'What's he like, your husband?' and she, in confidence, had answered, 'Try him.'

The cameo, the little Iris, was tucked into the pages of her diary. She pictured it there, making a friendly dent in the paper, close to the spine.

She hadn't wanted to share Hal's cigarette, or sip his brandy, and she checked her arms, where the redness was fading. He had hurt her, there would be blue bruises later, but that wasn't why she had stayed inside. It wasn't because of the way he could overlook the vicious crimes of his own men, as if they were insignificant; she could bear that, she could try to forgive him. She hadn't wanted to go outside with him because the smell of the smoke turned her stomach, and she didn't want to drink, even a little. Clara counted back in her mind to another night for which she must forgive Hal, and knew beyond doubt that she was pregnant. She had known for days. She had lied to herself.

Chapter Ten

Privates Francke and Miller were transferred and attached to separate units; they didn't see each other again. All three men went through the rest of their lives with no moment at which they were discovered or punished. Their consciences troubled them variously, and without consequence.

Hal was experiencing unpopularity amongst his men for the first time. Many of them had their pay docked because of the night in Limassol, or spent time in the guardroom, and Hal's responsibility for the banishment of Francke and Miller had made him their enemy, too. He didn't need love, just respect. He had them out on night patrols, down at the ranges or practising drill for hours in the daytime and discipline improved, if his popularity didn't. He counted it as a victory in a battle that had become smaller and smaller, with so little room for victory in it.

If Hal was unpopular, Davis was loathed. He had never found a comfortable place at Episkopi because of his connection with the SIB; it separated him, and now, with a reputation as a toad who would report his fellows – and then, worse, not stand by his own story – he was shunned. Davis felt their dislike keenly, and the hatred of the men, too, because he had betrayed them. Davis believed he sensed violence amongst them, directed at him. Unfamiliar with their class, he was fearful of it and, to avoid being left alone, forced into the reluctant company of the other junior officers.

Grieves had been attached to the REME, as part of a security detail, high in the Troodos. It would be the last posting of his National Service, which was due to finish in the autumn. He was in a tented camp, very uncomfortable and isolated; he wanted to write to Deirdre, a litany of lonely obscenity, but couldn't have done it without discovery by her husband, so there was no more communication between them.

Deirdre was left with a resentment she longed to express. She found Mark intolerable. Sleeping with Tony Grieves had eased the tension between them, in some ways; now she was focused utterly on him, but not to the good. He wanted a brother or sister for Roger. Deirdre obliged in the effort, grudgingly. Hal heard them through the walls during his long and sleepless nights, rowing and occasionally having sex, and remembered himself and Clara, as quiet as they could be, whispering into each other's hands and ears and necks.

Hal didn't know if Mark had any idea about Deirdre and Grieves, still, but he hadn't seemed to think any the worse of Hal for arresting him – unlike some of the others – and had even remarked, 'Have to root out the rotten apples, Hal. Just don't expect to change the world and win a popularity prize while you're about it,' which Hal had accepted with good grace, as fair enough.

There were ceasefire talks going on, and relative quiet from EOKA, who were taking the opportunity to re-arm. The British were trying to negotiate with the exiled Archbishop Makarios, and – though it stuck in their throats to do it – to treat him as a man of God and a politician, instead of the duplicitous terrorist they held him to be when a ceasefire was not being discussed.

With tensions between the British and the Greeks eased, the violence between the Greek and Turkish Cypriots expanded, as if to fill a vacuum. The soldiers at Episkopi and all over the island were occupied with quelling disputes between the two populations, separating them from one another with barbed wire, patrolling the streets they shared to keep the peace.

Cyprus shifted through an uneasy summer; Britain kept her slender grasp on empire and the Cypriots and soldiers continued to play out the long game of complicity and enmity, welcome and rebellion, the bloodshed entrenching each position as firmly as the friendship did.

Mark and Hal, accompanying a patrol through a Greek village one Sunday, found themselves the guests of honour at a wedding; honey and figs and rough, cork-stopped bottles of wine were heaped into their car while they were pressed, each in turn, to dance with the bride. The village was decked with flowers and ribbons. It seemed to balance over the vast, glittering view like an exquisite mirage. The next day two British soldiers were badly injured in an ambush two miles from the same village.

Then, towards the end of July, all of Cyprus's problems were dwarfed by President Nasser's nationalising of the Suez Canal. He did it dramatically, during a triumphant speech, heard on wirelesses all over the world, and the British, French and Americans were thrown into disarray and conflict, not only with Egypt but with one another. To the British, a gauntlet had been thrown down. At Episkopi and everywhere else the talk was almost exclusively of that. The usual polarity of extraordinary and ordinary, which characterised life in Cyprus, was made more extreme again. Troops flooded the island from Egypt and elsewhere, thrown off Egyptian soil, billeted in tented camps, under pressure to finish new airfields and repair old ones, moving vehicles and weapons in haste, while colonial life went on uninterrupted, staunch and defiant in the face of the coming crisis. The army wives still ran their poetry clubs and drama societies; bands were still booked into the Limassol Club. The women with families, or young children, like Clara, found they were left out of fun that was more stubbornly frivolous than it had been before, a society thumbing its nose at danger.

Clara knew she must tell Hal she was pregnant. She dreaded it. She scarcely owned it to herself. She decided she might as well just come right out and say it.

Hal was in the small garden with the girls. They were filling the paddling pool from the tap in the kitchen; Hal had a watering can and the girls their tiny beach buckets of painted tin. The three of them marched back and forth, the girls spilling most of the water on the tiles and the grass, and the paddling pool seemed to fill very slowly. Clara was cutting tomatoes in the kitchen, stepping aside for the girls, 'Mummy!' and Hal, 'Excuse me.'

The girls were in rompers, Hal had on a shirt, undone at the neck. He looked up from the spangled lapping water into the house and she said, 'Come in for a moment, Hal.'

'What is it?'

'Please?'

'Carry on, girls,' he said, and came inside.

She wiped her forehead with the back of her wrist. Her hands were wet on the knife. 'Hal,' she said. She would just say it. Once it was said, he would know. She sawed at the thick tomato skin with the knife.

'Careful.' He took the knife from her.

She turned and dried her hands. The water outside threw bright flashes into her eyes.

'Clara?'

'I'm pregnant.'

'Really?'

'Yes.'

'That's wonderful,' he said.

'Do you really think so?' She looked into his clear eyes and he looked into hers.

'Of course! When will it come?'

'I don't know yet. Perhaps in January. I need to go to the doctor.'

'Are you feeling all right?'

'Yes – fine.'

It was as if they had studied their words earlier and knew them quite well.

Hal put his hand on her arm and said, 'Well, that's marvellous news.'

Hal spent the next day rounding up possible terror suspects in one of the hilltop villages. He stood with his back to the church. The pen was set up in the bright glare of a shadeless corner. There were fifteen men inside it, guarded by soldiers. Hal was with Kirby near a very small café. You wouldn't have known it was a café, except for the row of old men who normally sat outside it on metal chairs. They weren't there now.

The village was tiny and the café, square and church were

tiny too, with narrow streets and the smell of donkey shit ground into the uneven stones.

The three-tonner with the informer in it hadn't been able to get into the square, being too wide, so it was virtually wedged into a side street about a hundred and fifty yards away, thick canvas hanging down over the back, with a frayed hole cut out of it for the informer to see out.

The men were to be paraded past, and the soldiers were ordering them into a line.

The glare came up off the streets, the whitish stone and plaster of the buildings, with their tattered wooden balconies and broken tiles on the sagging roofs.

Hal squinted into the bright light. His mouth tasted bitter. He watched the men being paraded slowly past the unseen informer. All of them were frightened, an assortment of ages and types made one by their captivity.

Davis was in the truck with the informer and the SIB. He and Hal hadn't spoken to one another, beyond what was necessary, since the summary hearing.

The church behind Hal was shaped like a small fat cross, with domes on each section. Beside him, Kirby lit a cigarette and the sharp smell of burned sulphur reached him. The sour smell started quick images in his mind – glaring sand, thick blood. He shook his head slightly, made irritable and bored by the intrusion, but his heart, ungovernable, beat huge and violently in his chest. Clara's weak body, pregnant, the pieces of bloodied men . . . 'They all know the routine,' he said to Kirby. 'If there was anyone worth looking at here, they'd have made a bolt for it when they saw us coming.'

'Always the way, sir,' said Kirby, comfortably.

Hal was very aware of the church at his back. He felt the

tilt of the hill sloping down under his feet on the uneven cobbles. The angle of his vision slanted towards the line of men shuffling past the truck, like a magic lantern of false perspective, in the hot day.

There was a disturbance in the line – some scuffling. One of the soldiers shoved an old man in the kidneys with the butt of his rifle. He collapsed with weak knees onto the ground, putting out a bony hand to steady himself.

Hal saw him fall, saw the brief pleasure of the nineteen-year-old private who had pushed him, and said nothing.

He turned, sensing something, but there was nobody there, just the church. A moment later he looked again, forgetting he had checked already, feeling a presence and uncomfortable.

He turned back to the church and found he had started to walk towards it. He glanced back once, then pushed the door open and went in. The building was oddly bigger inside than it had appeared. There was dimness and cool air, some thin candles dug into sand burning near to him. He felt their warmth. His eyes moved from dome to shadowed arching dome in the peaceful height of the church.

Churches in England had worn grey stone, dampness, dryness, dripping English trees outside, and he had looked at those leaded panes and stone arches a million times. He had always liked church, for its order and recitation, for the singing and the peaceful gap between one part of the day and the next. He felt at home there, in the boredom of school chapel and the joy of his wedding; it was home as England was home. This place was nothing like the churches he knew and yet it was familiar to him – uncomfortably so: the familiarity seemed to find him out, unpeel the layers of him, a feeling that was too sharp for comfort.

He walked down the aisle, between the pews, towards the altar, which, set deeply in another arch, he could hardly see.

Hal had spent more hours than he could count in the chapel at Sandhurst. Attendance was obligatory, enforcing the long contemplation of altar, ceiling, the white stone engraved with the rolls of honour, other men's heads, and, above their heads, the officers' collect, in stone too. 'Almighty God, whose son Jesus Christ, the Lord of all life, came not to be served but to serve.'

Approaching this altar, he had an idea he might pray.

There was no light except that coming through the windows above and the limited glow of the candles. The paint on the wooden altarpieces behind the gold candelabra was dark with age and poverty. There were two wooden panels, and the third missing – broken or stolen. The central picture, directly facing, was a Madonna and Child, with short perspective so that it looked as if the baby was held against her, with no legs or lap to support it. Both faces stared outwards, crudely. Hal saw that beside it – more strange because it lacked an opposite – was a painting of Christ, as a man, walking towards him, with a diagonal pattern of crosses on white over a robe Hal could not make out. Behind Him, in gold, were ranks of angels.

The rest of the small church was bare. There were no other panels, no curtains or carvings, just the stone, and this.

The face of Christ was Byzantine, a blank oval, arched lines for brow and nose, stiff white hand lifted in blessing as He marched outwards, leading the angels in their lines behind.

Hal stared at the painted face, and was filled with fear, a rush of sorrow he didn't understand. He turned quickly and went back down the church, feet loud in the silence. Pulling the flaking, heavy door towards him, he got out onto the cobbles, half stumbling as one foot tipped into a shallow channel.

The brightness blinded him. He felt very shaken; his hands were trembling.

Kirby was exactly where he had left him and didn't look round when Hal returned. It was as if going into the church had taken no time at all, or he had imagined it. He wanted to ask – had to stop himself asking – if he had gone inside the church, or been with Kirby all the time, seeing the line of frightened men pass the cut-out hole to be identified, and other men, uniformed, watching them.

Chapter Eleven

Davis, confounded by his treacherous weakness in bringing Grieves and the others to trial, was seeking an easier route to absolution: he thought about Clara. He tried not to, but she had the irresistible pull of the forbidden. Her being married was ecstatic danger enough. He knew it couldn't be an erotic obsession, she was a married woman, and a mother: it must be love.

A young boy, a boy of only about fifteen, had been brought into the guardroom, and SIB were deciding whether or not they would send him to Camp K. Davis did not allow himself to imagine what might happen to the boy, or what his own part in it would be. For the past few weeks the interrogations had been perfunctory, and he was thankful for that.

The boy was put into a cell and, although so far untouched, his presence was a constant irritant to Davis, a piece of sharp grit in his eye that would not come out, painful and affecting his vision. He would walk past the cell with the boy in it, his face slightly turned away. He dreaded the summons to question him and hoped it would not come.

It did come, though, on an overcast day when the flies hung lazily in the air with no breeze to push them away. Davis was smoking, fifty yards up the hill from the guardroom, when a private was sent to fetch him. It was late morning.

'We're going to have a go at Alexis Dranias this morning,' was all that was said.

Nothing had been done to the boy yet; perhaps nothing would be.

'What is your name?'

'Your uncle is Thanos Artino. Tell us about him.'

'What connection do you have to EOKA?'

'You are named in this letter signed by Dighenis himself. And this one. Why?'

Davis was surprised that his capacity for dread and disgust had not diminished. The boy was kept awake, standing, for hours at time, and with each interrogation, seeing his deterioration, Davis jumped through the same hoops in the circus of his mental process. Steeped in shame, he condemned himself, but always, in the back of his mind the thought: *This is still within the realms of acceptable. If something really bad were to happen, I'd do something.* He knew he had failed before, that Clara's husband had been right to call him a moral coward, but he couldn't easily give up the idea of himself as honourable. He clung to the notion that he had a limit, that his threshold lay somewhere, uncrossed, and ready to save him, if only he were given the opportunity. So far, he hadn't been asked to leave the interrogation and the boy was unmarked, but he felt disgust in the pit of his stomach, hot and rising, as he continued to translate:

'We know you are associated with these men. We have information about you. Answer the question.'

And the boy, unscathed and confident, looked back at him silently.

They questioned him for a long time, perhaps three hours. Then he was hooded and left, but not alone – not to rest – with his arms above his head, hands on the wall of his cell. Davis went into his small office, the SIB officers back into theirs. Cups of tea were made for them, and Davis's thoughts, battered to breaking, slipped away to settle on Clara.

Clara Treherne. In his innocence of women, he blushed at the thought of her. He tipped back his chair and closed his eyes and thought of her and thought of her, her image a balm to the cuts in his conscience, until he was calm and comforted, cushioned by familiar desire and rejection. Had he been a student of psychology, rather than classics, he might have examined why he was romantically fixated on the wife of a man whose authority and principle he admired and resented in equal measure.

On the last day of Hal's unit's two weeks on ops there were riots at the school in Limassol. Hal's vehicle had been well back in the wide street and he saw the schoolchildren – most were girls – running towards the soldiers in their white ankle socks. They threw rocks and bottles, while the British soldiers, behind plastic shields, tried to protect themselves. None of them wanted to be fighting little girls. They took injuries they shouldn't have – gashed heads, burns from improvised petrol bombs – just to avoid clashing with them. It was an ugly sight: the embarrassment and polite professionalism of his men, forced into slowly mounting retaliation by the angry, taunting children. Girls and young boys had been manhandled, reluctantly, and the Greeks were quick to cry, 'Not fair,' at the brutality of the British. The same day, a roadside bomb had killed one of Hal's men, Private Hopkins – the driver of a lorry – and injured three of his passengers.

Hal still had his regular meetings with Burroughs.

'Men all right?'

'Yes, sir.'

'We'll be getting even more crowded around here soon. Third Battalion the G— G— will be here by next week.'

'I see.'

'None of your boys hell-bent on revenge for Hopkins's death?'

'No, sir, not that I'm aware.'

'Spirits up, then?'

'Not too bad, sir.'

'Jolly good.'

Burroughs no longer asked after his father. Hal no longer confided in him any detail of his life – professional or otherwise.

Now it was paperwork, reports, and waiting to be back out there again.

Hal sat at his desk. The building was quiet around him. The door to Mark Innes's empty office stood open. He was at Evdimou beach, probably, with the others. The air was still. It was in the quiet afternoon hours when nobody else was there.

Hal, who had always felt clumsy indoors with pen and paper, forcing the tedious sentences to form, had stopped leaving his office in the late afternoons, stayed at his desk for the solitude, so he did not have to speak to Mark or anyone. Between desk work and schoolgirl riots he'd take the riots, and either one was preferable to going home to Clara's quietly examining face, the impossibility of relaxation and the intolerable sweetness of his daughters.

He was writing to Private Hopkins's family. 'Dear Mrs Hopkins, As your son's commanding officer, the sad duty . . .' The pen was slippery with sweat in his hand. It was important to get it right. Hal wrote slowly, making notes beforehand. He must imagine the man alive, the way he had been in life, what he could remember of him. He must imagine the effect the letter would have and also carefully not imagine it, not indulge himself: it wasn't his grief. He was lucky, it was only the fourth letter of this kind he'd had to write. The last had been to Private Jenson's mother. *Always popular with the other men. Was doing what he loved best.* In other wars, in real wars, the letters went out thicker and faster than they had in the few short months of his service in Cyprus. Other officers would do it properly, not like him; they wouldn't make such a meal of it, examining every little thing, going back and forth over it the way he did. They would have something better than 'he was driving a truck along the wrong road' to say about it. At least a battle – at least they would have the name of a battle to have died in, not just a row of Greek letters most of them didn't even understand, at least a country to fight against, or defend, not this small, dirty struggle. He took out his handkerchief and wiped his wet hands.

The heat was extraordinary. Even with the window open only hot air came in. It felt as if there was a furnace at his back, pushing the burning draught onto him, his shirt was wet with sweat and his neck was, too, his forearms. The high small sun had glazed the earth like a kiln and every metal, glass, wooden, flesh thing on the garrison was heated and heated so the very paper under his hand was damp and warm; the normally cool things – ink bottle, belt buckle, water glass – were slick with heat. The ink was drying brittle. His eyes were hot with blood that was heated in his moving veins. He would not go home. He would work.

Behind the wooden door to Mark's office the telephone rang. Mark wasn't there. Nobody else was there. It continued to ring.

It stopped.

It began again. The jangling rattle persisted. Hal stood up and went into the room, where papers were neatly stacked and the blinds drawn. 'Hello?'

'Captain Innes?'

'No. This is Major Treherne. Who's speaking?'

'Sergeant Wells, sir, down at the guardroom.' The sergeant was looking for an officer to come down. 'Private Nugent, sir, he's had some sort of fit. Can't locate the battalion MO –'

Private Nugent was one of Hal's. Hal had given him thirty days for drunkenness.

'He seems all right now, sir, only it's not my place to say.'

He shouldn't have picked up the telephone; it wasn't the sort of thing he'd normally bother with. 'Come on, Sergeant Wells, there's nobody else?'

'Sorry, sir, there's no officers here. All otherwise engaged.'

'Otherwise engaged' meant at home with their wives or at Evdimou beach; it was four o'clock in the afternoon.

'All right,' said Hal. 'On my way.'

He had let Kirby go, so he took one of the cars reserved for officers and drove himself to the guardroom. The vehicle had been left in full sun and the wheel was too hot to touch, he had to nudge it with the heel of his hand to steer, the old car dropping hard into the pot-holes as it growled down the hill.

He returned the salutes of the privates who were on duty as he went up the hollow rough wood steps to the entrance.

He'd never been in the guardroom before, which was funny, given all the men he'd sent down there. There was a desk, quite high, and behind it a sergeant, who saluted him sloppily.

'Major Treherne,' he said to the sergeant, a stranger to him, 'concerning Private Nugent.'

The entrance was crowded and messy, with rows of keys on hooks and stacks of box files with marbled paper spines peeling off them on thick wood shelves along two walls. There wasn't much light.

'Ah, yes, sir, thank you, sir. Just a moment.'

The sergeant went off through a door that had a dusty toughened-glass panel in it. Hal looked at the shelves and shelves of misdeeds. The files were stuffed and spilling with paper. The sergeant came back. 'Through here, sir,' he said, lifting the counter to come out and opening a door for Hal.

The corridor was clean-looking but stank of sweat and sourness that might have been piss or old wood, wet rags, creosote. Despite the heat that had followed him in and moved in the air, Hal felt a chill go over his skin – perhaps it was from the darkness: the windows were barred and covered with fine mesh in places too.

'Can you wait in here, please, sir?' said the sergeant, and opened the door into an office – at least, it was being used as an office: it had a desk piled high with papers and files, but had been a cell at some point; it was the right size for it, and the door was heavy with bolts on the outside.

He was left alone again. He could hear muffled sounds. He could hear boots, hobnails on the floors, and voices, a number of different voices, muted and broken. The walls were wood and plasterboard, the sound came through to him in different places, very quiet, in the honeycomb around him. And then a shout.

The shout was English, he thought, but the scream after it was unidentifiable. After the scream there was a return to just the sense of being in the middle of a building full of unseen men, some making noise, others moving about. And then there came a groaning, retching sound. Hal hadn't heard a sound like it before.

He went back to the doorway, next to the bolted heavy door of the tiny room, and looked both ways down the corridor. He could see no one. He could just hear the murmur of conversation, then metal cups or plates, or something clanging at least, a long way off.

He waited.

It came again, a gurgling, choking sound, then high laughter immediately after and a heavy thud. It was coming from his right, round a corner.

The sergeant hadn't come back.

Hal went to the doorway and stood, waiting. He couldn't see him anywhere, or anybody else. He heard shouting, muffled by several doors, but still very angry, out of control; insane rage.

Hal started down the narrow wooden corridor – a bleach smell overlying the sourness – and went through the door at the end. The shouting was louder now. He turned a right angle after twenty feet and saw another, similar corridor, with doors on both sides. The shouting stopped suddenly. Silence.

He waited. More sounds, confusing, then the gurgling retching he had heard in the small cell, louder now, then shouts, decipherable: 'Come on!'

Hal was a voyeur, with the voyeur's reluctant thrill of curiosity; he wasn't accustomed to feeling like a trespasser anywhere. The cell doors were closed, except one, halfway down. He went quietly, not noticing his own stealth but aware of the edge of the doorframe coming towards him and the need to see what was on the other side of it.

Because of the angle of his approach, and the smallness of the lobby, he was very close to the two men when he reached the door. In the room to the right of the lobby, stood a private and a prisoner.

The prisoner, with his back to him, was hooded with an empty sandbag and in the stress position, hands up high against the wall. His bony back was dark-tanned and bare, his baggy trousers stained, both legs shaking. Hal noticed that the floor – wooden boards that were sealed tight in places and gappy in others – was wet. There was puddling under his boots and seeping around them.

Standing a few feet away from him, was Davis. Then the shouting started again, unseen – very loud and angry – a stream of obscene, disjointed abuse.

Davis looked at Hal. He seemed to gaze at him with love and wonder, as if he were a small boy who had lost himself somewhere in the dark and, in confusion, looked up to see his father. Then the blood rushed into his face, as shame dawned on him.

The private, assuming from Hal's rank that his presence was authorised, saluted. Hal, ignoring him, turned so that he was in the tiny lobby and could see into the cell to his left. He had the sense that Davis was coming towards him, at his back.

The cell was crowded with people, it seemed. It took less than a second to take in everything.

A boy, a young boy, was lying on the floor. There was blood on his chest. The blood was pink from being mixed with water, in rivulets and drips and darker lines too, all down his front and running under his thin arms. His arms and stomach were red and marked with welts. His face was bruised and split open in places, the eyes swollen closed. His knees were drawn up to protect his genitals because his hands were bound behind him. He was barefoot. There was more blood and water on the floor, and a bucket of water on the ground. His breathing was noisy and laboured; he was coughing and trembling.

Sitting at a battered table were two SIB plainclothes officers, whose names Hal knew – he had seen them for six months, spoken to them, yet knew little of them. On the table there was another emptied sandbag, soaked, a wireless set, cigarettes and matches. Near them was a private, in shirtsleeves, sweating. He had wet clothes and was holding a wooden stick.

There was silence, apart from the strained breathing of the half-stripped prisoner.

'Who is this?' said Hal, without thinking.

Nobody spoke. The boy, lying there, stopped moving, alert and quivering. He looked up at Hal, or turned his face towards him anyway, but the blackish blood and bruises made it hard to see if his eyes were open.

'Who's this?' Hal asked again, hearing himself and wondering at the sound of his voice. 'What's going on here? What is this?' He was a man accustomed to answers. 'Davis? What sort of procedure is this?'

Davis, behind him, didn't answer.

The nearest of the SIB men stood up and came forward.

His voice was nasal; he spoke coolly. 'I'm afraid you've made a mistake,' he said.

'What mistake?'

'You'll have to go.' He came towards Hal, as if to leave with him. 'I have authority here,' he said.

Hal heard men coming fast along the corridor behind him. Their feet sounded loud, the noise banging around the walls as they closed in, but he didn't turn. Then a voice said, 'Major Treherne. Excuse me, sir?' and he did turn, slowly, to see the sergeant from the front desk, with another behind him. They saluted him. Davis had stood aside for them, and now was looking down. The sergeant spoke again: 'Sir. Would you come with me, please? About Nugent?'

Hal looked back at the SIB man, who smiled.

'Thanks awfully,' he said.

'Sir?' the sergeant said.

Hal went to the door. 'Davis. Follow me,' he said, without looking at him.

He went with the sergeants, away from the prisoners, past the first room he had been in. They walked quickly in front of him. Hal could smell the fresh air coming in as they went back towards the desk.

'We thought we'd lost you,' said one.

Hal couldn't hear Davis behind him.

'This way, sir,' said the sergeant. 'Through here.'

But Hal ignored them – hardly saw them – and walked past, out of the building, down the wooden steps and onto the hard ground in the glare of the sun outside. He was blinded. He stopped, not deliberately, just his mind stopping and his body winding down. He still couldn't see in the bright light, taking breaths of clean air as his eyes adjusted.

There was no Davis behind. He wasn't coming out. Hal looked about him.

'Sir?'

One of the sergeants' voices. Hal pulled the keys from his pocket and went towards his car, parked fifty feet away.

'Sir!'

'Not now.'

He pulled open the door, nothing in his mind but that he had to think calmly, away from the wood-smelling wet dim rotten corridors of that place, out of sight of it. He felt the blood pounding behind his eyes, his brain rushing to fight, save, act – but not doing that, doing nothing but trying to get away. The thin key went into the ignition, turned, metal pressing his fingers, but no sound, no spark – he switched off, turned it again, and there was an answering hum, but nothing more. The smell of the place hadn't left him, that the boy in there was bleeding. He turned the key again. The car started up, turning over slower than it should; he revved it, putting it hard into reverse and pulling away from the building with the engine protesting. The gears jolted into first, without stalling, and he got away from the guardroom up the hill.

Nobody came after him.

The track led up the hill to a dividing point. Hal, clear of the guardroom, stopped the car. He was on the brow of a hill. He couldn't see anybody. The windscreen was covered with fine dust.

Roads, made and unmade, converged here, uneven, marked by tyre tracks and signs sticking out of the dry earth. 'Officers' Mess', 'Lionheart Estate', 'Kensington'. He didn't need them: he knew the place. He knew it.

Roads meeting, joining, splayed and spreading as they found

their destinations. The one to his right led to the Burroughses' house where surely his servant, or wife, would know where to find him – but the thought died before Hal even had time to dismiss it. He had no ally. His country, his schoolboy land of just hierarchies, was defeated. It had no ambassador to send out any longer.

Chapter Twelve

Corporal Kirby had found that strong British tea and a roll-up, harsh and quick-burning, were very reviving, even when the mercury was up in the hundreds. Thinking he had the afternoon off, he was in the corporals' mess when Major Treherne sent for him.

'Righty-oh, lads, that's my holidays buggered up,' he said, draining his mug, and left them.

He found the major at his office. He was waiting inside, and didn't seem to hear when Kirby knocked on the door, just when he said, 'Sir?'

Then he jerked his head up, and looked at him. 'Run me down to Evdimou, would you, Kirby?'

'Sir.'

Hal crossed the blazing beach, walking towards the café; he had guessed Mark would be there, and he was, leaning back almost to the horizontal under the shade of the canopy with his boot heels dug into the sand. There was the tiniest of breezes coming off the dark blue sea.

'Fancy a trip into town?' said Hal, hearing, with some surprise, his voice come out as clipped and even as ever.

'*Avec* or *sans* wives?' said Mark.

'Without.'

'Absolutely.'

They went to Maxim's Cabaret, in Limassol, and were there as the doors opened.

Upstairs there was a brothel of some repute that neither of them intended to visit. They took a corner table, far back, and started with bottles of Keo beer, laying the foundations. Mark could see it was a determined effort of Hal's to get drunk, and welcomed it, whatever his reason.

Squares of sour herbed feta and sodden olives were brought along with each round; the table around them and the floor beneath were littered with cigarette ends and olive stones and still they hardly spoke. Hal was looking straight ahead, drinking fast, and Mark left him to it, not asking anything.

After an hour or so, the floor show started – dancing girls from around the world – and they moved on to brandy sours, ordering bread to soak it up, mixing the bland flat bread with dark tobacco and the strong liquor.

The Spanish dancer stayed on for a long time – too long. She had castanets and uttered guttural yelps that had the soldiers around them answering her and laughing. Hal and Mark were drunk now, thick-tongued with it, arguing over whether she was really Spanish and if she was a stripper on other nights, or a whore. They drank more brandies, without the sour, and a swollen clay jug of water was brought and ignored.

A Turkish belly-dancer, then respectable Greeks were followed by a girl of unidentifiable nationality with veils who might have been Persian and was almost definitely a stripper on other nights.

'You can bet your life old Kirby's availing himself of the upstairs entertainment,' said Mark, and they laughed at the idea of knock-kneed Kirby burning through his corporal's pay, taking his chances with VD and Military Police raids, while they watched the belly-dancing below him.

Their jackets were on the backs of their chairs. There were no women there apart from those dancing, just other soldiers and British civil servants or engineers with dark-tanned faces, making their eyes show up in the shadowed room where cheap, exotic lamps shone onto the red embroidered tablecloths.

They drank some more. Mark was leaning back in his chair watching the ceiling above him as much as the women. Hal felt the raw liquor burning him. The blotting out of pain, anaesthetic, escape – that was what other men found in it. His stomach turned over, rebelling, but he drank more, in need. Not absolution: oblivion, the consummation of nothingness. If he did not have decency then he might at least cut out the desire for it.

The back of his hand was numb against the mouth he tried to wipe.

He knocked over the water jug, which broke on the tiles, and neither of them noticed. A waiter, with his neat white jacket, crouched at their feet to gather up the pieces. Hal half took in the top of his head, bowed, as he cleared up for them, fumbling around the floor near their boots as the show ended. The music was louder. All the girls crowded the stage, surrounded by clapping, their heels drumming on the hollow wood – boots on the wooden floor of the guardroom – stamping, loud stamping on wood, and cheers in sudden darkness.

In the dark Hal closed his eyes. Blind.

'Fuck Jesus Christ Jesus oh God,' he said, into the anonymous noise around him. 'Oh, God. Please. Help me. God,' and the noise of men clapping, the shouts and whistles, received his words.

Dim lights came up slowly as the clapping stopped. The girls had gone. He put his head down into his hand, half resting on the table, but then straightened, not looking at anything.

Mark signalled for another drink.

'My wife's having another baby,' said Hal, surprising himself, because he hadn't been thinking about that. Mark didn't say anything stupid like 'congratulations'; he stayed quiet.

Hal started his next drink, losing the appetite for it. The room was slipping around him. He found he couldn't grasp the things that were tearing at him as sharply as before, and felt grateful. But then, in that defenceless relaxing, as he let himself fall inside his head, deep down, the old familiar horrors showed themselves. They had been waiting for him to let down his guard.

He could refuse the temptation to describe the sad innards of his brain; he could refuse to say, 'I saw a boy . . . I probably brought him in myself – there's nowhere for me to go for help and I can't help anybody.' He could deny the arguments with himself, knowing he was impotent, and had failed, but the images came back, fresh minted, mocking, all his various agonies, and he was helpless in the face of them and shamed.

'Come on,' said Mark. 'Let's get you home.'

They left the nightclub at midnight, stepping into a stiff wind coming in from the sea, and Kirby, moderately sober and sexually sated, drove them out of Limassol.

'How was your evening, Kirby?' asked Mark.

'Not too bad, sir, thank you,' said Kirby, turning the car onto the road.

'Glad to hear it. Glad to hear it,' said Mark, dropping his chin onto his chest.

Hal, beside him, who had longed for unconsciousness, knowing now there was no release in it, fought for control. He kept his eyes open, and watched the bright moon as it rode fast and high above them.

The moonlight striped the bed where Clara lay. She watched the shadows on the wall and tried to remember hymns, but couldn't. She remembered the words or the tunes but not together, and they were always in fragments. A strong wind blew the short curtains outwards into the room so that they looked stiff, like something hard but still moving.

She sat up in bed and tucked her hair behind her ears. The wind was pushing the catch of the window back and forth in uneven squeaks. Immortal. Invisible. Immortal. Invisible. She reached for her diary in the darkness and opened it, feeling through the pages blindly. Taking the cameo in her fingertips, she held it in the bar of silver light across her legs.

It was just a talisman; it couldn't help her. She was alone. Clara felt the slow, deep beginning of anger inside herself, so great it terrified her. It made her feel ashamed that she hid the cameo from Hal, that she had been flattered by the attention of a man in whom, really, she had no interest. She clenched her fist around the cameo, then put it down and away from her.

She felt a small tap, like a tiny finger, inside her, a tiny movement, as if she were being reminded of something.

Her baby was moving. For a moment she felt pure wonder, but it sickened.

She remembered this feeling, this first movement, from when she was pregnant with the twins. Then the realisation of life within her had been lit up and circled by joy, which now was telescopically distant in her memory. She imagined the small thing strengthening inside her with the blind assumption of her protection. Only inches of soft flesh formed the barrier between it and the dreadful air. She wasn't the strong cradle it needed. If it had a brain it would read her thoughts. If it even had a brain the size of a mouse's brain it would know it was unwelcome, had been unwelcome from its conception. She had tried to lie to it, and to herself, but she knew she had failed. The small tap came again, like a question.

Clara heard the car draw up, and Hal saying goodnight to Kirby and to Mark. After a time the door opened.

She sat up in bed again as he came up the stairs and stopped in the doorway.

'Hello,' he said.

'Hello.'

He didn't move, or start to undress, or come nearer, he just stood there, a soldier silhouette.

'I felt the baby move,' she said, her habit, in spite of everything, still being to tell him things.

He didn't answer her. She couldn't see his face.

'It was the first time,' she said. 'I wish you had been here.'

He didn't speak.

He could see that she needed him to. He came and sat on the bed, not looking at her. He felt her hand on his arm. 'Did you hear me?' she said. 'About the baby? Are you drunk?'

'No. Yes – I heard you. That's good, then.'

'What's the matter?'

'Nothing. I'm pleased.'

'For God's sake, Hal!'

His hand was on something small and rounded that pressed into his palm. He picked it up. 'Is this yours?' he said, and handed her the cameo. She took it, and he got up and went into the bathroom.

Chapter Thirteen

When he woke up, his head hurt all over and his mouth was dry. He sat up and watched his sleeping wife. Her face was turned towards him, unseeing, her arm flung out trustingly with soft, curled fingers. He thought that if he placed his finger in her palm they would close, like a baby's, and hold him. He lifted his hand to do it. She opened her eyes.

'Morning,' he said.

Slowly she looked back at him.

'Good morning,' he said again, waiting for her to warm to him. She didn't.

The twins cried out for her, so Hal went into their room and got them, and brought them in. Clara kissed them, she smiled and spoke to them. She had put on a character – the cheerful mother – as she might have put on a dress. What a marvellous effort that was, he thought, but he had seen her move from flat nothingness, to girding herself, to this brave artifice, and was chilled.

They all went down to breakfast.

Hal watched his household through the fog of his headache. The sun came in at the window. Clara was on her knees, doing up Lottie's dress at the back. Adile came in. Clara said brightly, 'Good morning, Adile!'

She looked at Hal, and smiled. An exuberant bird sang outside.

He was reminded of a film he had seen in Germany, one 'Thursday Night at the Pictures', in the gymnasium at the base. The giant room had been thick with smoke and laughter from the rows of men on folding chairs, and the white screen seeming to jump in bright light as the reels were changed. It had been a silly story, and Hal couldn't remember the name of it; he hadn't thought of it again till now. It had been about the population of a town. The townspeople were corn-fed American types, and foreign to him anyway. They were being taken over by creatures from another world, which inhabited their bodies so that even those closest to them didn't realise they had changed. They would walk and talk and do all the normal things, but they were unfeeling. Their very wholesomeness was an unnerving deceit because they hid monsters within themselves and didn't know it.

Kirby's quick double knock came at eight, as it always did, and Hal said, 'Yup!' as he always did, and stood up.

He picked up his cap and put things into his pockets – keys, cigarettes – from the counter by the door where he had left them the night before.

'Have a lovely day, darling,' said Clara.

He left the house. Kirby had turned off the engine and was smoking, half sitting on the bonnet of the car. When he saw Hal he stubbed out his cigarette. 'Morning, sir.'

'Morning, Kirby. Office.'

In his office, Hal closed the door to Mark's room, and the one to the corridor.

He sat, and picked up his pen. The shutters and window

were open behind him. The sun hadn't come into the room yet, and he was in relative cool. His desk was thickly varnished chestnut-coloured wood and it shone glassily. He took a sheet of fresh paper from the drawer and, in doing so, noticed that the varnish of the desk was smeared; the cleaner must have used a wet cloth to wipe it, and the water had dried in spots.

Hal rubbed the small spots with his sleeve. Some disappeared, but others were left, dragged out of shape. He took out his handkerchief and polished a small area, realising, as he did it, that the rest of the desk was still smeared.

He cleared the blotter, pens, hole-punch, rubber stamps and ink bottles from the top and put them onto the round table by the door.

In the service room, he washed out a cloth. It was grey, with a thin red stripe; the grey was dirt, not its real colour, but it didn't go away, even after he had wrung it out under the tap several times.

He wiped the top of the desk and dried it, with his handkerchief, the white one, with the red chain-stitched initials, until there were no more smears on the varnish. The handkerchief would need washing. He had thought he was quite ordered, but he was not. The drawers were filled and spilling over with paperclips, papers, receipts, letters from London, Nicosia, and internal correspondence too.

Hal got down on his knees. The corners of the drawers were slightly crumbly where the varnish had crunched against the wooden runners. There was dust and tiny sawdust streaks, fluff in the drawers, amongst the contents, which seemed to stick to his hands, presenting smaller and smaller asymmetries for him to address: pencils that were different lengths, papers with corners that were soft and creased, the grain of the cheap wood itself, raw inside the drawers, holding the dust and damp from the cloth in shifting, textured grooves that could not be perfectly flat, ever.

In the service room he rinsed the cloth, and wrung it out, counting the twists and the trickles of water running into the dirty sink.

Hal had lunch in the mess. There, all the talk was of an abandoned car that had been discovered on the road between Limassol and Larnaka the night before. It had contained the mutilated bodies of four Greeks. Their hands had been severed from their wrists, they were stripped naked, and their penises, cut off, had been forced into their dead mouths. The topic was lodged between menus and politics, the movements of troops and the latest news from Egypt. The mutilation – or so went the theory – was a religious act: the Muslim Turks believed that an enemy whose body was cut up in such a way may not enter Paradise. The killers had chopped off the genitals of their victims for theological reasons, then.

Naked corpses with their hands cut off, vichyssoise for lunch, rumours of a new governor, the illegal torture of a teenage boy – if you reflected upon it, thought Hal, one topic was pretty much like any other. It was comfortable to be surrounded by men: the eating, banging cutlery, cigarette smoke and noise, much more subdued than in the evening, were nevertheless consoling. He wished his hands didn't smell of the filthy cloth he'd used to clean his desk. After lunch he went back to his office to finish cleaning and to write letters.

The typewriter on the clerk's desk made a rhythmic, metallic sound as he hit the keys with jabbing, staccato fingers, punctuated by a small bell when the carriage returned with an oiled slip and halt; then the smooth revolving rasp of the paper being removed, and in the quiet that followed Hal, lifting his head a moment, thought, *Clara needs to be sent away.*

He put his pen down. The thought came again, like a bubble rising cleanly from a dark pool: *Clara and the children must get away from here.*

Clara was sitting on the sofa, trying to read a book. She had the doors closed to the hot night. Moths fluttered around the big orange shades of the lamps. The bobbled fabric glowed. There was the sound of tiny taps as their bodies hit the shades and thin metal struts supporting the bulbs. Sometimes the moths released themselves, feathery wings against Clara's hair, knocking against her, and she waved them away, glancing up at the door for her husband, waiting.

When he came in, she said, 'Hello,' and then pretended to read again.

He hadn't answered. She looked up. He hadn't taken off his belt, or his holster, but stood, as if completely disconnected from the room, staring at her.

'What?'

He moved then, as if unaware of having stopped. 'Girls asleep?' he said.

'Yes. What is it?'

He shook his head slightly, emptied his pockets, began to do all the things he did on returning home but Clara, alerted to some change, put her book down.

'It's very stuffy in here,' he said. 'Shall I open the door?'

'If you like.'

He crossed the room. The doors opened and blessed fresh air came in.

Clara stood up. 'Hal, I want to talk to you.'

He seemed surprised. 'Do you?' he said.

'Yes.'

They were facing one another, a few feet apart.

'Well, what is it?'

'I'm worried about you,' she said.

The clarity of the phrase surprised them both. He looked at her for a moment. He smiled a tight smile, narrowing his eyes in a sort of irony. She didn't think he knew he did it. 'I'm absolutely fine,' he said.

She searched for words. 'You don't seem yourself,' she said at last, in a small voice.

The commonplace little phrase lay between them in all its magnitude. He looked down at the floor, discovered. 'No,' he said.

'Hal . . .' Clara moved towards him. She put her hands on his arms.

He narrowed his eyes again, almost smiling but somehow not, and then he said, 'Clara,' as if he would turn away from her, but she kept holding his arms.

Without going anywhere, he was all movement, fidgeting beneath his skin, behind his eyes.

'Wait,' she said. She could feel the hard tension rising through him like a vibration, but he didn't move.

She placed her hand flat over his heart. She moved a little closer to him. She was breathing lightly, and he not at all. He was frozen as she approached him, carefully, and touched his neck with her fingertips. She could feel his heart beating very fast against her hand.

He did not take his eyes from hers. He blinked. She began to smile at him.

'I want you to go away from here,' he said.

There was silence. Then, 'What?' she said.

'I think the best plan is that you and the girls go to Nicosia.'

Clara took her hands from him. Her eyes were wide.

Hal put his hands into his pockets. 'I'm sure it can easily be arranged, I'll have a word with the housing officer about it, if you like.'

'You want me to go away from you?' She took a step back from him.

'Don't you think it would be the best thing?'

When she spoke, her voice was low and shaking: 'For who?'

'For you, of course. And the girls. There are doctors there, much better than Godwin, lots of English. You're not happy here, you'll be much better off, and then, when things have calmed down, we'll think again.'

While he was talking she turned away from him, and he spoke to her back. Her head was bowed. Above the top of her dress, between the covered buttons and the curl of her hair, there was bare skin, and he looked at it as he went on, 'Things have been pretty rough round here recently.'

'Have they?' she said, very quietly, without turning. Her hands were gripping the skirt of her dress, twisting the material.

'If you're in Nicosia, you'll be much better off. Things happen here that I don't like to have you – have anything to do with. The baby –'

She turned suddenly and her face was furious; anger he had never seen in her – that he hadn't known she had but, as she spoke, he realised he had felt for a long time – now surfacing, stripped bare. 'The baby?'

'Yes.'

'Don't you think I know what's best for me? Don't you think I know what's best for me and the girls and this *baby*?' She said the word as if she hated it.

'Yes, but –'

'Well, why, then? Why?'

'I told you. In Nicosia you'll be better off.' Hal tried hard to articulate. 'I'm not sure, I don't think I'm much good for you at the moment,' he said.

'Aren't you?' She laughed harshly.

'I don't think so,' he said.

'And if I'm gone you'll be able to get on with your work?' she said, not laughing now, bitter.

'It might be easier.'

'And you won't have to look at me?'

'I –'

'You hardly do. The only time you're with me, you *hurt* me, Hal. This *baby*,' she gestured, 'which you don't even *want* – and don't pretend you do, or that you've given it a moment's thought – and *yesterday*, when I *needed* you –'

What did she mean? Yesterday – the vision of the boy on the wet boards, the blood and water on his chest. Hal's mouth seemed to fill with hot mineral-tasting blood.

'When you were *drunk* –'

'I'd –'

'Our baby is *here*, Hal. It's in me, and do you know how I feel about it? I'll tell you. I don't bloody want it either,' she said. 'That *night* – that *celebration night* of yours, *hurrah*, jolly good, go home and have your wife. Don't you remember?'

'Clara –'

Her voice was raw: 'No! You say you want me safe, but you hurt me.'

'Clara –'

'No.'

She backed off, and sat down, suddenly, in the chair opposite him. She began to cry, hiding her face. It was desperate. He felt desperate. The vast realisation of her feelings, and of his failure, engulfed him. 'I didn't know,' he said.

'Didn't know what?'

He was her enemy. He hadn't known it. He went to the chair by the sofa, and sat down, rubbed his face with his hands, trying to order his thoughts. 'If I have made you unhappy, I apologise.' He sounded ridiculous, even to himself. Ridiculous and polite, unable to find any way to speak to her. She didn't say anything. He tried to salvage something. Perhaps he could take it back. She might stay, if he asked her. 'I don't know if you want – what you want,' he said, fumbling through the words, 'but perhaps you could –'

'Yes, Hal.' She stopped him. 'We'll go. Don't worry. We'll go – gladly. *Leave you to it*, as they say. You win. I surrender.' She gave him no quarter. 'I do. I surrender.'

PART THREE

Nicosia, September

Chapter One

The hotel in Nicosia was a big 1920s building of yellow stone, almost a whole block, close to Government House and not far from the old city wall. It had pointed arches on the windows, balconies and decorative cut-outs in concrete that looked Moorish to Clara. Nicosia was an interior capital; the drive from Limassol, across the plains, had been dusty and long. Climbing the wide stairs of the hotel, with the girls stop-starting, tripping behind her and under her feet, Clara felt nothing but exhaustion.

She opened the tall door to her room. It was a big, square, light room, quite plain, with twin beds and a door to a narrow bathroom that stood open. She glimpsed a much smaller room through it, with camp beds set up. There were salmon-coloured candlewick bedspreads and a chandelier with small orange-pink shades, not quite matching. Clara took off her gloves, which were dirty and damp. The sun came through the big windows pitilessly.

'Here Lottie. No, Meg, come here, darling.'

She showed the porter where to put the cases and he went down to fetch the rest. She walked across to the window. She was two floors above a wide street where British soldiers patrolled. The few cars went very quickly, it seemed, past the modern buildings. There was a zebra crossing under the window and Union flags flying from the rooftops. She needed to organise the girls' supper. Her legs felt thick and heavy. She sat down on the edge of the bed and the girls bumbled about, came near her, peering at her and tugging her skirt. The porter came in again, and behind him, a woman – an Englishwoman.

'You must be Clara Treherne,' she said, stepping around the porter. 'I'm Gracie Bundle.'

Gracie was bright blonde, with neatly painted lips and a light grey suit hugging her small and curvy body. 'Have they sorted a maid out for you yet?'

'I'm not sure,' said Clara, standing up.

She felt dizzy. She sat down again.

'You look fairly done in,' said Gracie. The girls were staring at her. 'Aren't they little poppets!' she said. 'Hang on a mo, I'll send down for some sustenance. Don't move.'

Clara hung on, and soon there was room service – bread and tea – a maid for the next day, and net curtains keeping the sun out of the room.

'I'll get my Miss Sila to come, shall I? Take your two off your hands for an hour or so,' said Gracie, and darted out of the room. She returned some minutes later with her Greek maid, a woman in her fifties, who was carrying a small boy and leading another by the hand.

'Say hello, Tommy, say hello, Larry.'

They didn't.

'Jolly good. Off you go, children,' said Gracie, and the four children and the maid, swept along by her energy, left the room.

'I should think you could do with a rest. Don't worry about

the children – I'll keep a beady eye. Shall we have supper together?'

'Yes,' said Clara, gratefully, and Gracie backed out of the room, gave a wink, and shut the door.

Clara looked around her. She ought to let Hal know she had arrived.

She picked up the telephone. There was a purring sound, then the desk answered, a high, scratchy Greek voice. Clara said, 'This is room two one five. Would you connect me with the operator, please? Thank you.'

The sound of several rings and vibrations, as the lines were crossed and cleared. Then another female voice, efficient, greeted her in Greek. Clara said clearly, 'Hello? Yes, it's a Limassol number, the Episkopi Garrison. The garrison at Episkopi.'

Another wait. Silence. Violent whirrings. Distant voices, as though she were eavesdropping on nations. Then she was connected. She heard a soldier's voice, with a London accent, asking for the name and extension number. 'Major Treherne, company lines, extension forty-three, please.'

A long pause. Clicks on the line. Ringing. The sound of it was almost contact. Ringing. Ringing. The distant rasping went on. The telephone wasn't picked up. She listened, each second falling from the last, each ring emptier, but she waited until the soldier's voice came back and said, 'There's no reply from Major Treherne, madam,' before she replaced the heavy receiver gently, and with relief, onto its black cradle.

Clara and Gracie had supper in the hotel dining room and Gracie told Clara all about Nicosia. The dining room was big and shabby, with a box-panelled ceiling and a dance floor at one end. They ate grilled chicken and drank boiled water from a decanter beaded with droplets. Clara felt unlike herself in this new place; she listened closely to Gracie, clinging to her words like a life raft.

'You're much better off here. It's practically Paris compared to Limassol,' said Gracie, who was the wife of Major David Bundle, in the K— R—. He had been stationed up in the Troodos for a year. Her two boys were at the English nursery. She took a photograph – black-and-white, with a white scalloped edge – from her small crocodile handbag and showed it to Clara. In the photograph David Bundle, roundly filling his uniform, was grinning. 'He's a shadow of his former self now, I should think,' said Gracie, laughing, and then, 'You look rather white. I'm a terrible talker. Are you shattered?'

They finished supper, signed for it, and Clara went up the wide stairs to the second floor alone.

Gracie's maid was on a gilt-framed chair in the long corridor, a tiny middle-aged woman in a black dress. Her empty shoes were placed neatly beside her, the thin laces stiff and curled. The corridor glowed with unnatural light, too bright for late night.

Clara took off her own shoes, and softly opened her door, stepping inside quietly so as not to disturb the girls.

She lay between the sheets, with the corridor light showing under her door.

She was alone. She moved on the unfamiliar bed, tentatively. The long journey lay between her and the last violent conversation with Hal. Contained and invisible, her anger had grown, but now she was empty, like a cool metal shell when the bullet is at last discharged – clean. She didn't miss Hal. She wouldn't think of him.

* * *

After Clara had left, Hal went to the café at Evdimou beach. He spent the afternoon there and, after changing at home, had dinner in the mess. He would have slept there if he could.

It was easier without Clara and his daughters. Once a week, he wrote her short cheerful letters. He wrote: 'Epi's the same as usual, poor old Mark still hounded by Deirdre and the food ghastly as ever', or 'Saw Evelyn Burroughs today and she asked me to give you Harold and Eileen Empson's number. Remember we met them at Krefeld that Christmas? '53, was it?' and always, after signing his name, he would fold the letter very precisely and fast, then put it inside the envelope, out of sight.

But she didn't write to him. The days went by, then weeks, and he never heard from her. He telephoned the hotel, to make sure she'd arrived safely, and although he was shocked that she didn't write to him, her silence was easier to manage.

In Clara's absence, Evelyn Burroughs invited him for supper at least once a week. 'How is dear Clara?' she would say, leaning across the table at him. 'Of course you miss her, but I honestly think it's the best thing all round, don't you?'

The colonel began to ask after his father again, and one night, finishing his soup and blotting his lips, he said, 'You certainly had a baptism of fire coming here, didn't you? All settled down, now, has it?'

Hal looked into his pale blue eyes and answered, 'Yes, Colonel, pretty much quiet now.'

'Good to get rid of those rogue elements, I think. Bit of spring-cleaning, eh? No more trouble from Lieutenant Davis?'

'No, no more trouble there. He hasn't come to me again.'

But then there was the undressing for bed.

He peeled away the layers each night, stripping his uniform

to the bare skin that wasn't nakedness for sleeping, or for his wife, or any other version of himself that he could stand. He began to spend the nights dressed, or half dressed, sometimes leaning up against the bedstead, sometimes in a chair, and then, in the morning, get up and wash and change his shirt. He found he could rest better that way, a half sleep for a half soldier, half clothed and better protected.

Lawrence Davis didn't know that Clara was gone until a few days after her departure. There was no reason why he would have known, but even not seeing her, he'd had a comforting mental picture of her there, in the barracks, and now she had been taken away from him. In his mind, she had become his confessor, and his fantasies about her were more romantic than sexual. They had been sexual too, of course, but Lawrence Davis was a virgin, and telling secrets to his mother was where he'd had much more experience.

It was Deirdre Innes who told him Clara had left Episkopi. He was in Limassol buying some shoelaces and razor blades and had seen her on the street. She was carrying a basket and had big sunglasses on; she had said his name first. 'Lieutenant Davis!'

'Good morning.' He had stepped off the narrow pavement to let her by.

'Thank you. What are you up to?'

'Oh, you know.' He had held up the brown paper bag with his purchases inside.

'Finding your fun in town now?' she had said and, seeing his confusion, enlightened him about Clara's departure.

'Nicosia? Oh.' He had felt quite lost suddenly, one of his anchors tearing free and leaving him to drift.

'Bit of a contretemps with her husband, as I understood it. I would have thought she'd have told you.'

'Why would she tell me?'

'Weren't you friendly?'

'Well . . .'

'You're blushing! You are!'

'I'm not sure what you mean –'

'Men are so prissy. You were friends, weren't you?'

'I suppose.'

Then she had looked around her and said, 'Listen, shall we go somewhere?'

He had been taken aback enough not to absorb her suggestion immediately. 'I have a car if you need –'

'No, not home. And I don't mean the club either. Come on, it'll be fun.'

He had taken her – or she had taken him – to a bar near the cinema. He had been in a state of sweating anxiety throughout. She had ordered three large gin-and-tonics and then they had gone into the hot, pitch-black cinema and stared blindly at *The King and I* while she put her hand on his leg and began to rub him there.

There was a thrill in doing what he then began to do with the wife of Hal Treherne's 2 i/c, and she certainly took his mind off his work. To meet Deirdre Innes, in one of the more deserted coves after dark, or the vehicle park amongst the three-tonners and the Fords, was intoxicating. Having her – the secrecy, the hard obliterating feel of it, knowing she didn't even like him – was in keeping with his new idea of himself. He wasn't sure what he'd say to a nice girl now; he wouldn't know how to act.

When he thought of Clara, it was with regret and shame.

She and the goddess Iris he'd left her with were like figures in a story-book that once he'd dreamed of but now had left behind, along with any fantasies about conscientious objection. Now, like Grieves, he was simply counting the days until demob.

As for Clara, she had lost the little cameo when she moved away from Episkopi. It must have fallen into the sandy folds of a suitcase, or dropped carelessly from a dress pocket on folding. It had never really comforted her; she hadn't known Lawrence Davis well, and the hiding it from Hal had taken any use it might have had away from her.

Chapter Two

Clara didn't tell Gracie she was pregnant. In late September, at four and a half months, if she wore her belts high and loosened them, she could just about get away with it – or convince herself that she could. For such a breezy person, Gracie was very tactful. Instead of prying, she told Clara all about her husband, David. 'He has leave in two weeks. We shan't have time to go anywhere – it's only a few days. Just long enough to try and feed him up a bit. David likes his grub, and he gets awfully low up there eating out of mess tins.'

Gracie's boys were three and five. She had two others at prep school in England. It was miraculous that her tiny body could have produced four boys and still fit so effortlessly into a girdle. Even her ankles were tiny. The five-year-old, Tommy, was learning to read and do his letters; Larry, the little one, had a scooter, which he guarded jealously and wouldn't let the twins play with. Gracie was forever saying, 'Now, Larry, I shall take it away from you if you're going to be selfish,' but not taking it away, while the twins ran after him across hot terraces and up and down the pavements of Nicosia.

They spent most of their days at the officers' club, avoiding the streets, which were crowded with Greeks and soldiers. The club was bigger than the one in Limassol, with a swimming pool, and they would take it in turns to go in the water with the children, or walk in the gardens and sit near the fountain in the shade of palm trees. The club had delusions of grandeur; it didn't know what a shabby lesser outpost it was in. There were always soldiers, carrying Stens or .303s, posted at the hotel doors, and at the club, but Clara, used to living in a barracks, barely noticed them, feeling the freedom of being in a city.

Gracie and Clara walked slowly around the garden, with the children. They stopped at one of the shaded dark green benches and sat. The traffic noise out in the city, beyond the walls, reached them, and the sounds of waiters laying tables for lunch on the terrace.

'Heard from Hal?' asked Gracie, pretending to dust small particles from her calves.

'I had a letter this morning.'

Clara had read the letter to the girls dutifully, then put it away, with all the others. There was nothing in it but trivia.

'He must miss you.'

Clara nodded.

'Larry! Larry! Stop that!' cried Gracie, as Larry vented his rage on Tommy, rushing him head first and pushing him over. The twins, pausing in their business, looked on with meek expressions.

'Look at your lovely girls,' said Gracie, getting up. 'Why don't I have girls?' She ran towards Larry, her very narrow skirt making her skitter.

Clara, in solitude for a moment, took a deep breath and let it out slowly.

She looked around her at the white-painted palm trees. Women in summer dresses with their men, mostly in uniform, went in and out of the club building, greeting one another at the pool. The sounds of their voices reached her, and the playing children. She heard a song start up inside, faintly, a wireless or gramophone in one of the rooms, upstairs. '*Hey mambo, mambo Italiano! Hey mambo, mambo Italiano . . .*'

A woman at a table by the pool got up from her chair. She was wearing a yellow two-piece and she danced a little as she shook out her towel.

What a silly song, thought Clara, and the careless beauty of the world, and herself in it, came back to her, like a mist thinning in the morning. She felt herself tremble. Small shivers touched her. She felt life. And then, again, the little tap inside her, the soft shifting of her baby. She closed her eyes.

She could hear Gracie, quite clearly but as if at some distance, scolding her child.

The thing about dancing with Hal, she thought, was that he looked at her all the time and made her feel beautiful.

Clara laid her hand on her stomach and little tapping bubbles seemed to answer her. She admired the tiny thing, spinning away inside her. It had stuck with her, hadn't been deterred by her weakness. She hadn't even been there, she thought, just a vessel for the carrying of it. She was rewarded by another little movement, nothing like a kick. Don't worry, she thought. I'll make sure you're all right. I promise.

She found herself smiling. She wanted to speak to it. She wanted to say, 'Look! We're in a nice garden, and soon we'll go and have lunch.'

She heard Gracie coming back towards her and opened her eyes. Gracie had Larry firmly by the hand, but he still held the scooter.

'What are you smiling about?' said Gracie.

'I'm pregnant,' said Clara.

'Oh, thank goodness. I knew you were, but I didn't want to make a gaffe,' said Gracie, and plumped neatly down on the bench, heaving Larry onto her knee. 'How far gone are you?'

'Just five months.'

'Gosh, you carry it awfully well. You must miss poor old Hal. It's been weeks.'

'We argued very badly before I left.'

'Oh . . . that's rough.'

'He was the one who wanted me to come here. I didn't want to.'

'It has worked out for the best though, hasn't it?'

'I suppose it has.'

'Who'd be an army wife, eh?'

'Quite.'

'Rather stoical sort of person, aren't you?'

'I don't think so. I'm a terrible coward.'

'Well, I think you're marvellous,' said Gracie, firmly. Clara had to look the other way to stop herself crying. Gracie patted her hand. 'I blubbed every single day when I was preggers with Larry,' she said, then, 'that's probably why he's so ghastly.'

Larry gripped his scooter harder and sulked.

When Clara had put the girls down for their nap, she sat in the dim bedroom and took out Hal's letters.

There were ten. The paper was white, quite thick, from a box her mother had sent out at Christmas the year before. Hal's writing was neat and accurate, with almost no crossings-out. He had signed each one 'With love, Hal'. Just that, and nothing else. He talked about the weather, 'Hellishly hot, had to put three men on a charge for sunburn'; about EOKA, 'Been a bit busy lately. Casualties.'

She held the letters in her hand. She remembered his letters from Sandhurst ('Food hell. See you on the 16th') and from Germany ('Can't stand this paperwork, rained all week').

One of the girls moved behind her, murmuring in her sleep.

She had always had to read between the lines with Hal.

She opened the drawer in the desk, and took out a sheet of blue writing paper that said 'Ledra Palace Hotel' at the top, in slightly uneven print.

She unscrewed the top of the pen. 'Hal,' she wrote, hesitating between sentences. 'I'm sorry for the extended silence.' The ink didn't flow at first, and the letters had gaps. 'I hope you are well. The girls are very well, and so am I.'

She crossed that out, and started again.

Do you remember all the letters we used to write? I wrote many more than you. Yours are what is known as 'opaque', I think. But I'm out of practice now, too, and can't seem to say what I'd like to. I feel so very badly about so many things. I did feel 'the wronged wife'. Hal – I even hated you. I've had a chance to think, and I've cheered up rather. Ought we to talk about my coming back? You have leave in November, but it seems a long way away. Shall we speak soon? Darling.

She stopped. Then, on a new line, she wrote again, 'Darling,' very deliberately, and 'Today I went to the club, with my friend Gracie . . .'

And she told him about the white-painted palms, David, whom she'd never met, Gracie and the little boys, the hotel dining room, that the girls missed the beach and that they had many more words. They could say 'bath-time' and 'Look at the water'. She told him about feeling the baby moving: 'Forget what I said about it before, please. It was wicked and not meant at *all*.'

She took the letter downstairs, tiptoeing from the room, and gave it to the concierge. Then she stood, with her arms around herself, just standing still. She seemed to see Hal in front of her, in his uniform, a little dusty and hot from the day, and out of place in the hotel lobby.

Chapter Three

Hal sat at the breakfast table and drank his coffee, looking at Clara's letter, lying near him. He had dismissed Adile the week before, embarrassed by having her around the house with him, a single man. A cleaning woman came in every few days. There wasn't much to do. He didn't make much mess.

He looked at Clara's looped, schoolgirlish handwriting on the envelope, which was lightweight and battered, as if it had been all the way to some sorting office in Scotland or Arabia before coming to him. Just seeing her writing undid him, as if she were reaching out her hand and touching him, and he was endangered by it.

He put one finger on the letter and slid it towards him. He took out his pocket knife. The point found the gap, the secret crease gave to the blade. He pulled out the letter and laid it flat.

'Hal,' she had written. Then he read the crossed-out part, and seemed to see her do it. He heard her voice. *Do you remember all the letters we used to write?*

This was no good. Just seeing her writing was impossible. He put his hand over the letter and looked up, out of the small window across the table from him. He lifted his hand, glancing down, and read sideways, out of the corner of his eye.

I did feel the 'wronged wife'. Hal – I even hated you.

He didn't have time now. Kirby was on his way. There was no time for this. He carefully refolded it, first along its original crease, then again and again, until it was a small, fat square, using the back of his thumbnail to force the folds. He got up and cleared his place, washing the plate under the tap and wiping the crumbs away carefully.

As he dried his hands he heard Kirby pull up outside. He folded the tea-towel. Passing the table he picked up the letter and put it into his pocket. He left the house.

Clara's breakfast at the Ledra Palace with the girls was far from solitary. It was a rowdy affair. There were the other guests, and quite a few children. Waiters with thick linen cloths carried heavy hot silver pots, dodging the chairs and sticking-out feet. Clara had no letter from Hal, but a week-old copy of *The Times*, much read, that she was trying to glance at between buttering the girls' toast.

'No! Meg!'

Meg had pulled a big corner from the paper, tearing off a large piece and closing her hands over it, trying to fold it in half.

'All right, here, then.' Clara helped her, folding the torn piece of newspaper neatly, once in half, twice, smoothing it with her thumb. 'See, darling? Like that . . .'

Meg patted it with her small hands, like starfish. Clara lifted one and kissed the dimples where the knuckles were.

'There you are!'

Clara looked up. Gracie was marching towards her, breakfasted already, makeup on.

'Shops today.'

The hotel was outside the old city walls. The streets within them were narrow and jumbled, more picturesque, but dirtier too. The best shops were inside the walls, though, and the main shopping street, Ledra Street, was where everybody went; it was a long straight road that ran the length of the old town.

The road that Hal's Land Rover was on was high and narrow, a track between villages that, without the army vehicles rolling over the baked ground, would have been little used.

It was a white road. On all sides the island reached away from it. There were the pine-covered hills to the north, a giant falling-away to miles and miles of dry rocks, troughs and gullies to the west, and ahead, the small road ribboned downwards and there was a scattering of leaning buildings, derelict.

Hal's vehicle, alone, crossed the spit between the villages and Kirby drove slowly. Hal, next to Kirby, had his hand in his pocket with Clara's letter, compressed, closed inside it. He had left Lieutenant Thompson's platoon at Omodos, and he was travelling to Kalo Chorio to get to McKinney and two sections that were doing a house-to-house there.

Ledra Street was lined with clothes shops filled with imported fashions, and cafés. Gracie loved going there, and would have gone every day if Clara had agreed. You could post your letters in the red post boxes. You could buy talcum powder, chocolates, gloves.

They would have the car drop them at the top, near the walls, then walk down, chatting and window-shopping, saying hello to people. They always saw people they – or at least

Gracie – knew: diplomats' wives, army wives, all kinds of other English people. Clara was coming to know them too.

'Here,' said Gracie to the driver. 'Just here, thank you.'

The bicycles were small-looking and far away along the white road. There were two of them. Thin white dust hovered over the road and shimmered.

Hal didn't think anything of them, apart from noting their approach, until one of the figures, seeing his vehicle, jumped off his bike and disappeared, down the steep hill into the bushes.

'Hello,' said Kirby, and Hal leaned out to see better.

The second bicycle stopped. They were nearer now, just a couple of hundred yards away. The boy – it was a boy – still on the bike was shouting down the hill to his friend, and the abandoned bike lay on its side.

After a moment, the boy stopped shouting, glanced towards Hal's Land Rover, and started towards them again. There was a basket on the front of his bike, covered by a cloth.

Kirby stopped the Land Rover and cut the engine. They could hear the bike squeaking as the boy laboured up the stony hill towards them on the white road. He was whistling. Nice touch, thought Hal, getting out. Kirby got out, too.

'Halt,' he said. '*Stamata. Dur.*'

And the boy halted. He was about fifteen. He rested on one foot, his forearms leaning on the handlebars, squinting at them.

Hal walked over to him. If the other hadn't stopped, he never would have noticed them. He was still in two minds whether to search him.

'What's in there?' said Kirby, not expecting to be understood, but gesturing.

The boy suddenly abandoned his pretence, and made a lunge away from them, but Kirby, nimble on his big feet, grabbed his thin arm with his big hand, restraining him.

'We would have passed him,' said Hal.

He went to the bicycle, which had fallen in the scuffle. A bundle in a white cloth had fallen from it onto the stony road. He picked it up and lifted the corners of the cloth. Inside it was a smoothly oiled pistol, standard British Army issue, a Webley .38. The boy wriggled in Kirby's grasp.

Stupid, thought Hal. Stupid. Some bloody uncle, or his father or some other sneaky Cyp bastard having kids do things like this. Bloody hell. And now – He looked at the boy. Now he'd have to take him in.

'Sir? What are we going to do? Take him on to Kalo with us? Where will we put him? We could go back to Epi with him.'

Yes. It was eleven o'clock. They could take him to the guardroom at Episkopi and still be up at Kalo in time.

The boy had gone silent and was staring at the ground. He could be in the Episkopi guardroom, in a cell there, waiting for questioning, in less than an hour.

'Which village are you from?' Hal said to the boy. 'Where's your mother? Are you coming with us now?'

'Sir,' said Kirby. 'He don't understand you, does he?'

Hal walked off, ten feet away from them. He was still holding the pistol. He took the cloth off it. The gun was sleek and heavy in his hand. He checked the chamber. It was empty. He walked fast up to the boy. 'Stupid!' he shouted. 'Stupid! Stupid! Stupid!' He held the gun up to the boy's temple and pressed it hard into his head, shouting, '*Do you know what will happen to you? Do you know?*'

There was silence for a moment, just the boy staring at him, then Hal lowered the gun and walked away again. Kirby, nervous now, wiped the sweat from his face with his free hand.

Hal stood with his back to them both.

Kirby looked up and down the empty road and said, 'Sir, he's old enough to know better.' After a moment, he added, 'We've taken in kids younger than him before, sir. That gun was on its way somewhere.'

Hal saw the other boy in his mind, the blood and water on him and the floor, his breath dragging in and out of his throat. He didn't know if that boy had been one of his arrests – he hadn't been able to see his face properly. He wouldn't be able to tell one from another anyway.

He turned back to them and came up to the boy and looked, one hand in his pocket, the other holding the gun loosely in his hand.

This boy, this particular boy, had jaggedly cut hair, short into the neck but growing out. He had a slightly flattened nose and high cheekbones, giving his face a Slav look. He had scars on his knees. Sweat was soaking in patches through his shirt and a wristwatch with a dirty canvas strap, much too big for him, hung down over his hand. This particular boy looked back at Hal bravely.

Hal didn't have a choice. 'We'll take him back to Epi,' he said.

Getting back into the Land Rover, he pulled his hand from his pocket, unthinkingly throwing the small thick square of paper away from him onto the road as Kirby put the cuffed boy into the back seat.

Clara and Gracie left the car at Eleftheria Square at eleven o'clock, walking through the darkness under the deep medieval arches as the clocks struck the hour. Clara hadn't wanted to be on Ledra Street, but Gracie was very keen to find a new dress to impress David. His leave was at the end of the week.

They had the children with them. The girls were in pinafores and Larry and Tommy had shorts and white shirts, Tommy with braces because his shorts always slipped down.

Clara had no sense of being followed or watched. Her anxiety, the current of fear that had run underneath everything, had quieted recently. There were crowds here, anyway, and open daytime normality, nothing to fear. 'I think I must surrender to the inevitable,' she said.

'Oh, yes?'

'It's smocks for me from now on. I may as well get used to the idea. I can't possibly keep on like this – look at me!'

'You'll be much more comfortable,' said Gracie, 'and cooler too. Perhaps we'll find something today.'

'I shall look like an old Greek lady.'

'Never. Elegance always.'

They had emerged into the inner city, and crossed the roads that circled it to enter Ledra Street, which, in late morning, was teeming.

The women held the children's hands firmly in the crowds.

'I saw a printed organza,' said Gracie, and – exactly at that moment – Clara heard the shots.

She didn't recognise them as shots. She couldn't place the sound. It was a cracking sound – a sharp knocking – and she saw Gracie going sideways away from her and falling.

The world slowed. Clara saw the crowds near them pull back as Gracie fell. A woman in a yellow dress was putting her hands up to her face, her handbag hanging from her wrist. An old man with a sagging belly over belted trousers threw his arms out wide. Then again, in that infinite second, the sharp high crack, and Clara felt a quick hot pricking feeling low down in her stomach.

That's odd, Clara thought slowly, letting go of Lottie's hand. She heard screams. They weren't hers. She saw that Gracie, falling, had pulled Tommy down with her into a heap on the dirty pavement. There were cigarette ends on the pavement. The strong heat was still there in her abdomen, but Clara didn't feel any pain. She thought, Poor Tommy – then her vision was splashed with black. There were dark fireworks across her sight. She looked down, aware of Lottie's face looking up at her, through the dark patches. She saw that her hand and the front of her dress were covered with blood. She didn't know where it was coming from. She was falling. She saw the pavement, detailed, come up at her but didn't feel herself hitting it.

Like Gracie, she had kept hold of Meg's hand, and they fell – with Lottie standing alone, watching – like people being tripped up in a race at a village fair, tumbling, and they lay, jumbled together, the blood fast pooling out, creeping shinily over the pavement.

The mass of people reacted, pulling back in a wave, then there were sounds of panic, people looking to see where the shots had come from, but the gunman, hiding the smooth pistol easily, had walked away.

After just a very few seconds, English people, Greek and Turkish, strangers to them, came closer. Somebody leaned down. Somebody knelt. The woman in the yellow dress tried to pull the children away, her husband helped her. Most, though, carried on walking, turning their faces away. Some covered their mouths, as if the two Englishwomen shot down were run-over dogs, to be passed with eyes averted and hurriedly left behind.

Gracie was lying on her back, with her hips and legs twisted in the opposite direction from her shoulders. Her eyes were unflinching in the brightness. The children began to scream. It was hard to tell which ones were screaming.

Clara's eyes were blinking fast. She was trying to sit up and see past the black shapes in her vision, but she couldn't seem to move at all. She was sharply aware of her children, and that she was lying down. The heat had spread out now through her hips and stomach and become the centre of her. She was trying to speak, and stuttering. A part of her could see she was lying on the street, but the rest of her was lost in it. She wanted to say, 'My girls, please, help,' but she couldn't speak. She could see people leaning over her. She didn't know any of them. There were strangers leaning over her and touching her. She couldn't hear anything. She began to be very frightened. She thought, oh no, oh no, oh no, oh no . . .

It took an hour to get back to Episkopi.

Hal put the boy into the guardroom, hating the time it took, the paperwork. It was hard to make himself keep standing there as the sergeant on the desk fiddled with the carbon paper, clumsily, unable to adjust it so that it wasn't creased, oblivious to Hal's tension and the fearful boy in front of him. The air was stifling in that place. It still stank.

'Just a mo,' he said, smoothing out the creases, registering the oiled pistol, tagging it, and it was nearly another hour before they could get away.

At last they were released, and the boy taken inside. Hal didn't watch him go.

He came down the steps. He got into the Land Rover. Kirby pulled away again, grumbling about the heat and his lunch being late, and Hal put his elbow out of the open window, resting his fingers on the doorframe.

To their left, a handful of men were playing football, shirts off, a layer of dust a foot thick making it look as if they were cut off at the knee, the heavy ball occasionally flying up to shoulder height. Their shouts reached Hal over the roar of the Land Rover as it slowed for the gate.

There came the rattle of the ball hitting the wire fence and bouncing back into the dust as the barrier sentry, instead of lifting it up, letting them go as he had let them enter, came out into the road, and raised his hand, signalling to them to pull over. He was talking to his companion over his shoulder as he walked.

Kirby braked. 'What have I done now?' he said. 'There's always bloody something.'

The Land Rover's engine idled. The soldier gestured, 'Stay!' He began to run heavily towards them.

Hal watched the sentry running towards them. He saw his boots in the dust, his face screwed up with intent, his Sten bouncing and steadied with one hand as he approached, and Hal felt, from nowhere, cold dread, the horror of absolute change approaching him, and when he heard what had happened, it was as if he had known it all along.

Chapter Four

Kirby drove him straight to Nicosia, to the hospital where Clara was. The drive, all four hours, was made in silence, with nothing to say or do except keep from falling into imagining. He had been told she wasn't dead when he left. When he left, she wasn't dead.

He stared out of the car at nothing, seeing the long white road and the young boy on it, the slick pistol, wrapped lovingly in white cloth, imagining blood on his thin child's body.

It had been the work of a quick and vengeful God, he thought, but she wasn't dead when he left.

The hospital was in the centre of the city. They were being held up by trucks stopping to let out troops, soldiers with metal barriers, and the Land Rover had to squeeze between them. Neither he nor Kirby said anything about it. It was distant to Hal. He didn't connect it with Clara or the other woman who was shot.

They reached the hospital, in a quiet street, and stopped as a straggle of civilians, running to their houses, skidded in front of the car. Hal had an impression of the building, rising in stone above him, high; the entrance hall was vast with a polished floor. He walked across the shining floor to the desk.

He did not run. He heard his voice: 'My wife is here. Clara Treherne.'

A soldier came over to him, introduced himself – some name, some regiment. They didn't make him wait, they took him upstairs. There were nurses, like nuns, in white head-dresses, quietly walking, the corridors were shiny too, the doors. Each one could have been hers. Passing doors, waiting to be taken to her, but then a doctor approached him.

Hal said, 'Where's my wife?'

'Come with me,' said the doctor.

'No. Where's my wife?'

'Please, Mr Treherne, come with me.'

The man was Greek. Why didn't they have a proper doctor? Why didn't he address him properly? If he didn't know a soldier – or how to speak to one – she was in the hands of foreigners, she couldn't be helped, where was she?

'Who are you?'

'My name is Dr Antoniadis.'

'I want to see my wife.'

'Let me explain to you.'

'Christ –'

'Here, please.' The man had a hand on his arm and Hal sat down on a chair in the long white corridor with the polished floors and cool blinds all along it.

'Is she dead?'

'No.'

'I can't, I'm sorry –'

'That's perfectly fine. You will see her. Let me, please, tell you the situation. Would you like some water?'

'Just tell me.'

'Your wife was shopping, with her friend, here in Nicosia.'

Hal fixed his eyes on the doctor's face.

'She was brought here at twelve o'clock. She was shot with a revolver. A hand gun. Do you understand?'

'Yes. Go on.'

'Twice. Here.' He gestured. 'In the stomach. I am sorry, sir, the baby inside is dead.'

He didn't care. He didn't care about the fucking baby. 'Tell me.'

'We have stopped the bleeding. She is unconscious. It's best if you know the situation. Please. Have some water.'

'I want to see her. Now.' Hal stood up.

The doctor stood up too. 'This way.'

The door was opened. Hal stepped into the white room. The air was suffused with bright, blurred light. He smelled disinfectant, mineral and sweet. Clara was lying on the bed. Her hair was the only dark thing in the room. It looked like a vision, to Hal.

The doctor was just behind his shoulder. Hal saw that she was breathing. A glass bottle, shining and full of liquid, hung above her. There were tubes going into her arms. Her shoulders were bare above the sheet, white bandages on her wrists, the backs of her hands. She had never been so still.

'Where are my daughters?' he said.

'They are safe.'

'But where?'

'They are here, in the hospital.'

Hal walked over to the bed. The frame of the bed was white. The pillows, blankets, sheets, table, floor – everything was white. Clara's hair and lashes were dark. Her mouth was red. There was a red stain on the sheet.

'She's still bleeding,' he said.

They sent him out.

He waited.

He sat in a chair in another room and a nurse brought him water and left the warm glass in front of him. He didn't know how long he sat there.

Another doctor came. An older man, in a suit. 'I'm afraid your wife is still very ill,' he said. 'The foetus is still inside her. Can you say with certainty how many weeks pregnant she is?'

'No. I don't know.'

'The bullet entered the placenta. The main thing has been to stop the haemorrhaging, do you understand?'

'Yes,' said Hal, thinking of tying off the stump of Taylor's leg on the beach, how fast the blood pumped from it onto the sand.

'We cannot think beyond keeping her stable for the moment. After that we'll see what to do about the pregnancy. I am very sorry.'

Hal looked at him. He had dark brown eyes behind glasses. The glasses made them seem bigger, peering at him. 'You can call the company lines at Episkopi,' said Hal. 'The battalion MO there, Major Godwin, he'll know how many weeks she is.'

The army sent people to help him. He didn't notice the things that were done for him. Nobody tried to make him leave.

They let him back into the room. It was empty – just the square room like a nightmare. His stomach dropped inside him, then her bed was pushed in past him – as if he were not there, just observing – rubber wheels on the polished floor. The bed was adjusted by the nurses in headdresses, who didn't look at him and left quietly afterwards. He didn't know what they had done to her out of the room, if she had nearly left him or if she was safe. She was in the same position. They had changed the sheets.

He sat down in the same chair. The doctor came in again and stood next to him. 'You can stay here now,' he said. 'We will make arrangements. Try not to worry.'

It was night-time now. He heard the wail of sirens at sunset. There had been gunfire outside, and the bells of police cars, but now it was quieter. He began to notice the building around him a little.

He could hear the business of the hospital, hurrying feet, voices and distant doors.

He sat in a chair by her bed, but not too close. At intervals, he didn't know how often, nurses would come in to check on Clara.

The checks were private, feminine work. When the nurses opened the door Hal would go to the window, looking out, far down into the street, where small cars passed the patrolling soldiers silently, until the door closed again. Through the night there were fewer cars in the street below, then none. Then after some time, the sky was paler above the buildings. The next time the nurse came, the pink sun was above the trees and roofs.

When she came back, it was not for Clara but for him: she had brought him tea. It was strong, Indian tea with condensed milk in a pale green cup with a saucer.

‘Thank you,’ said Hal, taking the cup politely, holding it in one hand near his thigh, like somebody at a tea party.

The nurse went away.

Strange, blank – he could hear cars again, trucks, people walking in the corridors, and there was Clara, lying there, not moving, in another day.

Frightened hot tears blinded him. He put the cup and saucer down on the floor, spilling the tea, clumsy, and pressed his palms to his eyes to get a hold of himself – except that instead his head went down onto his hands, bent over. More tears. Like a man before an altar, afraid, covering his face, he hid from the sight of her.

He prayed, but his prayers were just begging. He garbled silent fearful bargains behind his closed eyes, but it was too late for that. He already had God’s answer: his wife torn in half, his baby killed.

Later in the long morning, when Clara hadn’t woken still, but had moved her hand slightly and shifted in the bed, Hal went to see the girls.

They were on another floor, in an empty ward, sitting on the floor by a table where a sister was sewing. She handed them squares of coloured material and they pretended to sew, too. Hal looked through the glass door, down the long line of empty beds with folded blankets stacked on the ends of them, to where they were. He felt like a dead man, looking through glass into the living world.

The little girls were squatting, like people around a campfire, playing amongst the coloured felt near the legs of the sister, who bent down to them lovingly. Hal was far away, through the door, down the long line of beds. They looked the same, as far as he could see. They looked peaceful, intent.

He watched them for a little, flinching when they moved in case they saw him and were frightened. Then he went back to Clara.

In the middle of the day the first doctor, Dr Antoniadis, came and spoke to him. He put a hand on his shoulder. 'What is your Christian name?' he said.

'Hal.'

'And my name is Giorgios. We have a lady downstairs, she is asking for you.'

Evelyn Burroughs was standing in the middle of the vast lobby. Hal met her on the shining floor, stopping two feet away from her. He realised he was dirty and that he hadn't shaved. Evelyn was wearing a hat. Her nose was red. 'Hal, I'm so sorry.' She didn't meet his eye. 'I came as soon as I could. Is there any news?'

'Not at the moment.'

She looked at the floor. 'Good Lord. What a thing,' she said quietly.

They stood in silence.

'Now,' she said, her briskness was ironic, 'I've taken a room at the Ledra Palace. I shall collect the girls, if that's all right with you, and we'll go back there as it's home to them already. We'll try to make things as normal as possible, shall we? I shan't tell them anything. They're too little. They had an awful fright but I gather they're quite cheerful now.'

'Yes. Good. Thank you.'

'I'll keep popping by. And you're not to worry. Everybody is doing their best. How are the doctors?'

He couldn't speak; he was diminished. It was all he could do to stand there.

'Well,' she said, 'we're making sure she has the best care. I promise.'

She reached out a gloved hand, and put it on his, hanging at his side. She could have been his mother, closer than his mother had ever been, as close as anybody, as he had been to the soldier, Jenson, as he died, as close as he was to Clara when he was inside her. They had no secrets, no privacy.

'You look done in,' she said. 'If you change your clothes, and have a shave, you might feel better. Why don't you come with me?'

'Not now,' he said, trying to smile but wincing at the impossibility.

'I'll have some things sent over for you. I'm sure they'll let you have a room, or somewhere to change and clean up at least. A lot of people were brought in last night, after everything that went on, but I'm sure they'll find somewhere for you.'

He didn't know what she meant – *after everything that went on*.

In the afternoon Kirby – like a visitor from a different life – brought him a holdall, with clean clothes. They met in the lobby where Hal had spoken to Evelyn. Kirby was embarrassed and kept his eyes on the floor, shuffling and out of place. He didn't say a word apart from 'Sir' as he handed it over.

Hal shaved and changed his shirt in a long, tiled bathroom with a rubber curtain around the bath. The room echoed as he tapped the razor on the basin edge. The baby was dead inside her with a bullet in it. He didn't know how they would get it out.

Afterwards he sat by her bed again, regretting the brief time away from her.

In the afternoon she opened her eyes and looked at him, then closed them again.

In the evening the siren sounded for the curfew. Hal watched the streets clear as the nurses made intimate changes to her unmoving body. He heard the drips being changed. The glass bottles knocking against each other, instruments on the metal trolley. He watched the soldiers far below in the street. They looked like toy soldiers.

When he was a child, home from school for the holidays and alone again, he had played toy soldiers. His armies were vast and loved. At the back of the house, on the first floor, was a long landing, with doors on one side and cold windows on the other. The wooden floor had a runner down the middle, with brass fixings at each end, worn patches where the stitching had faded and gone. Hal would lie on his tummy with the lined-up battalions, their cannon and cavalry, all the flags, the minute courageous figures of his dreams. Above him, painted soldiers looked down from dull gilt frames all the way along the landing. They had seemed to smile at him. He had not felt alone. He had been surrounded by legions. But now it came suddenly and coldly into his head that, really, there had been nobody else there with him at all.

They brought a camp bed into the room and he slept on it, flat on his front with his arms thrown out, like a baby learning to walk, a sleep like death. He woke up at two when she said his name, but she hadn't moved; he was frightened he had dreamed she'd said his name because she was dying, and he was awake after that.

He lay in the dark listening to her breathing. Her breath

was shallow. He journeyed with her, each breath, in and out, then they waited together – too long – until once more, in . . .

Her hand had been cool when she'd come in from the garden with the flowers. She had smiled and held it out to him. 'Yes. Clara,' she'd said. He had felt the rain from the wet flowers on his fingers.

Her small breath travelled in and out. At their wedding they had walked under shining swords. He had made promises to her and the promises had held at first, untested. But when she had come off the ship to meet him, she had been so bright, and she had followed him. He had taken her into this place, and then he had deserted her.

The hours of the night went by fearfully and in dishonour.

The next day she was awake some of the time and they said words to each other. Hal didn't say any of the words he really had in his head. He said, 'Hello,' and 'Ssh'.

She looked out of her dark blue eyes softly, but her voice was a whisper. 'The girls?'

'They're fine. Don't worry.'

'Gracie? Gracie died.'

He held her gaze, nodded.

She seemed to wander. 'Am I all right?' she said. 'Is it all right?'

Her tongue was swollen, trying to lick her dry lips. The nurse dabbed at than with wet cotton wool. Hal felt it was an intrusion to watch, and looked away.

He spoke to her mother, in England, on the telephone in Dr Antoniadis's office. Moira and George had been told already, by the army, and the shooting was in the English papers – in the news all around the world. She had been told what time his call would come, and answered the telephone immediately it rang.

'I'm sorry George can't come to the phone,' she said. 'He just can't bear to.'

She was brave, asking him questions that he had a feeling she had written down first. Hal pretended confidence, reassuring her, waiting while she cried and recovered. He expected her to blame him, was prepared for it, and would not have defended himself, but Moira was subdued; her misery was beyond blame. She asked after the girls.

'They're well. They're fine.'

'Thank you, Hal,' she said. 'Thank you,' and Hal, in his shame, couldn't answer her.

The next day they measured the risk of infection against the risk of more haemorrhaging and decided to operate. The operating theatre was on the fourth floor. Hal watched while they made her ready, but didn't follow when they took her away. He stood in her empty room blankly, as the sound of the nurses, and the wheels of the bed, went away from him down the corridor.

Evelyn came for him. She took his arm, linking hers through his, and walked him out of the hospital into the street. They sat in the dining room at the hotel. It was where Clara and Gracie had sat – he didn't know – and Evelyn ordered food for him. He ate some of it.

'There's no reason to suppose it won't be all right,' she said.

After lunch they walked back to the hospital and sat together, waiting. There was dust in the sunlight.

Evelyn took a paperback from her handbag. 'Shall I tell you what it's about?' she said.

'Please.'

'Well, so far, we've met a fearfully glamorous viscount – it's set in the late seventeenth century, you see, and he's throwing away his fortune on wine, women and song until one day he meets a beautiful heiress . . .'

Clara did not die that day. She lived. They cleared out the torn placenta, her damaged womb, ovaries, and the foetus, which would have been almost eleven inches long, had it been stretched out, and a boy.

The patching up of a body is fairly crude, a matter of closing holes and sealing tubes, cutting away the things that are no longer needed; they had to put a lot of blood into her veins for all the blood she was losing.

The cut, from her navel to her pubic bone, was sewn neatly closed, but messier and wider where it met the bullet wounds. It was dressed with pads and gauze. When they told him she was alive, Evelyn cried, as if unused to it, turning her face away from him. Hal shut his eyes and saw an infinity of relief.

It occurred to him to thank his dead son for protecting his mother; if that was a man's first duty, that small life had performed it. There was more honour in its sacrifice than in any action of Hal's since his own conception.

Chapter Five

Then there was the telling. She had been in an in-between place, protected. He thought she was too weak still, and would have never said it out loud but 'The baby died,' she said, on the morning of the fifth day. 'I don't think it was ever going to stay. What did they do with it?'

'I don't know.'

'Was it a boy?'

'Yes.'

'I knew it was a boy.'

Her forehead was sweating. She was very pale.

Hal was close to her. He couldn't look at her face but dropped his head to avoid her.

'I'm sorry,' he said.

She slept after that.

The next afternoon, Hal brought the girls in to see her. They overlooked him in their eagerness to get to her. He had been right; they were unsettled by his reappearance. Clara had asked him to bring her makeup in, too. They waited outside for her to brush her hair and put on red lipstick. Evelyn had sent a bed-jacket with him, made of Greek cotton.

Hal kept the girls from climbing on the bed. Lottie tugged

at her mother's hand, jumping, while Meg stood close to her with her fingers in her mouth, listening.

He watched them, guarding her jealously from their love.

She fell asleep suddenly, and the girls were frightened. Hal was frightened too, and wanted them gone. 'Meg, kiss your mother, it's time to go home,' he said. The word 'home' was wrong, of course.

He pulled the girls from her, pushing them out of the door, not caring if they cried. He looked up and down the empty corridor; there was no nurse. He pushed the door against their small bodies. She hadn't wakened. He went back to the bed, with the girls crying in the corridor, and felt her head. It was both hot and cold. Quickly, quickly –

In the corridor he picked up one child and grabbed the other's hand.

'Come along, Mrs Burroughs now.'

He went down the empty corridor, feeling his panic in his chest. At the end of the corridor he saw a nurse. He knew this one, she didn't speak English – he thought suddenly of Davis; he would know the right words.

'My wife,' he said, pointing, 'my wife. Should she be asleep all the time? Please? Can you go? Can you check on her?'

The nurse smiled at him. She was going the wrong way – she hadn't turned round.

'Clara Treherne,' he said, pointing again. 'Please –'

She nodded kindly. 'Yes,' she said. 'Yes.'

He took the girls down to Evelyn and left them with her. They cried and had to be carried, wriggling. Hal didn't have any feeling for them.

'How is she?' said Evelyn, trying to wrestle them from him.

'I don't know,' he said, turning to leave.

'Hal, this is Captain Wallace, from Brigade HQ.'

'Yes?'

The captain, a pale man of about twenty-six with white lashes, stepped forward and saluted him.

'Major Treherne, would you be able to come with me, sir?'

'Now?'

The girls' cries made it hard to hear. Lottie gave a scream. Evelyn was trying to leave with them and Hal was distracted.

'Here,' he said, picking up Lottie round her middle and following Evelyn, who held Meg firmly by the hand, towards the entrance.

'Thank you,' said Evelyn. 'It's just to the car.'

The captain followed them, at Hal's shoulder. He was embarrassed. 'Sir, I've orders to accompany you to HQ, if it's convenient. There are a few things to sort out with your leave, sir, paperwork –'

'It isn't convenient.'

Captain Wallace opened the doors of the hospital for them and Hal and Evelyn got to the kerb, where a car and driver were waiting.

'My goodness, what a handful!' said Evelyn.

Hal bundled Lottie into the back of the car.

'You ought to go with him, Hal. It's just boring old procedure –'

'I'm terribly sorry, sir, but we won't take up much of your time, sir,' said the captain, holding the door of the car, and looking at Evelyn, struggling with Meg, as if he'd never seen a child before.

'All right. Yes. Come on, then,' said Hal, slamming the door after them.

The car pulled away and the girls' screams couldn't be heard.

'Is Mrs Treherne feeling better, sir?' asked the captain.

Hal nodded, but did not answer. The man had no business asking him.

It was a very short drive. Brigade HQ was a colonnaded building near the Archbishop's Palace.

Hal followed Captain Wallace into the peace of the shadowy entrance. Sentry guards saluted them. After the white foreign hospital the change in surroundings was profound. They entered corridors that were panelled and warm; their feet made an ordered rhythm. Typewriters could be heard in ante-rooms from the long corridors, which were lined with trophies and smudged photographs of past ceremonies. Even needing to get back to Clara, the arms of familiarity encircled him, as if lulling him into a dream state.

They came to a door.

The captain knocked twice and opened it.

The brigadier stood up.

'Brigadier Bryce-Stephens, this is Major Treherne,' said the captain, saluted again and left.

Hal stepped into the room.

'No need to stand on ceremony. Please. Sit down.'

Brigadier Bryce-Stephens was about fifty, his uniform, thick with medals, immaculate and at odds with his face, which was very tanned. A broad nose that had been broken at some point and re-set poorly.

'Can I say how sorry I am about what has happened to your wife?' His voice had the short flattened vowels of an aristocrat.

'Thank you.'

'We've been doing everything we can here to make things

run as smoothly as possible for you. I've spoken to Colonel Burroughs, at Episkopi, several times. Needless to say, everyone there has been eager for news. Mrs Burroughs has been a help, I understand?'

'Yes, she's been very kind indeed.'

'Can we offer you anything to drink? A cup of tea? Something stronger?'

'No. Thank you.'

'You're sure?'

'I should get back.'

The image of Clara, slipping away from him into mysterious sleep, played in front of his eyes. It didn't have the urgency it had before.

'I understand. I can't imagine how difficult it must have been for you. The funeral for Mrs Bundle will be on Friday. Will your wife be well enough to attend?'

Three days.

'I don't think so. She can't sit up properly.'

'We've received a number of cards from well-wishers. I shall have them sent on to you. Many of them are from England, not just people in the services. The general public . . .' He adjusted a pen on his desk. 'I don't know how much you've had a chance to think about what might happen next.'

'Sir?'

'Will your wife be going back to Episkopi Garrison with you?'

'No. She's going home.'

It was as if someone else had said it for him. The decision had been made.

'We'll need to arrange transport for her. She won't find a sea voyage very pleasant. I'll see what I can do to get her back by air. I'll have a word with the RAF, see if we can cadge a lift on a Valetta.'

Cadge a lift on a Valetta.

'Will it go directly back?'

'I would have thought so. Although with this Canal business, everything's rather up in the air at the moment, you understand.'

'She's not at all well.'

'Of course she won't travel until she's strong enough. Have they said when they'll discharge her?'

'No.'

'Which brings us to the question of your leave. I understand you were due a week, but not before the middle of November.'

'Yes.'

'The incident happened on Friday. Your company is on ops this week?'

'Yes, sir, for the next week and a half.'

There was silence.

'A shame things didn't fall the other way.'

'Sir?'

'There was rioting in Limassol yesterday. We're spreading ourselves pretty thin at the moment, as I'm sure you'll appreciate. Egypt –'

'There was rioting?'

'Yes. The schoolchildren. Not any more.'

Hal spoke quietly: 'The schoolchildren were rioting in Limassol.' He didn't know why he repeated it, just to hear the sound of the words in his mouth, he thought, picturing the schoolchildren, his men trying to stop them.

'It's calmed down now.'

'Fatalities?'

'None I'm aware of.'

'And here?'

'It was unfortunate here. Things got a little overheated. It was a despicable and cowardly act. EOKA deny all knowledge, of course, but it's hard to believe it was coincidence that the wives of British Army officers were the targets. It's been difficult for our boys to control themselves as they ought. As I say, it's all calmed down now. We'll lift the curfew tonight. Feeling was running high, after what happened to Mrs Bundle and to your wife. You know.'

Yes. Hal knew. The schoolchildren were rioting. Clara, with the long cut in her abdomen, their baby dead, could cadge a lift back to England on a Valetta.

'I can promise you I'll do my best to make sure your wife is given every care, every consideration. We'll see her safely home, Major. Normally we'd be dealing with this sort of thing at battalion level, of course, but in view of the circumstances, we'd like to give you a few extra days. I can extend your leave until next weekend. Your 2 i/c is a Captain Innes, is that right?'

'Yes, sir. Mark Innes. He's very capable.'

'Jolly good. I'm sure they'll get along without you for another week.'

Hal looked at the brigadier across the desk, knowing he was to be thanked.

He watched the people on the sunny pavements from the car.

The inside of the hospital was familiar to him, too, and like a homecoming. The reflections on the shiny floors, the echoing sounds – metal bowls being stacked, trolleys pushed through swinging doors – the sight of Clara's door as he approached, the weak sick fear he felt on opening it: all were known to him.

He went inside. Clara was sitting up in bed in Evelyn's bed-jacket. Hal felt absurd surprise at her being there; it washed through him. He wanted to say – to say something, to say –

'Hello. Feeling better?'

'A bit,' she said.

'You fell asleep. I was worried.'

'How were the girls?'

He had a picture of himself manhandling them into the car. 'Fine,' he said.

He went over to her, but didn't sit down. Inside this limiting white room he ought to be able to find words to say to her. 'They've given me extra leave. Until next Saturday.'

'What then?'

'Well, I'll go back to Episkopi.'

He looked down, tried not to look at the blankets where they covered her bandages. 'I thought you might want to go back to England,' he said.

'Without you?'

He nodded.

'Oh.'

Her blue look flickered towards him, and then, as if seeing something harmful, glanced away. 'I do want to go home,' she said.

As he was leaving, she said, 'Hal, would you go to the funeral? Gracie's funeral?'

'Yes, if you want me to.'

'Please.'

Chapter Six

Gracie might have been a general for all the soldiers there, mixing with the civilians amongst the gravestones. Major David Bundle stood at the graveside. His younger sons were not present, just the two older ones – little boys still – in dark suits, and next to them Gracie's mother, a wider version of Gracie, holding their hands.

Kirby drove him to the British cemetery outside the city. The watered grass grew neatly around the edges of the gravestones laid out in long rows. Hal was standing away from the family, with people he did not know. Soldiers carried the small coffin. The Cyprus sun shone onto them: their buttons, medals and buckles. It spread the smell of the grass and the flowers through the people.

There was silence as the coffin was lowered. The graveyard was very exposed, on flat ground in the glaring sun. A hot wind came sideways through the crowd, blowing the pages of the Bible the chaplain was holding.

Hal stood upright, following the coffin with his eyes as it went slowly down into the deep grave. He had not known her.

The coffin settled and was left alone in the ground. The chaplain began to read. '"I am the resurrection and the life," saith the Lord; "he that believeth in me, though he were dead, yet shall he live . . ."'

Hal looked from soldiers, to mourners, to chaplain; and at David Bundle, whose face had the same blank broken shock he felt himself, and thought what a helpless scrabbling for dignity it was, to put Gracie's small body amongst those of fighting men. Would it help her husband to have her grave amongst the noble, not the commonplace, dead? Gracie hadn't known she was bravely risking her life. She hadn't known she would be honoured for it. He thought of his letter to Jenson's parents, his search for heroism in the man's life or death, his failure in finding it. Jenson had been good with horses. Gracie had been kind to Hal's wife.

'"I know that my Redeemer liveth . . ."'

Afterwards, as the people moved away, Hal, aware of his duty, spoke briefly to David Bundle. He was repelled by him, as if by the brief contact they could be magically reversed, and it would be he whose wife was dead, not the other man.

David was fired up with the energy of his grief, wishing Hal well and telling him how often Gracie had written to him about Clara. 'Thank God *she* was spared,' he said, with apparent joy, grasping Hal's hand in both of his. 'Thank God.'

Hal let the family leave, and those who knew them well, too.

He walked slowly across the huge cemetery, past the rows of graves until, stopping, he read:

Capt. Thomas S. Thurlough

1888–1917

A gallant soldier, and a very perfect gentleman

He stood looking at the headstone for some minutes. He gave a short nod towards that favoured soldier, in envy and regret, and walked on.

Far in the distance he could see the mountains beautifully encircling them all.

The entrance to the cemetery was a tall iron gate set in a long black railing, like a garden square in London. Hal walked through it as light dust floated round the feet of the people getting into their various vehicles to drive back to the city. He had left Kirby there, a few hundred yards along the road, but he saw Captain Wallace, going against the crowd, approaching him.

'Sir?'

'What is it?'

'It's important you come with me, sir. I'm terribly sorry to bother you again.'

'What's this about?'

'Let's talk about it at HQ. The brigadier is waiting.'

Brigadier Bryce-Stephens met him at the door to his office this time and closed it, shaking his hand very firmly. 'Hal, there's been a change of plan. I've spoken to Colonel Burroughs, the situation in Limassol requires your presence. Luckily, this has coincided with my happening to procure a place for your wife on a plane. It's a Foreign Office plane – a lot more comfortable than she might have been – landing here at RAF Nicosia this afternoon. She can be at home or in hospital by this evening.'

His urgency and sureness were infectious and Hal, adjusting, felt the pull of unseen mechanisms. 'Just a moment,' he said.

'I'm sorry to spring this on you. Do sit down.'

'I'll stand. What situation in Limassol, sir?'

'I don't know the details. My office had a communication from your CO – I'm sure he'll fill you in on your return. The point is there's a change of plan. How is your wife?'

'To travel?'

'Is she well enough?'

'I've no idea. I'd have to –'

'The hospital had been planning to discharge her in a few days anyway. I believe she's anxious to be reunited with your daughters.'

'How do you know all this?'

'My office have spoken to a Dr . . .' he went to his desk, glancing down '. . . Antoniadis there.' He glanced up at Hal. 'There's a degree of urgency about this. Of course you wouldn't know all these things, being so much at the hospital, but I can assure you you're needed.'

It was resolved then. Hal said, 'What time will the plane be ready, sir?'

'Around eighteen hundred hours.'

'Then I'll leave straight after I've seen them off.'

Hal had Kirby drop him at the hospital, then dispatched him to the hotel to see about the packing. He didn't go to Clara immediately; first he found Dr Antoniadis.

'Yes, we were visited by two men, soldiers. I don't remember the names. It is very important for Mrs Treherne to go back to England, I understand this.'

'But is she all right to travel?'

'Yes, Mr Treherne, if she must.'

'You're sure?'

'There is no danger.'

'No danger?'

'No big danger, sir, of infection or haemorrhage, if she is sensible. But she is very weak. She needs to rest now as much as she can.'

So it was done. Clara and the girls would go back to England, and Hal would resume his duty.

Chapter Seven

They drove to RAF Nicosia as the sun went down. The sky was flame-filled and violent.

Clara and Hal sat in the car with the girls between them, the luggage piled next to Kirby and behind the back seat. Hal had his arm round both girls to stop them climbing on Clara. Dressing and the walk to the car had been very slow. She was leaning back now, as if she had no muscles at all in her body, and her hands were held over herself for protection, but when he had told her she was to leave that day, she had looked at him, alive suddenly and lit up, and said, 'Going home today?'

The bright colours in the enormous sunset faded slowly. They drove into the airfield, stopping for the sentry guards and checkpoints.

The car turned slowly past concrete buildings that had corrugated curved tops and breeze-block hangars divided by thin roads. The runways tapered into far straight distance, spotted with lights just showing, and black mountains behind.

The car stopped. Hal went round and opened Clara's door so that she could hold on to him getting out.

They were met by a flight lieutenant and a man from the

Foreign Office, who had flown in earlier that day with a minister on the plane that would take Clara home. They all stood in a tight group, lit by the big low sun, the half-disc slowly sinking.

Kirby was fumbling with luggage and pieces of paper as an RAF corporal tried to organise them. Clara was standing as if in a daze, her hands hanging by her sides, gazing at the plane – not a Valetta after all, but a twin-engined Hastings, with blocks under its wheels – waiting five hundred yards away from them. The girls were clinging to her skirts, motionless too. Hal looked at them, and then back over his shoulder towards the exit road to the gate and the sentries standing at it.

The luggage was in two piles now, his one or two things and his family's. Kirby had started to put Hal's back into the car, sighing at the effort.

Clara turned to him. 'Hal?' she said.

The man from the Foreign Office was handing over some papers to the flight lieutenant, neither of them paying his wife or himself any attention.

'What are you doing, Kirby?' said Hal.

'Sir?' Kirby paused in his labours, perplexed.

'All of those things are going on the plane.'

'No, sir, these ones are yours.'

'No. All of them on the plane, please.'

'Sir . . .'

'Just a moment.' Hal turned to the flight lieutenant. 'I hope there hasn't been another mess made over these arrangements. Would you check your manifest? The four of us are travelling. I'm sure it was made clear.'

The flight lieutenant blinked.

'No, sir. I understood Mrs Treherne would be travelling with the children alone.'

'You understood wrong. Does it seem likely to you that an ill woman would make the journey alone, with two children to look after?'

'The manifest –'

'See to it, then, please,' said Hal. Then, 'Kirby, look sharp,' and 'Clara, you ought to be sitting down. Lieutenant, when are we scheduled to leave?'

'Eighteen thirty, sir.'

'Can't you make it any sooner?'

'No, sir. They're refuelling now, sir.'

'Come on, Lieutenant, get on with it. My wife needs to sit down. Where?'

'I'm sorry, sir. Of course. Follow me, sir.'

Hal supported Clara as they walked. She held his arm, looking up at him. As they followed the lieutenant, she said, 'Hal?' but Hal was turned away from her, collecting up the girls, and ignored her.

As he straightened, with Lottie in his arms, Kirby caught up with him. 'Sir – sir?'

Hal stopped. He turned slowly. Kirby's face, pale, for all its hours in the sun, was damp and pasty; his eyebrows were knitted together. 'Sir. You're not going, sir.'

'Would you get those things loaded? Thanks very much.' Kirby didn't move. Hal waited, looking him in the eye. 'That's all, thank you, Kirby,' he said.

Kirby turned, and did as he was told.

They were put into a hot little office where an RAF corporal was typing up letters with two fingers. They sat on a very narrow wooden bench. The girls were clambering everywhere, trying to get on Clara's lap and being deflected by Hal. She had her eyes half shut, leaning back, but then she lowered her head and looked at him: 'Hal, what's happening?'

He didn't answer. She was breathing lightly through her mouth. She rested her head again. The corporal was trying to align the forms he was typing. He was fiddling with the carriage release, exasperated, tugging at the paper. Every now and then one of the metal arms would stick, pointing upwards, and he would free it, irritable, then bash away at the keys again.

Hal waited for the phone to ring. They had the manifest, no doubt in triplicate. The lieutenant wouldn't take long to get through to somebody at HQ. This was madness. The phone would ring – but the phone sat silently next to the typewriter, as the corporal bashed away at the keys with his two flat-ended fingers.

Hal watched the seconds going by on the clock above his head. The thin second hand sticking, moving, sticking. It was eleven minutes past six. It was eleven and a half minutes past six. It was twelve minutes past six –

The door opened. 'Sir?' The lieutenant looked concerned. He had a sheaf of papers in his hand. Hal's mind was numb. 'They're about ready for you to board,' he said.

Then the telephone rang. 'Sir?' said the lieutenant, over the loud ringing.

The corporal picked up the phone, 'Corporal Billings . . . In hangar five? You must be joking. Nobody told me about it.'

'Sir?' said the lieutenant again.

Hal stood up. 'Girls,' he said, 'come along. Clara?'

He held out his hand to her, and she took it.

* * *

The inside of the plane had been modified from military to government use. There were double rows of seats facing front, instead of benches, but the rest of it was untouched. The walls were bolted metal and very noisy when the engines started their raw deep sound.

Clara was pale, uncomfortable against the steep back of her seat. She had her feet up on a trunk that was lashed to the plane floor, as close to curled up as she could be. Hal had rolled up his jacket for her head and put it between her shoulder and the window; he sat behind her with the girls so that he could hold on to them.

Lottie put her hands over her ears and Meg reached forwards, trying to stretch her fingers between the seats to touch her mother. Hal patted the small of her back, but she pulled away from him, and went forward, to climb onto the seat in front. Hal stopped her, put her under his arm, and went forward to sit next to Clara.

'There,' he said, pulling Lottie up too, so that they were both on his lap. 'Be careful of Mummy,' he said, holding them. 'Sit still.' He glanced at Clara, who was resting her head on the rolled-up jacket. Her lashes fluttered closed.

Through the thick dirty glass he watched the flight lieutenant running back towards the hangar, and the short canvas straps of the rolled-up shades swung as the plane began to move. They made a wide, slowly rocking arc across the tarmac, then paused at the head of the runway.

'Are you frightened?' he asked.

'No, I'm not frightened,' Clara said, as the engines reached a pitch.

He looked ahead again. Past the pilot's shoulder, through the glass of the cockpit, he could see the gently bobbing nose of the aircraft. Lights shone a straight path. They started along it.

As the plane lurched into its steep take-off, Hal held both girls firmly. Lottie cried out, once, at the noise, but then was quiet. The plane rose and soared. He felt the high beauty of flight mix with the sharp falling realisation of what he had done.

He looked down: no jeeps fanning out over the tarmac, no signallers spelling out his crime, nothing but the fast-rising plane and the air, bigger and bigger, around it. He looked over his shoulder, behind, to see the buildings of the airfield slanted, diminishing, the wide evening all around and beneath them. Cyprus dipped, tilted, and went away from him.

Outside the aeroplane it was quite dark; there was no sense of height, or even of speed, and inside, the main part of the plane was unlit. In the cockpit ahead of him he could see the instruments, and the pilot silhouetted. Even the radio had fallen silent, so that just the sound of the engines, soon familiar, wrapped around them.

His daughters, surrendered and delivered to him by sleep, were heavy in his arms. Clara opened her eyes. 'I'm cold.'

It was cold, up in the sky, with just metal between them and the air.

'Jacket,' he said, and she took his jacket from under her head, and shifted over so that she was resting on his shoulder. She opened the stiff green wool jacket, with weak hands, and he laid it over them.

She went back to sleep, under it, almost immediately, and

Hal, with the warmth of all three of them touching him, turned his eyes to the window, where nothing could be seen at all. He would not move, he must not wake them; he would have hours of night-time with them, over the sea.

PART FOUR

England, October

Chapter One

They came down the metal steps of the plane at RAF Boscombe Down, after midnight. There was a breeze, a little chilly, smelling of petrol and cut grass. The sky above was a deep, quiet dark. Everything around them – aeroplane hangars, RAF vehicles – lay in darkness too, a variety of shadows, or lone caged bulbs to light the way, and occasional night-time voices, or boots on the tarmac muffled in the late-shift feeling of the deep night.

Both children were asleep. Hal carried Lottie, and the officer who had met them carried Meg, her baby cheek on his unknown arm. 'Welcome home, sir,' he had said, coming up the steps to help them.

Hal didn't know what he'd expected; he had a fugitive's anxiety of discovery, but the officer, very young and respectful, was only concerned with their comfort.

A car rolled towards them out of the darkness, its head-lights fanned across the underside of the plane.

'Sir, madam? Come with me, please.'

Car doors were opened, loud in the stillness. The family and the officer crowded into the small car for the short drive, a brief imprisonment, the compression of feet, close breaths in the cramped cold space.

At the edge of the airfield – Hal could see the perimeter

gate now – there was another building and the car stopped by it. Through the wet glass Hal saw a door open. A man was silhouetted against the lighted interior. He had a hat, a dark civilian suit, slightly stooping narrow shoulders – Clara cried out, 'Daddy!'

She was out of the car, away from Hal – George came to meet her, steadying her – and she was in her father's arms. 'Darling girl. Here, here, I have the car. Just over here –'

Hal got out slowly, protecting Lottie's head from the doorframe with his hand.

Clara walked as close to her father as she could, his arms supported her. Hal followed them, carrying Lottie, the officer with Meg next to him. At his car, George Ward turned to him. He spoke with perfect civility. 'Hal, welcome back. You must be exhausted.'

'Hello, sir. Not too bad.'

George didn't meet his eye. 'Oh, good . . . good.'

He knows. How could he know? Have they spoken to him?

'Clara's played out,' said Hal.

'Yes,' he said shortly. Then, 'Not too long now.'

It seemed to take an hour, the loading of them all and the strapping on of cases to the car. It was a Riley, built for beauty not luggage, and Hal took charge, with the flight lieutenant helping him, pulling the straps hard into tension, while George Ward stood by with his hands in his pockets, whistling through his teeth, an impractical man, and Clara sat bundled in a blanket in the back with the sleeping girls.

'There'll be nobody on the road, at least. Your mother waited up, of course. We shouldn't be too long.'

* * *

Hal sat next to her father in the front. Clara spread the blanket over Meg and Lottie as the officer said goodbye through the driver's window. Light slanted in from the open office door, striking the backs of the seats, illuminating the men in front. The back of Hal's neck, tanned, and the hair razored close into it, gleamed where it was bleached by the sun; her father's neck was white. Clara could just see the familiar jut of his nose in semi-profile, and pale, clean-shaven cheek. His hair, dark and brilliantined, was exactly the same as in her childhood. She closed her eyes.

The car glided past the guards, and then the sentry posts, finding the exits unhindered. It felt unreal.

Theirs was the only car on the road. They had left the camp behind and were in the deep emptiness of Salisbury Plain. The narrow road was lit just ahead by the wide yellow beams of the headlights, and inside the car Hal could see the wooden dashboard and George Ward's pale hands on the wheel.

Outside, just nearby, was the cool enormous mass of Stonehenge. He knew the stones, had touched them, and didn't have to see it. He thought of them rising from the bare land, and remembered his hands, hot from running, flat against the rock, when one summer day he had played amongst them as a child. He must have been very young, because for a long time he had thought the stones had been raised by King Arthur. He had pictured them, dragged across the plough and grassy fields by teams of shires, straining and snorting in their harness against the great weight as they travelled, overseen by knights. The stones had hummed beneath his hands with the magic of the long centuries.

His own house – his parents' – was less than twenty

miles to the west. The plain, in familiar vastness, was around him.

Hal felt the English night and his own soul greeting it with the quiet recognition of return, but he had stolen home uninvited. Connected and unconnected, he had cut himself off from welcome.

The Wards' was the only village house lit up at half past two in the morning. Moira Ward had heard the car coming through the village, threw open the door to meet them and all her greetings were made in half-whispers, muted exclamations of fearful delight – Clara home, but wounded. Hal, an even bigger presence than she remembered, and the girls – so brown!

Hal and George reached into the back to pick up a girl each.

'Mummy!'

'Darling!'

They all hugged and whispered over one another and Hal, after surrendering Lottie to Moira's arms, began to unstrap the cases.

The family – and Hal – went into the house and closed the door.

Inside, with more whispers, journeys up and down stairs to fetch things and feminine half-tearful kindness, they were all settled into various bedrooms, practical things saving them from the harder ones, and concern for Clara over everything. She went straight to bed – helped upstairs by her parents, with Hal behind – and gave the care of the girls to her mother.

The house went to sleep, each person, one by one.

Hal closed the door at last behind them. Clara was lying down, drifting. It was a kind room, with flowers on the walls and lace along the tops of the polished wooden furniture. He stood with his back to the door.

He was fully dressed still. The cases on the floor were dark hard battered things, only Clara's spilling open in pretty confusion, rummaged through to find her nightdress.

Hal took off his shoes so as not to disturb her, although the floor was carpeted. He went over to the window. It overlooked the garden. He could just hear her parents' voices through the walls, or along the wooden boards and skirtings. He opened the window, the frame stuck slightly, then smoothly rolled up with the sash-cord holding.

The night smelled of wet woods, grass and fallen leaves, with a chill to the air, sharp and welcome. There was the smell of woodsmoke too, which he had always loved. He separated that – bonfires and autumn – from the other burning smell, which wasn't real. He could hear the slow whisper of the trees and there was water, even in the air, quiet wood and water; sap, wet flowers, soil, lawn, all living in the vague night. Some way off, he heard an owl.

He looked back at the bed. Clara's eyes were closed. He went over to her and knelt at her side.

It was dark and he couldn't see her clearly, but he felt her presence; the clean paleness of her skin, her hands tucked into the warmth inside the covers. She was surrounded by pillows and quilts, all the different soft things that make up an English bed. He had brought her home safely, at least.

Moira, George and the girls sat around the kitchen table, the breakfast things disordered on the oilcloth – boiled eggs, toast, teapot, the mismatched plates and cups of a life of family meals and family spillages.

'I'll let them sleep,' said Moira. 'The doctor isn't coming until ten o'clock.'

'Extraordinary they gave Hal leave with this Suez business,' said George, reaching for the toast rack. 'Even with Clara, you'd think they'd have had him stay.'

The newspaper, thick, folded over, lay amongst the crumbs and butter knives. Under Imperial and Foreign news, the inky headline said: 'NAVY SENDING CARRIERS TO CYPRUS'. Clara's brother, James, was on his way from Malaya, on a troop carrier in the Indian Ocean.

'Everyone in on the fight except Hal,' said George, wiping his mouth with his napkin and reaching for the paper again. There was outrage in his every quiet word and in each small movement he made.

Clara had suffered this unspeakable attack, James was still away, but Hal was here, unscathed. George's dislike of Hal's profession and, by association, Hal, had been subjugated by Clara's happiness. Now, with her injury, it found purchase.

The twins were next to one another, in bibs, their chins barely above the table, having egg and soldiers distributed between them by Moira, who was out of practice and delighted by them.

'Here, Meg, let Granny do it,' she was saying, and 'Careful, careful, well done! Mummy later. Mummy's tired now.'

Then the telephone rang.

George stood up, brushing off his trousers, and left the room.

'Mummy!' said Lottie.

'Yes, we'll go up and see Mummy and Daddy in a minute,' said Moira.

Then the sound of George's feet along the passage again.

'It was Hal's father. For him. Had to tell him he was still in bed – he didn't like that much. Almost slammed the phone down.'

'Really?' said Moira vaguely, wiping Lottie's fingers.

Moira, Lottie and Meg knocked gently on Clara's door and opened it. Moira let the girls go in. They were shy at first, then jumping and scrambling up.

'Careful!' She stayed on the landing.

Clara pulled herself to sitting, wincing at the sudden pain, and using her arms to take her weight. 'Hello, darlings,' she said. 'Come in, Mummy . . . It's all right, Hal isn't here.'

Moira put her head round the door. 'Oh? Where is he, then?'

'I don't know. Perhaps he's gone for a walk.'

It wasn't until late morning, after the doctor had left, that they began to think he had gone. It was on all their minds that he wasn't there. Occasionally one of them would say, 'He still hasn't come back,' or 'No word from Hal?' but, apart from that, they all fell into their closeness and the looking after of one another quite comfortably.

Major (Ret'd) Peter Jameson drove from Warminster to the Wards' village house in the Buckinghamshire valley. It was a damp October day and he had to keep wiping the inside of his windscreen with the chamois he kept in the car, a Rover, especially for the purpose. He had been sent out on these recces before, but he'd never had to chase down a major. It was mostly subalterns, once a captain. He had something of a talent for understanding. They felt understood; they came back.

It was a pretty house, he thought as he pushed open the gate, went up the stone path and knocked. A woman in an overall opened the door.

'Good morning, sir,' she said.

'Good morning. I'm looking for Major Henry Treherne.'

'Yes, sir, just a minute.'

Another woman came to the door, attractive in a dark grey wool dress. The wife's mother, he guessed. She seemed very nervous.

'You're looking for my son-in-law. He's not here.'

'Do you know where he is?'

'I'm sorry, you are?'

Jameson smiled as warmly as he could. 'My name's Jameson. Like the whisky. Major (Retired) Peter Jameson.'

'Yes. Do you have business with Hal?'

'Hal? Ah. Yes. Look, I'm sorry to land on you unannounced. Do you think I might come in?'

Clara was in the drawing room making scrapbooks with the girls. She sat in an armchair, with them at her feet. It hurt her to lean forward and she did it stiffly. She looked up as Moira came in with Jameson.

'Darling, this is Mr Jameson – I'm sorry, Retired Major –'

'You don't need to bother with all that. How d'you do?'

'My daughter, Clara.'

'Hello,' said Clara.

The little girls looked up with round eyes. Light scraps of old magazines lay about them, small brushes from the gluepot in their fists.

'He's looking for Hal.'

'You don't know where he is, I suppose?' said Jameson.

'Should I? I thought there must be some army . . .'

'If there was, I'd know about it,' said Jameson, his cheerfulness fading. 'It's rather awkward. It seems he left Cyprus with you last night unofficially.'

He noted their shock seemed genuine. 'You didn't know?'

'No,' said Clara, slowly, her eyes fixed on his face as she absorbed this.

'Won't you sit down?' said Moira, and went to the door, calling, 'George!'

Jameson sat on the edge of a chair opposite Clara.

'I don't understand,' she said. 'Are you saying he isn't on leave?'

'Yes.'

'But that can't be right. He had compassionate leave. Because of me.'

'Yes, he did –'

George came into the room. Jameson stood up and they shook hands, introducing themselves.

'Nobody knows where Hal is,' said Moira, by way of explanation.

'He was here last night,' said George.

'But he's not here now.'

'Well, that's very odd.'

'Clara?'

Clara's eyes were wide. 'I don't know. We went to sleep. I went to sleep . . . I haven't –' She stopped, looking down suddenly and fiddling with the paper scraps scattering the carpet.

'I understand this is completely out of character?' said Jameson.

'Completely,' said Clara, shortly, not looking up.

'I just want to have a chat with him. We might be able to sort things out quite simply. But we need to find him.'

Clara began to paste glue onto the thick card pages of the scrapbook.

George spoke. His voice was quiet and deliberate, not wanting to create drama. 'This is serious, then?'

A short pause.

'Yes,' said Jameson.

A quick glance passed between Clara and her mother.

'My daughter has been through a horrible time recently. She's still very weak. Hal will worry about her, I'm sure that he'll be in touch as soon as – well, very soon.'

'Have you spoken to his parents?' said George. 'You might want to try there.'

'Yes. This morning. No luck.'

Moira stood back slightly, making the door available. 'Would you leave us a telephone number, in case we hear anything?'

Shortly afterwards Jameson, taking the hint, left.

Moira closed the front door after him, waited a moment with her hand resting on it, and then went back into the drawing room.

Clara, her head bowed, was absorbed in cutting out shapes – or pretending to be. George was standing by the window, looking out.

'Clara,' said Moira, and sat down near her. 'Darling?'

Clara didn't look up. 'I don't know where he is,' she said.

'Is he all right, do you think?' said Moira, very gently.

There was a pause. Clara said tightly, 'I've no idea.'

Chapter Two

Hal had walked in only partial darkness. A low yellow moon hung over the fields, showing him straight streaked clouds near to it and the dark-cut shapes of trees below.

His civilian shoes weren't good for walking, but he wasn't tired and he covered the miles easily.

Morning came, with a grey sky and drizzle that was surprisingly drenching – he had no coat – but he welcomed the feel of it on his face, having been used to the very hot sun.

He passed through villages, or walked round them, clear in his direction, cutting through fields where the long grass soaked his trousers and birds flew up suddenly from the high hedges and banks as they heard him.

Every hour or so he thought he would stop, get to a station for a train or find a lift with somebody, but the walking became a peaceful compulsion and he found he couldn't stop. He didn't want to stop to have to climb over fences, or find his way across streams as he came to them. He found it hard to stop at all.

At first he noticed the landscape around him because it was emerging from night, and to find his way, but as the walking took him over he was caught up in the fever of it and his sight became feverish too. The ground was heavy and infinite below his feet, the fields circled and ringed him under the sky. Wet grass, thick hedges, clouded dark branches of far woods and clear frames of near ones – whole valleys opened up to him. The country lay around him. Some fields seemed so small, as if he could put them into his hand. Then, close up, the reddish tangle of twigs deep in the hedges as he passed them were as vast as universes, with perfect symmetry that he could almost unravel, if only he had the calculation to do it. The sun, far behind the deep cloud, moved its vague light through the day. He saw the leaves of brambles, all different, yellowing, with brown speckles or tattered edges and tiny holes left by small fat caterpillars, and strung between with spider's webs that trembled as he watched. He saw small broken blackberries that had been scorned by birds. He saw wet red foxes slipping into secret woods beneath the big darkening sky. He felt the rain on himself and his own curious heat. His breath was regular, reliable, he was not tired, he was not lost, he would not stop, not, except, almost, when – on reaching the brow of a hill, coming out of thin black trees, with ferns wetly tangling his legs – he saw below him the barracks. There: the long buildings, the parade square, and far away, the town, threading through the valley.

The downhill was quick, a matter of moments, a numb gliding flight above the ground; the field, the fence, the metal road, the gate and stop. Then. Stop. Stop. Stop.

The sentry guard had seen him come down the long hill and walk around the perimeter until he reached the road.

He'd had two roll-ups while he watched him; it had taken that long. The man was wearing a shirt, which was wet through, and his face was burned brown by the sun, like a wog, with mud all over his trouser legs and his hands filthy too. But he spoke like a gentleman and had a proper haircut, so the sentry guard called him 'sir'.

'Come from where, sir?'

'Woburton.'

'In Buckinghamshire?'

'Yes.'

'But that's thirty-odd miles away.'

'Yes.'

'Wait here.'

The sentry guard wasn't about to let him just wander in, posh or not. They'd sent someone down for him.

There were guards in the corridor outside the office. The captain regarded him across the desk, frowning. 'Have you had any lunch?'

'No.'

'Breakfast?'

'No, I told you. I've come –'

'Yes, yes. Thank you. Just a moment. Wait here.'

The captain left the room. Hal, still walking in his mind, had his eyes on the horizon.

The door opened again.

'Why don't you come and get cleaned up?' said the captain.

After Hal had washed his hands the captain took him to the officers' dining room, which was empty. He sat at a long darkly polished trestle table, like a school table, and was given tinned tomato soup and white bread. The captain, a slight man with a moustache, sat opposite, watching, and didn't speak to him.

'Thank you,' said Hal, when he had finished.

The door opened. Another man, a major, came into the room. 'Ah, there you are, Harris,' he said.

'Sir.'

The major turned to Hal. 'We haven't met. Charles West. It's very quiet around here, Treherne,' he said, 'because they're nearly all on their way to where you've just run off from.'

He was put into a small single room to wait. At exactly half past five Captain Harris opened the door. Behind him there was a man in a brown suit. The suit was soft, but he had military bearing. 'Hal Treherne,' he said. 'You've led us a merry dance. My name is Jameson. Like the whisky. Major (Retired) Peter Jameson.'

Hal stood up. 'How d'you do,' he said, and they shook hands.

'Glad you've come back. Walk all the way from Woburton, did you?'

'Yes.'

'I expect you'll need a drink, then. Not a bad place just up the road. You might know it.'

'All right.'

The pub had dark beams and a dog sleeping by a gas fire. The small corner bar was curved and there was nobody there, but, even so, Jameson, having bought two whisky macs, gestured to a table in the far corner. The room was gloomy and, away from the glowing fire, cold, too.

'Shall we?'

He allowed Hal to go first, then sat opposite him and took out a gold lighter, laying it by the heavy cut-glass ashtray on the table and crossing his legs. He eyed Hal astutely. 'I live over in Chippenham,' he said. 'I went all the way to Woburton to find you this morning.'

'Sorry about that.'

Jameson lifted his drink and sniffed it. 'Just the thing for a wet day,' he said. He took a sip and reached into his inside pocket. 'Cigarette?' He held out a case.

Hal refused, with a minute shake of his head, watching him.

'You've had a rotten time of it, I hear,' said Jameson, lighting a cigarette for himself.

'No worse than lots of people,' said Hal.

Jameson examined the gold lighter, squinting through the smoke, then laid it down. 'Oh, I wouldn't say that. I'm not going to dig it all up. I'm sure you'd rather I didn't, but I can tell you, when they told me what happened to your wife – well . . . It was in the papers here. I'm most terribly sorry.'

'I'm not cracking up, if that's what you think.'

It was amusing to Jameson that they all said that, the ones who were and the ones who weren't. There was a silence.

Two men came into the pub, glanced in their direction and away again to order their drinks. They had old tweed jackets and drinkers' faces. The dog heaved to its feet on shaking, ancient limbs and stretched, yawning. It lay down again.

'I never said you were cracking up, old chap. Although can you tell me what you *are* doing?'

'I had to leave.'

'All right. But why?'

No answer.

'Let's look at it this way, Hal. Why don't you tell me what happened? At RAF Nicosia.'

'All right,' said Hal, levelly. 'I went along to put them on the plane. Clara and the girls. I was going on to Episkopi.'

'Yes?'

'I saw them there all right, and then, when it came to it –'

He stopped, as if he were facing a wall.

'Couldn't leave your wife? Your family? It must have been terrible.'

Silence.

'Still, I should think you're utterly appalled at yourself, just disappearing like that.'

Hal frowned. 'I can't seem to get used to it,' he said.

'Yes. It's all wrong, isn't it? Not the sort of thing you do at all, is it?'

'No.'

'The thing is,' said Jameson, steadily, 'it's all so easy to resolve.' He smiled. 'You're not "cracking up" you say?'

'Of course not.'

'Had a sudden rash impulse, then? Acted on it?'

A pause then Hal said, 'I suppose . . .'

Jameson pressed on: 'The army take a pretty dim view of unauthorised absence – for God's sake, I don't need to tell you. You're not some private, off on a weekend bender. But this is different. This is understandable. But only up to a point, old man. If you regret what happened, *truly* regret it . . . It can't be overlooked, what you've done, it can't be undone, but, look, we know your record, we can see this is entirely out of character.' He leaned forward. 'I don't need to remind you of the demands being placed on us at the moment. We're stretched to the limits. It's all hotting up out there. It needn't harm your career in the long term. Just one unfortunate episode. We can have you back with your unit, doing your job, within twenty-four hours.'

Jameson crushed out his cigarette, screwing it down onto

the hard glass. Still hunched forwards, he fixed Hal with a look and smiled. 'How would that be?' he said. 'How would that be, Hal?'

And Hal answered him: 'No,' he said.

Outside in the muddy road the wind blew the leaves round their feet.

'It's a great shame,' said Jameson, despising him now and ready to go home. 'This is going to get a lot more complicated from here on in.'

'What happens now?'

Jameson was putting on his gloves. 'I don't know. Out of my hands, certainly. I need to speak to your HQ. They'll take it from there. I'll drive you back up to the barracks. You'll be under guard. The longer you leave it, the worse it will be for you, I'm afraid.'

'Yes, I see.'

A few dozen recruits and the headquarters personnel were the only other occupants of the barracks, apart from Hal. As Major West had pointed out, most of the regiment's attention was focused on the eastern Mediterranean. Far away, the Israeli Army were on Egypt's borders, ready to invade, and RAF bases in Cyprus were so overflowing with British and French troops that Malta was used to take the strain. Soldiers were moved from one place to another with the slow scrambling haste that characterises the transportation of great numbers. War was imminent; lines were drawn on maps – thousands will be taken from here to here to begin the bombardment here – while the logistics of kit, rations and coupons, of feeding those thousands in floating canteens, finding them beds and boots, was the overriding experience. Communications were sent by telephone, radio, wire; orders were given and drawn up, mapped out and circulated from Nicosia to Port Said, from London to Malta, and Paris to Israel. Communications were made about Hal, too. The rapidly rising organised chaos of Suez, Hal's rank, recent history, his background, his record, all coloured the circumstances of his punishment. There were a number of players in the game of deciding his future; the stakes were high and precariously balanced.

Hal, in the officers' quarters of his home barracks, heard the company sergeant major bark his instructions, his voice bouncing off the walls and echoing, and the marching feet on the stones obeying him. He walked up and down as he listened, marking the passing hours with remembered routine.

Chapter Three

Clara could not drive. That is, she knew how to drive, but she had been told by the doctor that she was not allowed to, not for several more weeks. Her father drove her to the barracks while Moira stayed at home with Lottie and Meg. Her parents had tried to stop her going. 'I'm all right. I went on an aeroplane, didn't I?'

Clara dressed carefully, like a soldier preparing for battle. She wore an olive green wool suit, with a brooch that had been her grandmother's and a cream silk blouse. She put her red lipstick on in two coats, blotting with tissue and powder on the first layer, so that it would be matte and not wear away. She had to leave the back button of the skirt undone, because the waistband rubbed where the dressing covered her stitches. The bandage had been changed that morning. Underneath it she had seen the red, raised scar. She was grateful for the protection of the dressing, and the silk blouse, tucked in, felt smooth between her skirt and the bare skin round it.

Her father drove her to the entrance of the barracks then stopped by the wide verge. Clara looked across at him. He smiled at her. His eyes met hers steadily.

'Good girl,' he said. 'I'm sure it will be all right.'

He squeezed her hand. He was wearing driving gloves and she thin leather ones, so she couldn't really feel his warmth.

Clara passed the sentry post and walked towards the main building in the wet air, her heels tapping on the stones. She could hear shots, far distant, echoing, and rooks flying up from the woods in alarm.

She waited in the billiard room of the officers' mess, where at one end there were two sofas facing one another and a small coal fire. She watched the door, listening for Hal, and caught sight of herself in the mirror above the mantelpiece, white and frightened, the lipstick livid against her pallor.

The door opened. He came in.

The sight of him – a wave of relief: she hadn't expected to feel so much love so quickly. She was disarmed for a moment. He was different. No, he was the same. He stepped towards her, frowned; he was shy – and something else. He didn't look full at her.

'Are you all right?' he said, and put his hands into his pockets.

'Yes, of course.'

He came further into the room. He was agitated, too active. 'Sit down. They're bringing tea for you,' he said. He glanced out of the window. 'Who brought you?'

'My father. He's gone to the pub, I think.'

'No good waiting in the car.'

'No.'

They looked at each other. A piece of coal slipped down amongst the other coals.

'Please sit down,' he said, not abruptly like before but really asking her to.

She sat. He seemed undecided, glancing around again, then came over to her and sat too, on the other end of the sofa.

'You're under guard,' she said.

He nodded.

'I thought you had leave,' she carried on, just to say something. 'I had no idea. I wasn't very – I didn't really have any idea what was happening. When they phoned I –'

He took her hand suddenly with both his and she stopped talking. He looked at her hand, holding each side of it lightly. He kept staring at it. He pushed her diamond ring, fiddling with it with one finger, familiar as his own hand, as foreign as it could have been to him.

'I'm not sure what to do,' he said.

Clara felt the cut in her stomach burn dully, tugging at her. She hadn't taken the pills she had been given that morning because they made her feel sick and dizzy, but realised she felt it anyway and now had pain, too. 'It's all right.'

'I have to apologise,' he said, 'I have ruined everything.'

'You couldn't have known. And I'm all right.'

He looked up at her.

The door opened – Hal let go of Clara – a soldier came in, a stooped ancient corporal, with a tea-tray. 'Madam,' he said, and placed it with shaking hands on the table between them.

Hal was tapping the heel of his shoe very fast on the floor in tiny movements.

Clara felt a hard, hot strain in her throat. The corporal went away and closed the door. She stared at her knees, examined the green wool, the stitches in the hem. She said carefully, 'Please don't blame yourself, Hal.'

'If I hadn't –'

'You can go back to Cyprus.'

'No.'

'I'll be much better soon.'

'I know that –'

'Would you like us to join you?'

'Join me?'

'At Christmas, perhaps?'

'Clara – I can't.'

'I don't understand. How can you not go back?'

'I just can't.'

'They'll court-martial you.'

'I know.'

'Because of me?'

He didn't answer.

'Hal? Because of me?'

Hal was struggling to articulate. 'I can't –'

She, gently, 'Try.'

His words came out of him painfully. 'I just can't carry on with it.'

'Hal?'

'I don't know what to do. I'm sorry.'

'Please, don't –'

He put his head into his hands.

Clara waited. She looked around the room. Thin steam rose from the spout of the teapot; she could see the grains of vapour in the cold air. The curtains hung still against the yellow walls. The ceiling was white with plaster moulding, like a wedding cake. The room was still and clear, and she felt clarity, too.

It was as if she could see their lives from above, stretching out behind them – the children, houses they had lived in, the travelling, the love and recent cruelties, strange beds and familiar ones, suppers, homecomings, all leading to this room. And then – after this – carrying on. The worst had happened to her. She wasn't dead. She wasn't frightened. She felt quite strong.

She said, 'We were nearly two months apart this time, weren't we? That's longer than usual. You know how low I had been feeling. I was terribly upset at first that we'd quarrelled. And I'm sorry I didn't write to you.'

He lifted his head slightly, listening to her. She went on, 'Even with everything that's happened, I'm so happy to be home, and to see my family. And being in England. Isn't it lovely seeing the leaves? I think, don't you, that with time, and if we just – explain to everybody, how things have been, you'll feel better. I'm feeling better already. We needn't blame one another. Or ourselves. It's your job, it's everything to you. You should go back to Episkopi, and settle down again, and –'

'I can't, Clara.'

She was interrupted. She felt her confidence slipping. 'But then . . . what will happen?'

'I don't know.'

'What will happen to me and the girls?'

'I'm sorry.'

'You're sorry?'

'I have to clear things up.'

'Yes. And go back!'

'No.'

'They'll lock you up! For what? Why? What about me? What about the consequence?'

There was a long silence. Clara stood up, slowly. 'I have to go.'

He didn't raise his head.

Chapter Four

Colonel Burroughs put in a long-distance call to Hal's father in Somerset. Burroughs was in his office at Episkopi, looking across at the wall of 'wanted' faces; Arthur Treherne was in his cold study, seated by the draughty window, the trees outside moving in the wind.

Hal's fall from grace was dishonour but they had both known dishonour before and had risen above it.

'I've never heard of anything like it. If it were anyone else, Arthur, if it weren't for his rank, they'd have packed him off back here for court-martial. He could get fourteen years.'

'I'll speak to him.'

'Will you go there?'

'If I could knock some sense into him . . .'

'It's gone too far for that.'

'Did he not say – was there no sign of it at all?'

'I can only think this awful business with Clara unbalanced him.'

They both remembered *awful business* of their own. Brothers lost. Horrors encountered and absorbed. They had not gone absent. They had managed. The line crackled and split between them. It was a great shame. A shame.

Arthur Treherne had driven from Somerset to the barracks

the next morning. He walked quickly behind Captain Harris, not looking at the soldiers who saluted them as they passed.

'Well, at least you're not in the bloody guardroom,' he said, on seeing his son for the first time in more than three years.

He knew him, he had thought, knew everything that mattered to him, but the meeting was brief and fruitless. Hal had refused to go with him, or offer any explanation. The only time he looked at his father was when Clara was mentioned.

'What about her? What about your children?'

'I don't know.'

But he hadn't been able to get anywhere with him, and left more afraid than when he'd got there.

He spoke to his wife when he got home, by the front door in his coat, not bothering to pretend they were not in crisis. 'He says he isn't cracking up. That's what he kept saying, but –' They stood close to one another in their cold hall and unspoken words hung between them. All the thirty-one years of defining their son. *A man like Hal . . . Hal is the sort of boy who – Hal always –*

'I didn't like the look of him,' he finished at last. 'If he offers no defence for himself then – I don't know. He won't see sense.'

Hal remained under guard at the barracks for two more days. If he had gone absent, there would have been a summary hearing. He was a major. Majors did not go absent. It had never happened. He would be questioned informally, instead.

They met in the big room that adjoined the lieutenant colonel's office in the brick and white Queen Anne barracks – it was pretty, made with conscious beauty to house soldiers. Hal was to be questioned by Lieutenant Colonel Hay. His adjutant, Captain Harris, who had first dealt with Hal, was seated on his left, with Major West on his right.

Hal entered just as sunlight, finding sudden gaps in the torn clouds, filled the room, with quick urgency. The smell of beeswax polish and across the gleaming table, facing him, the officers – stiff-decorated, dark green uniforms, red, gold, brass – were lit sharply in the acid light. The sunlight faded from the room. Dimness returned.

Salutes. Chairs clunking on the thick carpet as they were pulled back. Throats cleared.

Hal was asked to state his name and rank, and did so. The three men watched him carefully; he seemed perfectly correct.

Lieutenant Colonel Hay had met Hal many times, shaken his hand, welcomed him, praised him, served with his father, and saw him now, disgraced. 'Sit down, Hal,' he said.

They had written evidence of him sent from Cyprus.

Captain Harris shuffled the papers, cleared his throat and read them out. There was a statement from Mark Innes, describing Hal as 'distracted . . . depressed', from Colonel Burroughs, citing his recent 'somewhat erratic behaviour' as evidence of mental disturbance, contrary to his normal 'exemplary running of his company'. They even had a statement from Kirby, about Hal's departure from RAF Nicosia: 'Of course I was surprised, but he said the orders had changed so I didn't think nothing of it . . . He didn't look any different than usual. He just went off.' Everybody allowed a smile at Captain Harris's dry delivery of Kirby's statement, a man of a different class.

Lieutenant Colonel Hay spoke to him civilly, and with real curiosity: 'Are you aware of the consequences of what you have done?'

'Yes, sir.'

'Do you have something to say in explanation?'

'No, sir.'

'No? You don't want to offer anything in defence of your actions?'

'No, sir.'

'Do you regret it?'

Silence.

'Surely, Hal, this was the behaviour of a man distressed by his personal circumstances?'

Silence.

'Let's try and have this out man to man. Was it planned, your leaving Cyprus?'

'No, sir.'

'So it was a spur-of-the-moment decision?'

'Yes.'

'Because of your wife's accident? And yet you aren't on your way back there. Why?'

Hal did not answer.

'Is there something else we should know? Was there some issue at the barracks, then, prior to your wife's accident?'

'Issue?'

'Anything that happened, at Episkopi Garrison, that might enlighten us.'

The colonel leaned forward. He said again, more slowly, 'I'll ask you again, Hal. Was there an issue at Episkopi that – in your mind – prompted you to leave in this way?'

Everything about Hal had altered. They examined him. The silence stretched out.

'Hal?'

'I can't –' A sort of smile.

'Continue. Please. This isn't sufficient. We're getting nowhere.'

A long silence.

'You're not being co-operative.'

'No, sir. I am. I am co-operating,' he said clearly.

More silence. All eyes examining him.

Then, at last, 'Am I to understand, then, that you, a senior officer in Her Majesty's Army, walked out on your fellow officers, and your company, leaving them in a time of crisis, and went absent, avoiding your duty, with no intention of returning, and that you have nothing *whatever* to say in your own defence?'

They waited.

'Yes, sir.'

'And what do you expect us to do with you?'

Silence. Then, 'I'll take the consequences.'

'Well,' the colonel was bitter, but it was because of his regret, 'there's nothing more to be said.' He got up abruptly, and there was a hasty pushing back of chairs and salutes to him as he left the room, not looking at any of them again, but on passing Hal, he stopped, and said fiercely, under his breath, '*What is all this?*'

Hal kept his eyes front. He couldn't have been expected to do otherwise.

Burroughs, at Episkopi, found he could not wait to hear from Lieutenant Colonel Hay and had a call put through to him the moment he thought the hearing might have finished. In response to his questions, Hay came straight to the point. 'Something's going on and he won't come out with it.'

Burroughs didn't respond, but the static on the line might have been his brain turning the thing over. 'Did he give the impression,' he said slowly, 'that his going was a matter of *conscience*?'

'Possibly,' answered Hay. 'Does that surprise you?'

Burroughs was decisive. 'It's completely unthinkable,' he said.

Hay spoke very lightly. It was as if he were describing the weather. 'Is he a loose cannon?'

'He could very well be.' Burroughs's response was brief, too, belying the threat.

'He's disgraced whatever happens,' said Hay. 'But I'll be perfectly plain: it's the disgrace of others that concerns me.'

'Yes, that's exactly my thought, too.'

Resenting his hand being forced, with distaste, Hay began to form a new plan for Hal. He telephoned General Marcus Emery – quite unofficially. They met at the Army and Navy Club at St James's where the general, since his retirement, spent much of his time.

The general was sanguine. 'Good man, I hear. Or was. Horrible business with his wife.'

'There might be more to it. His CO has the idea he might kick up a fuss.'

'The press? We can't have that.'

'We're still not clear what exactly he's up to. To say he's just "gone absent" isn't exactly right. He's a major, after all, and he has been through a uniquely difficult time.' Hay didn't say it in sympathy, but in calculation.

The general considered. 'Let the poor blighter go quietly – if he must go. No need to haul him over the coals. No good for anybody. Let's find grounds to do it nicely.'

Chapter Five

The long car passed the sentry guards at the gates to the Bulworth Military Hospital and pulled up at the main door. Lieutenant Colonel Hay and Hal, getting out of the car, paused for a moment before entering.

The hospital was a converted barracks of grey stone, two storeys high. It could have been a barracks still, but for the windows, which were barred on the upper floor; barracks windows are not barred.

They passed nurses and soldiers along corridors with small white wooden signs screwed to grey walls. 'Wards 1–3', 'Waiting Room'. The doors had divided glass panes in their top halves and were painted grey, too.

Through some double doors, along a narrow corridor, and on the other side of a small, square vestibule, with two chairs, was the psychiatric clinic. Dr Robin Tait was the consultant there. The colonel, having greeted him and introduced Hal, left them.

'Come into my office. Do sit down, Major Treherne,' said Dr Tait.

The room was not big; the desk took up most of it. Dr Tait was in uniform and had a neat moustache. He was a small, barrel-chested man; his eyes were hidden behind reflective glasses. He sat at the same time as Hal, folded his hands in front of him and rested them on the desk.

'You know better than I what this is all about,' he said pleasantly.

'There's no need for me to be here.'

'Do you think you're here so that I can pronounce you mentally incompetent?'

Dr Tait watched Hal with detachment. He thought he had a stubborn look about him. 'I'm fifty-seven years old, Major Treherne, and I have never once, in all my career, seen a major go absent without leave.'

'I haven't gone absent.'

'Aren't you supposed to be in Cyprus with your regiment?'

'Yes.'

The doctor smiled at him. 'Well, we need to sort a few things out, then, don't we?'

'I suppose so.'

'Now. Let's begin with preliminaries. There are things I need to be able to tick off. Do you mind if I just ask you questions, to start with, and you answer?'

'That's fine.'

'Good, thank you. I see your Christian name is Henry but you're known as Hal, I believe. What would you rather be called?'

'It's up to you.'

'No preference?'

'None.'

'Fine. Good. Let's get on, then. You had a medical at the barracks, is that right?'

'Yes. Monday afternoon.'

'And they passed you fit.'

'Fit for detention. Yes.'

'These questions are personal, and I'm sorry for that, but it's all necessary.'

'I understand. You have to do your job.'

'How are you sleeping?'

'Fine, thanks.' The 'fine' was automatic.

'Let's not beat about the bush.'

'Of course. I'm sorry. Not awfully well.'

'How long have you been sleeping badly? Is that normal for you?'

'No. I'm a good sleeper normally.'

'How long, then? Approximately.'

'A few months. Look, this is all pointless –'

'Can you date it from any particular incident?'

'We were fairly busy.'

'At Episkopi?'

'Yes.'

'And you found you were sleeping badly?'

'On and off.'

'When did you last have a good night's sleep, would you say?'

'I'm not cracking up.'

The doctor leaned forward. 'Why don't we just leave all that to me? I shouldn't think it's your area of expertise.'

Hal nodded. 'Fair enough.'

'Good, then. You've come home like this. Got yourself into all kinds of trouble. Now they've hauled you off to see me. What do you think might happen?'

'I think they want to get me discharged. Or put on long leave – I don't know.'

'If it were you, what would *you* want to do with you?'

'What do you mean?'

'You're a senior officer. How would you deal with yourself?'

Hal smiled. 'I'd tell myself to pull myself together,' he said.

'And you would, if you could, wouldn't you?'

Hal didn't answer him. Tait glanced down at his notes. 'You're good at your job, aren't you?' he said.

'I tried to be.'

'Shall I tell you something? I'm sure you know it already.'

'Go on.'

'Anything you say to me here is strictly between us.'

'Yes, of course.'

'No. Treherne, this is really significant to our conversation. I want you to realise, absolutely, that nothing we say here will ever leave this room.'

'All right.'

'Do you mind my asking you, does your wife know about the way things have been for you?'

'She's not well.'

'I know. Sorry to hear it. Is she feeling better?'

'I think so. I haven't –'

The doctor saw him suddenly look away. After a moment he looked back again. 'I haven't been able to explain to her.'

'What is it – take your time – that you haven't been able to explain?' He waited in silence.

Many of the men who were sent to see him, when it came to the crisis, looked down at their hands or out of the window. It was an almost predictable stage in the conversation: the confession. This man seemed to rise to his breaking, if such a thing were possible. He looked him in the eye and said, slowly, 'I am aware, I *know*, I have let everybody down. You can't say I'm mad or that I don't know – because I know, completely, that I have let everybody down. That I *am* letting everybody down. I should go back. Don't you think?'

'It's not –'

'Let's put all this aside, shall we?' Hal was clear, not hesitating at all, quite calm, and met Tait's eye all the time he spoke. 'All this medical business. Putting all of that aside, don't you think it's a pretty poor show?'

Dr Tait should have liked to allow him a break in eye contact, but Hal would not allow it in himself.

'I have let down my wife. I have let down my subordinates. I have let down my CO. I've let down my men. Do you understand? Everybody. You're an army man: you know what that means. I have let down *everybody*.'

Dr Tait said steadily, 'I imagine you had your reasons.'

Hal laughed. 'I don't think there are any reasons that are good enough, do you?'

'It's not for me to say. What were they?'

'What?'

'The reasons.'

'I can't –'

'Nobody will know. You could ask for leave. It was an awful thing that happened to your wife. Look for understanding. I'm sure you'd find it.'

'No. Because –' He stopped.

'Because?'

'I can't go on doing the things I was doing.' He was angry, but not in a rage – he didn't have that release. 'It's pathetic that I can't.'

He stopped suddenly. He said, almost lightly, 'My wife nearly died – lost our child and nearly died – because of an EOKA terrorist. They say it wasn't them. I don't know. But, still, I'm not prepared to go and do my job. To fight them. Doesn't that sound – if you're looking for madness – doesn't that sound like madness to you?'

'All right, but why can't you?'

'Why? There is no "why". Why is unacceptable. Whether or not I can *square* it with myself, the things that I was doing, allowing, agreeing to. Whether I can – *live with myself* doesn't matter – it doesn't matter.'

'Square it with yourself?'

'It doesn't matter. It's my duty. People are relying on me. You must see this! "*Why*" doesn't *exist*.'

'And yet you're here.'

'Yes. I'm here.'

'All right.' Tait sat back. 'I think I understand. Thank you.'

He picked up his notes again, carefully leaving Hal, unobserved, as if to rest. 'Let's get back to things that do exist then, Treherne.'

'Good.'

'This sleeping.'

Hal, perfunctory, 'One or two hours a night.'

'Nightmares?'

'Yes.'

'About?'

'Things that happened.'

'Such as?'

'There was a bomb, some casualties. I dream about them. It's all fairly standard, I should think.'

'Specifically?'

'I'd rather not say.'

'And when you're awake, are you troubled by memories?'

'Yes. No more than the average person, probably.'

'What sort of memories? Pictures?'

'Yes. Sounds sometimes. Often, which is silly, I smell things. I mean I smell burning.'

'Burning what?'

'Burning bodies.'

'Are you drinking more than usual?'

'Not usually.'

'How much do you drink?'

'Not very much. The odd beer in Cyprus. Some brandy. Occasionally.'

'Would you say you've changed?'

'Changed? Yes.'

'How have you changed?'

'In minor ways. I can't leave things alone. I was working longer hours than I needed to, just to – well, just to . . .'

'How's your temper? Are you short-tempered?'

'Sometimes.'

'Yes?'

'I was – I was not very fair to my wife. Once or twice. I'm ashamed of that. Amongst other things.'

'Amongst other things you're ashamed about?'

'Yes, as I said, amongst the other things I'm ashamed about. Anyway, all this, what are you trying to get at? Not battle fatigue?'

'It's not a term we use now. But why not?'

'Are you not familiar with my record, Dr Tait? I haven't been in any battles.'

'I think it's important to recognise when we have been under tremendous mental strain –'

'I haven't been. You're just looking for excuses.'

'If you like. But I'm finding them, aren't I? Your wife –'

'That's personal to me.'

'Surely the distress of that, on top of other things, the things you were facing out there –'

'I haven't been in any conflict but the most trivial. I haven't faced anything my father or his father or my CO hasn't faced a hundred times over. None of this is significant.'

'What were you facing in Cyprus?'

'Nothing much. Routine. One or two incidents. Small things.'

'And yet here you are.'

'Again. Yes. Here I am. If it were up to me I'd – well, it seems there's no honour in any of it, but if it were up to me, and probably you, too, it would be like those old stories. You'd go out and leave the pistol on the desk, have a cup of tea and come back to clean up the mess. Except for Clara. It's no good. There's nothing. There's no honour to be found in it.'

'I'm so sorry.'

Hal brought his head up sharply. 'What did you say?'

'I'm so sorry you feel this way. That you have been under such tremendous strain and have found yourself feeling this way.'

'Don't feel sorry for me. Feel sorry for the hundred men, one woman and two young children I've walked out on to indulge my –'

'Conscience?'

The word hung between them in the long silence. The doctor, determined to make him answer, waited.

Eventually, Hal leaned towards him. He was unmasked. 'I will not say a word against the army,' he said quietly. His hands were on the desk. He looked at Tait, open, hopeful. 'Do you think they know that?'

'I don't know.'

'I'd hate to think – I'd hate to think they, you – that I'm the enemy.'

'Nobody wants you disgraced.'

'Nobody wants it – but,' he was still reaching forward, he said carefully, 'I am disgraced. You know that. I know it. They can afford to be generous. I just want them to know I'll put up with it. I mean, I won't kick up a fuss.'

'I understand.'

'I can't seem to explain to anybody.'

'It's all right. I'm glad you've told me. It will reassure everyone.'

A long pause. Hal nodded.

'Is there any other erratic behaviour you've noticed in yourself recently?' Tait asked.

'What?'

'We were discussing your mental state, weren't we? The worry – we sometimes call it "anxiety neurosis" – that prevents you doing your job.'

Hal gave him a long look. He wavered. Tait saw the blood come into his face. Then he blinked, looking down.

'Come now. Perhaps you've found your appetite has suffered?'

Hal brought his chin up. He was changed. 'My appetite?' he said.

'Yes.'

And Hal answered, giving the doctor the reasons he needed to let him off, because he was weak, and had found, under pressure, that he couldn't manage.

Chapter Six

Clara's stitches were taken out the day after Hal had left the barracks. She tried to lie still as the cold steel point slipped between the skin and the thick black thread, and cut. She felt the tugging and stinging pain echoed by her muscles inside, yearning, it seemed, for what was gone. She had been told she wouldn't feel anything after a while. There would be no more periods, no more babies. She had her twins. She looked up at the ceiling, not at the doctor bending over her or the nurse standing nearby.

Her father was waiting for her. He had brought her up to London to the hospital. Clara felt a hot tear slide from the corner of her eye down her temple and into her hair. Her father was waiting. Her father. Her mother at home with the children, and she, without her pregnancy, or any other parts of her adulthood, was made a child again.

Hal had been taken back to his parents' house, too, by his father, discharged and baseless. Both of them children, alone, with everything taken.

'Here, just a moment now,' said the doctor, and dabbed her with sweet white pads.

Cyprus. It had been encased around and above in hard blue sea and sky. They had made their small home on it, been taken in by it, and she had lost him. Such a small place to lose a person, she thought, and now, released, they were both alone.

'Are you all right?' said her father, taking her arm, squeezing her fingers as they reached the door of the hospital. They heard the sound of heavy rain on the tops of the cars. A man, coming in, opened the door for them. Her father stopped to put up his umbrella but Clara had stepped ahead of him out into the rain.

Hal arrived home – his parents' home – with his father, when the rain had stopped, but their breath was in clouds in the wet air and their fingers raw with cold just from carrying the cases in from the car. They came into the hall. The tall gloomy hall, with cold tiles as hard as steel to walk on; in childhood it had been as comforting to him as Clara's was to her. Now the house, with its dark walls, gilt-framed pictures on chains, hanging too high to look at comfortably, carpets and corners that were discoloured by damp or light, hard dark frames of straight chairs and chilly corridors, this house now, gave him no welcome.

His mother came to meet them. She was a narrow woman, flat-chested, in a thick, dark green woollen suit. A single row of pearls lay rigid on the thin sinews of her neck. She'd had two other boys who had died in infancy; Hal was her precious survivor. 'Oh, Hal,' she said, touching him suddenly on his cheek with her flat palm as she kissed him. She couldn't meet his eye.

Hal's father was an older version of Hal, it had often been said and had always been a source of pride to them both.

They heard a door opening, a distant voice, and the thud

of the dogs hitting it as they came through. Then scraping paws on the tiles and breathy barks, and the two hairy muddy spaniels raced each other into the hall.

All three of them busied themselves with the dogs, who did not remember Hal, having been puppies when he saw them last.

He went upstairs. His bedroom looked out onto the grey grass, first of the garden and then of the plain, where in his childhood the cavalry had charged in their scarlet coats, mowing down the hapless enemy with shining swords as he watched from his bed, imprisoned by coughs and colds. He had heard the bugles and the cries of battle amongst the battering hoofs.

Supper was in the dining room, a room cold enough in winter to see your breath. Accustomed to a companionable silence, it was hard now for any of them to eat. When it was over, Hal's mother went away, to her room, or to write letters, and Hal and his father took the dogs out for the last time, before shutting them up behind the door to the boot room, guns and scullery.

The night was sharp and clear, with no moon. The dogs went off, noses down, into the darkness to do their business. Hal and his father stood shoulder to shoulder.

'Perhaps you'll go back,' said his father, not looking at him.

Hal felt his chest contract for him; it was not to comfort Hal that he had said it, but himself. 'It was good of them to call it leave,' he said at last.

His father looked across, checking his expression.

'What will you do now?'

'I'll have to see about a job. I'll go after breakfast. Up to London.'

'Can't think what, can you?'

'No.'

The dogs, hearing the flapping of a pheasant in the deep grass, set off barking.

Hal's father said, 'I won't insult you with a lot of rubbish. Pretending it's not as bad as all that.'

Hal nodded. His father turned away. 'Come on, dogs!'

They went inside, muddy footprints on the flags by the back door, his father drawing the bolt firmly behind them.

The next morning, after breakfast as he had planned, Hal put his things into the car and waited for his father. He had said goodbye to his mother already. She had been crying. He could not remember a time in his life when she had cried – certainly not over him, perhaps animals or at the death of her sister. She had touched his face again with her dry fingers; he wanted to be gone.

At the back of the house, the smaller staircase led up to the back landing, above the garden, where he had played as a child. There were doors to spare rooms, or maids' rooms, never used, with damp beds that had blankets folded over their mattresses and pillows stacked without cases. Hal found himself climbing the thin staircase.

He stood looking along the landing's greenish length, with the October light from the windows on his left touching the painted portraits and photographs.

He walked quietly. It was as if his feet kicked through the legions of toy soldiers that had once covered the floor. He looked at the faces in the frames, the uniforms, plumes, grey moustaches of old soldiers, hands on swords of young ones, gleaming oil-painted medals, resolute expressions of unerring valour. Faces that had fought, had led, and served. It was not for him, not for him any more; he was not one of them and he could not serve.

The train rattled past fields and autumn woods, through Somerset, Wiltshire, Berkshire, smaller and smaller country, and at Paddington the tracks met other tracks that became a mass. It passed sidings, abandoned carriages, sheds and chimneys; the sky became thicker and greyish as smoke met clouds and fogs and city mists. The smell and rumble of the big city hit him hard as he got off the train, porters pushed past him, commuters, families, who knew their way and were hurrying, had purpose.

He left the station, and stopped at a news-stand, pulling coins from his pockets with trembling hands to buy an *Evening Standard*. Opposite the news-stand was a café, and Hal sat by the misted window in thick smoke and the smell of bacon, bought a cup of tea and looked through the classified advertisements in the back, underlining numbers with a pencil.

In a few hours, he had found a room between Westbourne Grove and Bayswater. It was cheap, on the second floor of a boarding house. He paid the landlady a week's deposit, and a week in advance, although he didn't know if he'd stay that long. He hadn't thought about timing; he didn't know what might happen, but unpacked with his usual care, folding and hanging his things, preserving symmetry as best he could. Then he sat on the bed. There was a green armchair by the window, with an antimacassar on the back of it and a stained seat.

He knew he must phone Clara. She was still weak and ill with that cut in her and he was frightened, even knowing she was with her parents. Frightened for her but, if he was honest, frightened for himself, too: he couldn't imagine she would want anything to do with him. This sick fear was new to him; like shame, it had been unknown. Now he was well acquainted with both.

There was a telephone in the hall downstairs, on the wall, next to the umbrella stand.

There were two other rooms that shared the bathroom on the landing, then three more and a bathroom above that. The pipes were noisy, and noisier where they came out from the walls and ran along the ceiling of his room, which had been cut from a larger space. Hal sat and listened to the pipes, thinking he should get some change for the gas because the room was cold, but not getting up to do it.

The October dark came in early because it was a cloudy afternoon. He could hear a newspaper man repeating the same word over and over. Sometimes he would stop, then start it up again a little while later. The street lamps came on. Hal thought he should really see about getting some change for the meter so that he could get the fire going. He heard footsteps up the stairs, a woman's, then more, running, then quiet.

What about me, Hal, what about us?

He must telephone Clara, and let her know he was going to find a job.

He thought that before he could find a job he must try to sleep in this bed. The bed had a pink candlewick bedspread and the wardrobe tilted towards it, with a mirror on the front that he had not been able to look into. On the corner of the small table by the bed were two hairpins. It must have been a woman's room before it was his.

He thought of beds in barracks and officers' messes, all of them he'd known, and the schools too, the collective sleeping places of his life, those kindly institutions, the compounding of company. Beds in dorms, in shared studies, down hallways, other boys, then men, the ranks of beds, rows of doors, bedrooms in Germany, Sandhurst, London, Winchester. He had lived his life in companionship, held richly by it, knowing those around him, names, ranks, faces who lived above, below, alongside, around him.

He must ring Clara. She should know he wasn't letting her down – not completely.

He eased himself back on the bed, up, back against the wall, to half sitting, with the pillow doubled behind him. Closing his eyes, he was back in Cyprus for a moment, with Clara away in Nicosia, the intolerable weight of the hours ahead, and loneliness.

What about me, Hal, what about us?

He got up.

The telephone in the hall was occupied. A girl was using it. She looked like a secretary, perhaps, and had her hair in rollers, which she touched self-consciously when she saw Hal coming down the stairs, turning away from him.

'I know,' she was saying, in a West Country accent that reminded Hal of home, 'I know, but if he doesn't ask her, then they never will, will they?'

The front door opened, and a man came in, wearing a hat and a mac. He shook off his umbrella, and the girl on the telephone bristled, like a cat being splashed.

'Excuse me,' he said. He had a thick moustache and a case that might have contained samples. 'Excuse me.' He put his umbrella into the stand and slid past Hal up the stairs.

Hal wasn't used to narrow hallways, and carpet on the stairs: he was used to sun-bleached rock and cracked plaster, diesel fumes on dry wind. The smell of boiling vegetables filled the house, and the clatter of pots.

'I'd better go,' said the girl. 'There's someone waiting. Give my love to Mam.' She said goodbye and hung up the phone, glancing coyly at Hal as she went past, then running up the stairs in her stockinged feet, pulling her cardigan round her.

Hal stood by the black telephone. 'Bayswater 2254,' it said, in italic ink on the dial.

He picked it up, finding the coins, readying them carefully, in a stack. It was an old habit. They had used to talk for a long time when he called her.

Clara was sitting on the stairs, watching the telephone. She had done it when Hal was at Sandhurst, and in Germany, when he would arrange to call, or promise to try. Now she was waiting for him again. Moira and George saw her, passed by her on the stairs.

The telephone rang. Moira, in the drawing room, heard Clara, answering, say, 'Oh, hello,' knew it was Hal, and closed the door.

There was no need for Hal's stack of coins.

'Clara? Are you all right?'

'Are you? Where are you?'

'London.'

'You're not coming?'

'No. I have to get on.'

'I'll come there.'

'No, you shouldn't –'

'Hal. I'm coming. I need to talk to you.'

'I'll meet the train, then.'

Chapter Seven

The very heavy sky threatened rain. It was a little warmer than it had been. Hal had spent the morning in two appointments. One was with the unemployment office, the other with a friend of his father. The man was called Henry Featherstone, a wine merchant, and one of Hal's family's few non-military connections. He had an office in St James's.

Hal had fought his sense of unreality, climbing the stairs, not in uniform but in the dark suit he'd had for five years or more and hardly worn. The stairway up from the lobby was gold-edged and brass-railed; there were offices on each floor, and the secretary at Featherstone's was an efficient woman with freshly painted nails and a younger assistant. The place smelled of respectability and confidence, if such things had a smell. Hal gave off need and confusion, he thought. He felt foolish in his upright bearing, that straightening up was all he knew how to do and of precious little help to him in this wide world.

Henry Featherstone was a tall man, sixty years old and slippery with urbanity. They had been extremely polite to one another, with almost no allusion to Hal's whole adult life having been spent in the army beyond the observation that he did not have a degree. It was a foreign country more absolute than any peasant village in southern Cyprus or grim suburb of Berlin had ever been. He had left with no clear idea of whether Henry Featherstone intended to employ him, but very clear indeed about his own ignorance of vintages, regions and grape varieties, let alone the vagaries of the spirits markets. He had learned that much of his time would be spent at châteaux in France and the Grill at the Savoy.

'Willing enough, eh?' Henry Featherstone had said, with a sharp, insinuating look.

Hal had raised his chin. 'Of course,' he said.

He was thirty-one years old with no training or real education, no experience of any use to anybody. Hal had heard the expression 'As if he'd had the stuffing knocked out of him' before. He had thought it funny. He hadn't known the feeling. This man, this suave man, who wore a gold signet ring and sat so comfortably in his chair, must see he was hollow. He was meeting Clara at noon. She would see it, too. Leaving, going down the hot overlit staircase, it was if the air itself outweighed him. *Treherne out*, he thought, *clean bowled*, but it didn't help: no quick vision of green grass and a white pavilion, just the empty gilded foyer ahead of him, the silent lift and the rows of small brass bells. His feet made no sound on the carpet as he left.

He walked along the platforms at Marylebone Station, looking for the right one. The train whistles and shunting sound of expelled steam mixed with the smoky smell of the air and the damp coldness and he saw her – long before she saw him – getting carefully down from the train, through the people, slowly easing herself, holding onto the door, as if she were an old lady. He wanted to run towards her, hold her, help her –

but he was far away, frozen, observing. Then, jolted into action, he started towards her.

'Platform ticket,' said the guard, extending a uniformed arm. Hal waited, obediently.

She came towards him and began to smile.

'Don't carry that,' he said, taking her small case from her. 'Why did you bring it?'

'I didn't know if I'd be able to get back tonight.'

Outside Hal waved a taxi forward from the line and helped her into it. They sat back in the deep seats. Neither spoke. She gazed straight ahead. Her hand lay beside him on the black seat. He wanted to touch it, but was prevented. 'Are you hungry?' he said.

'If you like.'

'My room is – I'd rather not go to it.'

'Fine, then.'

They had the taxi let them out on Westbourne Grove, not knowing exactly where to go, avoiding his room and neither of them thinking sensibly. The pavement was full of people. Hal tried to shield Clara. They walked some way with just the occasional 'Here . . .' or 'Let's try . . .' until both stopped – ran out of ideas – and Hal guided her by the elbow towards the side of the pavement on the opposite corner from a cinema.

'This is hopeless,' she said.

'I'm sorry, I should have thought . . .'

They stood, still figures amongst the crowd, and it began to rain.

'Umbrella?'

'I didn't think of it.'

Around them, black umbrellas went up. Clara almost

laughed, didn't. He saw her face, looking up at him, his red, white and blue girl. 'You want to leave me,' he said.

'No,' she answered him, and, 'No, Hal.'

'Oh,' he said, relief like the cutting of bonds, frightened by his feelings. His eyes hurt. 'Damn it.' He looked around for somewhere to hide.

'Here.' Her fingers found his hand.

He turned from the crowd, from her.

'Hal – stop it. Look at me.' He couldn't. 'Darling . . .'

The rain, which had been thin, began in earnest, quite suddenly. Thick cold drops, impossible to ignore. 'Oh, Christ,' he said, 'you'll catch cold. Here.'

He pointed over the road to the cinema, where the crowds, even at that time, were quite thick around the door. They crossed the road, half running, and got under the canopy, lit by bulbs, and glancing around them. He took hold of the tops of her arms and held her, looking into her face. 'I went for a job.'

'Did you?' she said faintly.

'You should be sitting down. You look – this is no good.'

There was a queue at the kiosk.

'Just until the rain –'

'Yes, all right –'

He bought tickets, and immediately afterwards the woman pulled down the shutter.

'Sold out,' she said.

'What's the film?' asked Clara.

'I don't know.'

They pushed inside to the warmth and cigarette smoke, the felted darkness.

The white screen flashed brightly past the heads of the people jostling at the entrance. The dark silhouettes of strangers in rows, the smell of their scent and hair cream and moving bodies as the usherette passed the beam of her torch over them to find seats. The speakers blared loudly in the opening chords of Pathé News, sharp sounds and sharper picture, the plumed cockerel, all heads lifted and turning. This was the reason for the crowd; this was the urgency in the feeling of the place; this was the need that had dragged them there.

Hal let his hand drop from Clara's arm. He was pressed against the wall by people, not noticing them, or anything, just watching.

'Yesterday. The Canal Zone. Egypt. British and French troops began the invasion of Port Said . . .'

The big screen, huge pictures of the invasion, filled his sight. The parachutes, floating under triumphant music, the vast troop carriers . . .

'Twenty thousand troops began their dawn invasion,' said the commentator, his clipped, portentous tone sealing the jolt from image to image, and then Anthony Eden.

'Today in Whitehall, the Prime Minister spoke . . .' His magnified face, staring down into the crowd, it seemed, his voice resolute and passionate. 'Britain and France have joined in this action that will safeguard the world . . .'

Clara, shielded by Hal's body, looked up at him. He didn't see her.

All around him people, sitting and standing in couples, groups, fidgeting in their soft civilian suits, watching with their vague, ill-tutored civilian eyes, and he, forced amongst them in the thick city air of England . . .

'Hal.'

He felt her press close to him, her arms around him in the

dark. Her hand was on his cheek, forcing his eyes from the screen, and he, looking down, saw nothing and felt only her lips against his mouth.

'Here,' she said. 'Don't –'

There were boos in the crowd, the people, watching, shifted their attention. Some fell silent, looking for the noise, and others joined in with it, a low sound, almost too deep to hear.

'And we can bring peace and stability . . .' Eden went on, to boos and hisses. Somebody threw something at the screen, a whistle, laughter, catcalls.

'Let's go,' said Clara.

'Yes, all right. Come on.'

They turned away.

Behind them, scenes of protest, crowds, banners in Trafalgar Square, the voice followed them out: '. . . as meanwhile, in London today, a large crowd of protesters made their feelings known . . .'

He took her hand and led her out, using the suitcase to push people aside, apologising, until they came out into the deserted foyer.

Rain poured thickly down. It beat on the pavements, bouncing up, and ran in trickles and drips about the doors and glass panes, splashing onto the carpeted step, puddling. Hal looked down at Clara, who was white-faced, and when she looked back her eyes were almost black, the pupils dilating into the blue irises.

He couldn't imagine her walking, not through the rain. 'Here. It's not far.'

He picked her up easily, and the case with her. She tucked her face into him, putting her arms around his neck. He crossed the wide road where cars, blinded by rain, rolled slowly.

Hal, carrying Clara, walked fast up the pavement through the rain. In a minute or two they were at the door to his lodgings, drenched, him out of breath, her face wet, his hair dripping cold wet drops onto her face. Her skirt was wet, his trousers splashed and heavy. He set her down. 'All right?' He took his key and let her into the dark hall. 'Up on the left. At the front.'

The bedroom door was loose and light on its hinges. Hal had lit the gas and hung her skirt nearby to dry. They lay on the thin bed together, with no space, touching all down their bodies. He stroked her hair from her face, pulling the pink cover over her. It wasn't clean. They didn't look at it.

'You shouldn't have come all this way,' he said. 'I don't know what you were thinking.'

Her feet were wet in her stockings, darker where her shoes had been. The white skin of her thighs was very smooth. He lifted her blouse, lightly, from her stomach and Clara shut her eyes. She had a nylon belt for a sanitary towel, too, the fragile practicality of her femininity. He slipped his finger under the elastic of her silk knickers, it wasn't tight, he lifted the band away from her. The long cut was raised, slightly, the points where the stitches had been still red. She put her hand over his. 'Don't touch it,' she said.

'I won't,' he said, but stroked with two fingers the skin that was unmarred, in small strokes, where it was soft and wouldn't tickle her or hurt. 'Tell me about the girls,' he said. 'Anything.'

'They're so well, Hal. Much happier now. Meg says, "Don't do that," all the time. Lottie has been gardening with my mother . . .'

As she spoke, he tucked her things and the cover around her again.

‘They’re both finding it jolly cold, and woke in the night twice last night. They need proper flannel nighties. It will be a horrible shock for them.’

‘Hot-water bottles,’ he said.

‘Yes, but we’ve only the one.’

The gas fire popped and hissed. The dark rain fell outside, the constant sound, far faint drops and closer drums and taps, too. They held hands.

The silence lengthened.

‘Meg says “lub” for “love” . . .’ she said, slowly.

He waited until she closed her eyes. He shifted his arm uncomfortably. After a while, Clara, sleeping now, settled into him, and Hal, his eyes open, listened to the falling rain.

Chapter Eight

The next morning there was a row with the landlady about Clara, whom she had seen leaving the bathroom. Clara hid under the bedspread while Hal assured the woman, at the narrowly open door, that they were married, and apologised for using a single room for double occupancy. He hadn't been trying to pull the wool over her eyes, he said. It had been an honest mistake. He closed the door. 'Completely ridiculous woman,' he said.

'Come back with me today,' said Clara, so he did, keeping the room for the appointments he would have to travel up for.

They closed and locked the loose door on the pink bedspread and Hal's interview suit, hanging motionless in the cupboard, and went down the stairs, out onto the damp pavement, washed clean from the night before, to catch their train.

At Marylebone, Hal bought the paper. Clara looked out of the window of the train while he read it, and the extra section that went with it, devoted entirely to what was happening in the Canal Zone. He studied the blurry photographs closely. The other passengers were reading about it too, and passing remarks, but Clara, taking hold of Hal's hand, kept her face resolutely turned to the landscape going by.

'It doesn't help you to look,' she said.

There were two men, one in a hat and suit, holding an empty pipe, the other in plus fours, who kept up a conversation about Eden, bringing in everything from Communism to nuclear war. Hal focused on the luggage rack above their heads, paying close attention. It was an odd sensation, listening to them, a little like spying; he had always heard about this mysterious thing, public opinion, but had never really been a member of the public.

'Eden is stuck in the 1930s, dragging this country into another colonial war,' said the man with the hat, stuffing soft tobacco into the bowl of his pipe.

'I suppose you'd have the reds in charge?' said the plus-fours man, happily.

They were very talkative, scattering opinions lazily. They had that luxury, Hal thought, out of habit, and then – briefly – so do I, now, too.

In the Buckinghamshire village, the taxi left them at the door. Hal took longer about paying the driver than he might have done, putting off the moment. Moira, with George behind her, opened the door to their daughter and their errant son-in-law. The girls, next to her, bounced up and down.

'Mummy!'

Hal squared up to greet them.

'Here, Hal, what a miserable day,' said Moira, coming down the path towards them. 'Come inside.' She took his arm. 'How was London?'

'Busy.'

'Good journey?' asked George.

'Yes, thank you, sir.'

Inside the house, Clara went up to rest, Moira took the girls into the kitchen with her, to see about the lunch, and George, on his way into the drawing room, turned to Hal. 'There's no need to call me "sir", Hal. You ought to know this family by now,' he said, and left him, shutting the door behind him.

Hal, alone, stood looking at the closed door for a moment. Then, as one who does a thing because he must, because he doesn't often turn away, he opened it.

George turned, surprised at being followed. He was at the fireplace facing his son-in-law – the patriarch despite himself.

'All right,' said Hal, coming into the room and closing the door firmly again. 'I thought you might want to know my plans.'

George, tight-lipped: 'If you like. Go on.'

'I'm sorry about everything that's happened, and I'm – I'll – do my best to –'

'You'll *do your best*?'

'Yes.'

'Jolly good.'

'Sir?' It came naturally, he couldn't help it.

'I said *jolly good*, you'll do your best, while my daughter nearly died, and my son is out in Egypt somewhere, and you've . . . whatever they call *deserted* these days – you'll *do your best*? I see.'

Hal persisted: 'I'm sorry.'

'Sorry? *You're* –' He turned away quickly, shaking his head, as if arguing with himself, said, 'No, no, *I'm* –' and stopped talking.

There was silence, Hal resolutely facing George but George

having walked off a few paces towards the window. Half turning back, but not enough to meet Hal's eye, he said, 'I'm sure you know, Hal, I got in at the end of the First War, 1918. I got the end of it. It got the beginning of me.' He paused. 'In my opinion there are very few wars that are really worth the fighting, and none that I know of at this present time. Nevertheless when one didn't . . .' he felt for the words '. . . *decide not to take part* oneself, however tempting it may have been, it's extremely difficult to see another man do it and not resent him. Do you understand that?'

'Yes, of course.'

'And I'm sorry for that. I truly am. I should thank you. I wanted my daughter home, and now she is – home. I wish it were you who was still out there, and not James.'

He hadn't said it viciously: it was a confession.

'Yes.'

There didn't seem any more to be said, or any further degradation to be faced. Hal nodded to his father-in-law, and started to leave the room.

'Hal, you know I'll help you, if I can.'

'Thank you.'

And then, almost as an afterthought, George said, 'It would be easier if you had taken some sort of a stand.'

At the door Hal turned. 'Easier?' He narrowed his eyes in close scrutiny of the idea, and then smiled slightly. 'Yes,' he said, 'it would have been.'

Clara hadn't closed the curtains, and grey light came in at the window onto the faded flowers of her bed. Hal closed the door behind him. He didn't know if she was asleep or not.

He went to the window and looked out, his hands in his pockets.

Below, in the garden, Meg and Lottie were walking up the grass with Moira. He couldn't hear what was being said, but there was some earnest burbled chatter going on, and he could see from Moira's bowed head that she was listening intently. They were going to get vegetables for lunch. Meg was carrying a basket. The children walked very slowly, but Moira was patient.

She stopped to point something out to them in the grass, and all three bent over to look.

He heard Clara move behind him, and get up.

She came over to him, stood by him and they both looked down into the garden. She was warm from the bed, wearing her slip over her underwear, but no stockings, her dressing gown in her hands, held loosely.

He nodded towards the children in the garden, trying to smile, or say something about it, but with nothing to say.

'Our lovely girls,' said Clara.

Still, he could not speak. Clara reached up and pulled the curtain across the window. The heavy lined material tugged its wooden rings along the pole. It was dark now. She dropped her dressing gown, put her arms around his waist and her head against him. 'Here,' she said.

The silk was soft against him, against his clothes, her warm body underneath, giving; her cheek was by his heart. He put his head down to her; he didn't put his arms around her – he couldn't – but his fingers touched the material of her slip, and held it. He closed his fingers tightly on the thin silk.

'Ssh,' she said.

So close to him, she lifted her face.

She put her arms up, her fingers on the back of his neck, then above his ear, stroking his brow. His lips were against her skin.

'I love you,' he said, twisting the silk between his fingers, and he started to cry.

Chapter Nine

It was Sunday, 11 November. The Wards, who did not attend church every Sunday, nevertheless went often, and always at Christmas, Easter, the Harvest Festival and this day, Remembrance Sunday. Whatever their opinion of specific conflicts, they showed their respect to the war dead.

'You needn't come,' said Clara, to Hal, but she was wrong.

The twins were dressed in matching black coats, with velvet collars, that Moira had made a special trip up to town for, without Clara, the week before. They had red ribbons in their hair, at the side, attached to their hairclips, and patent leather shoes with woollen tights. All of them had poppies on their lapels, bought from one of the churchwardens at the door the day before. They walked through the village, joining others as they went.

In the centre of the village, opposite the church, was the war memorial, like any war memorial, in any village, passed unthinkingly most of the time, but now laid with wreaths, some still being carried, still being placed. It took some time for everybody to come from their houses. The sky was grey and thick above them, and they were all in black, with poppies, and just the sudden colour of a skirt as it showed beneath a coat or the bright gloves of a child to break the blackness.

People talked as they approached the memorial, but fell quiet – except for children's voices – once they stood grouped around it. The rain was very fine and made no noise on the umbrellas men held over their wives.

The church was behind him. Hal looked over his shoulder at it.

The door was open and he could see the flowers inside; their colours glowed under the electric lights that had been put on because the day was so dark and wet. He thought of the little church in Cyprus that hot day, and the heat and glare outside. He had not been inside a church since.

The Wards stood towards the back of the crowd, though not apart. Clara was in front of Hal next to Moira and George. At the front, near the vicar, stood the old men, with their chests thrown out, and medals pinned to their civilian overcoats. The Scout troop was beside them, and cadets nearby. It was a crowd of perhaps three hundred, joined in silent communication; those who normally passed one another without greeting now nodded and smiled.

The vicar looked around the people, who settled themselves, and began.

'Let us remember with gratitude
Those who, in the cause of peace
And the service of their fellow men,
Died for their country, in time of war.'

He unfolded a piece of paper.

'I will now read a list: the names of the fallen of this parish,' he said. 'Abbot, Tom. Antony, Wilbur. Brown, Edward. Bryant,

Daniel. Bryant, John. Bryant, Michael . . .'

There was absolute quiet as he read. Even the children and babies who had been fidgeting grew still.

'Diller, Andrew . . .'

Hal stood rigidly, eyes front. He could see, over the shoulders and heads of the others, the corner of the fluttering page that the vicar was holding and behind that the stone edge of the memorial. In his heart, as he always had, he bowed down to the names of the dead, and honoured them. He tried to feel pride in them cleanly but, after a moment, he could not, and looked down at the ground. The list went on, the dead were still the dead, with or without his feeling their companionship.

Clara leaned closer and he felt her warmth come into the air around him. She took off her glove and her hand wrapped around his cold fingers but he did not look up.

> 'They shall grow not old, as we that are left grow old:
> Age shall not weary them, nor the years condemn.
> At the going down of the sun and in the morning
> We will remember them.'

'We will remember them,' answered the voices of the people.

After a moment the church bells pealed the hour. As the last bell faded the silence began.

The winter air of England was silent all around and between the villages, stretching high up into the grey sky and over the hills, linking them, joining.

A nervous boy of perhaps fourteen stepped forward. He held the bugle in pink cold fingers. He raised it, drew a breath, and Hal saw again the white road with the young boy on it, and his own hand holding the gun to his head.

The Last Post sounded. The first two notes were like a blade through the air, and breaths were taken around him. The reaching sound went on to its last thin note, then died.

The gathered people stirred themselves to walk to the church. They parted for the vicar and then began to follow him. Clara looked up at Hal. He nodded to her, reassuring her – about what, he didn't know – but then let go of her hand and walked quickly away from the others, back, along the road towards the house, leaving the black crowd behind him. He heard Lottie say, 'Mummy!' once, imperiously, and knew, gratefully, that Clara could not follow him.

His quick steps sounded hard on the gritty pavement. The white gate swung wide when he pushed it and banged back against its metal catch behind him. The front door was unlocked.

He went into the hall, fast, on into the drawing room, the fire was burning brightly behind the guard, paintings, photographs surrounded him, the gleaming battered piano, vases of flowers, silver and the smell of lunch that filled the empty warm house. He went back into the hall – feet on the worn rug – back, through the dining room, table set with empty places, into the stone-flagged passage past the kitchen door, past the boots and the place where the shotgun was kept in the high locked cupboard, amongst the tins and garden poisons, out of the back door, onto the terrace.

He went quickly up the garden, past the borders with the

cut ends of rose bushes and tangled wet shrubs, over the sinking grass to the gate. There was the pasture beyond it and the path cut through the grass, but he turned away from it, because he could not leave again, because there was nowhere to go to.

He was blinded. It was as if the universe turned round him blackly and he, within it, earthbound and empty too.

He closed his eyes.

'God,' he said.

Quiet. Silence. Darkness.

'God,' he said again.

Then, with his eyes shut, he heard a small whispering sound. It was a still, complicated sound. His mind was alert to it, and only it, immediately. He opened his eyes.

Ahead of him was a small tree. It was perhaps twenty feet high. It was a very young oak. The trunk was soft grey-brown like the hide of a young deer or rabbit.

And, just then, the breeze moved around him. He thought it must be a breeze – at least – he had been touched. He saw that the dry leaves that still hung from tiny twigs were moving together and making the whispering sound he had heard. The leaves trembled, each one, as their outlines grew sharper. He looked at the shivering leaves and at the clarity of their edges. The oak leaf, embroidered in gold, dreamed of, promised to, betrayed and deserted. Here was not one, but many, not just the leaf but the whole tree, and it seemed to brighten as he looked. He thought the sun must have come out but the fine wetness still moved in the air.

He saw that there were, amongst the twigs and clinging leaves, the tiny, almost invisible beginnings of new leaves –

not leaves exactly, but the suggestion of them – and next to those, acorns, very small and fresh looking.

He looked at the lines and shapes of the bark where the branches grew, at the leaves and the clean trunk. He stood in the damp winter garden with the small oak tree and it might have been Eden.

He was glad that they were singing and wouldn't notice him coming in. The flagstones of the path were wet beneath his feet. The door was slightly open and as he pushed it wider and stepped into the church he saw his family immediately. Clara lifted her chin and turned towards him. Her relief and anxiety made him impatient to get to her. He wanted to explain to her; he didn't think he could. The church was full and loud. He had to go to the aisle, past some flowers on a stand, and then push by a row of people, apologising, not noticing them, until he was beside her, or nearly – the twins were between them. Too young for singing, they were facing one another and pressing their hands together in pleasurable boredom at some vague version of pat-a-cake. They glanced up at him and then continued. Hal had stepped into the half-space made by the people next to them, and stood a little sideways looking at Clara. The heavy organ and uneven voices insulated them. He could not hold her hand; there was a row behind, people were less than a foot away, standing, singing in the narrow pews. He remembered he had been shamed by the presence of these people – remembered it but let it fall away from him. The damp coats and dark wood, gleaming, the cool rising arches of the vaulted ceiling, the music and strong, restrained communion, all were known to him, and loved: he was at home.

Clara put her hymn book across the gap between them awkwardly and he, grateful for the convention, shared the holding of it. Meg, bored with standing, leaned back against his knee, thoughtlessly confident of him, and Hal looked into Clara's face.

They examined one another and there was no barrier, no sea, no act committed, not so much as a pane of glass between them; not even air, it felt to him. He travelled her face slowly and, returning to her eyes, saw that she was smiling at him.

Author's Note

Small Wars is a fiction. With the greatest of respect for history and those people who experienced life in Cyprus and England in the 1950s, I have occasionally amalgamated, compressed or otherwise manipulated places and events to suit my story. I should like to make clear, too, that all the characters in *Small Wars* – with the obvious exceptions of well-known historical figures – are entirely fictional.

Acknowledgements

For *Small Wars*:

I am grateful to the many people who gave of their time and knowledge during the writing of the book.

I should like to thank the website britains-smallwars.com, which not only partly inspired the title, but also gave me invaluable and detailed information, military, political and personal, in the accounts of soldiers who served in Cyprus and elsewhere. They are owed an enormous debt of gratitude.

In the course of my research, these books were helpful to me: *The Decline and Fall of the British Empire* by Piers Brendon; *Time at War* by Nicholas Mosley; *Hot War, Cold War* by Colin McInnes; *Bitter Lemons of Cyprus* by Lawrence Durrell; *Instruments of War* by Peter R. Cullis; *'Terrible Hard', Says Alice* by Christopher Wood; *Murder, Mutiny and the Military* by Gerry R. Rubin; *The Call-Up: A History of National Service* by Tom Hickman; *Unreasonable Behaviour* by Don McCullin; *British Infantry Uniforms Since 1660* by Michael Barthorp and Pierre Turner.

My thanks also go to the staff at the British Library; RMA Sandhurst; the Imperial War Museum; Bulford Camp, Wiltshire; Episkopi Garrison, Cyprus; and to Dr Ian Palmer. Thanks to Alexander Baring, and the other serving soldiers with whom I spoke and had email correspondence. They were without exception kind, helpful and informative.

Many thanks to Christopher Wood, for his help and interest.

I am also extremely grateful to David Patterson for his memories of Cyprus during his National Service, his wonderful diaries and his generosity in sharing both. Thanks to Rebecca Harris and Anna Parker, and to Julia Gregson for her Cyprus memories. Many thanks also go to Martin Bradley, and to Charlie Hopkinson, whose patience and rigour in answering my questions made an enormous contribution during the writing.

I would particularly like to thank Clara Farmer for her insight and dedication; she has been a true friend to the book. Also, many thanks to Sue Amaradivakara. I am proud to have *Small Wars* published by Chatto & Windus, and grateful to everybody there; it could not be in better hands.

Thanks also to Terry Karten at HarperCollins, New York.

Thanks to my agent and friend, Caroline Wood, for her energy, consistency and integrity.

For myself:

To Tim, Daisy, Tabitha and Fred Boyd; Evan, Joanna and Melissa Jones; and my good friends – my love and gratitude.

Sadie Jones,
London, April 2009